THE MOVING BLADE

Praise for The Last Train, the first in the Detective Hiroshi series

Solo Medalist Winner New Apple Awards for Excellence 2017
Winner Crime Fiction Beverly Hills Book Awards 2017
Winner Best Mystery Book Excellence Awards 2017
Gold Award Literary Titan Book Award 2017
Finalist Next Generation Indie Book Awards 2018
Top Ten Self-Published Books 2017 The Bookbag
Silver Award IBPA Benjamin Franklin Awards 2017
Silver Award Feathered Quill Book Award 2018
Finalist Book Readers Appreciation Group (B.R.A.G.) 2017
Finalist IANB of the Year Awards 2017
Finalist EPIC eBook Awards 2018
Semi-finalist Booklife Prize 2017

A five-star detective read. It is unique, intriguing, and will hook the reader from beginning to end.
Reader Views

For anyone who loves crime and cop novels, or Japanophiles in general, this is a terrific thriller.
Blue Ink Review

This exotic crime thriller is a lightning-fast chase to the finish line that'll leave hearts pounding and pages turning.
Best Thrillers

A well-paced and absorbing mystery, with quick action and a look at urban life, an utterly page-turning adventure.
Foreword Reviews

An absorbing investigation and memorable backdrop put this series launch on the right track.
Kirkus Reviews

Gripping and suspenseful, this fast-paced thriller unfolds on the streets of Tokyo, where a clever and cold-blooded killer exacts revenge.
Booklife Prize

Mystery readers will relish the progress of a detective torn between two cultures, the reader of Japanese literature will truly appreciate the depth of background.

Midwest Book Review

Tokyo comes to vivid life in this taut thriller, an unrelenting portrayal of a strong female character and the heart-pounding search to find her.

Publishers Daily Reviews

The Last Train is nothing short of electrifying, a masterpiece that combines action with humor and suspense.

Readers' Favorite

The Last Train is a fast-paced thriller that skillfully exposes readers to the seedy urban side of Japan and leaves readers anxiously waiting for the next novel in the detective Hiroshi series.

Feathered Quill

Written from knowledge rather than research, he knows a lot more than he has any need to tell us brings the city gloriously to life.

The Bookbag

The story behind Michiko Suzuki is compelling and engaging, you can't help flipping the pages to see what she is going to do next and find out why her victims were chosen.

Literary Titan

Pronko truly knows how to use the setting in the read, exploring the many facets of the city to maximum effect. The Last Train is a gripping read, and leaves you really wanting to dig into the next book in the series.

Self-Publishing Review

A heartfelt, thoughtful ode to a strange and beautiful city, in the way that so many classic detective novels are. Lyrically written, with plenty of suspense.

IndieReader

I would definitely recommend it to crime and murder mystery fans, especially those with an interest in Japanese culture.

Online Book Club

Praise for Pronko's Writings on Tokyo Life

Motions and Moments: More Essays on Tokyo

Gold Award: Readers' Favorite Non-Fiction Cultural
Gold Award: Travel Writing Global E-Book Awards
Gold Award: Non-Fiction Authors Association
Gold Honoree: Benjamin Franklin Digital Awards
Silver Medal: Independent Publisher Book Awards
Indie Groundbreaking Book: Independent Publisher Book Review

Pronko is an insightful author capable of seeing a deeper beauty in everything he writes.
SPR Review

Vividly captures the depth and beauty of Tokyo, bringing to life the city and the lifestyle.
Reader's Favorite

This book sparkles and succeeds as a love letter of sorts to Tokyo. The author's writing is a joy to read, with wonderful phrasing and vivid descriptions.
OnlineBookClub.org

This is a memoir to be savored like a fine red wine, crafted with supreme care by a man who clearly has fallen in love with his adopted city.
Publishers Daily Reviews

Each of his essays brought me closer and closer to an appreciation of the complex and complicated place Tokyo is.
Reader's Favorite

The Moving Blade
By Michael Pronko
First paperback edition, 2018
ISBN 978-1-942410-16-4

Typesetting by FormattingExperts.com
Cover Design © 2018 Marco Mancini, www.magnetjazz.net

* * *

For more about the Detective Hiroshi series and Pronko's other writing: www.michaelpronko.com
Follow Michael on Twitter: @pronkomichael
Michael's Facebook page: www.facebook.com/pronkoauthor

Also available by Michael Pronko:
Beauty and Chaos: Slices and Morsels of Tokyo Life (2014)
Tokyo's Mystery Deepens: Essays on Tokyo (2014)
Motions and Moments: More Essays on Tokyo (2015)
The Last Train (Detective Hiroshi Series Book 1) (2017)

THE MOVING BLADE
by Michael Pronko

Raked Gravel Press 2018

RAKED
GRAVEL
PRESS

It is said the warrior's is the twofold Way of pen and sword, and he should have a taste for both Ways.

「先づ武士は文武二道と云ひて二つの道を嗜む事是道也」。

Miyamoto Musashi, *A Book of Five Rings:*
The Classic Guide to Strategy

宮本 武蔵『五輪書　地之巻』

For the striking sword, there is no mind. For myself, who is about to be struck, there is no mind. The attacker is emptiness. His sword is emptiness. I, who am about to be struck, am emptiness.

「自分の刀の動きを気にすれば、自分の刀に心をとられ、打ち込む瞬間に気を使えば、それに心をとられ、自分の心の在りように気を使えば、自分の心に心をとられてしまいます。このようなことでは、自分自身は抜殻のようなもので、なんの働きもできません。」

Takuan Soho, *The Unfettered Mind*

沢庵 宗彭 不動智神妙録

Chapter 1

Hideyasu Sato rarely took jobs involving foreigners. They usually lived in tall apartment buildings, kept little cash and had bad taste in valuables. But this job was pitched as an easy in-and-out with good pay and a light load.

Getting into the house was, as always in Tokyo, a cinch. He slid a small tension wrench into the keyhole of the kitchen delivery door, levered it up, poked in a rake pick, and after a few tickles, the lock plug spun loose and he was in.

The homeowner had just died, so Sato timed the break-in during the funeral—the best time to rob anyone in Tokyo. After the long ceremony, cremation took an hour or so, depending. Since the owner was famous—Bernard Mattson was a name even Sato knew—the post-funeral chitchat by bigwigs would give him a further cushion.

Sato left his shoes by the door and stepped into the stately, old house in the Asakusa *shitamachi* "lower town" district of eastern Tokyo. The kitchen had surprisingly few modern appliances and looked a little like he remembered his grandmother's in the countryside—spacious, simple, functional.

Walking into the living area, Sato admired the exquisite wood beams and intricate wood paneling. A *tatami*-floored room in Japanese style, empty save for a scroll, statue and vase, opened to the right. The main living room was Western style, with parquet floors that were wide and open, with a sofa, chairs, tree-trunk table and Japanese antiques.

Sato found the bookcase-lined study, and sat down at the computer to copy the two files he'd been hired to retrieve: "SOFA" and "*Shunga.*" It would be easy to download the files to two USB drives and erase the

1

computer before carrying the drives across town, but the computer was old and slow, the fan whirling loudly as he downloaded the files. All around him, the wood frame house creaked like an old man's bones.

When he'd downloaded one file on each of two separate USB drives, he pulled out a DVD to wipe the computer clean. He rebooted and waited while it worked its magic. He turned off the computer. Waited. Turned it back on. A small arrow pulsed at the bottom of the empty, grey screen. Pressing the keys and clicking the mouse had no effect. It was wiped clean.

As he rose, Sato could not help but look around, impressed at the offset shelves, paulownia *tansu* chests, and bamboo-sleeved pot hook dangling from the ceiling. His grandmother had cooked with one of those. Many things in the room could be resold, but from the long shelves along the wall, he pocketed four easy-to-carry *netsuke* carvings: a smiling frog, a *tanuki* raccoon-dog, and two of couples locked in sexual embrace. The *netsuke* were like ivory diamonds—compact and easy to sell.

On the way out, Sato surveyed the kitchen. It was hard to guess where a foreigner would tuck away cash, if at all, but he went with instincts honed by years of breaking in Japanese homes. Inside an old tea cabinet, he found a cherry-bark box with a false bottom concealing a thick wad of ten thousand yen notes.

Not so different, Sato chuckled to himself as he stuffed the money in his pocket next to the *netsuke* and USB drives. He slipped on his shoes, closed the door, exited through the garden and walked away as if he had lived in the neighborhood all his life.

It wasn't until he was changing trains in Ueno that he noticed the foreigner. Over the years, Sato had been tackled, punched, stabbed and slapped so his ear drum burst, but by following his most basic rule of never stopping, he always got away. He couldn't run like a young man anymore, so he'd doubled up on caution. Now, he had something new—a *gaijin* trailing him through Tokyo.

He'd noticed him on the train, but many foreigners returned from Asakusa on the same route. This foreigner, though, wasn't checking his cellphone for directions or looking at his camera photos. He was staring out the window at the subway walls, too patiently, too attentive to nothing.

Sato got off in Ueno and glanced back to see the foreigner riding the escalator a dozen steps behind. He was so tall he had to duck under the metal ceiling panels. His hat hid his face and a black leather coat stretched to his calves. Sato hurried to the Yamanote Line platform without looking back.

When the train got to Tokyo station, Sato could see his head jutting over the crowd like a giraffe. *All that milk and beef,* Sato thought. It was trying to get milk and beef that pushed him into housebreaking fifty years ago. So, Sato decided to follow another of his rules—stay on the train. The rush hour crowds in the stations made it easy to lose anyone.

The best plan was to ride all the way to Shinbashi, hurry up and over and down to the next platform for a train back towards Tokyo Station, and push into the middle of the jam-packed car just before the doors close.

At Tokyo Station, he glanced back down the long, steep escalator of the Chuo Line.

The foreigner was gone.

As he rode up, Sato texted the address of the house in Asakusa to the crew waiting to get in, describing what was there and estimating how long they had to get in and out. He was glad to leave the heavy stuff to the Koreans and Chinese. They were younger, quicker and stronger. Braver, too, he had to admit. He was never sure where they hocked what they carted off, but that wasn't any of his concern. He trusted them for his cut, which was always sent promptly through automatic bank transfer.

At Shinjuku Station, Sato followed another of his rules and steered himself to the densest middle of the crowd. Outside the station, he blended in with the pedestrians hunkered deep into their coats against the winter wind, moving at their pace.

A bit more caution couldn't hurt, he decided, so he turned into the Isetan department store. The first floor was crowded for a perfume sale with neatly dressed Japanese women sampling scents. Sato slipped through the medley of aromas and down a stairway to the tight-set basement counters selling tea, jam, cheese, pickles, miso and dried fish—a maze no foreigner could manage. Sato zigzagged past middle-aged women sniffing out daily bargains as salespeople called out their wares in booming, froggy voices. At the back of the basement floor, the underground market ended at a door into a bland corridor with stairs up to Yasukuni Dori Street.

He finally stopped in the fresh air outside and lit a cigarette by a display window of fall fashions. He looked back and forth from the mannequins in their put-on poses to the glass doors he'd just exited.

He smoked all the way down to the filter. Maybe he was being too cautious but that was better.

People flowed around him on the sidewalk, so he huddled close to the big window to wiggle one of the USB drives into the cigarette pack for safekeeping.

He decided to smoke one more. When he finished, no one had emerged. *Lost him*, his instincts told him as he ground out the butt, smug he still had the knack.

Halfway downhill towards Golden Gai, he stopped to buy cigarettes at a small tobacco stand wedged into a four-floor building. He slid a thousand-yen bill under the glass counter and looked back the way he came. As the old woman gave him change, he caught her rheumy eyes set deep in her furrowed smoker's face—and quickly looked away. She was old and her cheeks hung from her head like worn saddlebags.

Sato stood there and tamped the fresh pack, then pulled out a few of the cigarettes, slipped the other USB drive in and tossed out the couple cigarettes that wouldn't fit into the gutter.

He walked on to a narrow intersection a few blocks down, and turned onto a small street cramped with beer crates, Styrofoam fish boxes, and plastic trashcans. Some of the spotlights from the tall nightclubs on the main street had clicked on, but it would stay dark and deserted in the arm's-width alleys of Golden Gai until customers started arriving much later.

Sato turned into a narrow dead-end with a patchwork of bars not much wider than their doors and stopped in front of the Pan-Pan Club. It was far ahead of the rendezvous time and Sato recited another of his rules: *Never rush things.*

But this time, he broke it. It would be better to get rid of whatever was on the USB drives and go have a drink and a good meal with the cash he'd lifted. Sato knocked on the door—the only one not slathered in thick paint or handwritten signs. He got no answer.

Before he could knock again, he sensed someone behind him. He fumbled for the handle of the stiletto inside his jacket and plucked the metal baton from his waistband, turning around with both hands ready.

"Hand me the files," the foreigner commanded in fluent Japanese. His tall, lean frame blocked the trickle of light from the alley beyond. A single overhead bulb cast their shadows in opposite directions.

Sato was surprised by how well he spoke Japanese, by how he knew about the files, by how he had, in fact, tracked him across the city, and managed to confront him right at that spot. *How could this have happened?* He'd never been cornered before.

"It's just easier if you hand them over," the foreigner said. He held out his left hand and reset his feet and shoulders. His leather coat gleamed in the dim light.

Sato reached into his jacket for the drive-wiping DVD and tossed it onto the pavement between them. When he bent over to get it, he'd kick the foreigner in the head, stab him, and take off. The sides of the small bars were only a step away, so he'd have to be careful getting past. Fifteen years ago, he could have done it. Thirty years ago, it would have been as easy as picking a lock.

The DVD shimmered on the dull gray of the concrete, but the foreigner did not even glance at it. From a sheath inside the front flap of his coat, the foreigner pulled a *tanto* sword as long as his forearm. Together, sword and arm could reach the walls of the cramped cul-de-sac encircling them.

Sato clicked the stiletto and telescoped the baton with a flip of his wrist. The sword whirred and Sato jerked sideways as the sword crashed into the door above his shoulder, splintering the cheap wood.

The sword pinched in place, Sato jabbed at the foreigner's chest but his arms were too short and the foreigner was fast and limber. Blade and baton whisked the air. Sato backed against the closest wall to rebalance, breathing hard, trying to think.

"The USB." The sword upright and his feet planted, the foreigner stared at Sato.

Sato's stiletto had no reach and the baton was too thin, but he swung them side-to-side in a defensive X as he broke for the opening to the alley.

The *tanto* sword caught him from right hip to left rib.

Sato's knees buckled and he folded over like a split sack of rice. In the instant before his mid-section gushed from top and bottom, one of the USB drives flew out of his cut-open pocket and dropped through the grate of the sewer beside him. The foreigner snatched at it, but the memory drive tumbled into the pipes far out of reach below.

Slumped over a concrete step, Sato wheezed and clutched at the warm stream of blood before his fingers loosened and his body slackened. He eyed the foreigner kneeling over the sewer with a small flashlight peering below, felt the ruffle of the foreigner going through his pockets, and dimly gazed at the tangled wires crisscrossing the alley overhead.

* * *

The jacket was as sticky-wet as body tissue, and so was the wad of ten-thousand yen bills, which he tossed aside. The *netsuke* carvings, he dropped on the ground. After wiping the *tanto* blade with a neat cut of rice paper and resheathing it inside his long leather coat, he picked up the DVD, glanced around and walked away.

Chapter 2

When Jamie Mattson saw her father for the first time since she was thirteen, he lay in the casket in the Shida Funeral Hall and Crematorium. The white silk kimono and fat brown beads in his neatly folded hands made him look like a Buddhist monk.

She remembered him more like the large photo on the wall behind the casket, a smile on his lips telling her funny stories during long walks around Tokyo. She pressed a handkerchief to her nose to block out the smell of sickly-sweet flowers and smoldering incense that filled the funeral hall.

Next to Jamie sat her mother, Sachi, who'd flown in from Hawaii. Jamie waited after her flight from New York to meet her at Narita Airport and come together to the funeral hall and crematorium on the outskirts of Tokyo. They switched into their black funeral dresses in a changing room in the private family area. In the mirror, Jamie was surprised at the leathery skin of her mother's island tan and the bags in her eyes. In their boxy funeral dresses, they could have been twins, but undressed, Jamie was fuller and plumper than her mother, who seemed to have shrunk.

Sachi's black sunglasses embarrassed Jamie, but she said nothing as they sat in the front of the hall for the service. After chanted prayers from a bald, white-robed monk, the first speech started. Sachi leaned over and whispered, "This guy was the chairman of Nippon Steel, an old friend of your father's. Runs an arts foundation now." Unsure why she needed to know this, she patted her mother's hand.

Jamie tried to listen to the next speech from another chairman of something, but she had hardly spoken Japanese over the years in America. She could feel the language stirring inside but couldn't grasp

7

much. Her father would have understood every word. Jamie could read his name, Bernard Mattson, in *katakana* under his memorial photo, but almost all the *kanji* characters on the floral wreaths were beyond her. She regretted not studying, but had let it go, along with the relationship with her father. Though never officially estranged, they had lost touch after her mother swept her away from Tokyo to a Massachusetts boarding school.

When he emailed her again after years of silence, she realized she had never been angry or alienated. They'd just drifted apart. She had no reason not to write back. She enjoyed their renewed contact more than she expected and they arranged a father-daughter trip to Kyoto, Mount Koya and Beppu *Onsen*. After that, they'd planned to revisit their favorite spots in Tokyo, where they used to walk together some twenty years before.

She got the news of his death exactly one week before the reunion trip.

When the last speaker finished, the priest asked the hundred-some people in the hall to stand. He started chanting, slow, indecipherable *sutras*. Jamie followed her mother to the front where she pinched incense from a bowl and sprinkled it on flat burners, sending up a thick stream of white smoke. They bowed and prayed and circled back to their seats. The crematorium staff handed her a white chrysanthemum.

"What do we do with this?" Jamie whispered to her mother.

"Drop them on him."

Jamie frowned and twisted the flower in her hand, watching as each person took a flower as they returned to their seats.

Sachi leaned over. "There's that goody-two-shoes first wife of his."

What? That was the first Jamie had heard of—*what?*—another wife, before or after or *when*? Before she could get a look, two white-gloved employees gently turned the casket towards the door and everyone faced the center of the hall. As the funeral attendants rolled Mattson's casket down the aisle, everyone placed a white chrysanthemum into the casket. On top of the flowers, around his body, people nestled in personal notes, handwritten prayers, old photos and a well-worn book or two. When they reached the door of the hall, two attendants fit the casket lid in place and everyone bowed deeply.

Jamie and Sachi followed the attendants pushing the casket to the far end of a long hallway. Jamie peered inside the other halls at clumps of silent people dressed in black, waiting. The attendants pushed the casket into a hall with a high ceiling. Light filtered in from frosted windows high above. Along one wall was a vaulted steel door, burnished to a dull matte, from which protruded a waist-high frame of rollers. The attendants pushed Mattson's casket to the end of the frame, lined it up, and then lifted it onto a large tray on top of the rollers.

Jamie walked over to the big white casket and put her hand on the smooth wood. She wasn't sure yet of the extent of her loss but thinking of the emails he'd written to her over the past year or two, so full of life and humor, so intimate and wise, she choked up. Tears rolled down. She was just one week away from seeing him again. At least she should have had that, his presence, their togetherness, once more. He had wanted that more than anything, he'd written, and so had she. Jamie wiped her eyes and walked back to stand by her mother, who stood silently watching behind her black sunglasses.

An attendant pushed a large silver button and the door ascended. A wave of dry heat surged into the room from the roaring burners inside. Sachi nodded, the workers pressed a button, and the coffin glided into the oven.

A burst of light circled the coffin as it entered the flames and the room resounded with a fiery crackle. The inner door slowly descended until all that could be heard was the muffled rumble of the burners deep inside.

"What do we do now?" Jamie whispered.

"Wait." Sachi whispered. "I told them to use high heat so it would not leave so many bones."

"Bones?" Jamie wondered, making a face.

A loud pop from inside the oven echoed through the hall.

Sachi smiled. "Always had to have the last word."

A short, plump Japanese man who had followed them to the room, but stood waiting at the door, came over and bowed deeply to Sachi and Jamie.

Sachi looked at him. "Shibata-*san*? Is that you?" She settled her sunglasses on top of her head.

Shibata smiled and held out his arms. He was bristling with energy. A smile played across his impish, curled lips despite the solemn surroundings. His bump of a nose was flanked by fleshy cheeks. He looked familiar to Jamie, but she wasn't sure why. Her mind felt clogged with insistent memories and murky feelings, with fatigue and nausea and grief.

The younger man standing next to Shibata was the most handsome Japanese man Jamie had ever seen, magazine model looks with long hair tucked behind his ears and light-brown eyes. He thumbed a bracelet of sandalwood prayer beads and held a leather clutch bag along his forearm.

Sachi turned to Jamie. "This is Shibata-*san*, one of Bernie's oldest friends. You probably don't remember."

Shibata bowed deeply and mumbled a polite phrase in Japanese before switching to English. "Jamie, I know you when you little girl. Your father great friend." He turned to the handsome man. "This Ken-*san*."

Ken bowed his head and offered formal condolences in a soft voice.

Shibata smiled at Jamie before speaking again in Japanese to Sachi. They talked quickly back and forth, her voice rising and shrugging off his questions and her hands gesturing at Jamie. Jamie started to remember him, inside a restaurant or bar she and her father stopped by during a walk.

Shibata turned to Jamie and said, "I have many thing give you, of your father, and many more tell you. Is important. You stop by my club, yes?"

Jamie nodded yes. "Where is it?"

Shibata handed her his *meishi* shop card with a sketch map on the back and his phone number. Without another word, Shibata and Ken hurried off, their black silk jackets shining.

Jamie asked, "What were you talking about? I couldn't catch anything."

"He kept asking about the autopsy."

"Actually, I faxed a form to the embassy saying to go ahead without one. That's what the woman recommended."

Sachi pulled off her sunglasses and glared at Jamie. "What woman?"

10

"An embassy rep called me in the middle of the night." Jamie looked at the oven doors. "They needed my OK, about the house, about the funeral. I was listed as next of kin. I was upset."

A Japanese woman many years older than Sachi, as tall and poised as a ballerina in a mid-length skirt and business top, entered the hall. She walked slowly, deliberately and stopped with her feet together for a quick bow to Sachi before taking Jamie's hands. "I'm Setsuko. I'm so sorry about your father," she said in English.

Sachi pulled her sunglasses over her eyes.

"Setsuko? Dad mentioned you in his emails, but..." Jamie frowned and blinked. Confused, she turned to her mother as Setsuko squeezed her hands.

"You have to talk to the police," she said, squeezing tighter.

Jamie's frown deepened.

"His stomach was cut open, like for ritual *seppuku, hara-kiri.*"

"He killed himself?" Jamie felt like fainting. Her feet shuffled, her knees not holding, and both of the older women moved to steady her. "It was made to look like that," Setsuko explained.

"Were they after his Japanese art?" Sachi asked, still gripping Jamie's elbow.

"They were after his work," Setsuko said, not looking at her.

Jamie couldn't piece together who this was or what she was telling her. "Are you...were you...?"

Sachi said, "Your father was married when I met him. To her."

Jamie looked back and forth at the two women, processing this about her father's life, then filing it to ponder later. "What work are you talking about?" Jamie asked.

Setsuko shook her head. "He said it would all come out in his talk."

Jamie looked at the oven doors, the fire still humming inside. "He wanted me to be there for his talk, at the conference. It was only a week away, our trip."

"What trip?" Sachi asked.

Jamie turned to her mother. "Our trip together. I was going to tell you, but he died too soon. It doesn't matter now."

"Will you give the speech in his place?" Setsuko asked.

"What?"

"The speech he was giving at the conference."

Jamie coughed. "I don't do speeches. I..."

"Well, someone has to. But first, we have to find the speech."

Jamie looked at her own reflection in the brushed steel of the oven door. It was contorted, the black of her dress clouded gray.

Setsuko dug in her purse. "Here's a key to his house. I run a small English conversation school. Near Takadanobaba. Will you stop by? Or should I stop by Bernie's?"

"Either way, but..." Jamie absently took the key and *meishi* name card from Setsuko.

Setsuko cleared her throat. "I don't want to stay for the bones." She walked out of the room without looking back.

Jamie turned to Sachi and held up the key. "I can't even remember where the house is. I haven't been there since—"

"Once you get to Asakusa Station, you'll remember the way."

Jamie took her mother's hand. "Mom, won't you stay? My Japanese is so rusty and I—"

"I had enough of all this, of him, of Japan. I only came for this to be with you. He had no other family."

Jamie stared at her blurry reflection in the rough-polished doors.

"Did you bring any money?" Sachi dug in her purse.

"I brought a credit card. Two."

Sachi put up her sunglasses. "Tokyo's expensive. I don't want to have to rescue you again."

"That was a one-time thing."

An attendant ushered them to a marble bench against the front wall of the hall, and Jamie felt relieved to be a small bit further from the rumble of the oven. Compared to the stifling warmth of the air, the marble was so cool it made Jamie shiver in her funeral dress. Side by side, they waited silently for Bernard Mattson's body to turn to ash.

Chapter 3

Hiroshi Shimizu leaned back in his office chair and smiled at his computer screen. "Got him!" he said to Akiko, his assistant.

Akiko let out a squeal of delight as she stepped over to read the English email on the other side of the small office. Hiroshi pointed to the email in the center of his desktop. Around the email a profusion of Excel sheets, bank statements, flow charts and contracts overlapped in offset layers.

Hiroshi read the rest of the email, scrolling down past two photos of the scam artist. In one he was bald and dumpy in a wrinkled suit, and in the other, he sported a thick gold chain over a buffed, tanned chest, gripping a drink at a beach bar.

"Is that even the same guy?" Akiko laughed.

"Yes. Wait. Oh, no. They're going to prosecute him there."

"At least they got him," Akiko said. "Let's go celebrate. Lunch outside someplace?"

"It's taken us six months to put all this together. The Hawaiian FBI gets all the glory. We do all the work."

Akiko hummed in quiet consolation.

"Let's at least celebrate with a couple of espressos!" Akiko said. An espresso machine gleamed from its perch on top of an old metal file cabinet.

The smell of fresh coffee would help cover up the disappointment, and the disinfectant. Hiroshi appreciated the rare privilege of having his own office, but it was converted from a janitor's supply closet, and still smelled of it. Far from the noisy main building, it was quiet enough to call overseas on international cases. He was the only one in the homicide department where he'd been assigned who could speak English well enough to work with overseas cases and the only one who could make sense of financial forms in either language. He should have had a separate department, but he was assigned to homicide. *Money and murder go together*, the chief said the one and only time he stopped by.

"I can't believe they won't send him back," Hiroshi said, shaking his head at the screen. "What he stole was from Japanese pensioners *here*." Hiroshi pushed back his hair, grown long since his hibernating instincts took over after the case last summer. It hung on both sides of his face like blinders keeping his eyes on the files, flow charts, account graphs, bank transfers, and victims' statements that filled his days, and since he wasn't sleeping much, filled his nights.

Hiroshi mumbled, "Those American lawyers are good, but..."

"It's not fair, but that's the way it is," Akiko said, pressing the button for a double espresso.

Unlike Hiroshi, Akiko was the most regular of workers, coming in promptly at the same time every day, usually leaving about the same time, and in between ensuring the office remained in order. Her tight skirts, chic haircut and big eyes drew appreciative stares on Tokyo trains, but went largely unnoticed in the homicide offices. The detectives were too busy and overworked for flirtation or fantasy. Besides, she was strong and forthright, not cute and demure. She looked at faces, not at the floor.

Hiroshi scrolled back to the top of the email and started reading it again, shaking his head, barely noticing the cup Akiko set in front of him as he started writing an email back. "Our prisons have room. Just for once, I want to see them convicted. Face to face."

Akiko went back to make a second espresso for herself. "Well, at least you can finally get to Boston. I'll rebook that flight for you."

"Cancel Boston."

She inhaled, watching the thick coffee dribble into her cup. Hiroshi knew what she was going to say. She'd canceled and rebooked the flight a dozen times as Hiroshi decided to go, then not go, to meet his girlfriend, friend, lover, whatever she was.

Akiko took a deep, yoga-style breath. "What happened?"

"Everything happened." Hiroshi sipped his espresso. With a loud series of clicks, he checked the last email from Sanae. He'd met her on the case the summer before, the one where he almost got killed. Since then, he'd been trying to go see her after she moved to Boston to put her daughter in high school. In between white-collar crime cases, he would book the visit. Then, Sanae would ask to reschedule. Then he'd rebook, or Akiko would. He was never sure if she still wanted to meet, was nervous about it, felt bad to ask him to fly there, or didn't want anything more to do with him. The back-and-forth had exhausted him.

Akiko said, "Why don't you just get on a plane and talk it out there?"

"Skype's talking."

"Not really."

Akiko took her espresso back to her desk and sat down, sipping it slowly and looking at her screen, purposefully avoiding looking at Hiroshi writing to the Hawaiian detectives.

Hiroshi leaned back from the screen. "I can't believe they're not sending him back for trial here."

"As for Boston, the last-minute cancellation fees you've wasted would have bought several tickets. All any woman wants is someone to make an effort."

"An effort." Hiroshi sighed. "That's what I—"

"You can't do this forever."

"I know. I can't send this email either." He deleted it, as he had so many others recently. He stood up to stretch, noticed the espresso, took a few sips and stretched some more, wincing a bit as he did.

"Still hurts?" Akiko asked.

"Before with the bone bruises, I couldn't move. Now, I can't sit in one place for too long."

"That means they're healing."

The injury had become an excuse to hole up in front of his computer. He drank too much coffee, ate from the convenience store, and slept in the office on a foldout futon chair. He knew all that was not healthy as his face turned pasty, his eyes puffy and his shoulders stiff. For days at a stretch, he talked only to Akiko or overseas investigators, but consoled himself with having cracked six big cases, about one a month, a record of sorts.

But none of the prosecutions took place in Japan, so everything he did felt done at a distance. He never saw anything more of the criminals than their financial records, just like he never saw anymore of Sanae than her face on the screen. Without Akiko, without her energy and the stream of espresso, he would be totally isolated. He'd even quit going to meetings, always coming up with an excuse to stay in his office.

Akiko got out of her chair, which she did when she could no longer stand either the monotony of work or Hiroshi's inertia, and went back to the espresso machine. When she got really exasperated, she found some excuse to go gossip with the staff in the main building. Hiroshi heard her shake the bag of coffee beans like a maraca.

"Yes, but just a single," Hiroshi said. "And I'm still not going to Boston." He didn't want to say that the best four years of his life had been spent there studying, and in love. He worried that if he went, he would never leave again, never come back to Tokyo.

Akiko refilled the coffee bean chute and pressed the button for another espresso. After the loud grind and quick brew, she took a cup to Hiroshi and then made another for herself. She took her cup back to her desk and flopped down into her chair, shrugging. She pulled her cellphone from her purse to see if any of her friends had called or texted.

"I need a new keyboard," Hiroshi said.

Akiko made a note.

"And a new mouse pad."

Akiko bounced her head sarcastically and wrote that down too.

"And more of that air freshener. The smell of cleaning fluids really lingers."

Akiko wrote that down.

Without Akiko, Hiroshi also knew he couldn't have gotten even the simplest of things done. Akiko didn't seem to mind the chipped veneer desks with stubborn drawers or the rust-edged file cabinets, but she knew just how to use department funds to acquire anything they needed new—ergonomic chair, LED lights, a trashcan. She had told Hiroshi she was relieved to have been transferred from the main detective offices to help Hiroshi with investment scams, embezzlements and accounting fraud cases. It was better than being in the constant chaos of the main office, with all the desks pushed together, heaped with teetering mountains of folders. She spoke English almost as well as he did, which helped with the investigative reports they sent overseas.

When the phone rang, Akiko looked at Hiroshi. He had promised to answer every other phone call, but he ignored the ringing until Akiko gave in—again—and picked up. After a minute, she held the phone up in the air and announced, "It's Sakaguchi. Important. He says your cellphone is off."

Hiroshi looked at his cellphone to make sure it *was* off and plunged back into his screen. "I'm not here," he said.

"He can hear you," Akiko wiggled the phone at him.

"I told you no calls."

Akiko went back to the phone, "As you just heard, he won't take calls."

Hiroshi went back to his screen, trying to shut out her continued conversation with Sakaguchi.

Akiko held the phone out. "He says he'll call the chief if he has to."

Hiroshi disliked the chief, and avoided him scrupulously, but he liked Sakaguchi. More than that, he trusted him. Sakaguchi had wrestled his way out of a working-class section of Osaka to reach sumo's *makushita* ranking, the third highest division, one of the youngest wrestlers to do so ever. When a knee injury wouldn't heal, he became a policeman in Osaka and started the path to detective, which was as long and steep and grueling as for sumo. When Sakaguchi was promoted—against his will—to Head of Homicide after last summer's case when Hiroshi got injured and Takamatsu suspended, most of the department felt it was neither entirely deserved nor entirely undeserved.

Akiko hung up after promising Sakaguchi that Hiroshi would call. "Sakaguchi calls. You don't answer. Takamatsu calls. You don't answer. Jim Washington at Interpol calls. You answer."

Jim Washington. He needed to call him about this Hawaii case. After last summer's near-fatal case, Hiroshi became convinced he would be healthier and happier—and safer—working at Interpol. His contact there, Jim Washington, hinted a permanent office position might be opening. Interpol would have an international mindset, computer support, travel expenses, and an office without the leftover smell of cleaning supplies. The Hawaii scam he just broke up would be the icing on his application.

Akiko continued. "Sakaguchi has always been on your side, and he needs your English."

"Well, you go then."

"I'd like to."

Hiroshi leaned back in his chair and put his feet up on his desk. He turned on his phone to find his inbox jammed with calls from Sakaguchi, and from Takamatsu, who was still on disciplinary leave for misconduct. He pressed Sakaguchi's number and tried to sip his espresso but the cup was empty.

Akiko kept her head down and pretended not to listen.

"Free sumo tickets?" Hiroshi joked when Sakaguchi answered.

"My old stablemates can get you some," Sakaguchi said. "But right now, I need you here."

"Last time I heard that, I almost got killed."

"I'm not Takamatsu," Sakaguchi said.

Hiroshi thought that over.

"I really need your English. Nothing more," Sakaguchi said.

"Where are you exactly?"

Chapter 4

Hiroshi almost turned back from the narrow lanes of Golden Gai, but several young detectives guarding the police vans on the main street pointed the way to where Sakaguchi waited. He walked obediently into the maze of arms-width walkways, turning sideways to let the crime scene crew get past him. Bright police lights illuminated the dead-end, throwing sharp shadows through the back alleys and side lanes.

Hiroshi found Sakaguchi balanced over the bisected, blood-oozing body in the small cul-de-sac. His sumo bulk was awkward against the delicate white crime scene booties stretched over his big shoes. Hiroshi stayed a few steps back, dodging the detectives and specialists hustling back and forth from the body to the evidence bags in the wider lane. Hiroshi moved closer and Sakaguchi stood up, blocking a full view of the body.

The medical examiner looked up from where she was crouched over the body. "Except for his spine, he's in two pieces. Short sword. Single stroke. Clean as a laser scalpel." She stood up, her white coat gleaming in the lights, and continued. "You get sloppier cuts from a sushi chef. For now, it looks like the knife entered near the hip bone, angled up through the liver, stomach and intestines, dipped under the ribs and just nicked the heart. The cut line is—"

"OK, OK, we got it," Hiroshi said.

One of the younger detectives back by the crime scene tape called for Sakaguchi. Sakaguchi, who nodded for Hiroshi to stay and listen. Hiroshi started to protest, but Sakaguchi twisted away back to where evidence was being bagged and filed. Hiroshi looked away from the body into the dark sky above the over-bright cul-de-sac and pulled his wool coat tight with hands deep in his pockets. He needed a new winter coat.

The medical examiner looked surprised at Hiroshi's inattention to her and the corpse. "Something wrong?"

"I don't like hearing it." Hiroshi examined the doors of the small drinking places and stared at the crisscrossing knot of wires overhead. How could that not be dangerous, all those wires in the tight warren of wood?

"Most people are the other way; they can't look." The examiner dropped her blood-splattered gloves in a bag.

"I can't do that, either."

"You can read my report later." She shrugged and walked off.

Hiroshi looked at her and looked away, wondering why Sakaguchi had called him, regretting he'd agreed to come. What use was his English here? A photographer was working on specific angles and areas to capture. Hiroshi felt relieved when the camera flash bleached out the reality of it all for an instant.

Out in the large lane, Sakaguchi was talking with Ueno, Sugamo and Osaki. The three hard-working detectives bowed to Hiroshi, not having seen him in months, but not asking where he'd been. All three were younger than Sakaguchi, about the same size, double or triple Hiroshi's. Ueno and Osaki had stocky rugby bodies, and still played in the police league. Ueno was taller and thinner than the others, but Osaki was small and solid, the number 8 guy at the back of the scrum. Sugamo carried his weight in his chest and gut, a former sumo wrestler, like Sakaguchi.

"Why am I here again?" Hiroshi asked Sakaguchi, more impatiently than he intended.

"There's a file I need you to see," Sakaguchi whispered.

"You brought me here to see a file?" Everything had been so neat, clean and simple in his office. "Why not just send it to me?"

Everyone paused. Saito the bureau chief's yes-man and second in command, had just walked in to the crime scene.

"I'll take him this time," Sugamo said.

Saito always showed up late, ordered everyone around, and left before the work got done. Someone had to head him off at every crime scene to keep him from screwing things up. It was Sugamo's turn to send him packing.

"I'll get the computer," Osaki said.

They both hurried off. Hiroshi had heard from them that during the interim after Takamatsu got suspended for conduct violations, Saito took over and managed to irritate everyone, except, apparently, the current chief who kept him on as assistant chief. After that, Sakaguchi's steady hand and calm formality was a relief.

Sakaguchi turned to Hiroshi, "Can you call Takamatsu and get him over here? He covered a sword case a few years back."

Hiroshi shook his head. "He's the last person I want to talk to, and he's not supposed to be here anyway. He's still suspended..."

Sakaguchi was not listening. All around them, the crew followed their meticulous routine. Hiroshi found himself the only person with nothing to do, so he called Takamatsu.

Takamatsu picked up right away. "You're talking to me again?"

"I'm calling for Sakaguchi. He wants to know about another case a few years back? Sword cut?"

"Got another one?" Takamatsu asked.

"Sakaguchi wants you to take a look."

"Can't. Stakeout. Love hotel. The girl's something. The guy won't take long."

"Send a fox to catch a fox."

"I might never come back to detective work. This pays better, and no paperwork."

"We're in Golden Gai."

Takamatsu hesitated. "Is the chief there?"

"Saito's here."

"Same difference."

"Sugamo's getting rid of him."

Takamatsu went silent for a minute, then cursed.

"What?" Hiroshi huffed, tired of Takamatsu's games.

"You made me miss my shot. He's got her inside already. Damn!"

"So, get over here." Hiroshi hung up and avoided the body by studying the signs over the doors of the small bars that lined the alley: Afterward, Hang 1 On, Here and Now, Pan-Pan. Even as other Tokyo neighborhoods were leveled to throw up bland humdrum buildings, Golden Gai's retro postwar vibe, fire hazard layout and scruffy comfort never changed. The alleys and the bars—seating six or seven at most—teemed with energy. Usually. With the police there, none of the places had opened.

Osaki walked over with an open laptop, rested it on an abandoned barstool, inserted a USB drive and clicked on a file. "I had it earlier, but it's a big file."

Hiroshi drew his coat around him in the cold and glanced back at the corpse slumped over a concrete step at the edge of the cul-de-sac. He refocused on the computer screen and moved over a little when Sugamo returned to the scrum around the laptop.

"You got rid of Saito?" Osaki asked.

"He said it was getting late." Sugamo gave a disgusted little snort.

Sakaguchi walked towards them but stopped to answer his phone. As he listened he pointed at Sugamo. "Go rescue Takamatsu. They won't let him past the perimeter."

Sugamo walked off and in a minute came back with Takamatsu.

Sakaguchi nodded towards the body.

Without a word, Takamatsu passed his hand-tailored jacket and European raincoat to one of the young detectives. He took off his cufflinks and rolled up his sleeves, then slipped on booties and gloves before starting to survey the entire grid, first right-left and then up-down, then the same in reverse, using his finger to mark off areas.

Hiroshi wondered who the dead man was and why he'd been killed so violently, and in such an unexpected place. He watched Takamatsu squat over the exposed corpse and get down close to the raw open viscera. Takamatsu was never fazed by anything. Hiroshi watched him walk a perimeter around the body, taking in the scene from every angle, then, he reversed the circle and did it all again. Hiroshi could barely look in the direction of the corpse, much less at the details.

Finally, Takamatsu pulled off the gloves and booties and came over. He spoke to Hiroshi in a loud, teacher-like voice. "It's the small things lodged in the back of your mind that often break a case. Put them in. Let your mind work on them."

Hiroshi pretended to ignore him, still miffed at Takamatsu after the case the summer before. Takamatsu's indiscretion, to say the least, had set up Hiroshi for a fight that nearly killed him. No one mentioned that it was a woman who had done the damage.

22

Takamatsu said, "That little stiletto wasn't much help. Check out that splintered door." The door had fallen in on itself, hanging from the hinges, exposing the small counter and stools inside.

The medical examiner oversaw the transfer of the corpse with a plastic liner that slid under the body. It took four of the medical staff plus the examiner several tries to get the body, the top and bottom nearly in two, into the body bag and onto the gurney. The medical examiner turned to get Sakaguchi's final approval to take away the body.

Stopping their work, Sakaguchi, Takamatsu and the other detectives put their hands together and bowed in prayer to the dead man as the attendants see-sawed the gurney back and forth around the tight turn of the narrow alley.

After he passed, Takamatsu cocked his head at Hiroshi, straightening his dark red tie and gold cufflinks. "It was two different guys, two different swords, before."

Hiroshi turned away but kept listening.

Takamatsu continued, "We never solved them. Unpaid loan, right-wingers, vendetta, who knows? One was a long *tanto* sword and the other a short *nodachi* field sword. Each cut leaves its traces."

"Like a bullet?" Hiroshi shook his head at Takamatsu's unending self-assurance.

"Yes. Like that. You need a specialist."

Hiroshi said, "And I suppose you're a specialist on sword cuts along with everything else?"

"Still sulking?" Takamatsu asked Hiroshi. "I'm the one who got suspended. And two months in the hospital. What did you get? A few bruises?"

"I almost got killed. You got vacation."

Takamatsu smiled and lit another cigarette, his gold lighter clicking shut. "Being suspended *is* like vacation. First one I've ever had."

Sakaguchi looked at Takamatsu. "What's your guess?"

Takamatsu shrugged. "Runner for some yakuza group. Money, messages. Independent contractor."

"The USB was driven so deeply inside, the medical examiner thought at first he might have swallowed it. She said it must have been the force of the sword. The packet of cigarettes was in there too. In pieces."

"More proof tobacco is bad for your health." Takamatsu looked for a place to grind out his cigarette, but seeing none, he pulled out a portable ashtray, slipped the butt inside, sealed it and put it back in his pocket.

Osaki looked impatient with the computer, but the heavy file opened at last, conjuring images pixel by pixel. When the first one filled in completely, the detectives stared at a Japanese *ukiyoe* wood-block print of entangled lovers. The man's over-large, wrinkled penis was half-in half-out of the woman's swollen vulva. The woman's face reeled back in open-mouth, closed-eye pleasure while the man's eyebrows bent sharply in concentration. Around the edge of the print were Post-it notes and pencil sketches describing the details of the print in English.

"That's what you want me to translate?" Hiroshi pointed at the notes around the outside.

Sakaguchi told Osaki to enlarge the image and go to the next one. The next print showed the open kimonos and swirling genitals of two lovers standing on the street with their *geta* sandals on. Through the window frame of the house, another couple curved together half-hidden except for their faces in ecstasy and their groins interlocked. At the bottom of the print, a dog was draped over another dog, leering while going at it. Long lines of dialogue in curved grass script filled the empty background. Even the dogs were talking dirty.

Takamatsu laughed. "Doesn't seem like a reason to kill anyone."

"There must have been another USB drive," Sakaguchi mused.

After a few minutes of silence, the detectives staring at the screen, Sugamo burst out laughing, his huge body relieving its tension for the first time Hiroshi had ever seen.

Takamatsu snickered. "It's amazing what you can find at murder scenes."

Still chuckling, Sugamo said, "I'll go check on the others and hurry up the new guys."

"So, what do the notes say?" Sakaguchi asked.

Hiroshi leaned forward and squinted. "It's just descriptions of what makes the print authentic, notes on the color, configuration. Stuff that a collector or curator would want to know."

"Nothing else?" Sakaguchi asked.

Hiroshi shrugged. "It looks like notes on the quality of the print, the authenticity of the colors. There's a few translations of dialogue. That's it. You think it's some kind of code?"

Sakaguchi shrugged. "I don't speak English."

"It's got to be connected," Takamatsu said. "It was inside him."

Osaki asked, "Want to see the others?" He clicked through a few more prints of entwined bodies, genitals and arms and legs and kimonos writhing in impossible positions.

"What do you call this style of print?" Sakaguchi asked.

"*Shunga*. Spring pictures," Hiroshi answered.

Sakaguchi's cellphone buzzed. He squinted at the message on the screen and turned to Hiroshi. "Do you know the name Bernard Mattson?"

Hiroshi did. Mattson was a well-known American diplomat and specialist on Japanese culture. He often appeared on discussion panels and history shows on the public TV station, NHK. From the frown on Sakaguchi's face, Hiroshi could tell he wasn't going back to the office anytime soon.

Chapter 5

At the door to the house in Asakusa, Hiroshi toed off his shoes in the large *genkan* entryway. He was in the last of three cars of detectives that traveled the half hour across the city from Shinjuku. Hiroshi came last in a car with two younger detectives whose silence gave him time to get over his irritation at being dragged to a second scene.

Hiroshi stepped up onto the wood floor of the old house and looked at the row of *ukiyoe* woodblock prints along the wall. On an offset *chigaidana* shelf, a stand held three swords of different lengths. Next to the swords was a newly wrapped funeral urn.

Wedged into the doorway of the living room was Sakaguchi, blocking the muffled voice of Ueno responding in lurching English to the rapid-fire patter of quick, angry English from a woman Hiroshi could hear but not see.

Hiroshi tapped Sakaguchi. "Where's the crew?"

"The murder was several days ago," Sakaguchi answered in a hushed voice.

"Then why are we here?" Hiroshi whispered.

"There was a break-in today during his funeral. Any crime that happens soon after a murder gets kicked back to homicide." Sakaguchi stood aside like a door opening and gave Hiroshi a full-armed thrust into the living room.

Seeing Hiroshi stumble in, Ueno slunk away to help Sugamo and Osaki. Sakaguchi retreated to the hallway to talk with the neighborhood policeman from the *koban* police box. Hiroshi walked to the middle of the living room and presented his *meishi* name card.

"Another name card." Jamie Mattson snatched it from him. "I don't need to know who you are. I need to know what you'll do about this."

Hiroshi raised his eyes to Bernard Mattson's daughter, Jamie. Her black dress stretched and pulled as she gestured with the loose energy of Americans. She kept her hips steady like Japanese, and though her eyes were American-style direct, she closed and opened them slowly and gently as most Japanese women did. Hiroshi took a breath and refocused, thinking what to say.

"I thought Japan was a low-crime country!" Jamie demanded.

Hiroshi cleared his throat and managed, "It's frightening to have your space violated."

"At least you can speak English," she huffed.

Hiroshi peeled his eyes from her and looked around the ransacked room. A glass case was cracked open. Antique ceramics and tea ceremony bowls lay strewn around. Sofas and chairs were upended. Wood shelves were broken apart and books tossed on the floor like broken butterflies. It must have taken decades to acquire what was now shattered, splintered glass, ceramic and wood.

"Why is your English so good?" Jamie looked at Hiroshi, then at his name card.

"I went to school in America." Hiroshi tried not to stare at her. "Boston. Undergrad and grad. Worked a couple years."

"I went to school near Boston, before I moved to New York," she said.

"But you're from here?"

"Sort of," Jamie said. "Sort of not."

Hiroshi let that go. "Can you tell me what happened?"

"Let me first tell you my name. I'm Jamie."

"Bernard Mattson's daughter. I'm sorry for your loss."

"I almost dropped my father's ashes when I saw this."

"To have this happen on this day."

"You know, you look like Toshiro Mifune, only taller," she said, waving the name card.

"Well, he's the most famous Japanese actor, I guess," Hiroshi said.

"I didn't mean it like that."

"I didn't either. Any idea what they were looking for?"

"I haven't been here since I was thirteen. Now..." Jamie gestured at the mess.

"You were estranged?"

28

"Not exactly. We were just...I was coming back to hear him give a talk, about Asian politics. Next week."

"At the global conference on Asian security?"

"He was giving a talk about his new view of things, I guess."

"Will you be giving the speech in his place?"

"No way. I don't even know what he was going to say."

It might be good to find out, Hiroshi thought, nodding at the glass case across the living room. "Are those photos of you?"

Jamie walked over to a set of framed photos lined up in order: a baby swaddled in blankets, a girl swinging in a park, a teenager playing tennis, a new graduate in college robes, a twenty-something club-goer with a pearl necklace on the party-bra curve of her breasts. Hiroshi closed his eyes. Her breasts were American full and Japanese firm—in perfect proportion.

"I didn't know he had these." She blinked back tears.

"What happened today?" Hiroshi asked.

Jamie took a big breath and shuddered at the thought of the funeral. When the oven doors finally opened at the crematorium, a long, wide tray slid out. Amidst the ashes was a long sharp splinter of bone, a curved hollow of skull and a white knot of spine. Jamie and her mother worked hard to transfer the bones from the tray to the urn with the long funeral chopsticks. Jamie worked so diligently to perform the funeral ritual perfectly her arms started to shake. The attendant helped them, plucking up the remaining bones and poking them into the urn with a crunch. He brushed the ashes into a scoop and slid them inside. After tying the cover on with a silk ribbon, he placed the urn inside a wooden box and tied the wood top with rice straw rope. After a long quiet pause, she looked up at Hiroshi. "I had to carry his remains all the way through Tokyo on the train. I should call my mother."

"Where is she?" Hiroshi asked, looking around.

"On a plane to Hawaii."

Hiroshi opened and closed his mouth, frowning. "They weren't close?"

"Divorced. A long time ago. When I was thirteen."

"When did you get to the house after the funeral?"

"About two hours ago. I kept dialing 911, but the number's different here, I finally realized. 110?"

"Yes, 110."

"I finally got someone on the line who could understand my childish Japanese. The local policemen bicycled over right away." Jamie fought back tears. "Oh, look at this mess."

The bureau chief bustled in, peeling off his dress coat, Borsalino hat and long silk scarf. None of the younger detectives offered to help him and he had to drape his coat and scarf on the banister of the stairs himself. He looked for a place for his hat and set it by the swords on the offset shelf. He was followed in by Saito. "What's the deal here, Sakaguchi?" the chief shouted.

"Owner stabbed to death four days ago," Sakaguchi said. "Burglary today. Kicked back to homicide."

"Saito, you were on this," the chief demanded. "Remind me what you concluded."

Saito—the yes-man who chauffeured the chief, echoed his orders and irritated everyone else—smoothed his wispy mustache. "Guy just came home at the wrong time."

The chief frowned. "This is that diplomat, right?"

"The American embassy wanted it resolved," Saito reminded him. "Before the SOFA meetings next week."

Hiroshi swallowed his dislike of the chief and spoke up. "Mattson was giving the main address at the meetings."

"Was he? I don't watch TV." The chief surveyed the mess. "Saito, when you talked to the embassy staff last week, it was all resolved, right?"

Saito frowned and took a step back. "They trusted what we told them. I had a translator."

The chief shook his head. "So, now I'll have to spend the whole day—again—with the American embassy and whatever ministry people."

The detectives fell into a patient silence. Hiroshi looked at Jamie, wondering if she understood Japanese. She was listening as if she did, but he couldn't tell.

"I'm putting you on it now, Sakaguchi. We've got no one else to spare. And you too," the chief jabbed a finger towards Hiroshi. "You speak English, so you're our firewall. I don't like these international things. Americans get pushy."

The detectives stood in silence, their eyes cast down, waiting.

"I want this all done before those SOFA global whatever meetings. We all have to be there once they start. Saito, you're in charge of conference security at the International Forum, so pull someone from there and set up a rotation to watch this house." The chief turned towards the entry hall but noticed Jamie. He looked at Sakaguchi to see if this was the relative of the victim. Sakaguchi nodded.

The chief spoke to Hiroshi in Japanese, "Please give her my condolences and assure her we will handle this with our best efforts." Hiroshi translated from the formal Japanese.

Jamie looked into Hiroshi's face and said, "Please tell him I want the murder and break-in investigated thoroughly."

Hiroshi cleared his throat. "It's best if you threaten him."

"With what?" Jamie whispered.

"Just say it in an angry way," Hiroshi said in a low voice.

"I demand you get this sorted out or I'll file a complaint with the embassy," Jamie brought her voice to a shout.

Hiroshi translated, embellishing her words with forceful Japanese phrases.

The chief growled, his view of Americans reconfirmed. "Tell her our investigation will be concluded successfully. In the meantime, it's best if she returns home to America. Get a contact address from her."

Hiroshi translated from Japanese to English for her and added, "Tell him you're staying until it's solved."

Jamie did as Hiroshi advised, and cranked her voice up loud enough to open the chief's eyes wide.

"American women *are* different," the chief said to Hiroshi.

"She's half Japanese." Hiroshi said.

"Saito, give her...no, Sakaguchi you're on this, give her your number."

Sakaguchi handed Jamie his *meishi* name card with a slight bow. The chief walked out to the hallway, reset his Borsalino hat, scarf and coat and waltzed out with Saito behind.

"Is he going to do it?" Jamie asked.

"What?" Hiroshi said.

"Look into my father's case more deeply?"

"He won't, but we will. The bureau chief just administrates."

The detectives set to work finding evidence. Sakaguchi walked upstairs, his weight on the staircase making the entire house creak with each step.

Jamie looked at the tatami room with hardly anything in it.

"It was here?" Hiroshi asked.

"I guess." Jamie walked into the small Japanese style room, hesitantly rubbing her sock on the *tatami*. "What does the scroll say?"

"The big two characters say *mujo*. And the four smaller ones say *shogyo mujo*. All things must pass and nothing stays the same."

"It's like he knew."

"Those kinds of sayings are traditional."

"Not in New York. What's that statue?"

Hiroshi walked over to a small statue of the Fudo Myo-o, a sword upright in one hand and rope in the other, a circular carving of flames framing the god's angry visage. "I'm not sure how to translate exactly, but he's a protective deity."

"Didn't work."

"I'm sorry," Hiroshi bowed. "He's a wrathful god, of Unmoving Wisdom."

"Unmoving sounds opposite to nothing staying the same."

"Buddhism's complicated."

Jamie smiled.

Hiroshi gestured with his hands, American style. "You can place his ashes in the *tokonoma*, right there on the shelf beside the vase."

"Oh, I forgot all about him. His ashes, I mean." Jamie went to get the urn from the hallway. She untied the rice straw rope from around the wooden box, took out the urn with both hands and placed it on the shelf.

They looked at the urn quietly until Sakaguchi came back down the stairs, each step a small earthquake through the old wood-frame house. He came over and whispered to Hiroshi.

Hiroshi translated for Jamie. "My boss..."

"He looks like a sumo wrestler," Jamie said.

"He was, actually. He wants to know if it's OK if we borrow one of your father's books?" Sugamo held the book out. "It might help us with the investigation."

Jamie shrugged. "If it helps."

"We'll return it."

Sugamo took the large art book, a book of erotic *shunga* prints, under his arm.

Jamie sighed and snuffled. "Statues, jet lag, incense, bones, break-in, what's next?"

"Sleep," Hiroshi suggested.

Jamie smiled in weary agreement. She walked to the stairs.

The three detectives, Osaki and Ueno and Sugamo, stood together in the entryway. Without a word, they pumped their thick arms in the air three times and then flipped their fists into fingers. Osaki and Sugamo made scissors and Ueno kept his hand flat like a sheet of paper. Ueno sighed in aggravation at having lost the *janken* scissors-paper-stone contest, and pulled off his tie.

Ueno righted the sofa with one hand, set the cushions back and flopped down for the night. His feet hung over the end and his shoulders over the side. He raked a pillow under his head and Sugamo tossed him a throw blanket. The sofa looked small beneath him.

Hiroshi stood at the bottom of the stairs and said to Jamie, "I'll stop back tomorrow. About noon? We can talk more after you've rested."

Jamie climbed the stairs, her steps a whisper after the rumble of Sakaguchi's heavy footfalls. At the top, she turned and said in Japanese, "*Oyasumi-nasai.*"

In soft voices, the detectives, impressed at her knowing the Japanese for good night, chorused back, "*Oyasumi-nasai.*"

Chapter 6

After Mattson's house, Sakaguchi and Hiroshi met Takamatsu at the *koban* police box near Yushima Station. He was chatting with the uniformed officers leaning on their chest-high *keijo* poles. He had them laughing, their faces amused under the only light on the dark street.

"I was telling them I got the photo!" Takamatsu said when Hiroshi and Sakaguchi came up. Sakaguchi bowed to the police inside, who turned back to their nightly routine.

"What photo?" Hiroshi asked, sighing.

"The guy I've been following. Cheating on his wife."

Hiroshi had to call London at six in the morning. He wanted to sleep before then, but he couldn't sleep on an empty stomach. Sakaguchi said Takamatsu wanted to take them to one of the best sushi places in Tokyo. He decided to eat quickly and head back to the office for a few hours on the futon chair.

"Photographing these cheats is an art form." Takamatsu chuckled as he led Sakaguchi and Hiroshi down a quiet, dark street to what looked like a two-story house with wooden slats across the front. There was no sign and not even a *noren* curtain to indicate the slat-covered panel—too small to be a door—opened into a restaurant of any kind.

Takamatsu ducked in and Hiroshi followed, leaning forward under the low doorjamb. Sakaguchi curved in sideways stooping low.

"*Irrashaimase*! Welcome!" the *master* shouted from behind the counter.

Instead of the expected solitude, though, two young couples sat along the counter chatting and laughing, their faces red from drinking.

The boys' spike-cropped hair and the girls' sparkle makeup clashed with the soft wood and indigo cotton interior of the shop. The usual aroma of fresh fish and cooked rice was overwhelmed by cologne, perfume and tobacco smoke.

Takamatsu made a face and the *master* shot him a "sorry" look. He gestured at seats along the counter and politely asked the four youngsters to move over. The four quieted and reluctantly scooted closer to the wall.

Then, all four fell back to giggling and joking. One girl slapped one of the guys on his shoulder, and the other kept saying, "*Uso, uso,* I don't think so," tugging her tight one-piece dress from riding up her thighs.

Hiroshi wanted to tell them to shut up, but since Sakaguchi and Takamatsu ignored them, he did too. Hiroshi eyed the array of fresh fish beneath the curved glass case. The choice was so select he did not recognize all of them. The *master* handed the detectives steaming *oshibori*. They buried their faces in the delicious cleansing warmth.

The *master* set out a small dish of black, tangled *konbu* with small white fish, another with a neat slice of tofu bathed in *wasabi nori*, and three white cups with blue circles in the bottom. He poured out cloudy, unfiltered *nigori sake* from a large green bottle to the exact lip of the cups, where surface tension held it quivering.

The three detectives leaned over to keep from spilling.

After the first sip, Takamatsu raised his cup and said, "Hiroshi, you're going to have to get over your bad mood. What happened last summer could have been done differently, but it wasn't. Now it's done."

Hiroshi had a hard time seeing Takamatsu with Sakaguchi between them.

Sakaguchi grunted assent and turned to Hiroshi with his cup in the air. "A few bruises and a close call are just part of the deal."

Hiroshi started to object, "I was almost—" but he gave up and held his cup to them with a reluctant mumble of assent, "*Hai, hai.*"

"*Kanpai.* Cheers." They drank in unison.

"Oh, master," shouted the dyed-hair boy closest against the wall. "These girls have never had *ikizukuri*. Can you do one for us?"

"That's usually for the start of the meal," the *master* said calmly, apologizing to the detectives again with his eyes.

"For the girls," the guy said his face pink and perspiring from drinking.

Hiroshi leaned back and took a sip of *sake* instead of clouting the kid on the head like he felt like doing. Hiroshi focused on the *master* with his cutting board and fish knife. From the small, bubbling tank at the side of his prep counter, he pulled out a small silver fish. It squirmed on the cutting board as he sliced one side of the fish in rectangular pieces down to the bone and slid the knife along the smooth arc of bones to lift off the glistening flesh.

He turned the fish over and sliced the other side into small squares and ran a skewer from tail to gill, curving the fish so both filmy grey eyes peered forward. The gills pumped like small wings and the mouth flexed open and shut. He nestled it onto a bed of fern leaves over crushed ice and circled the plate with a mound of white *daikon*, a pinch of *wasabi, shiso* leaves and a teensy blue dish for soy sauce. The mouth of the fish kept gaping and closing.

"*Itadakimasu!*" The young couples dipped the small slices of fish into soy sauce and tucked them into their flushed faces. The girls covered their mouths with their manicured, polished nails and cooed delight, wiggling their thin, bare shoulders.

The three detectives sipped their *sake* and glanced at the sliced fish being eaten half alive from its bed of ice.

Sakaguchi's cellphone rang, and he retrieved it from the depths of his jacket and stepped outside. Hiroshi and Takamatsu sipped their *sake* quietly.

"What do you have against Saito?" Hiroshi asked Takamatsu.

Takamatsu growled as if he was thinking about that himself. "He was a good detective when he was young, but like the bureau chief, he takes the easy route now."

"You think Saito hurried too quickly through the Mattson case?"

"The more you dig into a case like that, the more trouble you bring on yourself. Saito avoids trouble at all costs. Like the chief."

When Sakaguchi ducked back through the sliding door, the *master* asked the four youngsters if they were finished.

One of the young guys replied in curt, haughty Japanese, "We'll leave when we're finished."

Sakaguchi rose up from his stool and dropped a thick, heavy hand on the kid's shoulder, letting it rest there. With his other hand, he pulled out his badge and held it in the kid's face before tapping it—once, hard—onto the kid's nose.

The kid shook his head away and rubbed his nose, his eyes full of tears. The other three set down their chopsticks. The other boy said, "We're done anyway." His moussed wet-look hair bounced around as he flopped ten-thousand yen notes on the counter. The girls got up without another word and tossed their cellphones and handkerchiefs in their brand name purses. The boys tugged on their polyester jackets with dramatic sullenness.

Sakaguchi remained standing in the middle of the sushi bar, leaving just enough room for the four youngsters to sidle out, if they were careful.

Hiroshi waited for the one bump or the one word that would set off Sakaguchi in a *tachiai* charge.

The four young people kept their eyes down and eased out. The only thing that touched Sakaguchi was the scent of their over-used fragrances.

The *master* slid out from the opening under the counter to thank them in the politest Japanese. When they were gone, the *master* set a small "closed" sign out front and slid a wood latch to lock the panel door. The *master* picked up the platter of half-eaten fish, its jaws still gulping, and held it up as he asked, "What else can I get you?"

Hiroshi looked into the cold, grey eye of the fish in the *master*'s hand and said, "Just *chazuke* is fine."

Takamatsu refolded his jacket on the stool beside him. "Just *sake*."

"Something grilled, *iwashi* maybe," Sakaguchi said, sitting down.

The *master* slid back under the counter with a shrug and got to work. The cologne and perfume started dissipating, replaced by the inviting smell of the *master*'s cooking.

Takamatsu said, "There's a guy I talked to about swords. In Shinjuku. Knows his stuff."

"You got the address?" Sakaguchi settled back onto his seat between Hiroshi and Takamatsu, who moved over as the *master* removed the used dishes.

"Someplace." Takamatsu scrolled through his contacts on his cell phone. "I'll send it to Hiroshi. Get him out of the office. Look how pale he is, and that long hair."

Hiroshi started to protest, but didn't want to provoke anything more. He was too tired.

Sakaguchi handed Takamatsu the book from Mattson's. Takamatsu hummed interest as he pulled open the big, heavy art book and leafed through the pages with a smile. He closed the book and handed it back. "There's a shop in the used bookstore area of Jinbocho, Endo Brothers. They specialize in this. They'll know about the *shunga* prints and the *netsuke* carvings."

Sakaguchi wrote down the name. "I'll stop by, but I've never been much of a reader."

Takamatsu smiled. "You don't need to read, you need to talk."

Sakaguchi sipped his *sake*. "Osaki said Mattson's computer was completely blank. They must have erased it after they took what they wanted."

Hiroshi set down his sake cup. "Mattson was going to speak at the opening of the conference on Asian security and defense. Whatever he was going to say was probably on there."

Takamatsu sipped his sake. "You should start with it as just a burglary, and work up from there."

Sakaguchi tucked some pickles into his mouth. "This won't get done before the conference. The Chinese, Korean and American diplomats are already pouring into Tokyo. They get first priority."

"Saito's not in charge of security for that, is he?" Takamatsu looked at them, then groaned. "Oh, of course he is."

"Almost everyone's been assigned over there. No one's left in the office." Sakaguchi set the book aside and sipped his *sake*.

"Where's the file on Mattson?" Hiroshi asked.

Sakaguchi said, "I sent Sugamo to secure it. That's who called. He said the file on Mattson was de-prioritized once the American embassy accepted he was killed during a robbery."

"Let's reprioritize it," Hiroshi said.

"I just did," Sakaguchi said, holding up his cup for another pour of *sake* from the *master*. After he refilled Sakaguchi's cup, the master plonked the top on the large bottle and placed it back in the refrigerated case behind the counter. He pulled the *iwashi* sardines from the grill, the silver skin bubbled and browned. He set them on a rectangular plate in front of Sakaguchi.

Sakaguchi barely blew on the still-smoking fish before popping one hot and whole into his mouth and chewing it, working it, bones and all, down to an easy-to-swallow mash.

"Not much to go on, sword cuts, erotic prints and a blank computer," Hiroshi said.

"It's enough if you read it right," Takamatsu said.

Chapter 7

Nearby the sword shop, Hiroshi slowed to watch a long line of mainly older people carrying signs about the Fukushima meltdown. The chants of the elderly protestors echoed off the corridor of Shinjuku's tall buildings. All were against nuclear power, but some aimed their outrage at the government, while other signs denounced the power companies. Not much separation between the two, Hiroshi thought, as the crowd moved along steadily shepherded by desultory police officers.

The sword shop's heavy door hushed the bullhorn slogans. Inside, Hiroshi let his eyes run over the swords arrayed by style and length in neat wall racks and chest-high glass cases, their shelves softened by silk-covered cushions. Even in the low light of the shop, the swords caught glints of sunlight that made them glimmer with readiness.

The owner, a bonsai of a man with all but the keenest parts trimmed away, stood behind the counter explaining fittings to a customer. The tendons of his forearms flexed as he slipped collars and ray skin grips on and off, explaining precisely what worked and what did not. The owner's neat-cut ponytail and traditional *sagyo-bakama* work clothes made it seem like he and the customer, a salaryman in office clothes, were talking across centuries, not just a counter.

Hiroshi walked to a vertical rack in the corner holding *tameshigiri*, *tatami* mats rolled in tight round bundles. It took Hiroshi a minute to figure out what they were for—sword practice. Some were as tall as a man and varied in thickness from wrist to thigh to waist. Snatching only a few hours of sleep between the sushi place and the call to London Interpol at six a.m., his eyes were so tired he had to squint to read the elegant *kanji* characters stenciled into the intricate sword mountings.

The customer in office clothes pulled open the door to leave, letting in the bullhorn chants from the street for a moment before the door shushed shut leaving only the sound of the owner rubbing a cloth over the *menuki, tsuba* and *fuchikashira* fittings he'd just shown the customer.

"You must like swords," the owner said, as he finished tucking the fittings away in a felt lined box.

"I'm amazed at the patterns along the edge." Hiroshi's eyes roamed over the waves, zig-zags and asymmetric lines flowing along the silver blades.

"Each has a unique *hamon*, made with an application of clay during tempering."

"It sounds complicated."

"Swords are the most complex construction of pre-industrial Japan—a combination of technology, design, engineering and spiritual force." He ran the handleless blade across a cut of oiled paper, placed the blade on the shelf behind the counter, and carefully wiped his hands before retying the front of his cotton jacket.

"A colleague recommended I stop by. Your name is Suzuki, isn't it?"

"Would your colleague be Detective Takamatsu?"

"How did you know?"

"I thought you might be an actor when you first came in. Actors get cast in one samurai movie and then want their own sword. Keeps me in business. If detectives started carrying swords, though, it would really boost sales."

Hiroshi was not sure if Suzuki was joking or not. His strong jawed face and deep-set eyes remained serious. Hiroshi handed him his *meishi*. "I'm Hiroshi Shimizu. Takamatsu is my mentor *senpai*, or was."

"Until he got suspended," Suzuki said.

"You seem to know everything."

"I keep my focus inside this shop. That's enough."

"I was wondering if you could look at a photo," Hiroshi said. "It's rather grisly."

"I've seen the effects of swords. It's never pleasant."

Hiroshi placed the photo of the dead man on the counter, being careful not to look at it. The images of the dead man from the night before had lost none of their persistence, bubbling up again to make the air in the shop stifling. He should have gone to the bookstore and let Sakaguchi work these photos.

Showing no sign of being repulsed, Suzuki turned on a desk light at the side of the counter, examining the photo with magnifying glasses.

"A *tanto* short sword, I would say. Those right there." Suzuki nodded at a row of swords.

Hiroshi stepped over to look at the horizontal display of shorter swords. They all looked the same to him except for their length. Thinking of them cutting into human flesh made their beauty confusing and frightening. Hiroshi rummaged in his head for what to ask. "Don't all swords cut the same?"

"One sign of a *tanto* is how it makes a clean cut." Suzuki looked at him over the top of his glasses. "It was not a *wakizashi* sword," Suzuki nodded at another rack of swords, "which are typically longer, and usually wider. See those over there?" He pointed at another horizontal ladder of longer swords. "You can take one down if you want."

Hiroshi hesitated, uncertain of whether he should actually reach for a sword. He knew there must be some etiquette for handling the swords, so he kept his hands at his sides.

"Those long *katana*," he nodded at a much wider rack on the other side of the store. "Hard to carry through the city without being noticed," Suzuki said, taking off his glasses and looking up at Hiroshi.

Hiroshi wondered if each of the swords in the shop had actually been used. "How do you know what each sword will do?"

"If you cut into a *tameshigiri*, you see right away. The swords produce a distinct stroke. The practice targets are different than human flesh. And this is just a photograph, after he fell."

"This stroke looks practiced?"

"Very."

"Why is there a slightly upward angle?" Hiroshi turned the photo back towards Suzuki. He pictured the whole scene again, making him queasy.

"Perhaps he drew from the scabbard straight into the stroke."

43

Hiroshi frowned, thinking about the dead man's last moments on the street of Golden Gai, bleeding out, feeling weaker, feeling nothing, alone.

"There were no defensive wounds, right?"

"No, but it looked like he ducked and the sword hit a door, shattering it."

"So, he's fast, practiced and unafraid to kill." Suzuki nodded.

"Who would use a *tanto* sword so well?"

"That's a more difficult question."

"Narrow it down for me."

Suzuki folded his magnifying glasses and put them into their case. "He could have studied anywhere, and these days, buyers and sellers come from all over the world. But of course, the blade could have been purchased anytime in the past."

"There's a lot of past." What happened, he wondered, to all the swords made over the centuries? Hiroshi felt he might be wasting his time here. That was Takamatsu's fault. He should have stayed in his office.

"Check the list of purchases at recent conventions. Check that against the list of registered swords."

"How many would that be?"

"Two million. Registered. No one knows how many unregistered swords there are."

"That's a lot to check."

"Don't you have one of those computers?"

"Yes, of course, but even with that, it would take—" Hiroshi stopped, wondering if Suzuki was joking with him, but Suzuki's features remained taut and focused. Hiroshi tapped the photo on the counter and put it away. "Computers are not much help for some things."

"It's hard enough to focus on what's in front of your senses."

"Do you know anything about *seppuku*?" Hiroshi set out a photo of Mattson with a smooth red line straight across his pale belly and another in the chair where he died, blood dripping on to the *tatami* below him. Hiroshi breathed in, pushing his revulsion, and fatigue, aside. "What kind of sword would be used for that?"

"Traditionally, the samurai used a *tanto* sword." Suzuki took the photo and put his glasses back on. "Short *wakizashi* swords could be used, too. The samurai would select their favorite sword, one they knew well and used often. Let me get one for you."

Hiroshi stood waiting as Suzuki went in the back room and returned with a plain wooden scabbard. He set it on a cloth on the counter and with his thumbs at the opening and the sharp side upward, he gently pushed the hilt out and removed the sword.

"Why is the wood so, well, cheap?" Hiroshi felt embarrassed, and a bit ashamed, to know so little of Japan's culture. Maybe Takamatsu was right—he had been overseas too long.

"This is a *shirasaya*, a storage mount. All the fittings are attached when the time comes. You can see the *hamon* pattern here." Suzuki held the *tanto* blade up to the light, moving it slowly so Hiroshi could see the patterns along each side. "You can see how the point, edge, tempered line and back are all different. The inner steel must be pliable, but the edge and point tempered hard."

"Why is that?"

Suzuki looked at Hiroshi patiently, and explained, "The inner metal must bend under pressure, to not break, while the exterior layer must cut clean and hold its edge."

Hiroshi struggled to think what to ask next. "Committing *seppuku* must have taken great determination and tremendous self-control."

"Only trained swordsmen could ever bring it off. Not many of those anymore."

"Cutting oneself open across the belly, no matter how quickly, must be extraordinarily painful."

Suzuki shrugged. "So is whatever drives them to it. There was no *kaishakunin*, was there?" Suzuki asked.

"*Kaishakunin?*" Hiroshi had no idea what he was asking about. He would tell Takamatsu that his sources might have information but offered it reluctantly, in disordered fashion. He should have stayed in his office and looked up most all of this online.

"In ritual suicide, a trusted accomplice stood behind the samurai who was committing suicide. His job was to sever the head of the victim at the neck with one swift, merciful cut."

"He was cut across the abdomen, but not beheaded." Hiroshi was again not sure if Suzuki was testing him, or if Takamatsu had told Suzuki to find how little Hiroshi knew. Either way, he was being tested.

"The stomach held great symbolism in the past. Maybe it doesn't any longer."

Hiroshi slipped the photos back in his pocket.

"Was he tied up?"

"Taped up."

"The swordsman leaned down for a quick stroke with a slight downward angle."

Hiroshi pictured the situation, mentally editing out the blood and gore. "Would a *tanto* work for that?"

"What did the autopsy say?"

"There wasn't one."

Hiroshi could just hear the faint sound of the megaphone from the march outside. It had been going on quietly in the background all along, but with all the back and forth about swords, he had not even noticed. He looked out the window.

Suzuki said, "They've been by every day. You can almost set your watch by them."

"The renewal of the Japan-US treaties is next week. They're warming up."

"They want something new when they lose touch with the old."

Hiroshi put away the photos and in the politest Japanese said, "Thank you for your help."

"Actually, some of us dealers set up a hotline to stop swords from being exported outside of Japan. It's a national heritage issue, I know, but the police have not followed up on any case we dealers have called in about."

"I'll ask around," Hiroshi said. "I have to make some inquiries about that anyway."

Suzuki nodded his thanks and pulled the soft cloth from the counter and folded it carefully. "By the way, if Takamatsu is suspended, he might be interested in delivery work. It's extremely well paid."

"Takamatsu seems to be making a lot as a private detective already."

"The purchaser of this sword would be a good person to talk with."

"How so?"

"Swords are a good investment, especially if you handle a lot of cash."

"The swords are a way of laundering money?"

46

"Sword owners usually have as much information as money."

The shop door opened, letting in the protestors' fading shouts along with a *salaryman* in a business suit. Suzuki turned his attention to the new customer.

Walking to the station, Hiroshi cut through the tail end of the protest line, which was much longer than he thought. He read a few of the signs, but most had passed by, and wondered who made up the concise rhythmic slogans they chanted.

As he walked, he thought about his computer and the comfort of his office. He wondered if he should go back to the office or catch up with Sakaguchi or go talk with Jamie. He entered Shinjuku Station, and walked slowly along a low-ceilinged passageway that ran under a dozen platforms for different train lines, deciding which one to take.

Chapter 8

Along the main street of Jinbocho, store windows displayed journals, textbooks, magazines, *manga*, chapbooks, maps and prints—each store with its own specialty. Library carts, fold-up tables and string-tied stacks of used books spilled onto the sidewalk. Everywhere, people stood reading. Sakaguchi stopped in front of one book propped in a window that would have saved him years as a beat cop—a preparation manual for the detective exam. If he had come to Jinbocho, if he had known such a book existed, he might not have failed the exam six straight years, finally passing the seventh time, never knowing why.

Sakaguchi walked on to the corner of the street and stopped under a ginkgo tree that spread over a large carved wood signboard: "Endo Brothers Bookstore 1889." The sign's gold leaf characters flaked off the worn wood below. Inside the front window, woodblock prints, matted but unframed, were stacked neatly in rows, hundreds of them with one propped for display on top, the date and artist penciled on the matting.

Sakaguchi shook his head as he looked past the prints towards the rows and rows of books inside. Hiroshi should have taken this assignment instead. Sakaguchi couldn't remember the last time he'd been in a bookstore. Hiroshi read all day, even if most of it was numbers on a screen.

A bell rang as Sakaguchi yanked open the door. He had to turn sideways to shuffle down the narrow aisle of densely packed books. At the far back of the store, three men stood by a counter. The man facing out from behind the counter was dressed in a dark tweed jacket and black shirt. His clothes and his shaved bald head contrasted with

49

the other man's long white hair, jeans and cable knit sweater. They had the same round face with almost the same nose and eyes and chin, the same well-fed frames. Twins, Sakaguchi realized, or brothers at least.

To the side, a third man leaned on the counter, one leg propped on a stack of old encyclopedias. He was thin as a sumo judge's *gunbai* fan, with stringy grey hair down both sides of his sunken face. The taut pucker of smoker's wrinkles held his last comment unfinished as they turned silently towards Sakaguchi.

From his pocket, Sakaguchi pulled out a flash drive with copies of the files found on the dead man in Golden Gai. He held up the USB drive in his thick hand. "I'm wondering if you could tell me more about these. I'm Detective Sakaguchi, homicide."

"A cop," the thin man said.

"And you two are the Endo brothers? Twins?" They nodded. Sakaguchi turned to the thin man. "And you are?"

The thin man leaned forward and said, "Books never killed anybody. You're in the wrong place." He pulled around his walking cane to ratchet himself forward. His right hand hung loose, as if unstrung.

When none of the three said anything more, Sakaguchi pulled out his cellphone and thumbed through the address book, trying a trick he'd learned from Takamatsu. "Are your accounts in order? I have a colleague in the tax office."

The two brothers glanced at each other, each waiting for the other to respond.

"We're the owners. I'm Shinichi," the brother in jeans said.

"And I'm Seiichi," the brother in black said.

"Aren't those both names for first sons?" Sakaguchi asked.

The two nodded together. "We were born the same day, but our mother never told us who came out first. She didn't want a hierarchy."

Sakaguchi looked at the thin, angry man leaning on the books.

"And this is Higa," the twins said in unison.

The prong of Higa's belt buckle poked through a handmade hole, plaiting his pants around his scrawny waist. His jacket was as yellowed and worn as his tobacco-stained teeth.

"Unusual name. Where's that from? Okinawa?"

Higa nodded. Sakaguchi pocketed his cellphone and pulled out his name card. One of the twins took it without handing him theirs.

"Here are the prints." Sakaguchi handed the USB drive to Seiichi who looked for an OK from his brother before sliding it into a laptop behind the counter. Seiichi turned the laptop around. Shinichi hiked up his jeans and leaned over the counter to see. The embraces and ecstasies of the woodblock prints drew no reaction from either brother.

Higa said, "Those *ukiyoe* masters knew how to conceal politics in erotics. Power and pleasure have never been so well matched since. Censorship nowadays—"

"Higa, please," said the Endo twins, at the same time.

"Who would have these? Who would buy and sell them?" Sakaguchi leaned forward.

The Endo brothers looked at each other, barely concealing that they knew if not who exactly, at least who would.

Sakaguchi scrunched his sumo wrestler's face into a ball and leaned forward. "This is a murder investigation."

Higa pushed off the counter, leaning on his cane. His right leg was shorter than his left and his foot turned out at an angle when he set it down on the floor. "Someone once said all brave men are in jail."

"Higa!" Shinichi interrupted. "Save it for the next book, can you?"

Higa tried to say more but started coughing, doubling over with a hard, raspy wheeze. Higa caught his breath, about to speak, but his coughing only got worse. Shinichi stepped over to pat Higa on the back and put his cane in his left hand, as his right didn't have any force. Shinichi started walking Higa around the store and Higa's coughing eased as he hobbled down the shelves.

Seiichi whispered, "Higa hates police, but he's one of our most prolific authors. We always publish his works, but he's not always easy to take."

"He's a writer?" Sakaguchi asked. "You're a publisher?"

"Since those Koza riots in 1970, we've published about a book a year of his. I thought old age and bad health would slow him down, but his ideas and his prose keep getting stronger."

"Make any money?" Sakaguchi asked.

"He's got a loyal readership." Seiichi pulled a thin volume from a shelf and handed it to Sakaguchi, *The Okinawa Solution* by Tetsuya Higa. "This is one of his best, or least vitriolic. Please take it. He wrote it after he was beaten by police during the riots. That's why he limps."

Sakaguchi tucked the thin book into his inside jacket pocket with a bow of thanks. "So, what can you tell me about these?"

Seiichi clicked back to a print of naked men with engorged penises laughing as they ran towards a finish line. "There are only two or three of this print in the world. And this one," he clicked to a fleshy tangle of three lovers, kimonos as open as the mouth of the voyeur watching from the side, "Is almost certainly an early Koryusai. Very rare, less than a dozen left."

Sakaguchi nodded. "How do I find who might have these?"

Shinichi returned from the walk around the shelves with a calmer Higa.

Seiichi said, "There is really only one specialist who would know."

"Where do I find him?"

"You can't. He just died."

"What's his name?"

"Bernard Mattson," Shinichi said.

Sakaguchi kept the surprise he felt deep inside his well-padded sumo face.

"His funeral was yesterday," Seiichi said.

"So, he bought and sold prints with you?" Sakaguchi wondered if rare prints were expensive enough to kill for. Surely, the trade was controlled, refined and traditional.

"Mattson was going to publish with us," Shinichi said.

"Two books," Seiichi said.

"About *shunga*?"

"One book was, but the other..." Shinichi let Seiichi finish his sentence. "...we don't know exactly other than it was about SOFA."

Sakaguchi frowned at the foreign-sounding pronunciation of "SOFA," then realized they meant The Status of Forces Agreement with America. Sakaguchi could recite the list of crimes committed by American servicemen protected by SOFA—gang rape of a sixteen-year-old girl, murder-rape of a twenty-year-old—and the many problems with the bases—helicopter crashes, car crashes, weapons misfires—but that did not seem a reason to rob Mattson's place, much less try to silence him.

"Tell him," Shinichi nodded at Higa. "It doesn't matter now."

"I'm trying to find who killed Mattson," Sakaguchi assured Higa.

Higa looked away. "I saw him on NHK programs all the time, but before last year, I met him only once, on a panel an Okinawan peace group set up. We were on opposite sides debating nuclear-armed American warships docking in Japan. He showed up late and very drunk."

Sakaguchi nodded for Higa to go on.

"I almost walked off the stage because it would be no pleasure to win the debate. He took swigs from a half-full bottle of *awamori* liquor with a *habu* snake inside." Higa cleared his throat and resettled his leg on the stack of books.

"So, what happened?" Shinichi prompted.

Higa let a brief smile flutter around his smoker's lips. "He was the most brilliant speaker I've ever heard. Even in that condition. He spoke in support of the status quo, yes, but he explained the issue from both sides so well, I barely got to speak. Genuine criticism is rare from an insider like him. Usually it's total defense of the status quo."

Seiichi nodded for Higa to continue. Sakaguchi listened closely.

"He spoke without notes, but rolled off details that I would have had to look up. He was a passionate speaker, in fluent Japanese, with a command of data and a deep knowledge of history. He quoted Groucho Marx one minute and *Heike Monogatari* the next. So I let him talk."

Sakaguchi said, "And then you asked him to publish?"

Higa chuckled drily. "No, I went home to lick my wounds and rewrite the book I was working on. I never thought anything more about him until he called me last year. I don't know how he got my home number. I keep it secret."

The brothers nodded for Higa to continue.

"I was ready for him to be drunk, but he was clean, sober, calm and focused." Higa cleared his rattling throat. "We talked for hours that day in a Ginza *kissaten*, drinking straight black coffee. He asked if I wanted to edit a book of his about the SOFA agreements. He had a new vision of it and wanted to lay the groundwork for new agreements. I was taken aback because there's been almost no revision since they were written. I brought him here to the Endo brothers."

"Our publishing business has been taking off," Shinichi said.

"Just when selling old books and prints was declining," Seiichi said.

"Mattson knew how to connect the dots." Higa coughed, but took a breath and didn't cough again. "He wrote as well as he spoke, knew both languages, both cultures."

"What did he write?" Sakaguchi asked. "What was he going to write?"

Higa looked at the wall and shook his head, coughing from deep in his lungs. "I didn't even see a draft. He wanted to finish the whole thing first. It got so long, we had to set up a second, condensed version that people could read quickly."

Seiichi said, "Mattson knew where to find the inside info all the way back to the first drafts in 1959. He had his own carrel in the national archives. He knew all the pieces, all the documents and discussions and meetings that formed the basis of the East Asian Alliance."

Shinichi said, "The last time I talked to him, a couple weeks ago, he said he had only a few more details to fill in. He was supposed to deliver the manuscript the day of his funeral."

"So, where's the manuscript?" Sakaguchi demanded. "We need it to see..."

The twins shook their heads and shrugged, their eyes cast down.

Higa snorted and cleared his phlegm-filled lungs. "Only Mattson could write the truth about the SOFA agreement."

"Why's that?" Sakaguchi asked.

"He wrote the original."

Chapter 9

Hiroshi listened from the entryway of Mattson's home before walking into the room where he'd talked with Jamie the night before. There was no sign of Jamie, but Ueno looked up from the too-small sofa in the living room with sleeplessness written across his face. Late morning light filtered in through the windows of Mattson's living room and spilled over the turmoil of furniture and antiques.

Ueno pushed himself up and stretched. "I thought someone would come earlier."

"She upstairs?" Hiroshi asked.

Ueno shrugged, stretched and plodded towards the door. He pulled on his coat and slipped into his shoes.

"I'm not in charge of the rotation," Hiroshi called after Ueno, but he closed the door without responding.

Hiroshi spent the next hour looking around the study and living room. He tried to imagine the robbers at work and held up the photos of Mattson's corpse against the spots where they were taken, feeling queasy again at the scene. He called the tech guys at the station to come get the stripped-clean computer and see what they could do. He wondered why they'd left it.

"Good morning," Jamie called from the doorway.

"I didn't hear you come down," Hiroshi said. "Sleep well?"

"I took a sleeping pill my mother gave me. I couldn't wake up," she said, yawning.

Even her yawn was gorgeous. She looked robustly American in jeans and a sweatshirt. Her fine nose and delicate lips looked even better in the daylight. Hiroshi looked away, and then followed her when she padded into the kitchen.

"It's a little bit creepy eating my dead father's food," she said, opening the refrigerator. "But there's nothing in here anyway."

"We can go out. It's almost lunch time."

"Let me take a shower." Jamie went upstairs and came back down in her father's bathrobe. The bath was at the back of the kitchen.

From the living room, Hiroshi could hear the heavy door to the bathing area roll shut. He called Akiko to tell her to send prosecutors a preliminary report on an embezzlement case at a joint French-Japanese insurance company and to put off anyone else who called. Before he could finish, he heard the bath door rolling open and Jamie calling, "Detective, detective?" He told Akiko he'd call back and hurried through the kitchen to the bathing area.

Jamie stood wrapped in her father's bathrobe staring at the water heater knobs. "There's only cold water," she said.

"You have to turn on the gas first. Here, let me."

Hiroshi edged past her into the changing room as Jamie stepped aside. Hiroshi couldn't quite reach the knobs in the tiled bath, so he pulled off his socks to keep them dry. He leaned down beside the large cedar tub to crank the spark handle and twist the heat to high.

"When I was a little girl, I used to be scared to bathe alone in here," Jamie said, re-tightening the belt on her robe. Hiroshi stood trying to think what to say to that, the two of them awkward in the small changing room, his socks dangling from his hands.

The doorbell rang, scattering the moment.

"I'll get that," Hiroshi said.

"Thanks," Jamie sang out after him.

At the door were two foreigners, a square-shouldered woman and a tall, blonde-haired guy who looked like the Marlboro man. The woman's big-jawed face held a friendly smile. Her short haircut, bulging briefcase, and pinstripe suit were all business. The tall man's smile broke into two dimpled lines along his tanned face. His eyes were so light blue, they seemed focused far away. He wore a leather coat over a camelhair jacket and turtleneck sweater.

The woman looked at Hiroshi strangely, noticing but not asking why he was holding his socks in his hands.

"Are you a relative of Bernard Mattson?" Hiroshi asked in English.

"I'm from the American embassy. My name is Pamela Carica." She pulled a name card out of a small leather holder and held it out to Hiroshi.

The man pulled his name card from inside his leather coat and said, "I work liaison through the embassy. My name's Trey Gladius. Bernie and I go way back."

"I'm Detective Hiroshi Shimizu."

Pamela reached out to shake his hand. "Have you found out anything new about the case?"

"There was a break-in during the funeral."

Pamela drew back, startled.

They followed Hiroshi into the living room and stood looking at each other in polite hesitation before he turned away and pulled on his socks.

"Jamie's in the shower," Hiroshi said.

"Ah," they both said and looked around for a place to sit.

"Someone was here all night. On the sofa." Hiroshi pointed where Ueno had slept. They looked at the jumbled room, everything in the wrong place, and waited quietly.

"Visitors?" Jamie came in to the living room in her father's bathrobe, several sizes too large for her, with her long hair spread out to dry on a towel over her shoulders.

"I'm Pamela Carica. From the embassy. We talked by phone? Before the funeral?"

"Oh, yes, of course, I'm sorry," Jamie said. "I forgot you were coming."

"Are you OK?" Pamela asked. "Was anything taken?"

"I haven't been here in twenty years. It took me half the morning to find a towel."

Jamie looked at Trey. Pamela introduced him. "This is a friend of your father's."

Trey leaned forward and took her hand in both of his. "I cannot tell you how sorry I am. Recently, your father only talked about two things—his project and you. I couldn't make the funeral, just back from Korea. But I wanted to offer my condolences in person."

"I'm happy to meet people who knew him. It's all I can do now."

Pamela said, "I have a few things for you, but is now a good time?"

57

"After I change, it will be." Jamie excused herself and went upstairs, rubbing her hair with the towel. When she came back, she was wearing jeans and a sweatshirt under one of her father's wool jackets, the sleeves rolled up and a fresh towel under her long hair.

They pulled up some stray chairs and arranged them around the only piece of furniture in the room other than the sofa that wasn't out of place: a dining table against the wall.

"Your father was so well known in Japan." Pamela opened her briefcase. "I can't tell you how many times I read his columns and heard him on TV. He often came to the embassy. It made me proud to know someone could know another culture so deeply and could do so much good work. You'll be giving his speech for him next week, I guess."

Jamie, not really listening, nodded her head yes, but when the last sentence clicked, she said, "I'm not giving any speeches. I just want to get his affairs in order."

"I understand." Pamela set a small stack of papers on the table. "I'm sorry to hand you a batch of forms, but if you want to send the ashes to America, you will need these. I have everything in Japanese and English. For accessing his bank accounts, it's these. Did he have a will?"

"I don't know. I hadn't thought about that." Jamie looked confused and ran the towel over her wet hair.

Trey cleared his throat, leaning forward with his hands together. "I'd like to help your father's project move forward if I can. A significant work from him would influence Pacific Rim politics and knowing Bernie, it would be masterful." Trey leaned forward and smiled, dimples crinkling on either side of his white teeth. "I just want to be sure Bernie's legacy is handled right. I'd also like to show my respects by taking his daughter out to dinner one evening?"

Jamie looked into his faraway blue eyes. "I've never been asked out in honor of my father before. That's a first."

"There's another friend of your father's I want you to meet. I'll call you tomorrow morning, if that's all right?"

Jamie nodded OK.

"Great," Trey said.

The front door bell rang and Hiroshi turned towards it, thinking that Americans smiled too much and always said things like "great" and "fantastic" and "wonderful," exaggerated words they didn't really mean.

Pamela stood up and zipped her briefcase closed. "Sounds like someone else is here. And I've got to run. Another American citizen's death."

"Another one?" A wave of concern passed over Jamie's face.

"Well, yes, sadly. There are a lot of Americans in Japan. The military takes care of service members, so that's a little less for me. But still. I used to work with the Chamber of Commerce and never got out of the office. Now I'm out almost everyday."

Americans also always talked about themselves without being asked, a habit Hiroshi had never been able to understand. They also touched each other a lot, even strangers.

Pamela took Jamie's hands in hers. "Let me know if there's anything else I can do."

Trey confirmed, "I'll call you tomorrow."

Americans always expected yes for an answer, didn't even wait for it. Hiroshi eyed Trey's big loping American stride as Jamie walked them to the front door.

Waiting at the front door was Setsuko, Mattson's first wife. Setsuko bowed politely to the two Americans as they walked out. Setsuko turned to give Jamie a hug. Hiroshi wondered who she could be. Everyone was hugging or touching Jamie. Hiroshi stood back as Jamie walked Setsuko in to the living room. Setsuko set down several bags on the table. "I realized Bernie probably had nothing to eat in the house. He said not eating out in Tokyo was a crime."

"There was zero in the fridge. But I'm the same in New York."

"So, you're the detective in charge?" Setsuko said to Hiroshi, brushing her grey hair behind her ears and straightening her blue jacket. "I'm Bernie's first wife."

Hiroshi handed her his *meishi*. She nodded and tucked it in her pocket. From one of the bags she set down, Setsuko pulled out *onigiri* rice balls, handmade from brown rice with a thick wrap of *nori* seaweed, sprinkled with sesame seeds and dried fish flakes.

"I really miss these," Jamie said.

Setsuko went into the kitchen. "He's got tea at least. For when he didn't go out for coffee."

Setsuko came back out with a pot of tea and three handmade cups. She seemed to know where everything was. She motioned for Hiroshi and Jamie to eat and drink. Hiroshi took one, opened the wrap and realized how hungry he was.

Not waiting to be asked, Setsuko looked straight in Hiroshi's eyes. "He wasn't robbed for his art treasures. Bernie was finishing an important study about the origins of SOFA and what it meant. He had been going to the national archives every day for the past two years. He was almost done, right before—"

Hiroshi swallowed a mouthful of rice. "When did you see him last?"

"The day before he was killed."

Setsuko poured for each of them. The scent of fresh green tea filled the room.

"You saw him every day?" Jamie asked.

Setsuko smiled at her. "Almost every day. You know, or maybe you don't, but you need to know, that he left me for your mother, Sachi, all those years ago. She was so sexy and wild and half my age. He was drinking constantly then. He'd black out and I'd have to go pick him up. Or the police would drag him home. I was sick of it. I guess you have to let people hit bottom before they come back up on their own. So, that's what I did, and he did come back to me, when he finally sobered up."

"He was drinking that much?" Jamie asked. "I didn't know. I don't remember that at all."

"It came and went. He got worse after you left for America. Finally, he dried out at a hospital. Half a year. And then he went to a Zen monastery, the same one where we first met. After meditating, he was like he used to be, in the 50s and 60s." Setsuko shook her head and took the hot cup of tea in two hands.

Jamie blew on her tea and Hiroshi finished his *onigiri*.

"After I was sure he sobered up, I pushed him to get in touch with you." Setsuko smiled at the memory. "It took him a year or two, but he finally wrote you after I found where you were working."

Jamie looked down at her tea cup.

Setsuko seemed lost, then came back and turned to Hiroshi. "He kept delaying handing the book to the publishers. He wanted one more...something, he never said what, but something he had to have for the book to work. He insisted it was there."

"What was where?" Jamie asked.

Setsuko shrugged and held her palms up. "He wanted it to be a surprise when he gave the plenary address at the conference. I thought he was joking, but he was serious. I don't even know where he kept the speech. Every day he was rewriting, rethinking, never telling me a word."

Setsuko put her hand to her cheek, remembering, and then got up to clear the dishes.

Hiroshi stood up, wondering about the speech. He could hear Setsuko doing a quick cleanup in the kitchen. From the corner of his eyes, Hiroshi watched Jamie fiddling quietly with the bag that had held the *onigiri*.

When Setsuko came back, she took Jamie's hand and walked her into the *tatami* room. The two women knelt in *seiza* style on the mats in front of Mattson's ashes. The urn seemed to fit the shelf as if it had always been there.

"You need a photo and some incense." Setsuko patted Jamie on the leg. "And a bell."

Jamie nodded her head. "I'll get those."

Both women faced the offset shelves holding the urn, statue and scroll. Jamie put her arm around Setsuko, their hair falling around them as they lowered their heads without moving or speaking.

Hiroshi watched them from where he stood in the next room, a distance that felt very far away.

Chapter 10

The narrow alleys of Golden Gai doglegged in all directions. At the funeral, Jamie had promised Shibata she'd stop by his club. She brought Hiroshi to be sure she could find it. Hiroshi had put up no resistance. The arm's-width bars were still closed, but it was hard to tell because most had no windows, just doorways.

"Let's try this lane." Hiroshi walked down another alley, studying the names, each on a different variety of sign hanging on the front walls.

"Didn't we go down there already?" Jamie waved the *meishi* shop card in the air. "I'm sorry to have asked you all the way over here. You must be busy."

Hiroshi didn't want to admit that, so he walked over to a hand-painted map of the area bolted onto two rusted poles, but the layout on the map was sideways from the streets.

Hiroshi heard something fall and Jamie shouting and turned to see her picking herself up from a jumble of empty Styrofoam boxes.

"Yuck. These stink!" She pulled herself up, then stood holding her arms to the side, shaking off whatever was on her hands.

Hiroshi dashed over and handed her his handkerchief. "You have to pay attention in Tokyo. The concrete's uneven."

As Jamie wiped her hands, Hiroshi saw behind her, and the Styrofoam fish boxes, the sign for "Pan-Pan," Shibata's bar.

Jamie turned and shouted, "There it is!"

Hiroshi realized, suddenly, horribly, the alley was where the dead man had been killed. Though the blood was washed off, he could picture the body split open on the pavement. The slashed-open door had crime scene and duct tape over the opening. A bouquet of flowers was propped on the curb across from Shibata's place, where the dead man had lain, an offering for his departed spirit.

Jamie knocked on the door and Shibata's round head poked around the weathered door, one eye through the crack. When he saw Jamie, he pulled back the door. His face's plump features filled out and his eyes opened wide.

"Little Jamie-*chan*! I thought it might be police. Come in, come in," he pulled her inside and gave her an American-style hug.

"We had a hard time finding the place. This is Detective Hiroshi. He's been helping me," Jamie said. Hiroshi stood behind her, wondering how Bernard Mattson knew this bar owner, and from how long ago.

Shibata pulled Jamie inside, and Hiroshi turned sideways to squeeze in behind the six tall stools along the bar. Light came from a small back room behind a *noren* shop curtain. A sink, microwave and glass cooler took up the rest of the space.

Hiroshi leaned against the velvet wallpaper, his head bumping Mardi Gras beads and retro photos in silver frames. Crinkled, colored streamers and white mesh fabric soared up and over the ceiling rafters, leftover from a party, or ready for one.

"Last time I see you, you were little, little girl. Sit, sit, sit." Shibata sat Jamie down on a stool.

"I sort of remember this place," Jamie said, unbuttoning her coat.

"That different place. Burned down. But inside is look same. You remember?"

"I sat on the bar and chewed gum."

"You only six or seven then. So cute! People stop you on the street take your picture."

Shibata glided around the bar and fished inside the under-bar ice chest. With a flourish, he pulled up a bottle of champagne and fingered three champagne flutes from a rack above the counter and set them upright onto the polished wood counter. In a flash, he ripped off the foil and wire and popped the cork. He poured out the champagne and let it bubble over the top. "Bernie saying you come back. And here you are!"

Jamie said, "Too late to..."

"Hush now," Shibata said, wiping the spill and sliding the flutes towards them. "Never too late. *Kanpai*! Cheers!"

"So, tell me Mr. Hiroshi, why you helping this gorgeous creature? That one of your dad's favorite phrase, *gorgeous creature*."

Hiroshi set his champagne down on the bar top and handed Shibata his card. "I'm helping with the break-in at her house."

"Break-in?" Shibata froze and squinted at Hiroshi. "When?"

"During the funeral," Jamie said. "I hadn't been in the house in twenty years. I get there and it's ransacked."

Shibata looked away. "Things stolen?"

"I don't even know what was there."

"Print, statue, carving, pottery, all very, very valuable." Shibata swallowed a long, slow mouthful of champagne. From the curtained-off back area stepped Ken, the younger man who had come with Shibata to the funeral. Ken's tall, buffed, tanned figure made the place feel smaller. Shibata held up his glass, but Ken shook his head and ducked under the curtain to the small back kitchen and storage area.

"I know Bernie so long time. Since 1950s," Shibata gulped his champagne. "Tokyo not so big those days. Your father knew everyone. He speak Japanese, Korean, good Chinese, too." Shibata poured more champagne for them.

"I didn't know that." Jamie sipped her refilled glass.

"More you don't need to know," Shibata laughed. "Occupation, soldiers, *yakuza*, black market, buying, selling. My bars, open, close. Crazy time, but fun." Shibata turned serious. "You must get his thing from archive. Bernie going there everyday translating, writing. He leave important thing there."

Jamie shrugged and smiled.

"I have other important thing but not have now," Shibata said. "I give you tomorrow when I send you airport."

"I'm not leaving tomorrow."

"I get you very cheap ticket New York." Shibata pointed at Hiroshi. "Let this man do his work, then come back."

"I want to stay and get things sorted out," Jamie insisted.

Shibata rubbed the dome of his head. "You got bodyguard here, but go back is better. You like *yakitori*?" He took a napkin from the stack and started sketching a map.

"Another map?" Jamie said. "We could barely find this place."

"I call tell them you coming. Your father favorite place," Shibata handed the hand-drawn map to Hiroshi and explained how to get there, then pushed them towards the door.

Outside, Shibata gave Jamie a big hug while Hiroshi stood politely to the side with the napkin map. Shibata took both of Jamie's hands in his. "Listen, I know you stubborn. You Bernie's daughter. But best you go back New York, come back later."

"I'll think about that," Jamie promised.

When they got to the corner of the narrow alley, Hiroshi looked back and saw Shibata standing over the flowers on the curb for the dead man.

Hiroshi would need to talk with him again, in Japanese, alone. But for now, with Jamie, Hiroshi twisted the napkin map like a compass to steer them out of Golden Gai towards the nearby area of Korean barbecue joints, Thai restaurants, coffee shops and dark doorways. Jamie followed, the sights and smells stirring memories of the long walks with her father around Tokyo. She recalled nothing specifically, but everything intensely.

Hiroshi stopped in front of an exhaust fan gushing the aroma of charcoal-grilled chicken. From a plain sliding glass door, more divider than door, a young man hurried out to welcome them.

Inside, the employees shouted, "*Irrashaimase*, Welcome." A long wood counter stretched around the glassed-in grill area. The room was smoky-steamy and Jamie's shoe soles stuck on the rough, oily concrete floor. Jamie and Hiroshi sat down in the last two open seats at the counter. A waiter handed them hot face towels.

"What do you want to drink?" Hiroshi asked.

Jamie smiled. "I drink everything."

"That's your American side. Anything you don't eat?"

Jamie smiled again. "I eat everything."

"That's your Japanese side." Hiroshi ordered beer.

The menu hung along the top of the wall, each dish on a wooden plaque darkened by oily smoke, one or two were turned around, sold out for the day. The waiter listened while Hiroshi reeled off orders as his eyes roamed the walls.

The waiter then hurried behind the grill pit and slapped the orders onto an overhead rack. The grill chef worked steadily over the glowing coals on a rig of grates and bricks. Catching Jamie watching, he gave her a serious nod of the head. The beer arrived in frosted glasses and they clinked them together and drank.

Jamie twisted around to see the whole place, beer glass at her lips. "I love this place!" Jamie turned towards Hiroshi, "Why does Shibata want to get me out of Tokyo?"

"It's not a bad idea, actually," Hiroshi said. Having Jamie safely back in New York would make the investigation easier and free up detectives. At least they would not have to have someone spend the night there.

"I want to go to the bank, talk to a lawyer. I want to find his speech and the manuscripts of his books."

"I read a book of your father's on US-Japan relations when I was in college. I forgot all about it until I heard his name again."

"Did you study politics?"

"I studied history before I transferred to the States for accounting."

"That's a big switch."

"It was long ago. In America, I got lost between two languages, two cultures, two everything."

"I always felt Japanese there, but I feel American here. It's like I have two identities arguing with each other in my head. Two passports. I'm supposed to choose one, but I've kept both." Jamie looked up at the ceiling, sucking in a deep breath. She stared at the grill, but after several sniffles trying to keep it all inside, tears coursed down her cheeks. "I would've loved to talk to my dad, sitting here, together."

Hiroshi, wondering how to soothe an aching he knew himself, handed her his handkerchief.

Jamie put it to her face, then held it away. "Oh, this smells like fish."

"Oh, sorry. From when you fell." He signaled to the waiter for another *oshibori*, started to stuff the handkerchief back into his pocket, then set it on the counter. The waiter set another hot towel down. Jamie unrolled it and wiped her face and eyes. Hiroshi waited as she calmed down.

"You know, you don't seem like a cop," Jamie said.

"You don't seem like, um, actually, what do you do?"

Jamie shrugged. "I work in human resources at UNICEF."

"Sounds interesting. And important."

"Does it? It bores me to tears," Jamie said, and tears started again. "Different tears," she said wiping her face, sniffling. "Most days, it feels like *in*human resources. Everyone is always telling me Asians are more empathetic blah blah blah, so human resources is perfect for me, but I'm not sure it is."

"You don't hate it, do you?"

"No, but I don't love it, either. It is what it is."

"What about life outside work?"

"New York's great. I loved shopping, but I couldn't keep up with my rich friends."

"Try living on detective pay."

"Is it low?"

"I track down embezzlers, scammers and cheats who make millions, illegally, while I get paid a pittance."

"My pay's less than a pittance *and* it's boring." Jamie downed the last half of her beer in one go. The waiter looked to see if she wanted a refill, and Hiroshi motioned for another.

"I'll stay a few days and get his stuff pulled together. But, would you help?" she asked in a small voice. "I don't know how to—"

"Of course," Hiroshi said. "I can go with you to the archives."

The waiter reached over the top of their heads to the grill chef for their orders of grilled chicken breast ribboned with plum sauce, browned scallops with wasabi, and pearl onions flaked with seaweed, two skewers each set neatly on their own rectangular plates—turquoise, sea-green or grey-black. Hiroshi arranged them on the counter.

Jamie sipped her beer and blinked her eyes. "It was stupid not to come before. Now, it's stupid not to stay."

Chapter 11

The next morning was fresh and bright and the city busy and crowded as Jamie settled into the taxi beside Trey. She apologized as the grogginess took over and she yawned wide and loud.

Trey smiled his TV smile and patted her arm. "I know about jet lag, don't worry."

Jamie sucked in a huge breath to stifle the next yawn, and said, "My mother gave me these sleeping pills. They work too well. My body doesn't know what time it is."

"If I knew you were sleeping, I wouldn't have kept pressing the bell. But with yesterday's events, I got worried. There should have been someone there." Trey's tanned face dimpled whether he smiled or frowned.

"There was a detective here when I went to sleep last night."

"Maybe it'd be better to stay somewhere else."

"I'm better there," Jamie said. "Anyway, this sounds exciting. Does she speak English? I'm regretting how much I let my Japanese slip."

"She went to school in America. She's the third generation of her family to get elected, but the first woman. Strong in foreign affairs. Might even be in the next Cabinet."

"It's nice of you to take me to meet her, but why?"

"You'll see," Trey said, humming to himself.

The taxi drove south on the expressway along the Sumida River before crossing a bridge into central Tokyo. Traffic was just heavy enough to slow them down. As they pulled further into the city, the Imperial Palace came into view opposite a row of office buildings.

Jamie straightened to get a look at it. "My father used to ask me what I imagined it was like inside."

"The Imperial Palace? Impressive, isn't it?" Trey glanced at it and then at Jamie, then looked at the meter.

Jamie knew the imperial family still lived there, in sealed-off areas, but she could sort of remember, as if watching some official NHK video, the sweeping white walls and a beautifully sculpted garden. She and her father had climbed up the stone foundations of something, maybe the original castle that burned down, him telling her stories the whole time. Jamie looked out the back window as they went past and then settled in for the rest of the ride.

When they got out in front of the Diet building, Jamie instinctively took a few steps towards a circle of protesters carrying signs in front of the wide, stone steps. Trey walked towards the office building, but Jamie stayed where she was, watching the protesters quietly circling with signs held high. Policemen in riot gear lined each side of the crowd, watching indifferently.

"What do the signs say?" Jamie asked.

Trey frowned. "Some are against nuclear power. Others against the bases."

"The American bases?" Jamie eyed the slow-circling crowd. It was composed mainly of elderly people, dressed in thick winter parkas and colorful hats.

"I'm all for free speech, but the US-Japan alliance is the gyroscope of Asia." Trey directed them up the steps towards the large, brass doors.

Jamie stopped at the bottom of the steps trying to decipher the signs. "That one says '3.11.' The earthquake, tsunami and nuclear plant meltdown, right?"

"The Japanese nuclear power company failed to do its job. Worst thing you can do in Japan. On top of that, the cleanup's costing billions. Still, I don't know what the protestors think, the radioactivity will clean itself up?" Trey shook his head and walked a few steps higher.

"My father said Japanese were apathetic."

"Next week's conference has them stirred up. But if they think they can change the status quo that easily, they're in fantasyland."

"The right fantasy maybe." Jamie yawned again, shaking her head and breathing deeply before following Trey up the steps and inside the spacious, Western-style building.

At the front sign-in area, Trey spoke to the guard in Japanese and he waved them through the metal detector. The arched ceilings and marble walls spoke power all through the corridor. An elevator operator in white gloves pushed the button for the ninth floor on a gleaming brass panel. In the upper-floor hallway, their footsteps echoed in the emptiness until Trey stopped and pulled open the large oak door of Shinobu Katsumura's office. Her secretary stood up with a polite bow and ushered them into the inner office.

Low lighting veiled the room, but the silver and gold lettering still sparkled on the sides of legal tomes lining wall-to-wall shelves. The room was too warm, and the air a bit stale even with the high ceiling. It brought back all of Jamie's drowsiness and she blinked to keep her eyes open as Shinobu Katsumura, Lower House Diet Member, got up from her computer chair in the alcove and walked towards them.

"Welcome!" Shinobu's voice carried across the room. Under her stylish maroon jacket, a black turtleneck and pencil skirt clung to her petite figure. Her hair fell from a side part in clipped, curved layers and her eyebrows, plucked at a sharp angle, steepened when she took Jamie's hand with the ease of someone used to campaigning face to face. Shinobu said, "Please accept my deepest condolences."

Jamie nodded and smiled her thanks. She followed Shinobu's lead towards soft leather chairs circling a low table in the middle of the room. Jamie sat down and Shinobu folded her legs at a prim angle under her skirt as she spoke. "I wanted to tell you how sorry I am in person. Your father succeeded in brokering agreements, drafting treaties, resolving disputes. We'll miss his steady hand and sage advice."

"Thank you," Jamie said, looking down.

The secretary carried in three cups of green tea, which she placed on the table between them, along with a small pot with steam escaping from the spout.

"You know, at every reception, gala or dinner, everyone gravitated to your father. He always pulled people to him, discussing culture, politics, art, history."

"I keep hearing things like that," Jamie said.

"My father—who also knew him during his years as a Diet Member—told me your father secured the foundation for democracy in Asia. He respected that deeply."

"I'm sure many others, like your father, contributed as well." Jamie scrambled for polite replies.

Shinobu smiled. "You're just as humble as he was." Shinobu cocked her head, her small lips curving gently to a smile, then reverting to a thin line in the middle of her delicate features. She seemed to be considering every word and spoke English fluently.

Jamie shifted in her chair, unsure how to read the compliments. She brought the teacup to her lips, but it was too hot, so she cradled it uncomfortably in her fingers for a few seconds, and then set it back down. "I'm happy to hear all this about my father. I just wish—"

"Some wishes—" Shinobu looked away. "My father passed away recently, too, so I know what you must be feeling. The funeral formalities, the unpleasant practicalities, the memories and regrets. No time for the grieving and reflection you really need," Shinobu said.

"Yes, that's it exactly." Jamie looked down at her teacup, wondering when it would be cool enough to attempt drinking again.

Shinobu paused in her presentation to let Jamie take a moment.

Trey sat on the soft leather watching the two women.

When Jamie looked up again, Shinobu said, "I want to publish your father's writings. One of my uncles runs a publishing house. I know this is out of the blue, but I wanted to show my appreciation. It's a small thing, but something." She folded her long, slender fingers around her teacup and took a sip.

Jamie leaned back wondering why Trey didn't say this before. "I'm not sure exactly, but I think he has a publisher already. Setsuko, I mean, a friend of his, told me something, but I wasn't listening carefully."

"My uncle's press would be able to reward you at a higher rate than anyone else. That's part of the reason I wanted to talk to you so soon. I know you need time to process, but I didn't want this opportunity to pass."

"I'd have to check. I don't know where any of his work is either."

Shinobu sat forward. "You wouldn't need to do anything but give us an OK. Trey could oversee the details. He would check with you on major decisions and move forward with the day-to-day. We can work out terms with the smaller publisher if need be. Happens all the time. They'll be amply compensated."

Trey leaned forward. "All you have to do is give us your OK."

"And my father's manuscripts," Jamie added.

Shinobu's plucked eyebrows arched to a "V."

Trey cleared his throat. "I'd like to look through all your father's writing to get the full scope."

"I really have no idea what he was writing. I haven't seen any of it yet, but I'd like to read it first."

Shinobu gave Jamie a smile that would have pleased her constituents. "Of course, of course! I'm sure, though, that much of it is probably ready to publish now, so it would be best if Trey could get started right away."

Shinobu leaned forward to pour more tea, though Jamie had not drunk any. Jamie watched her fluid delicate movements, which reminded her of a tea ceremony with older women in kimono—graceful, calming and practiced.

Trey smiled. "This project would take a lot of work, considering the range of his expertise, but that's the pleasure too. And like Shinobu said, they would give you full rights, take care of any other contracts he might have, and do this right."

Jamie thought for a minute, and said, "I could move forward on this. I mean, why not?"

"I was hoping you might say that. My uncle prepared a letter of agreement." Shinobu walked to her desk with ballet-like precision, returning with a contract, in Japanese, on a leather clipboard folder. "This is just a basic letter of intent. I'll get you a copy in English later. This just says we can get started."

Trey leaned forward. "It's the biggest honor you could give your father."

Jamie scooted to the edge of the soft leather chair, looked at the Japanese document, and signed it. She set the heavy pen down on the table and closed her eyes to dampen the dizzy surge of fatigue inside her, wondering if it was from jet lag, grief or those pills?

Shinobu placed the letter of agreement inside the leather folder.

Trey said, "This will be a great project."

"Let's get started right away," Shinobu said, standing by the side of Jamie's chair.

"No time like the present." Trey slapped his thighs and stood up.

Jamie looked back and forth as she stood up, wondering why they didn't say anything more about the project. Like with the autopsy and the funeral, there seemed to be little explanation in Japan. Everyone was supposed to know exactly what to do and stay quiet if they didn't. Everything happened below the surface, which is where Jamie had always felt the weakest. "You'll send me an English copy?"

"I'll have Trey bring it to you." Shinobu smiled and took Jamie's arm as they walked towards the door. "So, where did your father keep all his manuscripts?"

There was something in her voice, but Jamie was too jet lagged to figure out what. "They must be somewhere," Jamie said. "But the detectives need to look through them. That's what you meant, wasn't it? To publish after the murder investigation is finished?"

"Of course," Trey reassured her, taking Jamie's elbow.

Shinobu's campaign smile stayed fixed in place as she led Jamie to the door.

Chapter 12

Trey and Jamie walked slowly across a large intersection in Ginza. Multicolored signs with store names in Japanese, French and English rose gently along the buildings, their lights shining into the darkness overhead. Clusters of salarymen and slowly strolling couples spoke in drunken or hushed tones about where to go next. Jamie felt comfortable inside the glowing, humming lattice of wide sidewalks and straight streets.

Trey paused at a busy corner and turned to Jamie. "I'd like to take you to another of your father's favorite places, just for a nightcap?"

"Jet lag is calling me home." Jamie resisted the urge to yawn again. She'd yawned so many times at dinner, the chef made a joke about it in the restaurant Trey took her to, a sushi-sashimi place so exclusive, they had their own chef right across the counter for just the two of them. He recommended fish and prepared them one by one, setting them down beside large blocks of ice that kept them cool for the few seconds they enjoyed their appearance before popping them in their mouths. She tried to see the bill, but Trey made sure she couldn't. It must have cost a fortune.

"We hardly saw anything of Ginza." Trey motioned towards the lights of Ginza. "At least a walk?"

"It's a bit cold and I've got to get some sleep." Jamie pushed her hair back and let it fall over her shoulders, making no move towards the subway entrance. "Did you go out with him often?"

"Your father? I'll miss him." Trey put his hand on her arm, his touch filled with sympathy.

Jamie looked away at the sparkle of lights. "My father said all American cities look like Ginza. Even when we weren't in touch, my father's words were with me somehow."

Trey kept his hand on her arm, his strong hand trying to comfort her.

Jamie said, "Shinobu seemed anxious to get going. I hope I didn't sound rude."

"She's enthusiastic about this project. Before next week, we at least need a press release about the books."

"Next week?"

"This year with all the protests about renewing the agreements and the nuclear stuff, everyone's paying attention. Shinobu wanted your father's book out as a gift, to him, and now to you. Let's get his ideas into the public debate."

"That's why she's in a hurry?" Jamie wasn't sure she was reading anything right. She felt another surge of tears and wiped her eyes. "I think the jet lag is making me emotional."

"You're lucky. It makes most people brain dead."

Jamie laughed. "It's doing that too."

"Do you have time tomorrow?" Trey asked.

"I've got to do tomorrow what I didn't do today. Go to the archives, the bank, the lawyer."

"Can I see you home? It's easy to get lost in Tokyo."

"This orange subway goes right there, doesn't it?"

"Yes, the Ginza Line. I don't mind riding with you."

"I'm fine," Jamie said, putting her hand over his.

Trey kept his eyes on hers, but Jamie dropped his gaze and looked around at the lights shivering in the cold. Tokyo seemed a good place to be as the grief worked itself out. She could sink into her bad feelings and get through them. She felt warmed by two nights in a row with two handsome men. Maybe they were just feeling sorry for her, but the dinners helped.

Trey patted her arm. "I'll stop by tomorrow."

On tiptoe, Jamie gave Trey a kiss on the cheek, looked once more into his light blue eyes and then started towards the subway. At the top of the stairs, she turned back to see Trey disappearing into the crowd talking on his cellphone.

At the convenience store near her father's house, Jamie bought milk, yogurt, cereal, bananas and juice, which were if her math was correct, extremely expensive. She walked back towards the house feeling guilty, and a little angry, to have put off coming back for all those years. Why would she so willfully ignore her younger self?

Now, with her father's death, and her mother's indifference, she was thrust into a relationship with herself, a relationship long ignored in the busy swirl of New York. The dull job, her bank loans, the micro-apartment and the hard partying friends had kept her too well distracted.

Coming back to Tokyo—despite the sadness and regret—felt like getting rid of a weight she'd carried for too long, the weight of distance, of being alone in New York. After two days in Tokyo, her rush-around, talk-talk, get-ahead life in New York already felt far away. Maybe Tokyo was a place she could stay and not feel in between.

A block from her father's home, she came across the *ramen* shop where she and her father shared bowls of noodles. She had been too young to use chopsticks and had to use a fork. The plastic displays of noodles and their handwritten labels were covered with a thick layer of dust and faded by the sun and time. As she walked on, she tried to remember the faces of the old couple, the aprons they wore, the jokes and sweets they made for her.

Inside the front door of the house, she toed off her shoes in the entryway, turning the lock and slipping the chain across the door. This was her home, too, or had been, and was now again. She headed to put away her overpriced groceries, wondering where the will was and what the bank and lawyer would tell her.

Steps from the kitchen, she spun around. Two voices spoke in low tones. She stopped where she was and turned towards the living room, the groceries dangling in her hand. Were they policemen? How did they get in? She looked at the kitchen door and the front door and treaded warily back towards the living room.

Two men in black tracksuits stared at her. They set down what they were about to put into their black bags.

The word for "who" came to her in Japanese. "*Dare?*" She searched for more to say, but the words stuck inside her.

They glided quickly towards her.

Jamie bolted for the front door and swung the bag of groceries into the head of the closest guy. Milk exploded over the entryway. She snatched at the latch chain and bolt but he pulled her backwards onto the umbrella stand, which crashed to the floor under her.

She sprang up and snatched desperately at the door, struggling to get the chain off before they grabbed both her arms and yanked her down hard onto the floor.

Jamie screamed when she hit the wood floor. One of them twisted her arm so hard she screamed again. Jamie flipped herself around and thrust a kick toward his balls that missed and caught his thigh.

He twisted her arm to flip her over on her stomach and then dropped a knee in her back, pushing until she quit wiggling. Jamie thought her back would break and her arm would twist off at the shoulder. Neither of the men spoke a word. She could feel their leather gloves on her skin as they yanked her up to carry her into the living room and drop her facedown on the sofa.

She could hear duct tape ripping from a roll and felt the tape tight around her wrists and elbows. She elbowed and kicked and butted her head back, missing with every try. One of them held her legs together as the other duct-taped her ankles and then her calves and knees, pulling the thick tape tight with each round. She tried to kick out again but could not even bend her legs.

Another rip of the tape covered her mouth and cut into her cheeks. She moaned as they wrapped turn after turn of tape around her wrists and ankles securing her to the woodwork of the sofa. Wrapped top to bottom, Jamie could only wriggle like a fish, staring at the wall with wild eyes and thinking of her father tied in the other room in the final moments before he was cut open and left to bleed to death.

Her arms hurt and she could feel her feet tingle as the circulation slowed under the tourniquet of tape. She sucked air in through her nose, desperate for more. They tossed a blanket over her head, making it even harder to breathe, and went back to work. She could hear them moving things nearby and dropping things onto the floor.

She tried to control her breathing by calming herself and inhaling steadily through her nose, but it was clotted with blood and snot and she had to suck in hard to get enough air. She bit at the tape over her mouth and caught an edge to gnaw open. She sawed at it with her teeth.

The sound of the two men got softer when they moved into the study. They seemed to be pulling books off shelves and dropping them on the floor one by one, kicking them around. Jamie could hear the kitchen cabinets opening and shutting. One of them walked upstairs, the house creaking under his steps. It sounded like every *tansu* chest and wardrobe was being pushed over upstairs.

Suddenly, the robbing and ransacking sounds stopped. She could hear one of them close to her typing a text message. She heard the two of them whispering to each other in quick sentences. She knew they were not speaking Japanese, maybe Korean, Chinese, Thai. The rhythm was different from Japanese but her head felt too swollen and sore to make it out.

Jamie snorted to clear her nose for air, feeling both hyper-alert and like she was going to black out. She moaned as loud as she could and squirmed harder from side to side. She heard another staccato rip of tape from the roll. Their hands checked the tape around her body and one of them pulled off one of her socks.

They ripped the tape from her mouth. She felt like her cheeks were torn open and in the instant her mouth was free, she cried out, "Please, I can't breathe. Please, my nose is stopped."

She sucked in all the liquid blocking her sinuses and spit it out. But before she could think how to plead in Japanese, they grabbed her hair and stuffed the sock inside her mouth, taping it in place with a fresh piece of tape.

The sock made it even harder to breathe. She tried to blow out the snot and blood from her nose to clear a path, but it kept filling back up, blocking any air.

Then, she heard nothing more.

Chapter 13

Hiroshi got to Mattson's house in Asakusa as soon as he could. After staying up half the night filling the French police in on an embezzlement case at a joint French-Japanese company, he'd gotten only a few hours of sleep before Sakaguchi called. The front door stood half-open despite the cold. Inside, Sakaguchi blocked the hallway, which was splashed with milk, arguing with Saito.

"You were in charge of getting someone here around the clock." Sakaguchi leaned forward towards Saito, as if readying an *oshidashi* sumo thrust that would send him flying.

Saito took a step back. "The chief put you in charge of this case."

"I'm taking my guys back from security at the Forum Hall." Sakaguchi stepped forward.

"You'll all have to be at the conference on Monday."

Hiroshi put a hand on Sakaguchi's arm to ease him back a step, despite wanting to see Sakaguchi stiff-arm Saito into flight.

In the living room, Hiroshi took in the cut strips of grey duct tape fluttering from the sofa. Cushion stuffing poked out from where the indigo-blue coverings were sliced to pieces. Ueno, Sugamo and Osaki were directing younger detectives to take photographs. Split books, shattered pottery, and smashed chairs littered the place, a worse shambles than before.

Seeing Hiroshi, Ueno nodded toward the stairway. "Upstairs."

Hiroshi took the stairs two at a time. He ducked under the overhead beam and stepped into the bedroom where Jamie was sitting on a folded-up futon mattress talking on the phone. Noticing Hiroshi's reflection in the mirror, she motioned for him to sit down. He kneeled on the tatami just inside the door. A floor lamp threw more shadows than light around the room. When she hung up, Hiroshi looked at her red and swollen face, but she would not meet his eyes.

"Can you tell me what happened? Or do you..."

"It's better to tell you now." Jamie looked past him at the wall and twisted the end of a blanket around her hands.

"Take your time," he said. The room felt small and close. Two large *tansu* chests, tilted at an awkward angle, must have been turned over and set back upright. Men's jackets, blankets and sheets, and a few women's underclothes and sweatshirts were piled randomly in the corner.

As she told what happened, Hiroshi wanted to reach out to touch her, but stayed where he was, kneeling on the tatami, listening.

When she was done, Hiroshi said, "I'm sorry."

Jamie looked confused. "It's not your fault."

"Of course not, but Japanese take the blame for everything."

Jamie hummed and wrapped her hands deeper into the blanket.

"Were they tall or short or...?"

"One tall, one short. They spoke Thai or Chinese or Korean. I really can't tell the difference."

"It wasn't Japanese?"

"Definitely not. When I couldn't see, I could hear more clearly, every bump and knock of them going through things. They texted someone too. Then, I couldn't breathe. They left me to slowly suffocate."

"How did you...?"

"I woke up, and bit the tape, chewed and spit, little by little. I finally got some air."

"You survived. You're here."

"None of it makes sense." Jamie dabbed cream from a small jar on the red skin around her wrists, and after pulling up her sweatpants, on the blue-green-yellow bruises around her ankles. The fear, like the tape, had stripped away her outside layer, leaving only her humblest, simplest, most uncertain self.

"My mother told me to get on the next plane out of here," Jamie said. "That was her on the phone. Maybe Shibata was right. You said the same."

"I'll take you to the airport right now," Hiroshi said.

Jamie looked at herself in the floor mirror, and shook her head no. "Now I have to find out what they were looking for, his speech, his book, his surprise. I have to."

Hiroshi wondered about the surprise. In Japan, the details for everything—a meeting, a conference, even a visit with friends—were worked out far in advance. The Japanese way of carrying out what was expected, of meticulously deciding ahead of time, left little room for surprise. Mattson would have been as aware of that as anyone. A surprise, especially in a speech or book, seemed unlikely.

Jamie looked up at Hiroshi. "I want to see his work published."

"We have to find it first."

Jamie got on her knees, wincing and resettling herself. "He always thought far ahead, like playing *Go*. It must be in the archives. Will you go with me?"

"We'll go tomorrow. It's probably there. But after that, it's better if you leave."

A few loud steps on the stairs and harsh words in Japanese drew their attention. Hiroshi stood up, leaning around the wood post at the top of the stairs, and saw Trey bounding up, Sakaguchi yelling at him to stop. Trey pushed past Hiroshi and went in to Jamie. Kneeling down in front of her, Trey wrapped his arms around her. Hiroshi watched the American hugging ritual with more than his usual envy. He had knelt on the tatami at a safe distance even though he wanted to embrace and comfort her. But he hadn't. He was there as a detective.

"I should have come back with you," Trey said.

"It's nobody's fault. My father's maybe. Or that's what my mother said." Jamie settled back onto the futon and curled into a ball, pulling the blanket tightly around herself.

Trey locked eyes with Hiroshi as he stood up. In the dark of the room, the floor lights cast shadows upwards to the ceiling. Both men looked at Jamie and again locked eyes with each other.

"It's the fault of the criminals. We'll find them," Hiroshi said, keeping his eyes on Trey's, but speaking towards Jamie. "Someone will be here at all times. You're not in any danger now."

"Not in any danger?" Trey scoffed.

"They got what they wanted or found it wasn't here. They're logical, thieves. They avoid people like night animals," Hiroshi said.

"You call this 'logical'?" Trey turned back to Jamie.

"Please, I've had enough for one day." Jamie kneaded the blanket from inside with her knuckles. "I've got to sleep."

Trey leaned over and patted her shoulder. "I'll stay downstairs on the sofa."

Hiroshi shook his head. "The police will handle this. There will be two police officers here tonight."

"The sleeping pill I took is kicking in and I want to be asleep before the shock wears off. Go now, both of you." She jutted her head towards the door.

Both of them looked at her again and headed for the door. Trey and then Hiroshi gestured for the other to go downstairs first, until Hiroshi finally gave in, looking back to make sure Trey followed.

At the bottom of the stairs, Trey switched to Japanese. "This is how Japanese handle cases? I'm going to contact Pamela Carica at the embassy and Shinobu Katsumura, the Diet member, to be sure this is handled right. In America, you'd have a lawsuit on your desk by morning."

"This isn't America," Hiroshi said.

"That's evident," Trey folded his arms over his chest.

"Where were you with Jamie this evening?"

"Not that it's any of your business, but I was helping her."

"Helping her with what?"

"Her father's manuscript."

"What manuscript? There's nothing around here that we've found."

Trey raised his eyebrows. "There's not? I thought the police would have everything in hand."

Hiroshi paused. "If you knew Mattson had a book ready, maybe you have an idea what he was writing about?"

"I know that whatever Mattson wrote was important. But I also know that Mattson's collection of *netsuke* ivory carvings should be in a museum. His tea bowls are priceless. Who knows what else he has in here?"

"You seem to have a pretty good idea."

"I knew Mattson, if that's what you mean."

"How long did you know him?" Hiroshi asked.

He pointed a finger at Hiroshi. "Look, a murder and two break-ins and you're asking me about his book? Shouldn't you have found it and read through it already?"

As Trey and Hiroshi squared off in Mattson's trashed living room, Sugamo, Osaki and Sakaguchi converged around them, Ueno two steps away. The six men stood in the middle of Mattson's living room staring at each other in silence. Trey looked around the bulky circle of detectives and then backed away, pulling on his coat and leaving without another word.

Hiroshi saw Takamatsu coming in the entryway folding his coat carefully over his arm and looking down at the milk on the entryway floor.

"What's with the milk?" Takamatsu asked with a grin.

"She smashed them in the head with her groceries," Ueno said.

Takamatsu nodded in approval. "I like those American women. Feisty."

"Who called you?" Hiroshi asked.

"This is starting to take time away from my private eye work. Who was that American guy?" Takamatsu pointed his thumb towards the front door.

Hiroshi shrugged.

"He didn't look too happy on his way out." Takamatsu chuckled as he draped his overcoat on the bannister and straightened his cuffs and tie. He nodded to Ueno, Osaki and Sugamo.

"So?" Takamatsu said to Hiroshi, as if he were not on probation.

Hiroshi sighed, knowing it was best to let Takamatsu in on what happened. "Interrupted the robbers. Taped her up. Took valuables. Destroyed others."

"The daughter is good-looking from what I hear," Takamatsu said to Hiroshi, looking upstairs with exaggerated curiosity. "That always makes things trickier. Better watch yourself."

"Good advice coming from you."

"The secret to life is to watch yourself, but not too closely. And not all the time." Takamatsu looked around the room. "You better get this resolved before the American embassy starts sticking its nose in."

"Too late for that," Sakaguchi said, coming in from the kitchen. "The media's been all over it too, the chief phoned to tell me. Takamatsu, take a quick look around. Then get out of here in case the chief stops by, or I'll be joining you on probation. Though that's starting to sound pretty good."

"The chief hasn't stopped by? Sent Saito instead?" Takamatsu smiled.

"I sent Saito packing," Sakaguchi growled.

"Give me fifteen," Takamatsu said, stopping in front of the sword rack in admiration before striding into the living room.

Hiroshi followed Takamatsu's systematic examination with his eyes and looked up the stairs every few minutes listening for any sound.

"I'll meet you two for a drink when you're done," was all Takamatsu said before picking up his coat on the way out.

Chapter 14

Hiroshi and Sakaguchi sat quietly in the taxi on the way to meet Takamatsu. They found him waiting at the *yattai* street cart parked at the end of a bridge that angled along a row of bushes and leafless trees, right where he said it would be.

When Hiroshi and Sakaguchi pushed inside, the *master* said, "*Irrashaimase*! Welcome!" and bowed his scarf-wrapped head for a moment before turning back to a rubbery octopus with a long, thin *takobiki* knife.

Hiroshi plopped down at the end of the short wooden counter and Takamatsu scooted over as Sakaguchi settled onto a stool between them. A small kerosene heater and gently smoking griddle warmed the interior. A thick curtain of plastic hung from the roof down to the pavement to keep out the winter night.

The *master* handed them steaming hot towels and set out two bottles of beer and three small glasses. They gave each other a quick toast as the *master* set out pickled vegetables and scoops of corn pâté in soup. Takamatsu took a polite sip of beer for the toast, then Sakaguchi and Hiroshi finished the rest in big, tired gulps. When the bottles were empty, the *master* handed them steaming glasses of *shochu* and hot tea.

"No place to hang your coat up in here," Hiroshi said to Takamatsu.

"He brought out a stool for me." Takamatsu nodded at his coat folded neatly behind him.

"Suspension gives you time for clothes shopping," Hiroshi scoffed.

"Less than you'd think. Divorce cases take time." Takamatsu chuckled. "Even though the causes are never hard to figure out."

"How do you know this *yattai* stall?" Hiroshi asked.

"I once thought of putting a GPS tracker on the undercarriage, but I can always find him through his roof."

"His roof?"

"Blue tile," Takamatsu said. "Like the roof of Mattson's house."

"I didn't notice the roof."

"No, you wouldn't have, with all there is to see inside. Like I told you, it's small details—"

"Enough. No squabbling tonight." Sakaguchi looked back and forth at them until they both went back to their drinks. Sakaguchi motioned for a refill of *shochu.* "What did you see?" he asked Takamatsu.

"It reminded me of that break-in from a couple years back where they killed the servant," Takamatsu looked around Sakaguchi to be sure Hiroshi was listening. "It's important to remember past cases. On that one, the servant, who doubled as chauffeur, came back for something the wife forgot. He interrupted the robbers at work and, though he fought hard, took a knife in the gut. The wife was at some gala event, while the servant bled to death at home."

The *master* set down octopus legs and fish paste balls in *dashi* broth.

"I talked to a couple old colleagues in Chiba and Saitama. They had the same kind of break-ins, but no murders," Takamatsu continued. "It seems like it's a Pan-Asian set-up. They work in rotation."

"What kind of rotation?" Hiroshi asked.

"Japanese come in first, take what they want, then tip off the Koreans. The Koreans come in and clean out what they want and pass the rest on to the Chinese. The Chinese from southeast Asia come first, leave the leftovers for mainland Chinese."

"That explains why the house got hit more than once," Sakaguchi mused, working his chopsticks.

"But wouldn't they do it all on the same night?" Hiroshi asked.

"I think that's the burglary ideal, but it doesn't always work. One group specializes in safes and secret closets, the next in computers and jewelry and the last snatches anything they can hock."

Sakaguchi frowned. "What about that ministry official killed last year? He was stabbed too. Any similarities?"

Takamatsu played with his cufflinks. "We found nothing. No clues. No leads. Nothing. They were good."

"But what about Mattson?" Hiroshi said. "Was it bad timing or did they want something specific?"

"Or, did they really go there *to* kill him, and to cover *that* up they made it look like he surprised them? I wonder." Takamatsu nodded at a shallow metal *oden* steamer filled with fish cakes, black kelp in thick knots, and grey triangles of *konnyaku*. The master ladled out a selection with broth on top.

"Either way, they know what they're doing." Sakaguchi took his bowl up to his mouth, slurping loudly.

"That ministry official had millions of yen in the house," Takamatsu said. "The family didn't want the police to tell the press."

Sakaguchi set down his chopsticks. "Only officials keep that much money at home."

"Donations, bribes, hush money, they have to hide it somewhere, poor things," Takamatsu laughed.

"You think Mattson was hiding dirty money?" Hiroshi asked. He tried to look out through the plastic curtain around the stall. It was fogged up from steam, closing them in with no view outside.

Takamatsu said, "Even if he was hiding money, that's not why he was robbed."

The *master* set out another round of *shochu* mixed with tea.

"Maybe he was robbed for the *shunga*?" Takamatsu laughed. "Can't get those out of my head."

"I'm sure you can't," Hiroshi said.

"You're no different." Takamatsu laughed again.

Sakaguchi swallowed the last of his bowl and asked for more. "The bookstore twins said Mattson would know who owned the prints. They were rare, those prints, and worth a fortune."

"Enough to kill for?" Hiroshi asked.

"Mattson was a specialist, but not a dealer. Maybe he owned a lot of rare prints. But more likely he just kept what he liked, sold the rest."

"Why would they steal computer images of woodblock prints?" Hiroshi asked.

"Maybe they needed the image to set the sale up?" Takamatsu said. "As proof or promise."

"Could be," Sakaguchi said. "We found where the *netsuke* carvings fit along the shelf. The dust left a perfect outline for each of the four.

So, the dead guy in Golden Gai was definitely at Mattson's. His name was Hideyasu Sato. A few prior arrests, but no convictions."

"Maybe he hid the original prints someplace before he was killed?" Hiroshi wondered.

Sakaguchi nodded. "Those twins also said they were expecting the manuscript, but it was never delivered. I believe them about that." Sakaguchi finished his bowl with a couple quick pushes of his chopsticks.

Takamatsu and Hiroshi looked sideways at Sakaguchi filling himself up.

Noticing their glances, Sakaguchi said, "This is lunch *and* dinner. I haven't eaten since breakfast."

"Don't you think that American guy is a bit suspicious?" Hiroshi asked. "I mean, how did he even know there was a break-in at the house?"

"He probably knows people."

"What people?"

"Americans who know. Anyway, I thought you were the pro-America faction?" Takamatsu said.

"I'm the pro-transparency faction. I'm going to make a few inquiries about who that guy Trey really is."

"On your computer? Or with your friends at Interpol?" Takamatsu asked. "I'm not sure I'd trust them. They never set foot on the street."

"I think I'll poke around, see who he is," Hiroshi said.

"I can tell you that. He's the knight in shining armor." Takamatsu smiled. "Isn't that how Americans think about themselves? They're going to save the world?"

Sakaguchi waved his chopsticks to quiet them down. "Chief told me Mattson was at every high-level meeting between Japan and America for the last couple decades. Why don't you follow up on that instead? See if someone wanted him not to speak next week."

"I'll do both," Hiroshi said. "I know someone who will know about Mattson."

"The woman whose husband I'm investigating owns a media group. She knows all the major players. I'll ask her, too," Takamatsu said. "She's been after some of these diplomats for years, has dirt on them all. She didn't have any dirt on her husband, though. Had to hire me for that."

"Jamie had no idea where the manuscript might be," Hiroshi said.

Sakaguchi looked at him. "The other guy in the bookstore, crazy left-wing nut from Okinawa, said Mattson was going to expose something shocking," Sakaguchi said.

"If Mattson put in all the shocking things about Okinawa, it would make a long book," Hiroshi said.

"Maybe it's gone," Sakaguchi said.

"We'll find it," Hiroshi said.

"It'll be fun looking. The daughter's gorgeous, isn't she?" Takamatsu asked. "I haven't even seen her and I can tell."

"You caused enough trouble last summer," Sakaguchi said, pointing his chopsticks rudely in Takamatsu's direction.

Takamatsu smirked.

Hiroshi tapped his glass on the wood counter. "That woman should have been arrested, not taken out to dinner and whatever else you did."

Sakaguchi got a call and stepped outside the plastic curtain around the stall.

Takamatsu leaned forward to be sure he could see Hiroshi's face. "I was doing my job. You think of suspension as punishment. I'd call it a consequence."

"You almost got me killed. And she might have killed you."

"If I didn't follow my instincts—all of them—I wouldn't have flushed her out and found who killed those men."

"There are safer ways to do it."

"Safe gets you nothing." Takamatsu took his pack of cigarettes out and started tamping it in his hand.

Hiroshi shook his head.

"Hiroshi, you think you can get by with computer programs. You can't catch bad guys through the web, or net or whatever you call it. The only way to work is with your feelings up front, and with the guts to follow where they lead. It's about people, not data. The street, not some information superhighway."

Sakaguchi came back in and sat down. He looked at Hiroshi and then at Takamatsu. "Didn't I say no squabbling? Let's focus on Mattson. He's the center of all this."

The *master* set out three small bowls of thick noodles, so hot the three of them had to hold them by the base and the rim as they brought the bowls up to their mouths, slurping loudly, not just to cool the broth, but to cover up the irritation of not knowing more than they did.

Chapter 15

The last time Hiroshi stood on his professor's porch he was dropping out of the history department and going to America to study accounting. Back then, after what seemed like hours, with his finger close to the doorbell, he finally walked off without a word of *sayonara*. More than twenty years had passed since then, but when Hiroshi called that morning, Eto Sensei sounded like Hiroshi had just missed last week's seminar. Maybe there was no need for the apology Hiroshi prepared in his head on the hour-and-a-half train ride to Yokosuka.

Eto Sensei was different from most professors. In class, he prodded students to think for themselves about government transparency, the rule of law and political reform. He revealed and explained his opinions as one way of thinking, not as truth to be followed. The afternoon seminars spilled over into late-night discussions in his living room where Eto Sensei's wife, Yoko, made sure no one went student-hungry for long. She brewed pot after pot of tea, set out *senbei* rice crackers and cooked rice-filled omelets. She was not afraid of giving her opinion too, as she bustled in and out.

Now, as he was about to press the doorbell, Eto Sensei's wife pulled open the front door, startling Hiroshi from his memories. "Hiroshi, don't just stand there. Come in. He's excited to see you. It seems like yesterday you were talking in the living room," she said.

"Several yesterdays," Hiroshi said, stepping inside and taking off his shoes. "This is a wonderful home, but I loved that old house too."

"We wanted to fall asleep to the sound of the ocean. Unfortunately, the Americans changed their flight patterns so fighter jets and helicopters go right over our house. You can't hear yourself think. Payback for his politics, I guess."

She beamed at him, wiping her hands on her apron as she showed him inside to the living room. Though the house was new, the interior looked as if it was transported entire just as it had been, even the books on the same shelves. Beyond the living room, a sunroom with picture windows opened onto a panoramic view of the Pacific Ocean stretching to the horizon.

Yoko said, "You're a detective now? That's something to be proud of."

"I don't think Sensei thinks that. If you're not doing academic research..."

"But a detective *is* a researcher. Only not in books, in the world."

Hiroshi paused, never having thought of it that way. Maybe his university studies hadn't been derailed, just rerouted. After Hiroshi's parents died in his second year of college, Eto Sensei found a scholarship so Hiroshi could continue studying. But in the end, Hiroshi caved in to pressure from his uncle, who took over the finances of the family, and steeled himself for the sensible, tedious subject of accounting, which his uncle deemed best. When Hiroshi finally returned from Boston, after delaying for years, he refused to join his uncle's company, as he was supposed to, and took the job as detective instead. He hadn't entirely escaped accounting. His uncle had barely spoken to him since.

"I see you remember an old man in his dotage," Eto Sensei's voice rang out with the same authority. No one ever whispered, daydreamed or doodled during his classes.

Hiroshi bowed level to the ground.

"Oh, please. I'm retired! My back is too stiff to bend over in return." Eto Sensei laughed. He was tall and thin with silvery hair that matched his black turtleneck sweater and grey wool jacket. His skin was more wrinkled around his neck and face, but his eyes brimmed with the same enthusiasm as years ago. He leaned on a cane that Hiroshi pretended not to notice.

Eto Sensei sat down in a chair that kept him angled forward. Hiroshi sat across from him on a leather couch. The living room was set up for a seminar with students who might never come. Through the open picture windows, the salt-fish smell and shush of waves floated up from below.

"Tell me everything," Eto Sensei said.

"What's a detective's life like?" Yoko asked, bringing in a teapot and cups. She arranged everything and then poured a cup for both of them.

"Terrible pay, heavy workload, and nothing ever gets finished."

Eto Sensei chuckled. "Sounds like academia. Must be interesting, though."

"I follow trails of stolen money all day. How they get it is the easy part. Where they hide it is the hard part." Eto laughed and Hiroshi was pleased his old professor had the same light manner over the seriousness inside.

"In the seminar, you were good at following arguments, though I'm sure illegal finances are more convoluted. Are you married?"

"To the job."

"What was that girl's name in our seminar?" Eto Sensei tapped his forehead. "I can't remember anything anymore."

"Ayana," Hiroshi said. Ayana. After the student debates wound down and the dishes were dried, Ayana waited for Hiroshi to take the train home from Eto Sensei's house. During the ride, she dismantled his weaker points and praised his bolder ones. Hiroshi snuck glances at her and stammered, "*Sono tōri desu*" or "*So desu ne*," meaningless phrases of agreement that made him sound more bumbling than silence would have. As with Eto Sensei, when he left for America, he didn't even tell her goodbye. He wrote her a letter asking her—begging her—to come visit him in America, but he ended up throwing it away at Narita Airport. The rejection would have been too much on top of the embarrassment of being forced—like an arranged marriage—to study accounting.

"Ayana, yes. Such a beauty, wasn't she? She wrote the best papers in the class. Often better than yours, Hiroshi."

"I'm not surprised. She had that demure side around others but didn't miss anything."

"I gave a speech at her wedding but couldn't even remember her name. That's old age: lots of experiences, only half-remembered."

"Ayana got married?"

"And divorced. She lived in America for a long time, went into library studies. She works at the national archives now, in the center of Tokyo. I thought everyone was in touch with everyone on what's that thing?" Eto Sensei snapped his fingers trying to remember.

"Facebook?"

"That's it. I knew it was about face. Your other classmates are all part of the bureaucratic machinery now, government ministries and corporations, not that there's much difference—or distance—between the two," Eto Sensei mused. "You're not in touch with Ayana or anyone?"

Hiroshi looked out the window, lost in what might have been.

Eto Sensei noticed and smiled. "On the phone, you mentioned Bernard Mattson."

"He died last week," Hiroshi said, turning back to the conversation. "Did you hear?"

"Yes. He wasn't that much older than me. I always thought one of the right wing groups would get him."

"Why would they...?"

Eto leaned back his chair with a shake of his head. "He was the one who ensured the Japanese military would never re-arm. So, the right wing blamed Mattson for keeping Japan subservient, from rebuilding the empire to its former glory after the defeat."

Hiroshi looked confused. "You mean, they blame him for the fifty thousand American soldiers stationed here?"

Eto waved his index finger, the same gesture he used to use for emphasis. "Exactly, but nowadays it's the left wing that wants the bases out of Japan. It's now the right-wing that cozies up to America. Hard to say who would hate him more."

"As you used to say, if you wait long enough—"

"Everything turns around," Eto Sensei finished the sentence for him. "Have you been following the protests?"

"I saw one of the marches pass by."

"The protesters are having some effect for once. I never thought that would happen."

"What other issues might make Mattson, well, a target? It's not even clear it's political, but we have to look at everything."

Eto thought for a moment. "He did so much over the years, it could be many things. He was the force behind the SOFA agreements, which spread to other countries. America has harbors, airfields, firing ranges, and supply depots all over the world."

"Japan was the model?"

"One he helped design. So, I was surprised to hear from colleagues that Mattson came out against extending the agreements. He hinted the bases should be returned."

"He did?"

"From Cold war architect to peacenik internationalist. Nice headline. Never too late, I suppose." Eto reached for his tea.

Hiroshi followed his lead, taking a small sip of tea. "Why would he do an about-face? His love of Japanese culture?"

Eto Sensei looked impatient with his former student. "Maybe he finally realized the monster he created. Japan is where the American empire got started."

Hiroshi was reminded of the lectures Eto Sensei gave on why the Americans had lingered so long in Japan, on what the atomic bomb really meant, on how Asia might develop, or fail to reform. "How much would Mattson know about that monster?"

"Mattson would know everything." Eto Sensei said, opening his eyes wide, humming about just how much he might know. "He might have access to documents others don't."

"If he changed his views, would someone want to—" Hiroshi hesitated to finish his thought in words.

"Do something to keep him quiet? They have in the past." Eto Sensei sipped his tea. "As with everything related to the SOFA treaties, there's a lot of money, and careers and contracts, tied up in the status quo."

"I don't understand why he—"

"Mattson was respected. That's much more important in Japan than almost anywhere else in the world. The forces of change could use his support, and a scandal or two might help tip the balance."

"He'd been going to the archives almost every day for two years."

"He must have been looking into something more than SOFA."

"Like what?"

Eto Sensei shrugged with a hearty chuckle. "The archives are vast. What's your guess?"

Hiroshi remembered how Eto Sensei would end class by leaving questions hanging in the air, forcing students to keep discussing inside themselves long after the bell had rung.

Eto Sensei smiled. "But, you know, he probably got killed over money or valuables. Politics isn't everything."

"That's not what you used to say."

"I've learned there's more to life than politics." Eto smiled.

They both turned their attention to the grey-blue ocean sky outside the picture windows. Hiroshi had not told his old teacher anything about himself, but he would come back.

Hiroshi stood up. "I've got to go. Thank you for all this. It was so good to see you."

"Of course. I'm happy to help anytime. Time is one thing I have." Eto Sensei called his wife, who hurried in with a copy of Eto Sensei's latest book. He signed it in the inner flap and handed it to Hiroshi, who took it with two hands, bowing deeply.

On the train back to Tokyo, Hiroshi looked out the window for a long time. When he finally opened the book, *East Asian Politics in Perspective*, he read the inscription above Eto Sensei's signature on the inside front cover.

It said, simply, "Welcome Home!"

Chapter 16

The icy wind overpowering the late winter sun helped wake Hiroshi from his fatigue. After talking with Eto Sensei the day before, he had dropped in at Jamie's to make sure the detectives were rotating the guard but found her asleep. He returned to his office to work on two new cases that came in from London—real estate transactions gone wrong. After catching a few hours of sleep on the futon bed in his office, he hurried to the National Archives.

Hiroshi waited in front of the archives staring across the six-lane road at the wide moat encircling the Imperial Palace grounds. The water in the moat was thick and green with algae. The white stones of the walls, hewn from massive rocks, were set tightly, precisely in place, ready against attack. On the other side of the moat, the surrounding wall sloped down to a bridge with an entrance to the inner palace. It was fortified with a modern defense of tire spikes, barrier gates and a guardhouse.

Finally, Jamie arrived. She got out of the car and walked towards Hiroshi. Ueno stepped out from the driver's seat and looked over the roof at Hiroshi, who told him to go get something to eat since it would take hours to look through Mattson's research. Hiroshi would call him.

"Feeling better?" Hiroshi asked Jamie as they went up the wide sidewalk to the National Archives.

"Yes and no," Jamie answered. "I kept waking up all night, even with a sleeping pill."

"We can pick up your father's research materials, but then you should follow Shibata's advice and get on a plane back home."

"Let's first see what my father had in here."

"One of my old classmates from university works here," Hiroshi said, as casually as he could.

"When was the last time you saw him?"

"Her, actually. Not since I was twenty, but she knew your father when I called to tell her I—we were coming."

The archive's large open first floor had a high ceiling with thick wood tables. Stacks of books lined shelves in a low-ceilinged area behind the counter and the black domes of security cameras attached to the ceiling eyed the room. As Hiroshi filled in a detailed registration form, his mind flooded with memories of Ayana and questions about her life over the years they'd been out of touch. He made a mistake on the form and had to ask for a blank one to start again.

When he finally got it right, he turned to see the tall figure of Ayana coming out of the elevator at the end of the room. Her ballet-dancer walk—tall upper body leaning gently forward, her long legs springy and strong—was just the same. As she came closer, her neat-cut hair, business suit and designer glasses made her seem a different person altogether. Was she still the college girl he had been so hesitant to talk with, but couldn't *stop* talking with? He remembered hugging her in the shadows outside the train station near her apartment, deciding whether to spend the night, he knowing it would be the last chance before he left for America, she not knowing he was even leaving. How could he apologize for not even saying a word about leaving, for never writing, for shelving his feelings and never returning? Until now.

Ayana pulled at the glasses dangling from a strap around her neck. "Is that you, Hiroshi?"

"Ayana. It's been—"

"Let's not do the math."

"Can we skip the accounting, too?"

Ayana blushed, and then smiled. "Yes, we can skip that, too."

"I—"

Ayana waited for him to finish his sentence and when he didn't, she smiled and said, "Do you still do *kendo*?"

"I haven't touched a practice sword in years. I'm not even sure where my outfit is. You?"

"I go once a week now, but I don't remember it hurting so much."

"That's *all* I remember," Hiroshi said before switching to English to introduce Jamie Mattson, who stood beside him smiling at Ayana.

Ayana handed Jamie her name card. "I'm Ayana, one of the archivists. I was so sorry to hear about your father. He was a regular here. Had all the staff charmed."

"He was good at that," Jamie said with a bow. "Thank you for helping him."

"We didn't have to do much. He knew where everything was. He requested manuscript boxes from areas we'd never heard of and files no one had looked at in fifty years. Let me take you to the room. He had a lot of notes." Ayana held the elevator door open for them with the same lovely, long fingers Hiroshi remembered tapping on his notebooks as they talked after class. In the elevator, Ayana asked Jamie about herself, and Hiroshi stood quietly behind them.

At Mattson's study room, Ayana pulled a coiled bracelet key chain from the pocket of her tight-fitting pants and unlocked the soundproof door. Inside, a half dozen book carts crowded against a desk piled high with folders, notebooks and manuscript boxes.

"Does everyone get space like this?" Jamie asked, looking around the small, glassed-in room.

"Your father was here every day requesting so many things, it was easier to give him this room to save reshelving," Ayana said.

Jamie opened up a manuscript box to find it filled with loose sheets of crinkled documents. "There's a lot of stuff here! It will take forever to get through it all."

"I'll leave you to it," Ayana said. She pulled the door shut softly. From outside, she looked in through the glass. Hiroshi met her eyes for a moment and it felt like an entire conversation, the kind they used to have on the train home together. Then she looked down and walked away.

Jamie looked overwhelmed at the boxes stacked on the desk. "Could he have read all these? In both English and Japanese?" She ran her hands over the boxes one by one, picked up a folder from the closest stack and started reading. "Looks like these are all from 1959 and 1960. Was that the end of the occupation?"

Hiroshi was photographing the labels on the sides of the first stack of boxes. "No, that was 1952. These are probably related to the security treaty and SOFA."

"Translation, please."

"The treaties demilitarizing Japan and giving the US total control over their bases inside Japan."

Jamie put the top back on a box and opened another. "I hope there's a draft of his speech in one of these."

"And his manuscript for the book."

They sat on opposite sides of the desk and slipped into the special quiet timelessness of libraries. Hiroshi sifted through a stack of folders from various ministries: the Ministry of Land, Infrastructure, Transport and Tourism, the Ministry of Agriculture, Forestry and Fisheries, the Ministry of the Environment and the Ministry of Defense. Sandwiched in between the ministry files were other documents and proclamations from the American Occupation. He wondered how all of them connected to SOFA, and to Mattson's death. He could hear Eto Sensei's voice imploring him to think bigger.

Hiroshi pulled out a copy of one sheaf labeled, *Agreement under Article VI of the Treaty of Mutual Cooperation and Security between Japan and the United States of America, Regarding Facilities and Areas and the Status of United States Armed Forces in Japan*. He wondered if this was the complete, official name of the US-Japan SOFA. If so, Mattson seemed to be reviewing his past work, work that had molded Japan's post-war history. He wished Eto Sensei was here to explain what these meant, so he started making a list of questions for him. Hiroshi moved to the next manuscript box, trying to keep them in order by photographing the labels to remember what he'd finished.

"This is interesting," Jamie said, holding up a declassified embassy cablegram. The paper was crinkle-edged and the typewritten ink blurred. "My father's name is on it, but the other name's blacked out."

Hiroshi set the cablegram on the desk and took a photo of it. "Your father would have known whose name was there."

"I feel like the important things are gone. All these documents from his life, I had no idea what he did."

"It was before you were born—"

"He never said a word about any of this."

"Weren't you too young to—"

"To listen? Maybe. All I can do now is read."

Hiroshi opened another box. It was full of legal documents about land use law in Japanese. Most were from the Ministry of Land,

Infrastructure, Transport and Tourism, though the ministries had all been renamed in 2001. It was the third or fourth box of such documents. But what did land use law and the environment have to do with the SOFA agreements? Mattson had written notes on the copies of almost every one, notes to himself.

The sound of Ayana pushing open the door to the room startled Hiroshi and made Jamie drop the paper she was puzzling over.

"Find anything interesting?" Ayana asked.

Jamie bent to pick up the paper she dropped but smiled up at Ayana. "I wish I knew what it all meant. I'd like to take his notebooks. And these copies of documents?"

"Any copies he made have already been approved, and of course, his notes are yours now. Just leave the originals here," Ayana said. "What will you do with all his work?"

"I'm going to publish his memoirs." Jamie straightened the copies in front of her into a neat stack. "But the police need to look at it first."

"I'll go get a few bags from my office, but it's no problem to leave things here for now." Ayana hurried off and came back with four big shopping bags. The three of them worked together to fit the notebooks and copies in neatly and securely.

"You might want to take these with you too," Ayana said, handing Jamie two thick albums with a bemused smile. "He used to work on these when he got bored with the other documents."

Jamie pulled back the cover of the album to see handwritten notes surrounding a photocopy of an erotic *shunga* woodblock print of two lovers flowing into one another, the thick outlines of their curving bodies joining in the exact center of the page. Mattson's arrows, sketches and comments filled the margins of the photocopied paper.

"Oh my!" Jamie said, leafing through the erotic prints, each one a fresh variation on sexual desire. "No permutation left out."

Hiroshi peered down from the side. The prints were similar to the ones on the flash drive of the dead man. Hiroshi looked again to be sure he was remembering clearly. He couldn't concentrate with Jamie and Ayana so close, both giggling at the *shunga* images, turning them and pointing. He took a step back from the table, ignoring the stirrings inside himself. He peeked over and looked away, breathing in the closeness of the two women in the small confines of the research room.

"Amazing, aren't they?" Ayana helped fit the erotic notebooks in the paper shopping bag with the other files and folders of Mattson's copies and notes.

"Amazing and heavy!" Jamie hoisted two of the four bags, then added a third in her right hand. The string handle cut into her palm, but Jamie picked them up, readjusting the bags and setting her shoulders.

"You sure you want to take all these today?" Ayana asked.

"We'll take them straight to the station by car," Hiroshi said. "It'll be fine."

Ayana locked the room and Hiroshi took the fourth bag. Jamie walked ahead at a brisk pace, looking excited.

Ayana pulled out her cellphone and exchanged numbers with Hiroshi. "Will you call me?" she asked.

"I'd like to hear—"

"About the last two decades?"

"And about now too."

Would she have come visit him in America if he had sent that letter instead of throwing it out? Hiroshi felt weighed down by the bags, by his past, by how much there was to untangle. Ayana walked beside Hiroshi towards the exit, quietly in step the rest of the way.

Chapter 17

On the wide steps outside the archives, Jamie slumped under the weight of the bags. "Would you mind if we sat down for a few?"

"What about the bench over there under the cherry trees? We can get a taxi at the corner if Ueno can't drive back to get us."

Jamie and Hiroshi walked over and set the four bags of her father's work on the bench. Jamie flopped down. Hiroshi stepped away to call Akiko to get ready, they'd be there right away with Mattson's work. What had gotten Mattson killed was in there somewhere and he wanted to lay it all out so he could find the connections between the materials and the murder. He called Ueno. He didn't answer, so Hiroshi tried again, staring absently at the gnarled bark of a cherry tree.

Just as Ueno answered, Hiroshi heard Jamie scream and the roar of a motorcycle.

Hiroshi spun around.

Jamie was lying in a heap in the dirt and a man in a black track suit, high leather boots and smoked glass helmet was hustling all four bags towards a motorcycle where the driver clutched the handlebars and revved the engine. The robber threw his leg over the back of the bike as the driver let out the clutch and zipped away.

Hiroshi shouted into his cellphone to Ueno, "Someone's taken Mattson's stuff. Call Sakaguchi. Get over here. Going south from the National Archives."

Already running, Hiroshi fumbled his cellphone into his pocket and tried to keep an eye on the motorbike swerving through the afternoon traffic. He tripped over the outgrown root of a cherry tree jutting up from the sidewalk. His arms windmilling to stay upright, he recaptured his balance and kept running. He stayed along the side of the street, running up on the curb to avoid cars slowing or braking. When traffic lightened, he cut over to the middle of the street for a clear path forward.

Ahead, the motorcycle slowed for traffic pooled at the cross street, weaving back and forth trying to find a way through, the bags hanging from the rider's hands over both sides of the cycle.

Hiroshi gained ground but felt his legs turning to jelly. He wasn't sure if they had seen him yet or not, but he barreled forward as they approached the turn which would set them on a wide westbound express road. He dropped to a steady pace. He realized Jamie was all alone, but he couldn't turn back now. Mattson's work could disappear forever, and with it the reason he was killed.

Hiroshi pushed forward, catching a glimpse of the driver up ahead twisting the handlebars to walk the cycle into an opening in traffic before taking off down the center line, the second thief balancing expertly behind with both bags.

At the corner, two riot police at a guardhouse by the moat in front of the Imperial Grounds noticed the motorcycle's odd swerving. They stepped out to look and Hiroshi saw one of them speak into his headset. Several more guards instantly appeared from inside the guardhouse.

Picking up their long wooden *keijo* staffs, two of them took off after Hiroshi and the cycle. Still running in the gutter of the street, Hiroshi felt the guards gaining on him.

Hiroshi vaulted over a hedge onto the empty sidewalk, picking up speed. He could hear the palace guards shouting to him, but his ears were ringing so he couldn't hear what they said. He lost sight of the motorcycle, but picked up his pace past the British and Indian Embassies.

If the motorcycle reached the intersection, they could head west onto the expressway and everything of Mattson's would be gone. Hiroshi heard the guards closer behind him and pulled out his badge over his head, gasping for air, shouting, "Motorcycle."

The two guards, surprised by the badge, jogged beside Hiroshi. "You're police?" one asked.

"Homicide," Hiroshi managed to say, pointing ahead. "Stop...motorcycle...thieves." The two guards pulled past him without a word. They were in much better physical shape and Hiroshi could see them, through his blurring vision, giving chase. He tried to keep up.

At the next corner, Hiroshi watched a square gray bus with wire mesh over the windows pull out from the right, martial music blasting from loudspeakers affixed to the roof. It was driven by one of the many rightist groups that constantly circled the sacred area around the Imperial Palace and *Yasukuni Jinja* memorial shrine. *Hinomaru* Japanese flags fluttered from roof poles and a "Support the Emperor" banner hung along the side. Unlike most typical right-wing protest buses that scrupulously followed traffic laws while spewing propaganda at top volume, this bus pulled across the intersection against the light.

The thieves' motorcycle gunned forward—straight at the bus. Seeing it too late, the motorcycle angled into a desperate right turn and Hiroshi heard the rip of the engine as the tires lost traction and the metal shredded and screeched along the pavement. An abrupt *whomp* signaled it was over.

Hiroshi ran through the cars down the center line, from where he could see Mattson's papers scattered across the road in all directions. The rider, back upright after the slide, yanked at the handlebar trying to dislodge the driver who was pinned under the motorcycle wedged under the truck. The rider pulled under the driver's arms, but gave up, grabbed two of the bags and took off.

The driver kept yanking at his trapped leg, scooting back and forth to get free, but one of the palace guards landed a solid crack of his *keijo* staff on his collar bone, then another on his wrist. The driver reeled from the blows. The guard pressed the *keijo* into his abdomen until the driver leaned his helmet back on the pavement in surrender.

The right-wing fanatics, two grizzled old men, clambered out of the front seat of the gray bus to see what happened, their high-volume martial anthems rattling windows on the surrounding buildings. The guard turned his *keijo* poles towards them and ordered them not to move. They grunted and stopped in place.

Hiroshi yelled, "Over there!"

Hiroshi took off after the thief and the other guard followed, quickly passing Hiroshi and gaining on the thief with the bags. The thief was surprisingly quick, despite the heavy bags. Hiroshi could see him charging through a group of workers who leapt back against the wall clutching their cellphones, their workplace ID tags hanging from their necks.

Hiroshi and the guard shot past them. They gained on the thief as he turned down a side street lined with small shops and metal dividers that marked off a walkway from the car lane. Hiroshi tried to get his legs to move faster as the guard pulled ahead and got close enough to push his *keijo* staff forward to try to trip the black-clad thief.

But at the crucial moment, the guard was forced to swerve out of the way of a mother bicycling with two infants in child seats, front and back. He spun around just missing the mother, and the thief sprinted ahead throwing one of Mattson's bags into the air. The papers opened up like white birds freed from a cage, flapping and flying over the small lane.

The guard skidded to a stop before stepping nimbly over the scattered pages. On the other side of the mess, he dug his feet into the asphalt and started running again.

When Hiroshi got to the slippery carpet of papers, his legs—already wobbly from running—shot out from under him and he slid into the outdoor display of a small drugstore. Shampoo bottles, detergent packs and bundles of toilet paper scattered across the small lane. Hiroshi shouted an apology to the store as he corkscrewed himself up and started running again.

Hiroshi caught up with the guard at a turn into a tangle of smaller alleys. Standing in the center of the street spinning in all four directions, Hiroshi tried to see clearly but red and yellow spots floated across his eyes. The thief was nowhere to be seen. Hiroshi raised up and walked in a circle looking in all four directions down the small alleys, trying to catch his breath. Knowing he had to get back to Jamie right away, to see if Ueno had gotten to her, Hiroshi coughed and gasped, pulling out his cellphone and holding it in his fist, unable yet to speak.

The guard called into his headphone for back up and said, "He won't get far."

Hiroshi said, "He already has."

Chapter 18

When Hiroshi got to the interrogation room, Sakaguchi was locked in a stare down with the motorcycle thief, seated at a thick, grey table. Hiroshi looked at the thief's sullen face and his leg up horizontally across a chair, the pant leg cut back for a temporary splint. His black tracksuit was ripped and dirty from sliding under the truck, his hands cuffed to the table.

Hiroshi's hip throbbed where he landed on it and his leg muscles felt wobbly. The cortisone shot and painkillers from the station clinic had not kicked in yet. The doctor and nurse had made him put his feet up for a few minutes and get rehydrated, but they couldn't do anything for what Hiroshi felt about losing Mattson's documents.

"Broken leg?" Hiroshi asked.

Sakaguchi shrugged.

"Don't tell me," Hiroshi said. "He doesn't speak Japanese."

"He can speak, but he won't."

The driver looked at the two detectives through thick-lidded eyes, waiting for whatever this was going to be to be over with.

"It's hard to say which way he wants to go from here," Sakaguchi said. "Sometimes, people don't realize what they're stealing."

"Or don't care."

"Other times, they know exactly what they're stealing."

"And for whom and for what reason." Hiroshi knew this was all on him. If only he had just left everything safely in the archives—or waited for Ueno to pick them up. He put Jamie in more danger and compromised everything. Whatever Mattson had so painstakingly constructed might be lost forever.

Sakaguchi leaned over the table. "I guess you're Chinese, am I right?"

The guy said, "Korean."

"See? He can talk." Hiroshi stepped to the side of the table.

"North or South?" Sakaguchi asked.

He nodded up.

"Do you want to go to jail here or there?" Sakaguchi asked. "We can work it either way."

He shrugged.

Hiroshi smacked him across the face, sending the thief reeling towards his splinted leg. The driver righted himself on the chair, dragged his cuff chains back in place and braced himself for the next blow.

Hiroshi pulled his hand back but stopped it mid-air and instead kneed the man's thigh just above the temporary splint.

The driver jumped sideways, shivering until the pain subsided, his breathing hard and fast as he bent over as far as he could to protect his leg. The cuff chain rattled without letting him reach his leg.

Hiroshi stared into his eyes, questioning.

"*Keitai*," the driver said in Japanese, opening his palm for his cellphone.

Sakaguchi went out of the room to retrieve his cellphone.

As soon as Sakaguchi shut the door, Hiroshi backhanded him across his face.

The driver reeled halfway out of his chair and tottered upright, reseating himself with his arms up as far as he could on the chain, no longer proud, just self-protective, his splinted leg quivering until he could calm it.

Hiroshi leaned across the table and said, "You better be glad it's you that got hurt and not me or the girl. If I don't get all those documents back, I'll personally hand you over to the North Koreans."

Sakaguchi came back with the cellphone and handed it to the thief. He pulled his cuffs around with a clank, put in the password, which Hiroshi made him repeat out loud, and showed one of the numbers in his phone to the detectives.

"No name?"

The guy shook his head no.

Sakaguchi motioned Hiroshi out into the hall. A uniformed policeman came inside the room and stood by the door.

"We already ran the numbers from his phone, so it'll just take a minute to check this," Sakaguchi said as they walked back to the homicide office. A few detectives and staff were at their desks, but the room still crackled with restless energy. Ringing the walls were whiteboards loaded with scrawling and cork boards pinned full of notes on top of notes. Desks piled high with folders and out-of-date computers formed two long rows.

Sakaguchi shuffled through a stack of folders and slid out the list of numbers from the cellphone, the printout teensy in his big hand. Sakaguchi dug through his desk for another folder, flipped through several pages and hummed. "It's the number of the guy from the other night."

"What guy?"

"Hideyasu Sato, the guy cut in two in Golden Gai."

"He gave us the one worthless number."

"His idea of a joke."

Sakaguchi waved one of the office staff over and told him to find all the calls made to and from that number. The number would likely be burned and tossed already, but it was worth trying. Sakaguchi slumped down in his chair. "It's going to take a while to break this guy down. Why don't you get Jamie home? The schedule for the all-night guard is set up. She's waiting in your office."

"My office?" Hiroshi asked.

"Where should I have let her wait? In the lounge with the detectives?"

"Is Akiko there?"

"Didn't she phone you?"

Hiroshi walked off through the long, dimly lit underground corridor that led to the annex building where his office was. His feet, legs, and back ached and his hip throbbed. He had not eaten lunch and had only drunk water in the station clinic.

In his office, Akiko and Jamie were deep in conversation, both of them sipping from small espresso cups.

Jamie stood up from the futon bed-chair when she saw him. "Are you OK?"

"I'm fine," Hiroshi said.

"How did those guys know where I was?" Jamie stepped towards Hiroshi, examining him.

Hiroshi pretended he was fine. "They must have followed you. Or me."

"Are you really OK?" Jamie checked him over again.

Hiroshi waved her off.

"Why would they want my father's notebooks?" Jamie asked.

"Same reason they broke into the house," Akiko said.

"Which is what we don't know," Hiroshi said.

Akiko stood up and spoke softly "Why don't you take her home? It'll be easier to look through all this after I've put it in order."

Hiroshi poked through the materials from the retrieved bag. The notes and papers were dirty and wrinkled from being tossed on the ground during the chase. "That's less than half of what we took from the archives."

Jamie looked at the pile and shook her head.

"Let's get something to eat," Hiroshi said. "I've got to keep moving or my body will seize up. Are you hungry?"

"I should be, but I don't feel hungry," Jamie said, touching her stomach. "Akiko, won't you join us?"

Akiko looked at Hiroshi, plucking at the handle to the one bag that survived intact. "I'm sorry. I, uh, need to get these in order."

"Are you sure?" Jamie asked her.

"Next time." Akiko bowed her head lightly and sat down in front of the papers poking out of the bags they had shoved everything in after gathering them from the street.

"Best cure for anything is *ramen*." Hiroshi pulled his coat on.

Jamie pulled her backpack over her shoulder and stood ready.

* * *

The *ramen* shop had seats at the counter, but Hiroshi steered Jamie to a small table by the window. He bought tickets at the small ticket machine on the wall and handed them to the chef behind the counter. Only one other customer huddled over a bowl.

The prep chef brought Jamie a small bib and a hair tie. She leaned back smoothing her long hair before pulling it into a bundle and slipping the hair tie on. Jamie shook the bib out, circled it around her neck and then smoothed and tugged on the bib until it draped over the full curve of her breasts.

Hiroshi tried not to watch. He closed his eyes and reached for chopsticks from the box on the table. He handed Jamie a pair, and took another for himself. They sipped water until two steaming bowls of noodles arrived.

Jamie cracked open her chopsticks and surveyed the *nori* seaweed, *chashu* pork slices, green scallions and seasoned egg swimming in steaming broth. "I feel like a little girl again. My father always shared his *ramen* with me at a place around the corner from our house."

Hiroshi tried to think what to say. He could not stop looking at her, feeling she was even more beautiful than the first day, her face flushed from eating and softer than the other day. The food relaxed her, letting her just be there.

Sweat broke out on their foreheads after the first spoonfuls of miso broth and chopsticks full of noodles. Jamie became more animated as she ate, purring and humming with pleasure. Both of them lost in restoring and refilling themselves, they ate straight through. Jamie finished first, setting her chopsticks across her bowl and staring out the window.

Across the small lane, a flower box ran along a windowsill on the opposite building. Just above the window was an air conditioning unit on a wall bracket wrapped for winter in thick plastic and grey duct tape. Jamie looked back down at her bowl and took a sip of ice water. Her eyes wandered back to the grey strips of duct tape.

"I think we should go," she said, tucking her bib under the bowl. She tugged on her coat, grabbed her backpack and walked out.

Hiroshi slurped the last two mouthfuls of soup, wondering what he had said or done—or not said or done. He hurried out after her to where she was waiting in the cold a few steps away towards the brightly lit main street. "What is it?"

"I was just, well, I...Over there." She pointed down the small lane. It looked like a typical Tokyo back lane. Small houses and low apartment buildings stretched to the end of the curving road in the dark. He looked at Jamie, confused.

"On the wall there," she said, looking away, her backpack slipping off her shoulder. Hiroshi looked at the ramen shop where they sat and followed a line to where her gaze would have fallen. It was the air conditioning unit wound with duct tape.

Jamie started to cry.

"It's all right," Hiroshi said, reaching for her.

Tears streamed down her cheeks inside the curtain of her long, thick hair.

Hiroshi put his hands on her shoulders and looked into her face. "It's OK. You're all right. It's over."

"No, it's not over. I still feel the tape all over me. I didn't know where you went. I don't know what I'm doing here. My father bled to death. His work is gone."

"You're safe now." Hiroshi wished saying made it true.

Jamie wrapped her arms around him and buried her face in his chest. Her backpack, one strap in hand, bounced against his legs as her body convulsed with sobs, distress and confusion streaming out in wet heaves.

Hiroshi pulled her tight against him, turning her away from the duct tape and patting her back. He felt her body loosen and relax in the darkness of the back lane.

"It's all right," he repeated until her crying slowed.

"I can't go back to my father's tonight," she said, clearing her throat, her face still plastered against his chest.

"There will be two officers there."

"Can't you take me somewhere else?"

"Where?"

"Any place."

"Okay."

"And stay with me?"

"Okay."

Chapter 19

In the taxi, Jamie fell asleep on Hiroshi's shoulder. As they waited near the ramen shop for a taxi, she took a sleeping pill, swallowing it dry, and after a few minutes, he felt her head lolling on his shoulder, her hair spilling over the two of them. He unbuttoned his jacket, lifted his arm and let her burrow into him. When they got to his apartment building, Jamie was sleeping so soundly he had to lean her against the door and walk around the back of the taxi to lift her out from the other side.

"Is she all right?" the taxi driver asked.

"She's fine." Hiroshi held her upright.

"Did she drink too much?" The driver leaned out his window.

"We're fine," Hiroshi reached for his badge with one hand and kept Jamie upright with his other arm.

The badge registered right away, but the driver asked, "This is where you live?" The driver peered up at the eight-story apartment building.

Hiroshi didn't answer, but put his arm under Jamie's shoulder and walked her towards the door. He stuck his key into the elevator panel and pressed the button. Her head hung down, long hair over her face. He never imagined such a beautiful woman would be so heavy.

A couple got off the elevator and pulled back surprised. They stepped around and walked off without a word. Hiroshi pressed the button for the seventh floor, and once there, maneuvered her along the open-air walkway to his apartment, ignoring the usually soothing view of Tokyo's nightscape, the vast stretch of lights to the black horizon.

After he clunked open the deadbolt on the thick metal door, his next-door neighbor, a busybody housewife who was always at home, stepped outside.

"*O-kaeri-nasai*, welcome home," she chirped. "I took a delivery for you, signed for it. I hope that's OK?" Seeing Jamie, she fell silent, unlike every other time she cornered Hiroshi, when she rambled on about the other tenants or the latest TV crime show until he could get away.

Hiroshi twisted Jamie around to take the cardboard envelope from her. Posted from Boston, it was from Sanae. "Thank you." Hiroshi fumbled for his key and the door, straining under Jamie's weight. The neighbor backpedaled to her apartment, closed the heavy metal door and, Hiroshi could hear, opened the kitchen window to listen.

Inside the *genkan* entryway, he kicked aside the week's unread newspapers and eased Jamie against the shoe rack, gently sitting her down. When he bent down to take off her shoes, he sighed at the dust, dirt and mold. He held her shoulder as he toed off his shoes and stepped onto the floor. In one pull, he hauled her up from behind.

Jamie twisted around, her arms loosely around him. "I'm, just, need, sleep," she mumbled as he slow danced her down the hall to his bedroom. He had not changed the sheets in a long time, but had hardly slept in the bed, sacking out in his office instead. He plopped Jamie down and peeled off her jacket and sweatshirt. After gently lowering her head onto the pillow and lifting her legs, she snuggled in, moaned and coughed and growled a little before falling more deeply asleep.

Hiroshi knelt down beside her and looked at her face. She was just as stunning asleep. Awake, a succession of feelings and thoughts flitted across her features. Asleep, her deeper self—calm and serene—rose to the surface, like a *bodhisattva* statue hidden in the side shadows of a temple.

He stood watching her and then went to the living room. A couple blankets and throw pillows were tossed around on the sofa, where he'd slept more often than in his bed. The pizza boxes stacked on the coffee table and the "on" light of his stereo were the only other signs anyone lived there.

He went to the kitchen, pulled open the refrigerator and quickly shut the door on the emptiness inside. He took one of the two chairs from the kitchen island counter and dragged it back to the bedroom with a blanket. He set the chair an arms length from Jamie, rolled himself in the blanket and sat down in the half light of the room to watch the alluring rhythms of her sleep.

Jamie squirmed deliciously, snored lightly, rolled over, her chest in the air, her face flushed with the warmth of sleep. Her shoulders, sketched with black brushstrokes of thick hair, were as broad as a swimmer's. Hiroshi's eyes blinked open and shut, opened on her face, her body, her curves, her breathing, closed on the floating, fading images from the day, the documents and *shunga* prints, the chase and the thieves, the *ramen*, all of it blocking out thought, and dragging him to sleep.

* * *

Hiroshi walked behind his college *kendo* team after a post-match meal in an old *okonomiyaki* restaurant near Kotoku-in and the *Daibutsu* in Kamakura. The others in the university *kendo* team headed towards Hase Station, but Hiroshi and Ayana dawdled, tired of carrying the *kendo* gear.

When they got to the Enoshima Line station, Hiroshi and Ayana looked at each other. None of their classmates was anywhere in sight.

"Where did everyone go?"

"We were talking too much."

"I'm exhausted."

"Let's sit for a while."

Duffle bags on their shoulders and still talking, they headed across the highway towards the beach. In the sand, they took off their shoes. They dropped their gear halfway to the shoreline and leaned back side by side, watching the sunset as the evening chill came on, neither of them saying a word about leaving. Hiroshi got up to buy *onigiri* rice balls and cans of tea from a rundown beach shack that was just closing.

As Hiroshi and Ayana ate, the sunset turned to stars. After the last of the beachcombers finished their walks, they moved their stuff against a rack of windsurfing boards chained to the tide break wall, and snuggled under the awkward pile of *keikogi* uniforms and *kendo* gear, musky with sweat, warming each other.

117

They kissed for a long, long time as the darkness blanketed them. Little by little, Hiroshi found a way inside her sweatpants and she a way inside his, until they were making love. They didn't notice the sweat or the sand or the open air until they were spent and lying beside each other, sticky and satisfied, thrilled and confused. They curled up together, pulling the thick clothes over them for warmth.

When the sun woke them, they walked down to the water barefoot and splashed water on their faces, shivering from the cold. After brushing as much sand as they could off themselves, they took the first local train to Kamakura and found a breakfast spot with a *moningu setto* of buttered toast, boiled egg, salad and coffee, embarrassed by their duffle bags of *kendo* gear and grungy clothes as all around them neatly dressed salarymen and *OL* office ladies ate their usual morning meal. Hiroshi and Ayana stared into each other's eyes as they nibbled their breakfast and the workers left one-by-one for work.

Two weeks later, Hiroshi left for America, unsure of himself, angry at having to leave, unable to even send Ayana the letter trying to explain what he was doing and asking her to visit him in Boston.

* * *

The doorbell rang and Hiroshi rose up on one elbow. Hiroshi swung his legs around to sit up. He'd been so tired he couldn't remember when he moved to the living room sofa. He listened to the shower, imagining Jamie under the flow of warm water. The doorbell rang again, sounding more insistent. He staggered towards the door as he turned his cellphone on. It rang right away. "*Moshi moshi?*"

Akiko said, "Ueno is on his way to pick you up."

The front bell rang again. "I think he's already here."

"Sakaguchi is going to the bookstore in Jinbocho," Akiko continued. "He wants you to go with him. Everyone's in a stir this morning."

Hiroshi clicked off and unlocked the door.

Ueno looked around the edge of the door, set a thick paw on the heavy, rusting metal and pulled it open with a quizzical look on his face. "I hope she's here," he growled.

Hiroshi nodded.

Ueno stepped in. "Sakaguchi sent me to drive you to Jinbocho."

Hiroshi waved him inside and led him away from the bedroom towards the kitchen. The sound of flowing water ceased with a knock of pipes and Ueno looked in the direction of the shower. The water pipes clanked, and Hiroshi imagined her toweling off. They could hear Jamie padding back to the bedroom.

Hiroshi could tell from Ueno's expression he was waiting for an explanation or an apology, but Ueno said nothing until he pulled his cellphone out. "He's here. Yes, also." He listened, nodded, staring at Hiroshi. When he hung up, Ueno said, "Sakaguchi spent the night monitoring the search we had out for her."

"Search? All night?" Hiroshi sighed and scratched the back of his head, nodded and went to the sink to rinse his face. He looked around for a towel and finally had to use paper towels from a roll on the counter. All he said to Ueno was, "I'm not Takamatsu."

Jamie came out in the same clothes as the day before, but her jeans, white sweatshirt and father's wool jacket looked perfect. She had a big smile for both of the detectives, and didn't seem at all curious why Ueno was there. She looked recharged and, as if nothing had happened the past couple days. "Shibata wants me to stop by his club in Shinjuku. And Setsuko wants to talk with you. You'll come with me, won't you? I don't want to be alone."

Hiroshi thought of all the things he was supposed to do that day— writing up a real estate rip-off from London, going through Mattson's materials, apologizing to Sakaguchi, visiting the sword dealer, who called again, and dealing with the unopened envelope from Sanae— but said, "I've got plenty of time. Ueno can drive us."

Jamie beamed at him.

Chapter 20

The call from the Endo brothers early that morning came as a surprise since Sakaguchi assumed they wanted nothing to do with the police. They asked him to come right away. Sakaguchi had Sugamo go with him since Hiroshi had infuriated him by not answering his calls and not letting him know where Jamie was. Hiroshi was getting as bad as Takamatsu.

Sugamo pulled the car under the spreading ginkgo tree in front of the bookstore in Jinbocho. When Sakaguchi got out, he instantly understood why they'd called—the front window was a spider web of splintered glass.

Sakaguchi pushed the door open and shards of glass tinkled to the sidewalk. The bookstore shelves, formerly overflowing from ceiling to floor, were emptied. Knee-high jumbles of *ukiyoe* prints, antique manuscripts and rare books made it impossible to enter without crunching something underfoot.

The twin brothers Seiichi and Shinichi did not notice Sakaguchi come in. They were bent like rice farmers picking silently through the bedlam at their feet. Shinichi, in jeans, stood up to stretch. His long grey hair, loosened from his ponytail, fell down to his shoulders. Seiichi had sweated through a black T-shirt, his tweed jacket nowhere in sight.

Sakaguchi stood by the front door, too shocked to even clear this throat.

When the brothers finally noticed Sakaguchi, they stared at him blankly for a moment, their former businesslike manner turned to anguish, before setting the books in their hands on the closest shelves. The twins came to the front holding the empty shelves for balance.

Shinichi brushed the glass splinters off a stack of woodblock prints. Seiichi picked up a leather-bound book and wiped it with his hand-kerchief.

Seiichi said, "Who would think bookselling could be so danger-ous?"

Shinichi said, "It's book publishing that's dangerous."

Sakaguchi asked, "What do you have that's expensive?"

The brothers spoke over each other: "Everything's valuable."

"The really high-value stuff is kept where?"

"Some is out here, or was," Shinichi said. "The rest is in fireproof safes in the back."

"Let me take a look." Sakaguchi nodded for Sugamo, who'd parked the car and hurried in, to watch the door.

The twins and Sakaguchi picked their way over the mess to the back. Sakaguchi bent double under the low-hanging ceiling and stepped over the jumble of invoices, letters and receipts tossed out of the filing cabinets that were jimmied open. A half flight of steps dropped down to a narrow hallway running to the back of the build-ing. A dozen in-wall safes with hand-size dials and large L-shaped handles were set into the brick wall at chest height.

"Why do you have so many?" Sakaguchi asked.

"We added them one by one over the years." Seiichi said.

"These two bigger ones?" Sakaguchi asked.

"Rare books and prints," the brothers answered together.

"That small one above?"

"Hard drives and publishing data."

"Nothing missing?"

"Untouched."

"The Endo Brothers Bookstore and Publishers must be doing some-thing right," a familiar voice shouted from the front of the store.

The three of them walked up the stairs. Standing next to Sugamo at the front of the store, was the writer Higa, with a bitter grin across his mottled, intense face, leaning on his cane surveying the mess. Standing next to him was a young, sallow-faced man with round, jutting cheekbones and long, stringy hair. The man dangled a laptop bag, and looked like what Higa must have before the sepia wrinkles set in from years of chain smoking.

Sakaguchi touched Higa's book, the one that Shinichi gave him the first time he came, still unread in his inner coat pocket.

"Looks like publishing deadlines will be postponed," Higa shouted.

"Some permanently," Shinichi shouted back.

The twin brothers and Sakaguchi found a path to the front of the shop.

When Sakaguchi got there, he looked at Higa. "You must have some idea what Mattson was going to say, an outline, a synopsis. You were editing, right?"

Higa nodded and looked around at the quiet chaos of the store. "Because of his stature, I, we, trusted him. Mattson seemed like he was about to expose all the false promises with clear evidence. We didn't want to scare him off."

"Scare him off? False promises? What—"

"The treaty structure kept American bases in Japan as a staging ground for the Korean War, the Vietnam War, and the Iraq War too. Who knows where the next one will be? Japan has no say in how its own land is used."

Sakaguchi nodded for Higa to continue.

"The ruling party in Japan has always let the Americans stay. The political left is weak and powerless, so we were waiting for someone like Mattson to make the case."

"Mattson seems an unlikely savior," Sakaguchi said.

"The Cold War diplomat had changed his mind. But someone must have found out about it. It's no coincidence he was killed right before an important speech." Higa shifted on the cane, looking for a place to sit down, but found none.

Sakaguchi turned to the twin brothers. "As publishers, why wouldn't you have him send you something, anything, about what he was writing? Why keep it a secret?"

Seiichi nodded his head and looked at Shinichi. "We asked for an overview, but he wanted to do it his way, and we trusted him. We had to. He was the only one who would know where to find the archival documents to support his claims."

"But anyone could access the documents in the archive," Sakaguchi said.

"Mattson knew the details of the American bases, from Japan to Guam to the Philippines to South Korea," Higa explained.

"He was writing about all of Asia?" Sakaguchi asked.

"From what he said, his focus was mostly Okinawa," Shinichi said.

"If it was going to be published before the speech, how could this have been edited so quickly?"

Higa smiled. "I set aside everything else to do it. First, we'd finish a simplified version in time for his speech. The unabridged version would have been released two months later."

The twins spoke at the same time: "We were happy to stir things up, but not this much."

Higa said, "The right wing in Japan will stop at nothing."

"That's who did this?" Sakaguchi asked.

The young guy with Higa said, "The American bases take up a lot of land. Tens of thousands of American personnel are stationed in Okinawa alone. But no one outside the US military command has any idea what's going on *inside* the bases. It's all secret. A slice of America transplanted into Japanese soil."

"Who is this?" Sakaguchi asked Higa.

Higa pointed at the young man with the handle of his cane. "This is Iino. He runs a blog about the bases—crimes, pollution, accidents, protests. Gets a lot of hits these days."

Iino moved his laptop to the crook of his arm, scrolling as he spoke. "The problems are not *with* the bases. The bases *are* the problem. Mattson was in touch with me about small details."

"What kind of details?" Sakaguchi asked, peeking at what Iino was scrolling through on his laptop.

"Mattson seemed to already know the answers to the questions he asked," Iino said, tipping the screen away from Sakaguchi. "It seemed like he was probing me to find out how much I knew."

"He wanted confirmation?" Sakaguchi asked.

"He wanted to know if he was the only one outside the military who knew about how the bases were really run."

"What questions did he ask?"

Iino shook his head. "I thought back over it after I heard the news. But it was never really anything that specific. He did ask several times how porous I thought the bases were. He used that word many times."

"What did he mean, porous?" Sakaguchi looked back and forth from Higa to Iino for the answer.

Higa leaned on his cane and put an elbow on an unbroken section of the front glass case. "In the past, the American bases in Japan were like open ports. Everything snuck through. Guns and drugs mostly, anything prohibited in Japan. Now, there's more oversight, but take the American military budget, add in complicit Japanese politicians, and you get corruption."

Sakaguchi felt irritated Hiroshi was not with him to remember all these details, but he continued asking questions. "Why would Mattson's book be so shocking if you know all the details already?"

"We don't. That's the thing. Whatever we say has no footnotes, no annotations. He had facts, dates, people, amounts. He was an insider. He understood the details," Higa said.

Iino nodded in agreement. "And he had the voice of authority."

Shinichi said, "He always explained things clearly. People trusted his word. If he said the system was out of control, which is what I think he was going to say, people would listen."

Sakaguchi frowned. "And you didn't have so much as a description of what he was working on?"

Higa leaned on his cane and rocked forward. "Mattson was trying to finalize the work by painting the eye of the dragon."

"What does that mean?" Sakaguchi asked.

"In the old Chinese story, an artist painted such skillful, realistic paintings that when he painted in the last dot—the dragon's eye—the dragon came alive, peeled itself off the wall and flew away," Higa said.

"The eye of Mattson's painting," Sakaguchi asked. "What was it?"

"We don't know, but we're sure he found it," Shinichi said.

"He definitely found it," Seiichi said.

"How do you know?" Sakaguchi insisted.

"If he hadn't found it, we'd be talking with him instead of with you," Higa said.

Chapter 21

After navigating the neighborhood maze, Hiroshi and Jamie were surprised to find the door to Shibata's bar open a crack. Hiroshi pushed Jamie back with his hand, wondering if he had forgotten it was open, or he was in there airing the place out. They both looked at the flowers set on the curb where the thief, Sato, was killed.

Hiroshi stepped forward cautiously and pulled the door open the rest of the way, rusty hinges creaking. A sliver of midday sun found its way through the tangle of overhead wires and fell into the hazy interior onto the bar stools set upside down along the counter.

Hiroshi heard nothing as he took a step inside.

Before he could take another step, Shibata came shuffling out from the little kitchen area, holding his hand over his eyes to block the sun. "I hate hate hate morning. I got something for you, Jamie."

"It's afternoon." Jamie squeezed around Hiroshi and went to give Shibata a hug.

Ken emerged from under the curtain looking even taller and more muscled in daylight. He nodded politely without a word, and ducked back into the kitchen. Shibata batted the curtain aside with a wave of his hand and brought out a shoebox in both hands.

"Looking everywhere and find with tax stuff. I forgot these thing, and other thing, too." Shibata pulled off the top and rummaged through a disordered batch of old photos.

Shibata handed Jamie a black and white photo of her father in a khaki uniform standing in front of the Great Buddha in Kamakura. Her father stood arms akimbo smiling straight into the camera, looking a bit like Hemingway with a bushy mustache.

Jamie smiled back like a wide-eyed child.

"That's when he married Setsuko. She nice, calm, smart, not wild." Shibata dug for more photos.

"My mom was wild?"

"Depends on thinking. But, yes, very. Look at this one. Taken before Setsuko."

Shibata pulled out another photo of her father in uniform with his arms around two Japanese women in flower-print dresses, their hair in elaborate swirls and their faces in lipstick and rouge. They posed formally, but it looked like they had just been dancing, sweat beading on their foreheads.

"Inside my nightclub," Shibata said.

"Was that the one I went to?"

"No, no, before. Everything Japan changing then. Bernie love jazz and booking for me American soldier, Japanese and Filipino cats. Everyone play bebop, then. The country changing, opening, growing. Hard work, that club. But it burn down."

"Burned down?"

"Insurance problem." Shibata laughed. "I downsize now. No one insure this place. Too small." He handed Jamie another photo of her father standing with a tall, handsome Japanese woman, about her father's height.

"This girl nice. *Takarazuka.*"

"What's that?" Jamie said.

Hiroshi said, "*Takarazuka* is a theater with all female actresses. This woman must have played the male parts she's so tall."

"She only play men. Big star that time. Famous. She love your father, but she kill herself."

"What?" Jamie said.

"Not because your father, because she crazy. Your father very upset. Sad, she so pretty."

Ken came out of the backroom where he had been preparing coffee, carrying a tray with dainty cups. His thick, muscled arms, in a tight cotton shirt, flexed as he set out the cups.

"This photo 1959," Shibata said. Her father stood with young Japanese men in baggy button down shirts, pleated pants and round glasses. "Some these men at funeral. Your father, he respect Japanese people. That time, most military and American looking down us. We don't like them either most time, but have to get their money, right?" Shibata let out an explosive little chuckle.

Jamie looked at the crinkle-edged prints and faded photos. Her father looked calm and relaxed, like she remembered him. He was never drunk around her that she remembered. A photo of him reading a book reminded her of when she used to sit in his lap and read books with him in the study, not always understanding the content, just loving the music of the words.

In the next photo, Jamie, her father, mother, and school friends sat in a boat on the Sumida River, everyone in light summer kimonos. For her, the best day of the whole year was the fireworks festival. Her father rented a small boat with a little kitchen and a rice-stalk mat roof. Boats jammed the river, vying for the best view of the phosphorescent colors that burst and dripped and dissolved into the black canvas of the night.

"I loved Tokyo summers! Oh, I lost so much," Jamie said. "Can I make copies of these?"

"Copy? No, no, you take all. They all yours." Shibata pulled another one up.

"Is that me?" Jamie asked, holding the photo of a young girl on a swing in a park. She could recognize her mother and father holding the chain on either side of the swing.

Shibata touched her shoulder. "You a beauty even then. I take that photo. In Asakusa. That playground still there maybe. Just across street. Your father joke it is Jamie's private playground."

Hiroshi politely looked at the photos one by one as Jamie passed them to him, then handed them back to Shibata.

Shibata put the top back on the shoebox and handed it to Jamie. "So, you go to archive, get his things?"

"We got robbed outside the archive." Jamie dropped her eyes.

"What?" said Shibata, his eyes wide with alarm. "What happen? They take everything?"

Hiroshi set his coffee cup down.

"Hiroshi chased them and got some of it back." Jamie touched Hiroshi's arm.

Shibata looked at Jamie touching Hiroshi, pretended not to notice, and pressed for more. "What they look like? They speak Japanese?"

Hiroshi said, "They were Korean, maybe a gang that robs houses. We caught one, but he won't talk."

Shibata rubbed his head. He patted Jamie on the hand. "I talk detective in Japanese, OK?"

Shibata switched to Japanese to speak to Hiroshi. "When I talked to Bernie, he was going to publish what he found in the archives, but he said it's better I don't know."

"You don't think he stumbled on the robbery by accident?" Hiroshi asked.

"How many times do you police need to hear things before you get it?"

"How do you know it wasn't bad luck?"

"I know. I came to the bar one day, last February or so, and Bernie was here, so drunk he couldn't walk. He had a key to my bar, from long ago, so he let himself in and proceeded to get 'stinko,' as he said."

"I thought he stopped drinking."

"He did, but he got nervous. Fell off the wagon. He kept saying 'poison, poison,' but he was so drunk it made no sense."

"Poison?"

"Then, he started singing." Shibata finally laughed. "He was lying right here on the floor, until we put a blanket on him, and Ken and Setsuko and I took him back to the detox hospital."

"What poison?"

"I don't know. And don't tell Jamie about his one time drinking again. Maybe she understands a little Japanese." Shibata glanced over at her to see if she caught what he'd said and then went to the back room, quickly returning with a small spray bottle that he handed to Jamie. "Here, take this."

"What is it? I can't read it. Perfume?" Jamie started to open it.

Shibata snatched it from her. "Pepper spray. Strongest kind. You spray anyone come close you, OK?"

"I don't need this," Jamie said, setting it on the bar top back towards him.

Shibata pushed it back towards her. "I get from guy who come my bar. He say best brand."

Jamie shook her head and left it on the bar.

Shibata reached over and put it in the inside pocket of her jacket. "You stubborn like you father. I say again, you go back New York today. Come back Tokyo later."

Jamie shook her head no.

"He's right, you know," Hiroshi said. "You should go back to New York."

Jamie looked up at Hiroshi. "I'm not leaving until I get my father's manuscript and his speech and find out what happened to him."

The bar had gotten dark as the sun dipped below the tall buildings on the main street and a chill came in through the half-open door. Shibata slid a colorful *furoshiki* under the box of photos, pulled the corners up and tied them to make a handle on top to carry the box. He handed it to her with two hands and a pleasant little bow of his head. "Take to New York."

Jamie took the shoebox of photos with both hands as tears welled up. Shibata and Hiroshi both steadied and comforted her, one on each side. She nodded she was all right. "Oh, this jet lag," she said, and sniffled and smiled.

"I have other thing from your father, papers he gave me. I send you in New York is best. What your address there?" Shibata said, not meeting her eyes.

Jamie sniffled again and said, "Send them to my father's house."

"It not his house anymore. Is your house," Shibata said, his eyes opening wide to see if she understood. He handed her a set of papers.

"What is it?" Jamie asked.

Hiroshi took the documents and looked them over. "The deed to the house, and instructions for you to have it in the event of his death."

"I sorry, he give me that and I forget where is. I think there is one more document, too. Important, so I look again. So long ago, he give me these, for safe keep. I not so good organize."

"We have to go. I need to meet Setsuko." Jamie gathered up everything on the bar and gave Shibata a hug.

"Is better return New York," Shibata said again. He looked at Hiroshi, pleading with his eyes.

Outside the bar, Hiroshi looked at the flowers placed on the curb for the spirit of the thief, Sato. A wrapping of clear plastic kept the flowers from freezing and drying out too quickly in the cold.

Jamie smiled and hugged Shibata again. Ken came out and stood beside Shibata in front of the bar, both of them bowing again when Hiroshi and Jamie looked back one last time.

Chapter 22

When Hiroshi pushed open the door to the sword store, Suzuki, the sword dealer, was knotting a string around a sword handle. Suzuki was not in his *sagyo-bakama* work outfit, but in a more formal *iaidogi*. The shirt, sash and pleated trousers were all neat, clean and sharply pressed. The blue and grey chrysanthemum pattern matched his tight, grey ponytail. Takamatsu's contacts, Hiroshi had to admit, were different from everyone Hiroshi knew.

"You seem to be taking an uncommon interest in swords, detective. Are you considering one for the young lady?"

"I'm less interested in the swords than in the people who use them."

"Swords are often the more interesting. Each sword lives its own life in the world."

Jamie walked over to the sword racks and put her hand out to touch one, then pulled back. "Are these real?"

"What did she say?" Suzuki asked Hiroshi.

"She wants to know if they're real," Hiroshi said.

"Are all foreign women like that?"

"She's only half-foreign." In English, Hiroshi told Jamie, "They're real, all right."

Jamie ran her hand over the scabbard of a long *katana* sword and walked around the store, standing before the racks and racks of swords, mesmerized.

Suzuki pulled out a sword and set it on the counter for Hiroshi. "This is a *tanto* sword, the kind we discussed last time. Using the shorter *tanto* sword is a lost art. For samurai, the shorter swords were just as important."

Hiroshi wondered why Suzuki was showing him this, but tried to push down his American impatience. If he let Suzuki talk, he'd eventually get to the point of why he called. He'd seen Takamatsu chat for an hour with an informant to get one little tip. The relationship, Takamatsu had said, was more important than the information.

Suzuki kept working as he talked. "My father fed us during the war by retying the special *tsukamaki* patterns the officers liked. After the war, the officers had to sell their swords to feed their families—the last treasure sold in any household. It was like selling your soul and the souls of your ancestors. My father bought them for next to nothing."

Hiroshi observed his quick, practiced method of pulling two strands of braided string taut over the ray skin handle, and doing the same on the other side. Suzuki pulled the tip of the string around, pressed it under and over the grip and tucked its end into and under itself.

"My father was detained when the Americans rounded up all the swords, hundreds of thousands of them. The Americans dumped them in the Akabane Arsenal, where they rusted. It would have been like dumping priceless European artworks in a barn. That raised the price for the remaining ones, but if you were caught with a sword, penalties were severe."

"Your father hid them?"

"He never told me where. Outside Tokyo, I guess, until the Occupation was over. My father always made sure the string fit perfectly at the end. I never learned how he gauged the length on the final turns of the knot. Lots of small skills like that get lost." Suzuki held the sword up, turning it back and forth under the overhead light.

Hiroshi took a step away from the counter. Jamie came over and leaned close.

Suzuki wiped the blade from handle to point with a dry cloth and dusted fine powder along the steel. He wiped the blade clean and checked for blemishes under the light. At last, he put small drops of *choji* mineral-clove oil on the blade, working it in with a cloth and wiping off the extra with a cut of soft paper before sliding the blade into a black lacquer *saya* scabbard on the counter between them.

Hiroshi waited until he was finished and pulled out a list from his pocket. "We compiled a list of sword buyers. I wonder if you recognize any of these names?"

"Did you check these buyers against the registered owners?"

"They were all registered."

Suzuki put on his glasses to appraise the list, slowing his finger next to a few names, but never stopping, until he came to the end with a shrug. "I've heard some of these guys sell historically valuable swords abroad."

"So, no one on this list is worth checking into," Hiroshi sighed. "Another dead end."

"In Tokyo, there are no dead ends."

Hiroshi folded the list back in his pocket.

"Did you ask Takamatsu about transporting a sword for that collector?"

"Is that why you called me?" Hiroshi wondered if Suzuki was finally getting to the point.

"The payment is high. Sword collectors have money."

"And information?"

"The buyer knows swords and knows people. Runs a restaurant in Shin-Okubo."

"Korea-town."

"When Takamatsu goes, he'll find out what you need to know."

Hiroshi should have listened the first time to what Suzuki said. That's why he called again, to insist Takamatsu go to the sword buyer. But maybe Takamatsu wanted Hiroshi to know about all this, too, to participate in the process. If it were just about money, Takamatsu would have done it on his own without involving Hiroshi. "I'll get Takamatsu to do it."

Suzuki said, "Have Takamatsu call me here. I'll give him the number." He picked up the sword he had just cleaned and polished. "Want to try this?"

"Where? Here?" Hiroshi looked around the small shop, confused.

"Out back," Suzuki said. He locked the front door and turned the "Open" sign to "Closed."

"I don't know how to handle a sword," Hiroshi said.

"The girl will like it," Suzuki said.

Hiroshi turned to ask her. "Jamie? Want to see one in action?"

Jamie jumped. She was standing by a row of short swords, and shook her head as if woken from a dream. "I shot a gun once."

Suzuki nodded for Hiroshi to translate, and then replied, "With a sword you look your opponent in the eye, both of you equal distance from death. Guns are made in factories and used from far away. They are machines. They dehumanize and intervene in the moment before death. Swords are extensions of human beings. They move as a human moves."

Hiroshi didn't translate for Jamie. He was thinking about what Suzuki said as he followed him into his workroom. Three worktops were covered in handles, hilts and tools. Screw-handle clamps held blades and scabbards. The far side of the room was lined by sliding doors with sagging, rippled glass that rattled when Suzuki slid one open to reveal a garden outside.

From the threshold of the sliding door, Hiroshi took in the simplicity of the garden's design. Tall shrubs grew thick along one crumbling brick wall. Bamboo lattice concealed the other two. Pine trees pruned as tight as Suzuki's ponytail arched over a cascade of rocks. A dry pool of light-grey pebbles was raked into undulating waves, with a few pebbles scattered out of place.

Suzuki stepped into wooden *geta* clogs to walk across the thick carpet of moss. In the middle of the garden, he set up a *tameshigiri* woven tatami mat on a bamboo holder that stood as tall as a man's shoulders.

Jamie stepped down from the wooden overhang into a pair of wooden *geta* clogs watching Suzuki's every move. Hiroshi stayed where he was on the overhang close to the sliding doors.

"I've been working on this blade for a long time." Suzuki adjusted the target. "I'll probably give this one to the sword museum, get it designated non-exportable."

Suzuki brought his body to perfect stillness two steps from the practice target. He set one foot forward and the other back, working his feet in for traction. He drew the blade from the scabbard and pointed it straight ahead. To Hiroshi, the garden seemed to fall still, as if all sound and motion had ceased.

In two whispering strokes, two angled pieces of target toppled with soft thumps. The remaining piece trembled in place. Suzuki stood immobile with the sword pointed away and his right foot forward until the cut-off tatami pieces came to a rest. Stepping back with a sharp sideways snap of the sword and the traditional *chiburi* swipe of the blade to ritually cleanse it of blood, Suzuki slipped the sword into its sheath with a soft click.

Jamie said, "That was so fast, I couldn't even see it. What...?" She leaned forward, trying to process what she had just witnessed.

Suzuki turned to her and spoke in measured words. "Like water, swords exist in different states. A moving blade is unseen, hidden in the blur of motion, felt but not perceived. The rest of the time, its stillness allows its beauty to be revered."

Hiroshi translated as Jamie stood entranced.

Suzuki turned to Hiroshi. "Want to try?"

"I was in the *kendo* club at high school and college," Hiroshi explained. "But that was a wooden practice sword. I've never used a real sword before." Hiroshi thought back to the *dojo* practice room for *kendo* at college. The grill-front helmet and thick pads blocked the blows of wooden swords during the long after-school practices.

"You aren't Japanese until you do," Suzuki said, stepping towards Hiroshi.

"Are you going to try it?" Jamie asked Hiroshi.

Hiroshi shook his head no. "It's harder than you think."

He remembered how liberating and invigorating it was to shout and strike an opponent with full force. He remembered, too, the look of Ayana's flushed, sweaty face when she peeled off her helmet and shook out her hair, walking across the practice room to see how he was at the end of the workout.

He had given up Ayana, given up *kendo*, just like he'd always given up on the most important things too soon, stopping when they started to move toward greater meaning, shying away when they started to touch him closely, never letting people or practices or even work deepen inside him.

Suzuki—finished—bowed to the cut mats and turned to Hiroshi. "Let Takamatsu know right away about this sword delivery."

"*Hai*," was all Hiroshi could answer.

Chapter 23

Hiroshi had a hard time finding the *kissaten* coffee shop where they were supposed to meet Setsuko. The grid-like streets of Ginza, rebuilt during the Occupation, were just as confusing to Hiroshi as the winding, twisting alleys of the rest of Tokyo. He kept giving new directions to Ueno, apologizing each time since he suspected Ueno was about at his limit with Hiroshi after the night before. After helping Saito with security preparations at the International Forum, Ueno had to come back to chauffeur Hiroshi and Jamie around.

When they finally found the *kissaten* on a long, straight backstreet, Hiroshi was about to tell him to take a break, but Ueno held his hand up to silence him and pulled off without a word.

Hiroshi held the door of the *kissaten* open for Jamie. Inside, the *kissaten* had dark wood walls, a long European style mirror behind the counter, and hundreds of antique coffee grinders, hand cranks frozen in place.

At the back of the coffee shop sat Setsuko, Mattson's first wife. When she saw them enter, she put down her reading and got up to hug Jamie as if they'd known each other much longer than a couple of days. "This was your father's favorite seat," she said, motioning for Jamie to sit beside her on the banquette.

A row of siphon vacuum coffee makers bubbled over low blue flames behind the glass counter, the glass bulbs lined up evenly along the brown wood top. A piano sonata was playing over the speakers, Debussy or Satie, Hiroshi wasn't sure.

"Bernie loved to watch the coffee go up and down the glass chambers. Said it helped him think."

"We were robbed yesterday," Jamie said. "I didn't want to tell you on the phone."

Setsuko twisted in her seat. "Are you all right? Where were you?"

Hiroshi said, "In front of the archives. They wanted whatever Mattson had there."

Setsuko leaned back. "They were following you."

Jamie nodded. "They must have been."

"I'm not surprised. I've—" Setsuko stopped when the waiter came to take their order. Setsuko ordered coffee for them and patted Jamie's hand, "Your father said the coffee here was the best in Tokyo, but I think he just liked the theater of the whole thing."

"It's old, this place?"

"I came here when I was a girl," Setsuko said. "So, yes, *old*." She laughed. "But it's changed. My father was a doctor and all the best doctors—who studied in Germany—lived in Ginza. After the war, nothing German remained. Your father liked to write his scroll here."

"Scroll?"

Setsuko laughed. "I know it sounds ridiculous, but he started to keep a journal, for you, on a scroll."

"You mean like paper wrapped around wood rods?" Jamie laughed.

Hiroshi let the two women talk. Coffee bubbled along the counter, filling the air with a rich, roasty aroma, a pleasant accompaniment to the music.

Jamie said, "I remember sitting at the kitchen table practicing calligraphy with him, copying each one I mastered on a scroll. My mother wasn't ever much one for books."

Setsuko looked away.

The coffee *meister*, dressed in a jacket-less tux, brought three cups of coffee on a lacquer tray, setting them down on the dark wood of the table, turning the handle precisely to the right to be picked up more easily.

"Your mother was a different kind of person. Who could resist her good looks?" Setsuko said. "Beautiful as she was, she couldn't stop whatever was eating Bernie up. And she wanted your father to do something he didn't want to do."

"What was that?"

"She wanted to live in America."

"She got her wish," Jamie said. "She said I'd be better off there, too, but I'm not so sure."

"When I first met your father, he was into Zen and tea. We met at a retreat at Koya-san."

"Koya-san? We were going to go there. Together. On our trip."

"At that time, the late 50s, he was criticized as having 'gone native' by his American colleagues. They were running the country but could hardly speak Japanese. Always on about Communism, which was the least of everyone's problems."

"That's when he started drinking?"

"Your father started getting in arguments at work and coming home staggering drunk. He screamed about the idiots in Washington."

"It must have been a stressful time."

"Diplomatic cables were slow then, but the one agreeing with his view of SOFA never arrived. When the final version was delivered, it was nothing like what he'd argued for. He disappeared for two weeks. Drunk, I guess, with some woman. Maybe your mother, but there were others. I moved out."

"What did you do after you moved out?"

"Japanese women could get divorced, choose our jobs, even vote and remarry. I worked in shops for a while, then got a teaching license and a teaching position at a women's school. Eventually, I set up my own school. I'm teaching women now whose grandmothers I taught!"

"And you didn't see my father..."

"Until I took him to rehab three, four, years ago. A year in rehab and a year at a temple on Koya-san, the one where we met, and he was as good as new. Right after the earthquake and nuclear meltdown in Fukushima, he felt he was being called back to service."

Jamie smiled. "Well, everything will come out now. I signed an agreement to get everything published."

Setsuko and Hiroshi set their coffee cups down and looked at Jamie.

Jamie smiled, pleased with herself to divulge this secret.

Setsuko said, "Who did you sign an agreement with?"

"A Diet member," Jamie said.

"When was this?" Hiroshi asked.

Jamie said, "She wanted to meet me at her office in the Diet building."

141

Setsuko and Hiroshi exchanged glances.

Setsuko said, "What was the Diet woman's name?"

"Shinobu Katsumura. She knew my father and wanted to publish everything. Someone in her family owns a publishing house...what?" Jamie looked at Setsuko and Hiroshi.

Setsuko patted her hand.

Hiroshi excused himself. He stepped outside the *kissaten* onto the street, ignoring calls from Sakaguchi, who would only scold him, and from Akiko, who he could guess had everything organized. He called Eto Sensei instead.

"Are you visiting again or have you got more questions for me?" Eto Sensei had more energy in his voice than anyone Hiroshi talked with.

"The latter. Do you know a Diet member by the name of Shinobu Katsumura?" Hiroshi asked.

Eto Sensei was quiet. "I certainly do. Why do you want to know?"

"Apparently, Mattson's daughter met with her and she wanted to publish Mattson's entire memoirs."

"Well, they would do that, wouldn't they? One of the dynasties in Japanese politics, they made their fortune as land speculators and now run numerous businesses. They moved into publishing a few years ago, and since they know people in all the ministries, they took over high school textbooks."

"Textbooks?" Hiroshi felt confused. None of the questions he asked went where he expected. Inside his office, everything was comfortably unsurprising.

"That's where the money is. Most of what they publish is standard right-wing bunk—revisionist history, moral instruction, patriotism. Other works tried to disprove the Nanjing Massacre and comfort women. Their usual targets."

"So, why would they want to publish Mattson's work?"

"Well, that's just it. They wouldn't. Once they get the materials, they'll probably do what they do with textbook proposals they don't like—sit on them."

"They want to buy the rights to Mattson's work to *not* publish them?" Hiroshi couldn't quite get it.

"Exactly. One of my former students had a textbook manuscript quashed after signing with the Katsumura's. He called it 'shelving the truth.' A very Japanese sort of censorship."

"Do you think they—?"

"They wield power in a slow, steady, wear-you-down way," Eto Sensei said. "In Japan, that usually works."

"I wanted to ask you to look through some documents if you have time? I could really use your expertise."

"I'm finishing another manuscript of my own, but this sounds urgent. I hate to make you bring them down here, but if you could, that'd be easiest for me."

"I can do that."

"And I'll check with my younger colleagues about Mattson. They might know more than I do."

Hiroshi bowed, automatically, with phone in hand as he thanked Eto Sensei. He and Akiko would have to look through everything, and go again to the archive for the rest of Mattson's research. Hiroshi went back inside the *kissaten* and sat down next to Jamie and asked, "Did you turn over any documents, notes or writings of your father's to them?"

"No, not yet. Why?" Jamie looked confused. "I signed a contract. But I couldn't even read it. Trey—"

"Trey took you there?" Hiroshi asked, as calmly as he could.

Jamie breathed out, her eyes averted.

Setsuko said, "You could have asked me to read it for you."

"They promised to send me an English version. Maybe it's at the house already?"

"I just explained that Bernie was going to publish with a small press in Jinbocho," Setsuko said.

"Yes, I know. The Endo Brothers. My colleague, Sakaguchi, talked with them," Hiroshi said.

"Is this connected to the people following me? Us?" Jamie asked, picking up her empty cup, then setting it down.

"Speaking of being followed," Setsuko said. "I've been followed since Bernie's death."

Hiroshi and Jamie looked at Setsuko.

"That's why I wasn't surprised when you said they followed you too," Setsuko said. "I can't go anywhere without one of them following me."

"One of who?" Hiroshi asked.

Setsuko locked eyes with Hiroshi, "They take turns, but one of them is sitting at the table closest to the door."

Chapter 24

Speaking with feigned calm, Hiroshi sent a text to Sakaguchi telling him to come right away to the coffee shop in Ginza. He glanced at Setsuko, and at Jamie. "Why didn't you tell me you were being followed? And Jamie, keep talking and don't look around."

Setsuko shrugged. "Tokyo's so crowded, there are always people close by, so it's usually safe. It's only when no one's around that there's a risk."

"But that's what they're waiting for—the moment when no one's around."

The man by the door folded and refolded a newspaper, pulling it close to his face. Dressed in a grey wool suit jacket over a black sweater, he lined up his coffee, cigarettes and cellphone precisely at hand. He looked like no one in particular, with a flat face, a small nose and thin eyelids that let him watch without anyone knowing he was watching.

In a calm voice, Setsuko said, "They take turns, but this guy and one other are the most common. There are about four of them altogether. I wonder if they know I know?"

"Since when have they been following you? Jamie, don't look around."

Jamie trembled, her coffee cup clinking against the saucer when she set it down.

"For a couple months. I didn't want to distract Bernie. Now, I realize I should have. He was working so hard on his book and the speech." Setsuko turned to Jamie. "Won't you give his speech for him? He would want your voice to carry his words?"

Jamie rubbed her wrists, still raw from the tape. "I can't give a speech. Let's just get it into print instead."

"It won't matter once you start speaking."

"It will matter."

"Your father was nervous about public speeches, too, but once he got going—"

"We don't even know where the speech is."

"I'm sure it's there somewhere. He hid things all over the place."

Jamie leaned back and tried not to look at the man by the door. "Look, I'm not standing up in front of a huge group of people. I've never done anything like that. I was a student, then an HR director, a shopper, consumer, and debtor, I guess."

"Your father learned by doing."

"My father was reconstructing the world at my age. Of course, he could give a speech. I'm the opposite." Jamie rubbed her wrists again, nervously.

Hiroshi's cellphone buzzed, startling all three of them. Sakaguchi and Sugamo were on their way, ten minutes depending on traffic. "Just keep talking," Hiroshi said to Jamie and Setsuko.

Perhaps sensing he'd been made, the flat-faced man took his check to the counter. Three coffee bulbs were just finishing siphoning, so the coffee *meister* bowed with an apology and asked the man to wait by the register.

Hiroshi leaned across the table to Jamie and Setsuko. "Do not leave this shop no matter what. I'll be back to get you."

After paying, the flat-faced man left. When the bell on the front door stopped tinkling, Hiroshi got up, pulled on his coat and hurried out to the narrow road of shops outside.

The man moved quickly, hugging the tall buildings along the Ginza back street. At the first major crossing, he turned onto a busy sidewalk, scooting around window shoppers staring at jewelry, fashion, and furniture displays. The flat-faced man picked up his pace, cutting diagonally into the six-way crosswalk as the light turned yellow.

Hiroshi ran to get across before the light changed. When he got to the other side, he heard honking from Sugamo who had just pulled up at the corner. Sakaguchi hopped out and hurried ahead. Hiroshi let him take the lead, texting Ueno with instructions to find Jamie and Setsuko and stay with them in the *kissaten*.

The man turned into a small alley between an artisanal chocolate shop and a luxury pet goods store. Sakaguchi turned after him. Hiroshi hurried after. Turning the corner, he found Sakaguchi plunging down a long thin alley full of greasy trashcans and mops flopped over rope lines, drying.

The man was gone.

Hiroshi ran after Sakaguchi, pulling on the back doors on the left. Sakaguchi yanked the door handles on the right. All locked. The end of the alley was blocked by a large dumpster and a tall fence too high to scramble over easily. To the right, a door into the kitchen of a Chinese restaurant was tied open with rope. Sakaguchi burst in with Hiroshi right behind.

The cooks stopped chopping, stirring and frying when Sakaguchi held up his badge. Sakaguchi pushed through to the front of the restaurant, as Hiroshi waited by the door. After checking back down the alley to be sure they hadn't missed anything, Hiroshi ducked through to the front of the restaurant, a red-walled area with eight or nine Chinese-style tables. None of the half dozen customers looked anything like the guy.

"Did anyone come through here?" Sakaguchi asked one of the waitresses.

She answered in thickly accented Japanese. "People come through all day," she said. The cooks stepped to the door holding their cleavers and long wood spatulas, unsure what to do. The young woman shrugged.

One of the cooks came over and pulled off his white cap. "Why don't I call the owner for you?" The cook and the waitress started arguing in Chinese and the cook went back into the kitchen to get his cellphone.

At the side of the dining room, Hiroshi pulled back the *noren* curtain to a stairway so steep it was almost a ladder. Stacked along the side were pickling tubs, brown storage pots and fermenting vats of liquor. The aroma of vinegar, onions, shrimp sauce and chili pepper made Hiroshi sneeze. He pulled himself up the unlit stairs sideways, struggling to find a place to put his hands. When he got to the landing, he popped his head around the corner, then pulled back and did it again, but he could not see or sense any presence. He ran his hand along the wall by the doorframe but found no switch. So he pulled out his cellphone and held it up to illuminate what little he could of the room. He pushed against a stack of boxes. It didn't budge.

"Hiroshi!" Sakaguchi yelled from below. "Quick. Next door!" Hiroshi climbed down as quickly as he could, his hand on the ceiling to keep from hitting his head. He rushed out the front door of the restaurant. Sugamo—who must have pulled around the corner, parked and run down the front alley—waved him towards the door into the next building.

Sakaguchi was waiting just inside at the bottom of a long flight of stairs up to a purple glass door with the characters for "mahjong" in large gold letters. A thick haze of tobacco smoke hung in the air at the top of the steep stairway.

Hiroshi went up first with Sakaguchi and Sugamo right behind. The three of them paused at the top of the stairs and with a glance, burst in to the crowded game room. The noisy clack of mahjong tiles instantly ceased. No one looked at Hiroshi, Sakaguchi and Sugamo, but everyone at the dozen felt-covered tables froze. Light trickled in through frosted windows along one side of the room and got lost in the cheap wood paneling on the other three sides. The air was thick with cigarette smoke.

Sakaguchi and Sugamo fanned out to the sides of the room and Hiroshi checked every face of the men at the tables. He checked everyone again to be sure.

Sakaguchi saw Hiroshi's disappointed face and barked out, "Where's the fire exit?" in a rough Osaka accent, more *yakuza* threat than cop command.

Everyone remained quiet where they were.

"Last chance," Sakaguchi said. "Where's the fire exit?"

No one moved.

Sakaguchi stepped to the nearest table, put his thick hand under the edge, and dumped it over with a *yori-taoshi* throw. With his left hand, he tossed the nearest players' cart. Mahjong tiles, drinks, and ashtrays scattered across the floor. All around the room, the other players leapt to their feet. With nowhere to run, a few players backed towards the windows, while others stood where they were.

"If I have to ask again, the rest of the tables are going over, and this parlor will be closed for a very long time." Sakaguchi put his hand under another table.

A young man with a buzz cut in a tight grey sweater took a step forward from a table in the back. Without a word, he pointed towards a frayed curtain in the back corner.

Hiroshi and Sugamo yanked back the curtain to reveal a metal door. When Hiroshi pushed it open, no alarm sounded as it should have, and he stepped out onto an old metal grate fire escape. When Sugamo came out after Hiroshi, the landing dipped under his weight. Sakaguchi put one foot out on the landing and stopped when the metal creaked beneath them. Hiroshi grabbed the rusty metal of the rail.

The fire escape zigzagged down to an alley empty in both directions save for dumpsters. They didn't bother wasting their time climbing down. The ladder stopped at the second story, from where it was a long drop to the concrete. Hiroshi felt the fire escape swaying and tightened his grip on the rail.

"What now?" Sugamo asked. After looking up at the higher floor where the grate stopped, Sugamo stepped back towards the wall, sending a rattling shiver through the fire escape.

"We send Takamatsu to deliver a sword," Hiroshi said, edging back inside, unsure if it was strong enough to keep holding them. "And I'll talk to my contact at Interpol."

"That's all we have? A sword for Takamatsu?" Sugamo asked. "And an Interpol contact?"

Hiroshi put his hand on Sugamo's back to prod him inside.

Sakaguchi shifted his weight to the floor inside the mahjong parlor, and the entire landing jolted and clunked against the brick wall.

"We'll try the sword and Interpol," Sakaguchi said. "Unless you want to keep running around the city like this?"

Chapter 25

The walls and storefronts of the street abutting the Yamanote Line tracks in Shin-Okubo were jammed with signs in Chinese, Thai, Vietnamese and Korean. The smell of spices from different cuisines floated in the cold night air. Video soundtracks in different languages and the four-beat precision of Korean pop blasted out of knockoff stores, their racks protruding into the lane with a jumble of clothes, kitchenware and used video games. Faded arrows pointed up the dingy stairwells of the narrow buildings to more and more of the same. Most of the teen-oriented food stalls had closed, leaving only the smell of sizzling beef soaring out of tin exhaust hoods.

The detectives circled together at a V-split in the lanes. Sakaguchi slapped his hands together to warm them. "Get in and out as quickly as you can."

"These things have their own pace," Takamatsu said, readjusting the sword secreted inside a leather golf club bag over his shoulder.

Sakaguchi checked his cellphone. "Sugamo and Osaki are by the window to the left. If you need them."

Takamatsu shifted the sword to his other arm and adjusted the belt of his camelhair overcoat. "If nothing else, I'll make a few bucks and the guys will get a good meal."

"And if that guy finds the GPS in the case?" Hiroshi asked without looking up from his cellphone. He was still calling and texting Jamie, but got no answer, and none from Ueno.

Takamatsu smiled. "I have a hunch he'll find it eventually."

"Your last hunch ended you up in the hospital," Hiroshi reminded him.

"No, that was because I didn't follow my hunch." Takamatsu slung the sword bag to the crook of his arm to light a cigarette.

Sakaguchi stood in front of a large poster of a ten-girl Korean pop group taped to the wall, their super-cute dimples and big child-like eyes frozen in place, thin bodies trapped in a robotic dance pose.

Hiroshi tried again to call Jamie and Setsuko. Getting no answer, he slipped his cellphone back in his pocket.

Sakaguchi stretched his legs back and forth across from the restaurant. Red, blue and gold carvings climbed up the front pillars. Long strings of Korean flags fluttered from the second floor down to a row of small lion statues. Takamatsu ground out his cigarette and walked into the restaurant. Hiroshi and Sakaguchi huddled against the cold and watched him go.

Inside, Sugamo and Osaki kept their heads down, eyeing Takamatsu as if he were a stranger. Around them diners picked the flesh from crabs split and boiled in spicy, sour tofu-cabbage broth. The smoky scent of marbled beef slapped onto smoky grills mingled with *shoju* liquor and cigarette smoke.

When Takamatsu told him who he was, the headwaiter in a dark blue vest spoke into his cellphone ear bud. He led Takamatsu through the swinging doors into a kitchen crowded with silver racks and tall pots, stacks of cabbage and tubs of pepper paste. Square choppers rested on blocks made from whole tree trunks beside where cooks worked, washed and cooked in oily white uniforms.

The headwaiter beelined through the kitchen to a door at the back. It opened into a plush, carpeted hallway lit by dark blue lights. Takamatsu blinked to adjust his eyes. From a door at the end of the hallway, a short man in a bright red vest stepped into the dark. His gourd-shaped head was shaved to the scalp and one ear pierced with a run of silver rings. He held up his hands, indicating he would pat Takamatsu down. Tattoos ran to his knuckles.

Takamatsu held his hands up while the gourd-headed guy ran his hands inside Takamatsu's overcoat and jacket and down both pant legs. When he gestured for Takamatsu to hand over his overcoat and the sword in the golf club bag, Takamatsu stared him in the eye for a couple seconds, and then handed them over.

"That's camelhair." Takamatsu nodded at his coat.

Without another word, Takamatsu and the gourd-headed body-guard stepped into a room with high walls of textured concrete ringed with soft downlighting. In the middle of the opposite wall, a huge black lacquer cabinet—embossed with a stylized character for long life and thick brass fixtures—stretched floor to ceiling.

Behind two large computer screens on the leather-lined desk stood a tall, broad-shouldered man with backswept hair and a glowing tan. He wore a white, multi-pleated tuxedo shirt and tight black pants. He smiled at Takamatsu, looking too young and handsome to be in charge of a restaurant, club or anything else. The bodyguard set the sword on the long black lacquer desk in front of him.

"Thank you for bringing this to me. It's hard to find anyone to trust. I'm Kim Dae Hyun," the man with broad shoulders and backswept hair said, letting his pleasant face open up as he came around the desk.

"I'm Takamatsu." Straightening his cuffs, he offered a short, curt bow.

"Mind if I take a look while you're still here?" Kim smiled and unzipped the tie on the golf club carry bag and set it on the desk. He unwound the silk cord and slid off the cloth. Pulling the sword from the scabbard, he held it with one hand on the handle and the other around a soft cloth to protect the steel.

"Gorgeous. It's Korean. Taken during the occupation." Kim surveyed it from all angles under the spot lamps over his desk.

"Occupation?" Takamatsu asked.

"Japanese occupation of Korea." He stood behind the desk circling the sword gently right and left, marking a sideways eight in the air. With each soft move, the intricate collar and *tsuba* hand guard, tempered in gold, caught the downlight in glints and flashes that lingered in the air. The fluid silver gleam of the blade made the cavernous room feel small and close.

Kim examined the sword, speaking in a quiet, focused voice. "What amazes me is that in both Korea and Japan, we revere an object which must nearly be destroyed before it can find its proper shape. Heated, beaten, cooled, pounded, folded, and heated again."

Takamatsu listened without saying a word.

"From its weakest moment, the layers of steel are built back to a strength, an energy, that no other weapon, no other object, ever

153

achieves." Kim set down the sword beside its scabbard on his desk, shook off its spell and turned his attention to Takamatsu. "You probably want to be on your way. I don't know how to pay anyone anymore, much less cops." Kim said something to the bodyguard in Korean who went back behind the smoked glass wall.

"Actually, you could pay me with a piece of information," Takamatsu said, using the humblest of phrases while keeping his eyes straight on Kim's without a hint of humility.

"There's the cop in you." Kim walked to the side of his desk and leaned against it. "I thought you were retired."

"Probation."

"Did you do something bad?"

"Nothing that didn't need doing. I'm looking for someone."

"Information is the currency you prefer, is it?"

"I could take both."

Kim smiled. "First, some information for me. Are those big guys in the front room colleagues of yours?"

Takamatsu nodded yes.

"I don't want them hanging around here. It's bad for business."

"It takes time to feed someone their size."

Kim nodded in amused agreement. "They can finish their meal. In fact, it's on me. But don't bring them next time. It disturbs my customers."

The bodyguard came back with a thick envelope of cash, which he handed to Takamatsu. Without looking at it, Takamatsu tucked it into his inside jacket pocket.

"Could you let me know if you know this guy?" Takamatsu pulled out his cellphone and found the photo of the broken-legged thief who snatched the bag from Jamie and Hiroshi in front of the archives.

Takamatsu took a step forward, but the bodyguard held up his hand and took the cellphone from Takamatsu and walked over to Kim.

After a quick glance at it, Kim shrugged. "There are so many Koreans in Japan."

"He was North Korean."

"There are so many North Koreans."

The bodyguard spoke to Kim in Korean. Kim said, "He looks like a guy who cut crabs for us last year."

154

"Any contact address?"

Kim smiled. "We sell so many crabs."

"And have so many crab-cutters." Takamatsu finished his sentence for him. "He's still in your employ?"

The bodyguard shook his head no and handed the cellphone back.

"Actually, he's now in jail, which is sometimes a risky place for people with a lot of information," Takamatsu said.

"Information must be handled correctly." Kim nodded.

"He's connected to a ring that breaks into houses. I want to know who knows him." Takamatsu used polite phrasing, with the same haughty glare as before.

"The wealthy homes of Japanese turn a profit no doubt. Good, clean work."

"Except when people get killed."

Kim looked suddenly serious. He raised his eyes up to the camera positioned in the corner of the room, which Takamatsu had not noticed. With a gesture from Kim, two tall men, lanky and buffed in dark suits and shirts and ties, immediately came out from behind the smoked glass door.

Takamatsu glanced at the entrance where he came in, gauging its distance and waiting to see where the men would position themselves.

Kim came around the desk with a sweeping gesture. "Maybe we can talk again next time. There are several other swords I'm looking at in Tokyo that need delivery."

"I need to know about the burglaries. Not all of them. Just the ones where people got killed."

"The people involved need to take responsibility, is what you're saying? Crime never pays and so on?" Kim folded his arms over his chest.

"They got overzealous with the wrong person."

Kim walked behind his desk. "I prefer a calm approach in all business activities. This kind of thing just muddies the waters." Kim thought quietly for a minute and then smiled at Takamatsu, shrugged and nodded at the tall men. "Give them the photo and the dates and places. I'll have them look into it."

Chapter 26

Outside the Korean restaurant, Hiroshi kept dialing Jamie. Where was she? Did her cellphone and Setsuko's both need recharging? He called the coffee shop, but the shift had changed and the staff had no idea. Sakaguchi insisted—over all his protests—that Hiroshi back up Takamatsu in Shin-Okubo, so he had come. Hiroshi wanted to go look for the two women. Ueno wouldn't answer his cell either.

Hiroshi's fingers felt stiff from the cold and he needed a new winter coat. The last one he bought was years ago, and since he'd been inside all winter, he didn't even know where his sweaters were—probably in a storage box somewhere. He kept moving around the small lane while Takamatsu took his time inside. Sakaguchi fingered through a bin of video games, looking up from time to time at the diners stumbling out red-faced, slowed and sated from eating and drinking. Until Jamie answered, all Hiroshi could do was wait.

He dialed Jim Washington at Interpol in hopes he found something. Washington didn't want to talk by phone, so they set up a time and place to talk.

"I've got to go," Hiroshi said to Sakaguchi, his breath clouding in the winter air.

"This is about you or the girl or what?" Sakaguchi glanced impatiently at the Korean restaurant.

"I still can't get a hold of her..."

Sakaguchi took out his cellphone, but Ueno came walking up, surprising them both. He shook his head no.

Hiroshi started to say something to Ueno, but Sakaguchi waved his hand to quiet him, speaking to Ueno. "Take Hiroshi wherever he

157

needs to go and stay on the phone in case we need you back here. And don't let Hiroshi disappear all night again."

"Now you're tracking me?" Hiroshi walked away from Sakaguchi and the Korean restaurant to where Ueno parked the car at end of the tangle of alleyways and small lanes in Okubo. Ueno followed with a sigh.

In the car, Hiroshi called Jamie again as they drove across Tokyo. Ueno pulled up and stopped where Hiroshi told him, in Ginza in front of a broad, open plaza that bisected a department store, closed but still lighted from outside. The last trains had left, leaving people to hunt for a taxi or hotel or all-night coffee shop.

"I'll pull around the block and wait on the other side where I can watch you," Ueno said.

"Don't worry. This guy works for Interpol."

"It's better if I stay close," Ueno said. "In case we need to go."

"You don't answer me all day, why stay in touch now?"

Ueno looked away.

"He's got it backwards. He lets Jamie wander free and keeps an eye on me?" Hiroshi slammed the door shut, walking off and leaving Ueno shaking his head.

Jim Washington, the one pushing him to take the position opening at Interpol, waited by a huge movie poster for the latest high school baseball drama. Washington was tall and fit, with a patient stance and calm eyes. His small beer belly and big grey mustache rode easily on his lanky basketball player frame. Washington said, "Let's walk. It'll warm us up."

Hiroshi fell in step with Jim as they headed towards the smart boutiques, pricey clubs and trendy restaurants of Ginza, most closed for the night.

"Thanks for getting back to me," Hiroshi said.

"I don't sleep much anyway. Calls from headquarters in Lyon all night," Washington said, picking up the pace.

"That's why you get so much done."

"Wish that were true. I nap when I can."

"I've come to prefer napping."

"Dangerous when you get to that point." Washington laughed, keeping the quick pace through Ginza's latticework streets. He stopped in front of a wine bar, its front window lined with bottles top to bottom.

"Are you a wine drinker?" Hiroshi asked.

"I've come to love *sake* after being posted here," Washington said. "Such nuance and complexity. Without something, I wouldn't sleep at all."

"I know a good *sake* place near here. It's closed now, but let me take you there sometime."

"Maybe after your interview next week. You all set for that? The Asian bureau chief will be here. He's interested." Washington looked at Hiroshi.

"I'm ready," Hiroshi said.

"Interpol is a different kind of workplace."

"That's what I'm looking for."

Hiroshi had come to trust Washington most among all the people he interfaced with, after collaborating on several cases, and because they were both up all night for overseas calls and because he had to trust someone. The two men turned onto a small cross street with new trees, still wrapped in cloth, dropped into the earth along a new stretch of sidewalk, their branches bare and sparse like fingers reaching up to the sky.

Washington looked over at Hiroshi. "Did you inform your boss, or HR, at the station? I don't know all the complexities of the Japanese workplace, but—"

"Not yet." Hiroshi quickened his pace a little.

Washington stopped for a step. "I hesitated to make the move, too. You're a shoo-in for this spot."

"I'm falling a bit behind with our reports. I got dragged into another case that keeps escalating."

"At Interpol, we like to get cases completed before they escalate. Otherwise, you start thinking it's all connected, which it is, so you never finish anything."

Hiroshi sighed, knowing that was true.

Washington turned at the next block, looked back and asked, "That's your colleague back there, isn't it?"

Hiroshi turned his head and saw Ueno in the car behind them.

"If he gets a call, I'll have to rush back."

"Well, onto business then," Washington said. "The guy you were asking about, Trey Gladius, is presently in country, right?"

"Very much so."

"There's no info about him on our database."

Hiroshi stopped in place. "Maybe there's a computer glitch?"

"His name isn't on any database that he can keep it off."

"What's that mean?"

"It means he works for an agency that doesn't like its people noticed."

"Because?"

Washington took a breath, and then looked at Hiroshi without slowing down. "Tell me why you want to know and maybe I can tell you more."

"What do you know about Bernard Mattson?" Hiroshi asked.

"Japan specialist. Influential. Respected. Killed in a robbery at his home."

"Only it wasn't a robbery. The thieves wanted something he had."

"Something more than money or valuables." Washington hummed. "Any idea what?"

"A few."

They walked to the end of the block, crossed an empty main street and turned down a side street with only a few people, walking alone.

"What I'm wondering is why would Gladius show up at Mattson's place not long after his murder?" Hiroshi asked.

"How do you know Gladius isn't working parallel to you?" Washington asked. "Happens all the time."

"From the American side?"

"Probably just a lack of coordination, and territoriality."

"My hunch is he's not." Hiroshi shook his head, realizing he sounded like Takamatsu.

Washington nodded. "Probably he's one of ours."

"Ours?"

Washington squinted for a second. "I mean, he's not a criminal."

Hiroshi looked down as they walked a few more blocks, wondering if he was totally off about Gladius. He couldn't be that wrong. He could feel it. He waited for Washington to continue.

Washington slowed for a second, then started walking quickly again. "I haven't known you to be wrong, though, so I asked an old friend in Singapore with access to check some old databases, unofficially. Turns out Gladius had a few detainments years ago for transporting stolen goods across international borders. He's listed as a translator for one of the new security agencies, or rather one of the contractors to the agencies. Hundreds of them popped up after Iraq and Afghanistan."

A group of red-faced Japanese businessmen tumbled out of a tall building followed by a bevy of hostesses in expensive dresses and swirling hairdos. The women stamped and shivered on the street as the men, stumbling drunk, laughed and waved goodbye and clambered into taxis. The hostesses gave them cutesy waves until the men drove off, and then let their faces fall as they hoisted up their dresses and scurried back inside.

"Ginza's another world, isn't it?" Washington chuckled.

"Having money is another world."

"What was Mattson working on, do you think?"

"Something about the bases."

"American bases?"

"Any other kind?"

Washington smiled, "Guess not, but that's sensitive territory."

"It's territory Japanese can't get into at all."

"Wonder what next week's talks will produce? Big changes? I doubt it."

Hiroshi asked, "How much immunity do you think Gladius has?"

"Those new agencies are off limits to us. I'm surprised my friend could even find anything on him."

"So, what's your thought?"

"He sounds like a person who can do what needs to be done. They like to keep that type in the field. Speeds up operations. They overlook his quirks."

"Quirks? Might be more than that. I wish I could figure out which hornet's nest Mattson was poking and why Gladius would care."

"Why not poke the nest yourself?" Washington chuckled. "You're good at that, Hiroshi. Why we need you at Interpol."

Hiroshi nodded his head, thinking about how Interpol would be a better place to work. Much better. "Jim, thank you for this. I already owe you for setting up the interview."

"We want the best we can get. Once the Interpol Asia chief talks with you, you can start planning your move."

Hiroshi looked around for Ueno. He had pulled to the next cross street and was waving Hiroshi to hurry over.

"Are you sure Gladius is involved?" Washington asked. "If so, I can—"

"I'm sure."

"I'll ask that friend in Singapore again. Before he left the Tokyo post, my friend was working on a drug smuggling case at the American bases, so he might know something more."

"I doubt it's drugs, but anything would help." Hiroshi bowed and hurried off to where Ueno was waving frantically through the open window, leaving Washington to walk on his own through the late-night Ginza streets.

Chapter 27

As soon as Hiroshi got into the car, Ueno took off. Hiroshi rubbed his hands in front of the car's heating vent.

"Jamie must be back by now. Did you—"

"We're going to Kanda," Ueno said, making a U-turn in the late night street.

"What? Wait."

"Sakaguchi and everyone else are there."

Hiroshi looked over, but Ueno said nothing more. Hiroshi could tell he wasn't going to, either, so he left another message for Jamie and turned up the heat in the car.

Ueno parked on a wide street of drab buildings near Kanda Station. Along the first floor, a *gyudon* beef-rice shop, manga *kissaten*, and two convenience stores spilled dingy yellow light onto the empty sidewalk. From the surrounding buildings, office lights shone through window blinds and fell onto the street in mute stripes.

Ueno and Hiroshi got out and hunkered against the cold wind whipping through the buildings. They spotted Sakaguchi down the street talking with the chief, a thick cloud of breath from their argument floating over the chief's Borsalino hat. Avoiding them, Ueno and Hiroshi went the other way around to the back street.

TV crews were running up camera cranes from the back of their trucks to angle a shot down into the interior of the crime scene. Their lights—stronger than the police lights—turned the area as bright as noon. Blue tarpaulins ringing the murder site billowed in the wind and yellow crime scene tape marked off the entire street, a short, narrow space with ten-story buildings rising above it. The crime scene crew worked taking photos, collecting samples and looking for any fragment of evidence. Plastic markers with numbers dotted the asphalt next to bloodstains.

Hiroshi walked to where Takamatsu stood a few steps from the body lying under a thick black plastic sheet. "Want to see?" Takamatsu asked.

"Not really," Hiroshi said.

"You better." Takamatsu led him forward and stooped down beside the body.

"Why?"

"So you'll remember."

He didn't want to remember this.

Takamatsu pulled the sheet back at an angle.

The cheap, worn clothes and thin, frail body was like a homeless person. The oversize coat barely covered the wounds. Bony arms and thin legs flailed out at impossible angles and a walking cane lay to the side. His wrinkled face turned upwards and his jaw hung loose.

Hiroshi nodded at Takamatsu to pull the sheet back over, and whispered, "Sword?"

Takamatsu nodded. "Angled upwards and all the way through. Got a second cut in this time."

Sakaguchi stormed over. "I can't believe this guy's dead."

"You know him?" Hiroshi asked.

"If you had come with me, you'd know, too." Sakaguchi pulled a book from his inner coat pocket. Hiroshi took the book, *The Okinawa Solution* by Tetsuya Higa, and pondered the photo on the back cover of Higa as a young man with forceful, angry eyes. "Mattson's editor. Met him at the bookstore. He attacked power relations in Japan."

"Enough to get himself killed?" Hiroshi asked.

Sakaguchi stared at the thin, lifeless body. "He was good at pissing people off."

Takamatsu lit a cigarette, cupping his hands to get it lit in the wind. He leaned back with a billow of smoke. "So, this killer is the same as before."

"Higa had a bad leg, so he couldn't run. He talked so much, I wonder what he said at the end." Sakaguchi turned away to sign forms on a clipboard held by a young detective. Seeing the media trucks inching up over the tape, he looked around for Sugamo, but shouted instead at Osaki, who was talking with a police photographer: "Osaki, I thought I told you to get those TV trucks out of here?"

Osaki stopped talking with the police photographer and walked off to get the trucks to pull back from the scene. Sakaguchi followed him.

Hiroshi followed Takamatsu's gaze up to the lights from the windows above, wondering if anyone could have seen anything. The back of the closest building had a delivery bay with a loading dock and a guard station with a glassed-in area big enough for a chair and a clipboard. The street was too small for surveillance cameras, but the entrance to an automatic parking garage with a turnaround floor seemed large and busy enough to have one.

"Let's take a short walk," Takamatsu said, leading Hiroshi past the crime scene tape and around the corner. He stopped to examine the streets every few steps, and lit a cigarette. Hiroshi watched his direction, but saw only the steadfast streets of Kanda.

"How did the sword delivery go?" Hiroshi asked.

Takamatsu inhaled his cigarette and shrugged.

"Was he any help, or just another Korean restaurant owner?"

"Bit of both. And a sword collector. Those clean-looking types are always the ones that have their fingers in the deepest."

"You think he was involved in—"

"He's in there somewhere, somehow, but he knows how to work the police."

"He's from Korea or *zainichi* Japanese?"

"We didn't get into family residence, but he's making money, no matter how long he or his family has been here. His lair was fitted out for business."

They arrived back at the other side of the crime scene. Takamatsu looked back where they had walked and shook his head.

Seeing them back, Sakaguchi stopped talking with a young detective and stormed over to Takamatsu. "Did *you* call the media? That woman?"

"Saori Ikeda?" Takamatsu shook his head. "It wasn't me. They find out no matter how secret we are."

Trying to distract Sakaguchi, Hiroshi said, "What about this guy? Any guesses?"

"Too many." Sakaguchi thumbed his cellphone. "He didn't seem the type to have a lot of family or friends. I'll have to call the Endo Brothers. Add this to their woes."

"Used to be more people like him in Japan," Takamatsu said, and lit another cigarette.

"Like what?" Hiroshi frowned.

"People that would speak out. Better warn those bookstore twins they could be next." Takamatsu blew the smoke high in the air. "Where's the girl?"

"I think I better go find her." Hiroshi said, feeling confident she'd leave now, after this new killing. "Get her on a plane out of here." He'd insist.

"I think for once Hiroshi's on to something. Check out that American guy who's been hanging around," Takamatsu said.

"Who?" Sakaguchi asked.

"The Marlboro man. I used to love that brand."

"I already did," Hiroshi said. "Trey Gladius is secret service, emphasis on secret."

"Where did you get that?"

"Interpol."

"They know everything." Takamatsu smiled, rolling his cigarette in his fingers. "Show them how good you are, they might offer you a job."

Hiroshi looked away. He did not want them to read his face since he already *had* been offered an interview. He checked his cellphone.

Sakaguchi shouted at a group of young detectives shivering in the cold. "Check the area for surveillance cameras. And start canvassing every one of these buildings. Check the public phones around here, if there are any. He was paranoid. Said the police tapped his phone lines. He might have used one."

Takamatsu looked for a place to grind out his cigarette on the pavement. "I better get out of here. I am meeting Saori Ikeda later."

"A bit late for a meeting," Hiroshi said.

Takamatsu laughed. "We should quit and set up our own agency. We'll make a fortune with our combined experience, and my instincts."

"Instincts aren't everything. You told me that." Hiroshi shuffled in place to stay warm.

166

"No, but sometimes there's nothing else." Takamatsu straightened his cuffs and walked off into the night.

Sakaguchi stared at the TV people at the end of the alley, pushing for better angles from which to grab sensational footage. "Three sword-cut bodies, a ruined bookstore, two robberies, stolen documents and a taped-up girl. And the chief says to wind it up or postpone it. The Foreign Ministry told the chief to be sure this does not disrupt the conference."

"Still four days away."

Sakaguchi looked at his watch. "Three. The delegates and staff have already started arriving. Have to put on a nice face for them."

One of the cameramen ventured inside the barrier with his camera on his shoulder. Sakaguchi charged at him. The cameraman scurried away dragging his camera behind him. The soundman's microphone pole clattered to the ground. Sakaguchi kept going, yelling at the reporters and the young detectives in equal measure. Sakaguchi demanded more tape and more tarp to expand the perimeter. The youngest detectives scrambled to get it.

After his outburst, Sakaguchi came back.

"Feel better?" Hiroshi asked.

"If I'd got a hold of that cameraman I'd have felt better."

Hiroshi stared into Sakaguchi's eyes. "Why didn't Ueno answer me all day?"

"He was busy."

"With what? What did you have him do?"

Sakaguchi stared at Hiroshi. "In sumo, using your opponent's momentum against him is the most effective technique of all. All it takes is a step to the side, or a step back. Or both."

"Is that why Ueno left her alone all day?" Hiroshi asked.

Sakaguchi stood quietly, looking at the TV camera lights.

"Are there detectives watching Jamie or not?"

Sakaguchi turned to Hiroshi. "We might have had the guy already if you hadn't taken her to your apartment all night."

Higa's body bag was wheeled out on a gurney. The general hubbub of the site fell quiet and still, everyone glancing at the body, and then bowing their heads. Sakaguchi and Hiroshi put their hands together and bowed in prayer as the body went past.

When the body was loaded into the medical truck, Hiroshi turned to Sakaguchi. "You want to use her to draw them out. As bait."

Sakaguchi looked off into the night. "Even when you step back, or to the side, you don't let go. I pulled the detectives back, but they're still there."

"Still where?"

"Where you come in."

"Where I come *in*? I already *am* in."

"Stay with her after you find her."

"Find her? I can't even get her to answer the phone."

Sakaguchi took a call. Quickly hanging up, his face furious, he waved for Hiroshi and Ueno, shouted for Sugamo and Osaki, and turned Hiroshi around with a heavy arm. "Find her later. Right now, I need everyone. We'll need Takamatsu too."

Chapter 28

After Ueno dropped her off from the coffee shop at her father's home, or her home, or whatever it was now, she opened the door, putting aside the memory of the last time she entered. This time, Jamie knew there were going to be detectives there. But when she stepped in to the *genkan*, she could not see or hear any sign of them. She pushed the front door closed, but left it open a crack, in case she needed to bolt, and stepped up onto the floor, walking slowly, peering into the living room. Nothing.

She padded into the kitchen, checked the door to be sure it as locked, and that the bathing area was empty. Walking back to the stairs, she ascended, listening carefully in between the creak of each step. Her clothes and the futon were unfolded, as she'd left them. Where were the guards? Maybe the detectives were outside and she just had not seen them on the way in.

She thought about calling Hiroshi, he'd left messages all day and she was sure he'd come right away, but she reassured herself that if Setsuko was not afraid of being followed, she should not be afraid either, or she'd try not to be. Finding the scroll from her father would help. Her father's words would give her direction, something she needed badly. Following Setsuko's explanation, Jamie went downstairs to her father's office, took down a painting and pushed different spots until she nudged out a wood panel. Behind it was a wall safe.

She twisted the dials with her birthday as the combination, as Setsuko told her, but the numbers didn't work. She called Setsuko, but got no answer. So she called her mother, Sachi.

Sachi picked up right away. "Where are you?"

"In the study," Jamie replied.

"Of the house? I thought you'd be back in New York?"

"The combination is supposed to be my birthday, but it didn't work."

"The combination to what?"

"His safe."

"There's nothing worth the trouble of—"

"He left something in there for me."

"How do you know?"

"Setsuko told me."

"Listen to your mother. Pack your things. Get on a flight. You were just—"

"It looks like it needs four numbers."

"Try the lunar calendar," Sachi said.

"What?"

"Put in the year of the monkey—that's the ninth in the cycle—and then your year, Showa era fifty-two, and then eight for August and then fifteen. You had a very auspicious beginning. Nearly killed me."

"Not that again. Which order?"

"Try the nine first and if that doesn't work, put the nine last. Eight and fifteen in order."

"Stop talking for a minute and let me try," Jamie said. She dropped the cellphone into her pocket without turning it off and tried the numbers in different orders until she heard a soft click and the thick door of the safe eased open. "Got it!" Jamie shouted down to the phone.

Sachi kept talking, her voice muffled inside Jamie's breast pocket.

From inside the safe, Jamie pulled out a dozen envelopes thick as her grip, wrapped tightly with tape. She tore into the side of one of them to find a stack of ten thousand yen notes.

Jamie picked the phone out. "What do I do with all this money?"

"How much is there?"

"A lot!"

"That's why your father got killed. Take it to one of the international banks, deposit it, and go back to New York. Are you listening?" Sachi shouted into the phone.

"I'm listening, mother, but I'm also trying to do what father said."

"What Setsuko said your father said."

"I can't just ignore what he asked me to do."

170

"Yes, honey, you can. I always did."

Jamie clicked the cellphone off and ignored the buzzing when her mother called back. Jamie tiptoed up to look all the way to the back of the safe, but there was no scroll. She weighed the packets of money in her hands, thinking how this cash would pay things off in one go, getting her out from under the crushing penalty interest rate on her credit card debt. Her mother was right—take the money and go.

In her job in human resources, she had overseen other people, making decisions about their lives, hiring, firing, transferring sections. That was easy. But she was not used to making decisions about herself. There'd been nothing much *to* decide. Now there was. She would publish her father's manuscript—once she found it—not with Shinobu Katsumura, but with the publisher in Jinbocho, or one in New York.

She ran through the combination again to memorize it as she reset the panel and framed print, adjusting it carefully to be sure it looked right.

When she turned around, she screamed and dropped the money.

"Trey! What are you doing here?" She held her hand over her heart, to stop it racing, fumbling with the envelopes in her hand and bending towards the fallen packets. The envelopes had tumbled onto the desk and onto the floor at her feet. She left them.

"I didn't mean to startle you," Trey said, holding up his hands to calm her, his blue eyes shining in the dim light. "I wanted to be sure you were all right."

"How did you get in?"

"The front door was open a crack. I was going to drop these in the mailbox, but I heard someone moving around in here. I thought it might be another burglar."

"It was me."

"You're not a burglar?" Trey smiled from the door of the study, his black leather coat over his arm.

"How long were you watching me?"

"Were the manuscripts in there?"

"Isn't this a little late for an editorial meeting?"

"Maybe your father stored them somewhere else."

"Where would he leave them if not in his safe?"

"I'm not sure, but I have one idea." Trey waved Jamie into the kitchen, folding his leather coat carefully over a chair.

Jamie hesitated. She wanted him gone so she could find the scroll. Keeping her eyes on him, she picked up the envelopes of money and set them on the desk in a neat stack, as if it were nothing more than old paper to be used as a notepad. She didn't even glance down at the money. She did not want Trey to get suspicious, so she followed him to the kitchen—her kitchen.

Trey looked around. "Now, what I'm thinking is this. This is an old house, but the kitchen is missing one thing."

Jamie stayed in the doorway. "What's that?"

"A storage place under the floor." Trey gestured to the center of the kitchen floor.

Jamie shouted, "Oh, of course! I used to hide in there when I was a girl." That would be where her father left the scroll, not in the safe, which she didn't even know about. It was a game with her father. If she got angry or upset, as she often did, she would drop down into the storage chamber with the ceramic vats of pickles and jugs of *umeshu* plum wine. "Where's my pickle?" her father would shout after giving her time to calm down. After a few minutes, she would pop out, smiling and happy again.

"It's gone, though, look." The floor was paneled in long grey planks.

"This flooring is paulownia wood, the lightest, strongest wood in the world." Trey kneeled down and gave the planks a tap with his knuckles. The planks, wide as a hand and long as a *tatami* mat, gave out a resounding tone.

"So?"

"So, these planks look new, don't they?"

"Sort of."

"They're covering the old floor." Trey took one of the thick choppers from the knife block, hefted it confidently, knelt down and worked it under one of the planks, levering up at points along its length. The board popped up and the next ones eased out with a tug on the tongue-and-groove joint.

Trey set the chopper on the counter.

Below the new flooring were two small doors. Trey yanked on them and they opened. At the top of the storage chamber was the scroll. Trey handed it to Jamie. She took the two round cylinders, untied the silk sash, and unrolled a section to read what her father had left for her.

"What does it say?" Trey asked.

"It will take me a long time to read this." Jamie rolled it up and retied the silk sash.

Trey's blue eyes honed in on hers. "You should read it in private. But look at these."

Stacked inside the storage space were small wood boxes. Trey pulled one out, unwrapped it and lifted the top. Inside was a tea ceremony bowl. Trey held it up, turning it gently under the light. The shape was rough and uneven, the glazing a mottle of earthy browns, dark orange and greenish blue with a rough, hand-pleasing texture.

"It looks kind of sloppy to me? Why would he put them down there?"

"These are worth a fortune," Trey said.

Jamie hugged the scroll to her chest while Trey pulled out the others, running his hands around to check for more.

The scroll under one arm, Jamie kneeled down and pulled the top off another of the boxes. Tears started in her eyes. "This one...I used to eat from it." She set down the scroll to pick up her once-favorite bowl, the one she used every morning to eat rice porridge. The colors had been her favorites, orange and pale pink and yellow. Could it have been so expensive? Her father let her use it as a child.

"What should I do with these? Take them back to New York?"

"These are probably designated as treasures, so it's kind of a grey zone."

"You mean it's illegal to export them?"

"You'll get a lot more in New York. Getting them there is the problem, but I can help."

"How?"

"Through Guam. I used to help an antique dealer, so I know the route. And Guam's an easy place to crash out for a few days. You need that after all you've been through. Let me take you."

What would her father want her to do? She had no idea. What did she want to do herself? She had to read the scroll first. She nodded yes, looking into Trey's eyes.

Trey smiled his dimpled smile. "I'll show you how to pack them to carry on the plane."

"You really have done this before."

Trey set all the other bowls back inside and slid the paulownia wood back into place, tamping the boards down with his foot. He picked up the stainless steel cleaver and after wiping it clean, slid it back into the knife block on the counter. "I'll arrange everything for Guam, tickets and hotel. It's just three hours away, but it's America. You'll be safe there."

"He left a lot of cash, too."

"You can change it in Guam. Just double-wrap it and tuck it in your bras and underwear. If they even open it, the customs inspectors won't look there too long."

Trey picked up his coat and slung it over his shoulders. She was sure it was better to humor him until she could read the scroll.

"Day after tomorrow?" Trey said. "We can get some work done on your father's papers in Guam, too. If you feel up to it."

"I'll meet you at the airport," Jamie said.

"I'll call you tomorrow about the tickets. I have a couple things I need to do first."

Jamie nodded quietly. "Me too." She didn't know what else to do so she leaned forward and kissed him on the cheek.

Trey looked outside. "It looks like there's a festival here tomorrow. You don't want to stay for that?"

"I'll be coming back." She was sure about that.

"Is one day enough to get things together?" Trey asked at the front door.

"I'll be ready," Jamie said. Very ready, she thought.

Chapter 29

As soon as Trey was gone, Jamie rested the scroll on the *tatami* in front of her father's urn. She pulled a blanket over herself and began reading, unrolling one side and rolling up the other. In elegant handwriting it read:

"To my wonderful, beautiful, intelligent daughter, Jamie. If I'm right beside you as you read this, you'll know what a silly old man I am. But if you're reading this and I'm not in the next room or even in the same city, it means I'm dead. I've been followed for months now. If you're reading this without me, you'll be in danger too. So, skip this first bit about my life—too much melodrama anyway—and go to the section near the end titled, 'To my pickle.' It'll tell you what to do. I love you and always have and always will, more than you could ever know. Go to that section now, read, hurry, act!"

Jamie read the words again, hearing her father's voice deep in her mind. Her body shook once, twice, before she fell over in to what she'd resisted since first hearing he died—the wide inner space of grief. Her body curled up and pulled tight, letting the scroll unspool over the *tatami* with her father's story splayed out, exposed and waiting. She cried in big painful spasms, floundering in the undertow of feelings.

When she rose back to the surface, she wiped her eyes and nose with the blanket, pulled her hair back, and tried to focus through the flux of confusion, wondering how her father could know all this in advance. She wanted to read what he wrote about his life, to know his story as her own, but that would have to wait. She kept rolling and unrolling until she found "To my pickle."

"My book is finished, and my speech, too, so you just need to find them. Just think about what I'm saying and you'll know where it is. The book, the long version and the short one, is ready for publication, but this scroll is just for you. The book is about how I changed my mind and changed directions. I was always on the inside, working within the system. Doing that meant cooperating with powerful people and accepting powerful forces. I consoled myself with incremental changes. It wasn't enough. After getting sober this time, I realized I was done with that. I still had a chance to shake the foundations.

"The American military bases in Japan have become intolerable repositories of the worst instincts of America—the lust for power, conquest, dominance. The military was keeping the world safe for democracy after the war, but now, things have reversed, and it's democracy that provides cover for military proliferation.

"I helped write the SOFA agreements, but I wanted them to stay in place only until Japan recovered. I never imagined America would allow anti-communist paranoia and the lust for power and profit to disrupt diplomacy. My book explains how the American empire got started and why it should be curtailed. What I found in my research was the extensive corruption underlying all this. It left me more disappointed and more despondent than I'd ever been in my life. I had to do something.

"Enough on that for now. If you don't think you can do this, take the money and use it and don't worry. I will, from the grave, or the urn, or wherever I end up, love and respect you no matter what you choose.

"If you want to help, here's what you must know: trust Higa, the Endo Brothers, Shibata and Setsuko. Do not trust anyone else, no matter what they say. The manuscript is easy to find once you know where it is. Just think of this: You're my pickle. And remember our special times at breakfast, your mother still sleeping, and that bowl you loved."

Jamie had to stop: pickle...breakfast...bowl...she read on.

"If something happens to the Endos or to Higa, go back to New York and find a publisher there. Do not let yourself be followed. Going through Narita is too obvious. Take the *shinkansen* bullet train south to one of the airports in Kansai, Osaka or Fukuoka. It's easier to get on the train without being noticed in the dense station crowd than at Narita. From there, take a flight to Korea or Hong Kong, whatever leaves first. Just get out, and quick. In New York, I have a lawyer who will help. If I'm dead, he'll find you.

"There is money in the safe. Your birthday will get you in. It's enough for you to do what you want with your life. The bowls you'll also find, my little pickle, can be sold if you need to, but get out safely. With your smarts and my directions, you'll be fine. And never forget that I love you."

Jamie rolled up the scroll, went to the safe and spun the dials. Each ten thousand yen note was about one hundred dollars, the stacks as big as her grasp. She shoved several stacks into her travel bag, then went upstairs to get her suitcase. She wrapped stacks of ten-thousand yen notes in small nylon bags and tied them tightly. The money was heavier than a big bag of groceries, but her suitcase had good, strong wheels.

She ran upstairs for her clothes and carrying them in her arms, stamped down the stairs and dumped two armfuls of clothes on the *tatami.* She wrapped the scroll in a sweatshirt and nestled it at the top of the bag so it wouldn't get squashed. She pulled out all her undershirts, bras and underwear and put them around the bags of money, tucking and stuffing them inside another bigger nylon bag, hoping any customs agent would be too embarrassed to dig deeper.

She looked up at the calligraphy hanging on the wall, *shogyo mujo,* "nothing remains unchanged," took it down and put it next to her father's scroll. She went to her father's desk and from one of the busted drawers took out a stack of her father's notes. It was sad to sacrifice them, but she knew her father would understand.

She put the heavy notes into large manila folders and then one by one into her backpack. The backpack became so heavy with the weight of the thick paper, the padded straps pulled deep into her shoulders when she tried it on, but it worked. She left what did not fit in a pile on the desk, zipped the suitcase shut and locked it with a small padlock. She rolled the bag back and forth to test its weight and balance. It was heavy but rolled smoothly.

She went to the kitchen, took the chopper and knelt down to lever up the floor boards. She pulled the top of the storage area up and took her old breakfast bowl out. She pulled the wooden top off again, confused. She tapped the empty box and got a hollow tone. She reached inside and pushed hard, then harder, until the bottom eased up on one side, and she could pull the false bottom out.

Below, taped to the bottom corner was a USB drive. Was this what her father was killed for? She slipped the USB into her bra, the stretchy cloth pressing the hard plastic into the soft flesh of her breast.

Carefully, she put everything back, tamping the floor boards with her foot to settle them back in place. She took the breakfast bowl with her. It would fit in the bag with the money. Her father's computer had been trashed and she had not brought her laptop from New York. She would have to take it to the Endo brothers. They'd have one.

She would wait until the *matsuri* festival started. It would be easier then to lose the detectives she assumed were still guarding the house, though they had done nothing to stop Trey coming in. She could slip away through the festival crowd, go to the Endos and talk to Higa, the editor. She would take the bullet train, get a flight to Seoul, and from there to New York. It would be the first real story of her life, a start to catching up with her father. She'd never done anything, and her father had done everything.

She went back to the *tatami* room and knelt in front of her father's ashes. To be Japanese in respect and American in determination was a balance she had never achieved before. She bowed to her father. A wave of self-satisfaction swept through her. She was sure she was doing right by everyone—everyone except Hiroshi.

She pulled the *zabuton* cushions into a line in front of her father's urn and pulled the blanket, still wet from her tears, over her. For a few hours before she left, she would try to sleep. She'd hardly even really gotten over her jet lag, anyway.

Chapter 30

Sakaguchi already had the door open as Ueno pulled to a stop in Shin-Okubo. Always spare with words, Sakaguchi fumed in total silence in the car from Higa's murder site. Before Hiroshi could say a word, he was stomping down the alley toward Kim's Korean restaurant—the only place open along the emptied-out street, its shops shuttered and the food smells long gone in the night air.

Osaki and Sugamo ran to catch him before Sakaguchi tried to bust in on his own to the fortified seclusion where Takamatsu had delivered the sword. Hiroshi slowed his pace to watch behind for Takamatsu, pulling his coat tight around him against the cold wind blowing from both directions.

Ueno caught up with Hiroshi, both of them waiting for Takamatsu, who finally hopped out of a taxi to join them. Hiroshi, Takamatsu and Ueno turned towards Kim's restaurant, unsure why they were there a second time.

Osaki and Sugamo had wedged themselves between the front door of the restaurant and Sakaguchi pacing like a sumo wrestler in a pre-bout *shikiri*. When Sakaguchi saw everyone assembled, he pulled open the door, and led the charge, Osaki and Sugamo at his heels, Takamatsu, Ueno and Hiroshi a few steps behind.

Inside, Sakaguchi forearmed the headwaiter out of the way. Sugamo grabbed him on the rebound and wrenched him up by one arm. Osaki yanked out his ear phone and lifted him from the other side. Only a few customers sat eating and drinking at this late hour, but they all turned to watch the blur of detectives frogmarching the headwaiter through the dining area towards Kim's inner rooms.

As they burst into the kitchen, Takamatsu shouted, "Back of the kitchen, on the right."

Hiroshi, pulling up the rear, eyed the startled kitchen workers, their square choppers and long bamboo spatulas frozen in place as the kitchen quieted to the bubble of soup and sizzle of woks.

At the door, Osaki shoved the ear phone back in the headwaiter's hands while Sugamo lowered him enough he could stand. The headwaiter stared them down for a moment before taking the ear phone and speaking in Korean, glancing at the surveillance camera overhead.

When the door to the dark hallway clicked open, Sugamo shoved the headwaiter forward. The gourd-headed bodyguard, right inside the door, lost his footing, tattooed arms flailing, and fell back surprised against the two tall bodyguards in suits.

Takamatsu shouted, "All the way to the back. There's a door on the right."

The detectives strode down the dark corridor to Kim's office. The door slid open and they shoved the headwaiter inside. The two suits and the gourd-head guy scrambled in after them, quickly circling the detectives. They stood sideways with their left feet forward, elbows cocked, ready to spring.

Sakaguchi stood in front with Sugamo and Osaki on either side, while Ueno edged several steps to the right, spreading the range. Hiroshi and Takamatsu stood behind.

Hiroshi waited for everyone to stop moving. When they did, he surveyed the cavernous room. A gleaming, floor-to-ceiling cabinet took up one wall, its front embossed with a massive character for long life. In front of the cabinet, at a wide leather-lined desk, Kim, the restaurateur and sword collector, sat calmly under soft down lights.

Kim clicked off his laptop and slowly walked around his desk, trailing his fingers along its edge until he was right beside his bodyguards and the headwaiter. He leaned quizzically to the side, ignoring the bigger detectives, and spoke to the one person he knew. "Detective Takamatsu, all this melodrama isn't really needed, is it?"

Takamatsu, behind the huge detectives, shrugged. "Apparently it is."

"No sword today?" Kim flipped his long hair back like a teenager and smiled boyishly.

"No sword today." Takamatsu fiddled in his pocket for his cigarettes but left them in his pocket.

"Aren't you going to introduce your colleagues?" Kim asked, his voice echoing in the large concrete-walled room.

"I assume you know who they are," Takamatsu said.

Kim smiled. "I do, more or less."

Sakaguchi stepped forward and the bodyguards coiled. Sakaguchi had calmed himself enough to speak. "Is he here?"

"Is who here?" Kim asked back.

"How did you get him out?" Sakaguchi demanded.

"Get who out?" Kim's voice dropped, impatient.

"Who do you know on the inside?"

"Inside?" Kim snorted, then chuckled. "Wish I did. Detective Takamatsu and I just met the other day. Other than that—"

Sakaguchi took another step forward. The bodyguards reset their stance. Ueno, Sugamo, and Osaki tried to conceal their confusion. Hiroshi wondered what Sakaguchi was doing.

Kim put his hands up. "Does it matter? He's out of your way."

"Ah," Takamatsu said, and chuckled. "You sprang the motorcycle thief? That was quick. You are good."

Hiroshi tried to figure how many hours—not even days—the thief had been inside. He could have been held for twenty-three days without bail, so to get out in under two was unheard of. Judging by their anger, neither Sakaguchi or Takamatsu had heard of it happening before, either.

Sakaguchi, insistent, stood where he was. "Where is he?"

"By now, I'd guess Shenyang, Liaoning, somewhere in north China. On his way to North Korea? Who knows?" Kim shrugged and smiled amiably.

"How did you work it?" Sakaguchi demanded.

"Here's the big secret—lawyers." Kim wiggled his head with mock surprise. "There are so few of them in Japan, they always make a big impression. Look, could we sit down? You're Detective Sakaguchi, right?" He waved everyone towards a Korean-style tea table.

Sakaguchi made no move to sit.

"And you're Detective Shimizu?" Kim looked around Osaki and Sugamo to make eye contact with Hiroshi.

Hiroshi didn't respond, still wondering how Kim managed to get the thief out. He imagined the guy would be there three full weeks, minimum, so they'd have plenty of time for another go at him.

Hiroshi's legs had not even stopped hurting from the chase and the thief was already out of the country.

Kim did not seem perturbed at their refusing his offer to sit down. Instead, he walked to the floor-to-ceiling cabinet. He reached in his pocket for an electronic key. A green light flashed and the heavy floor-to-ceiling panels swung open as overhead spots clicked on.

Inside the case were three dozen swords of various sizes. Behind the swords was a background of yellow silk on which a red-blue-green dragon with thick, scale-covered legs and sharp, spread claws stared menacingly. On tiptoe, Kim reached to take down a sword with an ornate handle.

In a single, nimble motion, Kim slid off the scabbard and sighted down the bare blade. "Here's the one you brought me the other day. Only two hundred years old, but the detail is fantastic. Strong *kissaki* point. Elegant *sori* curvature. Exceptional *hamon*. The best qualities of humanity—inner resilience and outer strength—also make the best swords."

Kim swung the sword in a sweeping arc which lingered silvery-white in midair before an abrupt standstill straight out from his chest. "It's seen battle. That's why it's so alive."

Kim set out a felt cloth and rested the sword on the desk in front of him, the handle close by his right hand. "As you said last time, Detective Takamatsu, information is more valuable than anything. I couldn't agree more. To get information, though, you need other information."

Sakaguchi stepped towards Kim. The bodyguards tensed. Sugamo and Osaki reached forward to hold Sakaguchi back.

Kim paused, deciding something, it seemed. "I do have something for you." Kim bent behind his desk and pulled a large shopping bag onto the desktop. "We Koreans love giving gifts, just like you Japanese."

Hiroshi walked towards the bag and Kim nodded to his bodyguards to let him through. Hiroshi dug into the bag, pulled out a notebook, flipped through the pages. They were Mattson's. Hiroshi was as relieved as he was curious. Hiroshi turned to Sakaguchi and Takamatsu. "This is what they took from me outside the archives. It's not all of it, but most of it."

Kim pulled a fake sad look on his face. "No gift is ever perfect."

"Where did you get this?" Hiroshi asked.

"Someone left that on my doorstep," Kim said. "I have to work with a lot of people. I can't always be choosy."

Hiroshi spoke slowly. "If you're involved—"

"I'm not," Kim quickly cut in. "But after Takamatsu showed me those photos, it reminded me that I had been pushed out of a very appealing business deal."

"Legal or illegal?"

"Taxed or untaxed, you mean?"

"You said 'business deal'?" Hiroshi asked.

Kim nodded. "Before I diversified into this restaurant and club, I ran a small waste management business. We had good contracts and a nice profit for years. But after the Tohoku earthquake, things changed. So much to dispose of and nowhere to put it. Emergency work, emergency budgets."

"A windfall for you."

"So I thought. Unfortunately, American companies tried to snatch up all the contracts. That pushed the Japanese government, always so nationalistic, to award the contracts to Japanese companies. A poor Korean like myself couldn't compete." His hand drifted to the handle of the sword.

"That's business, isn't it?" Hiroshi said.

"I didn't even try for storage contracts, where the real money is. It would have been a lifetime of work transporting debris *and* storing it. Whoever got those contracts would make a fortune."

"But how does that—?" Hiroshi stopped mid-sentence. His mind raced back to the file folders in the archives. He could not figure out why Mattson had so many files from so many different areas—safety, transportation, warehousing, environmental law. He thought Mattson was researching his own history with SOFA. But maybe Mattson was looking into a lot more.

"No one wants radioactive water, soil and debris nearby, but it has to be in someone's backyard. And for a very long time." Kim paused, thinking. "So, when I heard the stolen papers were Mattson's, I remembered he was the one who set up most of the deals."

Hiroshi wasn't sure if he believed Kim, but he'd check into it as soon as they got out of there. If what he said was true, he'd missed where they should have been investigating from the start. Moving fast in a half wrong direction is much worse than moving slow in the right one, Professor Eto had often told students.

Kim smiled at the detectives. "I decided early retirement from the hazardous waste business would be wise. There's always a time to sheathe the sword." His hand moved to the sword on the desk in front of him. "Perhaps I'm destined to be a subcontractor all my life."

Hiroshi's mind raced to remember what else was in Mattson's files. He'd have to go back. Pamela at the American Embassy said she worked with American companies bidding for contracts. He'd have to call her.

Kim spread his arms wide, the swords and the dragon gleaming behind him. "I do have one more thing that might interest you."

He gave a nod and the gourd-headed bodyguard carried an old, flip-top cellphone over to the three detectives. He clicked through several pages and held it out towards them.

Hiroshi leaned down to look at the small screen. On it was a photo of Trey Gladius, with phone number and contact email.

"Why do you have this?" Hiroshi passed the cellphone to Sakaguchi.

"Whenever we do business, we find out about our competitors. He spoke good Korean, they told me. I'm always impressed by people who speak several languages, aren't you? Especially Americans."

Hiroshi frowned, thinking. "So, Trey Gladius contacts your North Koreans when he needs something special done?"

Kim smiled. "You got it backwards, detective. They contact him when they need something special done."

Chapter 31

Outside the Korean restaurant, Hiroshi fumbled through the name cards in his wallet and found Pamela Carica from the American Embassy. He called her, his hands reddening in the cold night air as he followed the other detectives down the small lane towards the cars. Pamela picked up, though it was after midnight.

"This is detective Hiroshi Shimizu. I met you at the home of Bernard Mattson."

"Yes, I remember. How is Jamie doing?" Pamela's voice was husky and deep, unlike most Japanese women's, but there was an insistent impatience to it that was purely American.

Hiroshi cleared his throat. "She's fine. Recovering. Listen, would you be able to meet me to answer a few questions?"

"Right now? I'm still at the embassy. No one is allowed in at this time of night except for employees," Pamela said.

"Working so late must be the Japanese influence?"

"With the conference coming up, we've been working overtime."

"You said you often met Bernard Mattson?"

"He was here a lot after the earthquake, but I never talked with him."

"He was helping businesspeople?"

"That's all we do at the embassy, assist American businesses, military contractors. I'm supposed to be the NGO liaison. I was stuck with the American Chamber of Commerce the entire year after the earthquake."

"Did American companies get many contracts after the earthquake and meltdown?"

"American companies have a lot of expertise in nuclear waste."

"Japanese companies didn't outbid them, or block them out?"

"The American Chamber of Commerce handles the final stages. We just help smooth the introductions."

"Are there records of those introductions?"

"Not really."

"Hazardous waste was not exactly Mattson's specialty." Hiroshi stopped in the middle of the small lane, the other detectives waiting for him by the cars. He held his hand up for them to wait.

"He was the only consultant who knew about the bases."

"Some of the contractors are military?"

"Or both military and civilian."

"Do you know the names of the companies?"

Pamela hesitated.

"Can you send me a list?"

"I'd have to check on that."

"It'd help Jamie and help us find who killed her father."

"I'm not sure the list can be shared."

"I can get it through the Japanese ministries, but you'd speed things up for me considerably if you could share it."

Pamela paused. "I'll check."

Hiroshi wondered if he really could get the list through the ministries but knew it would take forever even if he could. He waited for Pamela to say something more. Maybe he was shutting her up. Another tack might be better. "Do you know who Trey Gladius worked for?"

"I never saw him before the clean-up contracts. And never saw him after. Until a few days ago."

"He said he knew Mattson from way back."

"I never saw them talk," Pamela said, speaking slowly. "We have people like Gladius foisted on us all the time. Wish they were all like Mattson."

"So do I," Hiroshi said. "If you could send me that list, it would be very helpful."

At the end of the lane, Sakaguchi told Hiroshi Trey's photo would be in every police box in Tokyo, Kanagawa, Saitama and Chiba by eight a.m. Hiroshi got in the car with Ueno and asked to be dropped off at his office. He called Akiko.

"It's the middle of the night," she complained.

"I really need your help in the office. I'll make it up—"

Akiko growled and hung up without saying no.

Hiroshi got out at his office and sent the other detectives home. He needed time alone, and then Akiko's help, to figure out the connections between Mattson's research and the companies. The middle of the night was always the most productive time. The daytime background buzz quieted, allowing him to think more clearly, more connectedly.

Hiroshi was on his second espresso when Akiko arrived. She hung up her coat on the rack and in a crabby voice, asked "What's so important to drag me in—"

"I know this is early."

"It's not even early. It's late," Akiko huffed.

Hiroshi waved his hands at the files on his desk and computer screen. "I can't find the files from the bankruptcy last year, the waste management company, you remember?" He got up to make her an espresso.

"Those files are in the main building." Akiko flopped into her chair and yawned.

"Could you go get those?" The espresso started trickling out, filling the room with the wake-up tang of fresh coffee.

"Now or after my coffee?"

Hiroshi handed her the cup with two hands.

Akiko took gulps of espresso, growled and hurried to the main building. Before she returned, Hiroshi's inbox pinged with the email list of the companies from Pamela. He felt sure she wouldn't help, but she also maybe didn't care for Trey, or the jobs she had been assigned. Hiroshi recognized a few of the names but started looking up the ones he didn't. It would take time to find them all, even longer to know whether they were connected or not.

When Akiko returned, she dropped the file on Hiroshi's desk and went to make another espresso, letting the coffee bean grinder resound a little longer than necessary.

They worked in silence for hours in the early morning calm of the annex building, trying to see which companies finagled contracts, which cooperated with Japanese companies, which subcontracted, and which gave up.

Akiko hummed. "Many of the Japanese ones seem to be cement companies. They use the debris as fuel." She got up to stretch. "I don't get it, cement?"

"I wonder if they mix radioactive debris into the cement?"

"I hope not. Listen, I need a break. You should take one too."

"The archives will be a break. Most of these American companies work through the military bases. None of that makes sense, though. The archive doesn't open until 9:15, so we've got a few more hours."

"You're not going to sleep?"

"I want to get this done, get to the archives and then—"

"Go find Jamie."

Hiroshi looked at Akiko, grateful she always understood, never judged, and only complained about things so small they both knew they didn't matter. He'd have to tell her how much she helped, how much he relied on her and trusted her, show her in some way. "Can you get the scanned documents onto one file? To take with us. And leave a backup here."

"Already done. Get an hour or two of sleep. Helps bring things together."

Hiroshi rubbed his eyes and pushed his hair back, knowing she was right. He pulled the foldout futon chair to the side of the office and flopped down. Akiko made a face when she sniffed the lap blanket he kept on the sideboard—it needed a good cleaning—but she threw it over him anyway. Hiroshi snorted and breathed in and out, his body quickly finding sleep.

* * *

At 9:15 sharp, Ayana met them at the front door of the archives. She walked them upstairs, twisting and rolling the key chain coiled around her wrist like a set of prayer beads.

Akiko whispered to Hiroshi, "I see why you wanted to come back!"

Hiroshi ignored her comment. Stealing glances at Ayana, he was not sure of all the reasons he was there, but he'd wanted to call Ayana to talk, even in the middle of everything else. There'd just been no time.

Ayana said, "Yesterday, one of the librarians found a memory stick, USB, whatever you call it, in an archive box. Mattson must have forgotten it when he sent the box back to be reshelved." Ayana walked them towards the elevator to the floor for Mattson's room. "We also found what you asked for last time—the record of all his requested materials."

"It must have been a lot of trouble. He'd been researching for years." Hiroshi looked at her as they waited for the elevator. She looked refreshed and cheery, younger than she really was. He knew he must look older. He felt older.

"Actually, it couldn't have been easier. Mattson kept a list in one of his notebooks. He wrote it by hand."

"Why didn't we see that before?" Hiroshi asked.

"Because he forgot it in the same archive box with the lost USB," Ayana laughed. "He didn't seem absent-minded to me, but I guess everyone—"

"He left it there on purpose, for safekeeping," Hiroshi explained, walking out of the elevator. The two women paused before following him.

"He *was* here almost every day for the past two years, and *was* always careful with everything," Ayana said.

"Was there any request that seemed out of the ordinary?"

Ayana cocked her head and plucked at the springy key chain. "He said he was writing an article about the tsunami and earthquake in Fukushima. He requested things so recent the other archivist had to check document after document to approve them for release."

Akiko groaned. "Fukushima! Three core meltdowns and still not under control. People lost homes, family members. Entire communities gone. What a mess."

"It was those kindergarten kids that really got me," Ayana said. "Teachers led them in the wrong direction. No emergency plan."

"And it's far from over," Akiko added.

Ayana shook her head in disgust.

Hiroshi interrupted them. "Did Mattson ask for newspaper articles or legal records or...?"

"I'm sure it's all in his folder. He was meticulous." Ayana unlocked his room and the three of them went in. The USB and the notebook were in the center of the table.

The notebook pages were divided into four columns, date requested, title of material, date returned, evaluation, all written in a neat, tidy hand. The entire hardbound notebook was filled top to bottom about two-thirds of the way through. After the last requested material, one day before his death, he had drawn three thick straight lines.

Hiroshi leaned back, staring as he flipped the pages back, then forward again through Mattson's list. "Last time we were here, I thought he was researching the military bases, with all the documents from 1958 and 1959, and the Occupation in 1951 and 1952."

"What was he really looking for?" Akiko asked.

"That's what we're going to find out." Hiroshi took the laptop Akiko had carried with them and turned it on. Worrying briefly that the files would again be nothing but *shunga* erotica prints, he slid the USB into the side of the computer.

Akiko took over and sat down to click open the first file.

All three of them bent down towards the screen to see what was on the USB Mattson intentionally kept safe.

Chapter 32

The computer whirred and the large, heavy file slowly opened. It was a long string of PDFs, scans and photos of documents, cables, internal memos and official orders all connected to the Occupation. Akiko scrolled down, skimming the endless flow of images.

"Skip to the very end," Hiroshi said, pointing down, trying to hurry her.

Akiko sped up so the images didn't fully open. Finally, she reached the last files—documents from late 2011 that seemed like invoices for work orders and shipment manifests.

"Try the other two files." Hiroshi leaned back and stretched, embarrassed to hear his back pop and crack. Dry eyes and a stiff back, but still better than if he hadn't gotten the couple hours of sleep in his office.

The next file opened: "American Military Bases in Japan, from Occupation to Radiation."

Ayana twiddled the coiled key chain. "Is that the book?"

Hiroshi said, "It's 30,000 words. Must be the shorter, simplified version the Endo brothers were going to publish first. Let's open the other one and hope it's the full, unabridged version."

Akiko closed the file and opened the third one.

The title was the same, and the file size larger.

"That's it!" Akiko shouted.

The three of them leaned towards the screen. The table of contents covered everything from the origins of the Occupation to problems with the military bases, cooperative efforts, types of agreements, limitations and environmental surveys. There were chapters on crime, pollution, violations, protests, cost estimates and interviews with soldiers. He wondered how any of this research could lead to his murder.

"We need to take this to Yokosuka," Hiroshi said.

The two women looked at him.

"I wish I knew what it all meant, but I don't. My professor, Eto Sensei, will. He'll see the crucial junctures we might miss. Somewhere in here is the reason Mattson and the other two were killed."

Akiko stood up and started gathering the papers and the laptop, putting them all in order.

Ayana said, "We don't have murder investigations here very often. Ever, in fact. Though I suppose in one sense the archives hold a vast history of murder."

"All well-recorded." Hiroshi looked at Ayana. "Is it OK to leave everything else here? No one can get in here, can they?"

Ayana said, "Not without permission. But you know, a foreign guy came to the desk asking about Mattson's research."

"When was that?" Hiroshi asked.

"Yesterday."

"What time?"

"Just before closing."

Hiroshi dug in his cellphone for the photo of Trey. "Is this the guy?"

"Yes. How did you know?"

"Did you let him in?"

"When I showed him the application forms, he said he forgot his ID and would come back again."

"If he comes back, call me, and the local police, right away, OK? And do not let him in."

"OK," Ayana said. "Let me walk you out."

Akiko took the computer bag and walked ahead.

Hiroshi lowered his voice and said to Ayana, "What can I do to repay you?"

"It's just good to see you again." Ayana pulled the strap of the reading glasses around her neck before letting them drop.

"I've got to run," Hiroshi said again.

"Call me?"

"I will." Hiroshi turned and repeated, "I will."

Outside on the steps of the archive, Hiroshi looked carefully in all directions, hurrying Akiko along. "I hope Eto Sensei can work quickly."

"Your professor and I can get started. You better go find Jamie."

"She's fine. I'm going with you."

"No need," Akiko said.

Hiroshi moved towards the street and put his hand up for a taxi, keeping a close eye on the traffic in the nearest lane. In the taxi, he called Eto Sensei to tell him when Akiko would arrive. They rode to Tokyo Station and when they got out, Hiroshi hurried them inside and through the ticket gate. As they walked, he thought of what Takamatsu told him, that sometimes it's necessary to go outside the department to get things done. He couldn't be in two places, much less three. So, he called Suzuki, the sword dealer. The stillness of the shop, and of the man, seemed to flow through the phone, canceling out the bustle of Tokyo Station around him.

"Suzuki *san*, I want to ask what you do about the illegal export of valuable swords."

Suzuki said, "Sword dealers can't do anything without the help of the police and customs officers. We have to stand by and watch national treasures disappear like sand from the shoreline."

"If you know something is being taken out, what do you do?"

"When we get suspicious about one buyer or another, we contact authorities. But nothing ever happens. Why are you asking?"

"I'll let you know later, but for now, I need your help."

Silence for a moment before Suzuki asked, "Help with swords?"

"I'm wondering whether you can disarm someone carrying a sword."

"Few people needing disarming have attained a high level of swordsmanship. But for those that have, it's very difficult."

Hiroshi thought about that for a minute. Anyone who reached a high enough level should have—must have—taken in the ethical, spiritual elements of swordsmanship. He knew the police practiced a group method for capturing someone with a knife or sword, but he had never done that training.

Hiroshi asked, "Can you tell the level of someone with a sword in hand?"

"Yes, usually, but swords are dangerous in anyone's hands, whatever their level of training."

"I need your help, then."

"I'm listening."

Hiroshi explained what he needed Suzuki to do. At the end of his explanation, Suzuki paused and said, "You're starting to act like Takamatsu."

"I'm starting to feel like him."

As Hiroshi walked Akiko down to the Yokosuka Line platform, he thought of the speed with which Suzuki had cut the *tameshigiri* practice target into three pieces.

Akiko turned towards Hiroshi as the train pulled in. "Listen, Takamatsu used to take me out in the field all the time. I know how to handle myself. It's just one train from here. I'll get a taxi from the station directly to Eto Sensei's house."

"I'm going with you." Hiroshi looked at the train pulling in, then up at the signboard.

"The other night, when you didn't sleep in your office...look, go find her and come to Yokosuka after that. I've carried bags on a train before." Akiko reached for Hiroshi to hand her the other bag.

He handed her the bag as the train pulled in. Akiko rolled her eyes and lined up by the door.

From the platform, Hiroshi watched her get on the train and sit down, pulling the bags onto her lap and settling in for the hour-long ride. When the boarding bell rang, Akiko waved once, the doors shut and Hiroshi watched her go. When the train was gone, he walked up the escalator checking for messages from Jamie.

As soon as Hiroshi went out the ticket gate, he stopped and turned around. Above him, over the row of ticket machines, was an intricate map of Tokyo's trains and subways. The map's multicolored lines, boxed transfer points and rounded rectangles webbed in all directions, a schema for navigating Tokyo's countless interconnections, the city's endless choices. Around him, commuters bustled in crisscrossing trajectories, each of them making a decision, a thousand decisions, through a single day's commute. He turned around in the center of the hall, watching people deciding where to go and how to get there.

The scam artists and con men he spent most days tracking knew how to make decisions. It amazed him, their ability to decide on the lies, repeat them, embellish them, make them seem real, waiting for that one moment—one mistaken, inattentive, confused moment—when the victims allowed the hook to sink in and they started wiggling on the line. He could use half their decisiveness, and much more of their persistence.

Sakaguchi was right about Jamie. He would have to trust the detectives to watch her, to see if they could catch Trey, or whoever went after her. Someone would be near her, watching.

But Hiroshi realized he was wrong to leave Akiko alone, to have let her and Mattson's work out of his sight. If they'd followed Jamie—or him—once, they could do it again. They were as patient and practiced as scam artists. And more violent. They had to be. That was their scam—violence.

Hiroshi went back inside the ticket gate, calling Akiko. She always picked up. Except now, after his decision to let her get on that train alone. He hung up without leaving a message and called again. If she got off at Shinagawa or Yokohama, one of the big, safe, crowded stations, she could wait for him at the *koban* police box inside the station. He called again. No answer. He tried again. No answer but left her a message.

All he had left was Sakaguchi. "We need to get to Yokosuka," Hiroshi blurted when Sakaguchi answered.

"What's there?"

"Akiko, my professor and everything Mattson found."

Sakaguchi sounded as if he had just woken up. "You let Akiko go alone with all that?" Sakaguchi paused. "Tell her to get off at Shinagawa and go to the *koban*."

"She's not answering." The train arrived and Hiroshi got on, still talking.

"Where are you?" Sakaguchi asked.

"Tokyo Station."

Sakaguchi cleared his throat. "We'll head down the Shuto Expressway and pick you up outside Shinagawa Station."

Hiroshi hung up. What had he been thinking? He hadn't been thinking. He stared out the window, feeling as if the speeding train was barely moving.

Chapter 33

Jamie woke from her nap to the loud chants and tweet-thump of flute and drums coming from the *matsuri* festival outside. Women's shrill shouts of "*sa, sa*" mixed with hard-blown whistles that pierced the steady slam and jump of festival rhythms. She uncurled herself from where she napped on the *tatami* and listened.

From the time she could remember until she left for America, she helped carry the *mikoshi* portable shrine with the neighborhood children through the streets of Asakusa. A few parents had to help carry the end of the beams and steer them, but the kids liked to feel they did it themselves. After parading, they sat at tables on a side street eating fried *takoyaki* balls and shaved ice loaded with sweet adzuki and drenched in *macha*.

In the afternoon, the streets filled with adults carrying the ornate gold towers of the adult *mikoshi*. Each one needed two dozen men and women to carry and even more to raise it overhead in front of the main shrine, the gold phoenix on top clinking and swaying to appease the gods. By evening, the crowds swelled and merged into a single exhilarated, drunken, human mass lifting, pushing, dancing, chanting and—though it was outlawed—riding on top.

With portable shrines coming from every *chome* near Asakusa, the streets became so jammed with people that nothing—neither police, barricades, nor bullhorn pleas—could contain the pulsing, surging crowd. It was the perfect time to escape the detectives and get out of Asakusa—and out of Japan.

Jamie slipped her father's sport jacket over her thick white sweatshirt and pulled her hair into a ponytail under an old newsboy cap of her father's. She balanced the backpack on top of the rolling suitcase, slung her travel bag over her shoulder and reset the USB in her bra. She'd have to reach in and pull it out in front of the Endo Brothers and Higa when she got there. The backpack would go to Shinobu Katsumura. The suitcase and travel bag would go with her on the bullet train.

Jamie drank the last of the green tea and rinsed the cup and pot, setting them carefully on the drying rack in the kitchen, spreading the tea leaves in the sink to dry. She folded up the blanket and stacked the cushions neatly, double-checked her passport and cash for the train and plane. Then, she kneeled again in front of her father's ashes, aching to speak with him, even for an instant. She would leave his urn on the shelf in the *tatami* room. He'd be fine.

She eased out the kitchen door, and softly shut it behind her. Squeezing sideways, she yanked her suitcase up and shoved it through a divide in the hedges into the garden next door. She dropped her backpack after it, and with her travel bag over her shoulder, pulled herself over the low wall limb by limb, checking down the sightline of the house to be sure the detectives posted in front did not come around.

In the neighbor's yard, she hobbled along as stealthily as she could, the suitcase awkward over the dried out moss and gravel of their yard. She used to play there as a girl, but wondered if the neighbors would remember her, should they come out.

A small door in the wall opened onto the street. She pulled the handle and pushed gently, then harder, but it was locked. She un-twisted the push button latch, twisted it again, but it would not open. Holding the push button as she jiggled the handle, she cringed at the creaky noise it made, checking the house to see if anyone noticed. After another jiggle, the knob unlocked. She ducked through the door, set her bags in the small lane, and merged into the crowd.

The festival streets were jammed. A flute could be heard from the Kaminarimon Gate, or maybe further away. The entirety of Asakusa bustled with people dressed in bright kimono, samurai-like *kamishimo* jackets and *hakama* trousers. Wooden *geta* sandals clonked like horses. A few barefoot men sprinted around with *happi* jackets over *fundoshi*, their butt cheeks hanging out around the cotton loincloth.

With the colorful traditional outfits filling the streets, the two men in the alley outside her house stood out. Both were clad in black sports gear and leather coats. One had a mustache like dead grass, and the other smoked placidly, a night of cigarette butts crushed out at his feet.

Jamie concentrated on jockeying through the crowd towards the main street where she could hail a taxi, at least when crowds had not taken over the streets and police not blocked off the roads. She was too busy moving forward with her plan to even turn around as the two men wormed their way through the crowd after her.

Jamie waved down a taxi just as the police were setting up a wooden barrier to direct traffic away. She ran towards it, struggling with her luggage past the festival-goers, her body directed and tense. She put her bag in the trunk, thanked the driver, and settled in. She would come back to enjoy Tokyo when this was all over.

She would have the house and everything would be settled. She'd hate leaving New York, but her friends could visit. She would explain to Hiroshi and they would go out again. She would get her Japanese back, find a job, join one of the neighborhood groups and carry the *mikoshi* again—with the adults—chanting and hopping and drinking and feeling alive.

As the taxi pulled past the subway exit from which people kept emerging to join the festival, she finally thought to turn around and check behind her. She didn't know what to look for, but for her own peace of mind, she needed to look. When she turned forward again, she noticed, in the rearview mirror, the worried expression in the driver's eyes. She settled in to the seat and stared ahead.

The taxi dropped her off in the bookstore neighborhood of Jinbo-cho, in front of the Endo Brothers Bookshop, she struggled her bags to the sidewalk. When she turned around, ready to walk in and turn over her father's manuscript to the publishers, she gasped, bending over double, the wind knocked out of her by the scene.

A huge blue tarpaulin was stretched over the front of the store, held tight by roped grommets. She walked up, pulled back the tarp and cupped her hands to peer inside. The damage and disorder were worse than at her father's. Books were tossed thigh-high below the empty shelves. Stacks of woodblock prints lay in oddly-angled piles.

She peeled her eyes away from the chaos and examined the street in both directions, pulling her bags close against her. She turned back searching for a phone number or note or map or something, but found nothing.

And where would she find Higa? Her father left no contact info for him, saying only to go to the Endos. She hurried to the street corner, balancing the two bags on her shoulders and tugging the rolling suitcase behind her, thinking where to go. If they had been hurt, or killed, Hiroshi would have told her. But she hadn't heard from him since his last call, which she had ignored.

She hailed a taxi and told the driver, "Golden Gai." Shibata would help. The driver looked at her, curious why a young woman would want to go there in the middle of the day with a suitcase and backpack. On the way, Jamie tried to mentally reconstruct the path to Shibata's club through the small back streets.

The driver let her out at the same spot on the large street where she got out with Hiroshi two days before. She pulled the bag behind her with the other two over her shoulders, heading straight into the warren of lanes, turning and turning again. She remembered a low-hanging, rusted-out light socket and knew she was going the right way, surer still when she passed the neighborhood map neither she nor Hiroshi could decipher. She turned the corner to the small dead-end and let out an involuntary cry.

Police tape stretched across the door of Shibata's place. Jamie took in the smashed-in door, a broken stool on its side and what looked like blood stains on the pavement in front Shibata's door. The dead-end was otherwise empty except for a uniformed police officer posted in front of the club.

Jamie exchanged glances with him and he took a step towards her, about to say something. She threw him a naive, "little girl lost" look, flashed a big fake smile, and hurried on through the tight lanes.

She tried to head towards the big street but got turned around. The suitcase kept bumping into the Styrofoam cartons, trash cans and air conditioning units that jammed up the alleys. Moving clumsily, she searched for an exit, a small alley or walkway of any kind along the endless rows of small doors.

Finally, she saw an opening down a long narrow lane onto a bigger street. She checked behind her. When she got to the street, she called Shibata. If he had been hurt, Hiroshi would have called her and left a message, despite her not answering his calls. But if he wasn't hurt, whose blood was that in front of his bar? Someone had busted in their front door and the stool was theirs.

She crossed at a light and headed up an incline past love hotels and host and hostess clubs. The bland, clunky old buildings had been spiffed up with glitzy signs and theme-park exteriors, the faces of the hosts and hostesses smiling to lure in customers. Jamie felt the oversize head shots urged her to keep moving.

She called Hiroshi, wondering if he'd forgive her, if he would come, then stopped, turned around and looked behind her. The late afternoon was beginning to draw out shadows and a few customers. She clicked off the call to Hiroshi and started walking again. She called Setsuko but got no answer.

She tried calling Shinobu Katsumura. Her secretary answered and immediately forwarded her call. Jamie told Shinobu she would stop by her office within the hour. Looking both ways, she stopped a taxi, put her luggage into the trunk and clambered in.

Chapter 34

At Yokosuka Station, Akiko roused herself. With the heater under her seat toasting her bottom and thighs, she had let the train lull her to sleep. Outside the station, refreshed in the winter air, she walked briskly towards the taxi rank.

English signs for American chain stores blanketed the walls of the surrounding buildings. Foreigners from the American navy base—large men with big biceps—walked with their American wives or local girlfriends. The area felt more like Hawaii than Japan. Akiko climbed in a taxi, dropping the computer bag and her purse on the backseat, still drowsy.

Akiko's taxi let her out in front of the ocean-view home of Eto Sensei. Eto Sensei's wife had been waiting and opened the door with a smile. "We've been expecting you. I'm Yoko. Sensei is very excited to help."

Akiko bowed deeply. "Hiroshi has told me so much about you. I am sorry to bother you at home."

"We love to have visitors. Since retirement, he loves to work more than before. And I've got a space cleared for you." Yoko took Akiko's arm and led her to a large dining table.

Eto Sensei came into the room, leaning as lightly as he could on his cane. His eyes crackling with interest, his maroon turtleneck and tweed jacket worn just right, he looked ready for class. "Where's Hiroshi?"

"He got detained. He'll be here later." Akiko answered, bowing deeply.

"He's easily led astray." Eto Sensei laughed.

"He often is. You have a wonderful place here. The view of the ocean is spectacular!" She took a step towards the back windows looking over the ocean.

"In between takeoffs, it's nice. The jet fighters rattle your teeth," Eto Sensei said.

"Hiroshi was so intent on getting your input."

"Was he?"

"He's been talking about your book the past several days."

"Has he?"

"All he talks about usually is work, so it was a nice change."

"He's probably too busy to read much."

"Usually, it's just accounting books and police reports."

"I suppose that might be interesting." Eto Sensei draped his cane over the edge of the table and settled into his chair. "I called a few old contacts. Several magazine editors are waiting to know what we have here. We can get a summary and excerpts out right away. Do you know what happened to the Endo brothers? I can find someone else to do this if they can't."

"Hiroshi said they were robbed, their store trashed, but I don't know if that means—"

"It means Mattson must have found something important." Eto Sensei beamed. "This is going to be a pleasure. Anyway, let's see what we have. Hiroshi said he wasn't entirely sure how it all connected."

Akiko checked her cellphone and saw many calls from Hiroshi, but she would call him once they found something to tell him. Akiko hovered over the table, setting up the computers. She handed Eto Sensei the notebook detailing all requested materials and then spread out a list of what documents were in the bags and what Hiroshi remembered that was stolen. She arranged the two laptops—the professor's and the detective's.

Eto Sensei opened Mattson's handwritten notebook. "Let's start here. I liked the old days when information took its time."

"There's this USB, too." Akiko set Mattson's USB from the library by the laptop she brought.

"We'll look at that in a minute. Let's dig into Mattson's list of requested materials first, see if we can find any patterns." Eto Sensei started to make notes on a large piece of paper, sketching in circles and squares with swooping arrows between items.

"That's a big piece of paper."

"I used to use this butcher block paper when teaching. I'd make notes and then hang it up on the blackboard. I still have a roll or two left over. Probably classrooms don't even have blackboards anymore now that you can use projectors."

"Blackboards are too expensive to remove." Akiko sat down to start copying the companies he jotted down and start a database for reference, just as she did with all of Hiroshi's cases.

Yoko came in with a pot of tea, cups and a cherry bark tea caddy. "Having young people visit makes it seem like old times. Akiko, you must..."

Eto Sensei cut her off, "Yoko, please. Work first, chat later."

His wife *tsk-tsk-ed* him and shuffled back to the kitchen.

"Mattson did his homework." Eto Sensei looked over his bifocals at her. "My whole career, I've never come across this much information. But a lot of what's here seems to be about hazardous waste and the American bases."

"Why would he care about...?" Akiko looked at Eto Sensei for the answer.

Eto Sensei shrugged a little and looked off at the windows. "Maybe he's thinking of American land use on the bases. If they can secretly store napalm—"

"Napalm?"

"Okinawa was the staging ground for the Vietnam war. The bases stored surplus barrels of everything toxic for decades. It was discovered leaking into the ground water a few years ago."

"So, if they can get away with *that* on the bases..."

"They have a lot of land, but let's see what Mattson found out."

Yoko came in with sweet boiled chestnuts and rice crackers. Picking up one of the small USB drives on the table, she said, "Things get smaller every year, don't they?"

"But the problems get bigger," Eto Sensei said.

"I guess you didn't have any lunch?"

Akiko was about to answer, but Eto Sensei looked up sharply. "Can you just wait until we get this all done before you start the parade of food?"

"*Hai, hai, hai.* The tea is ready," she answered, heading towards the kitchen, leaving the tea steeping.

Akiko giggled at the old married couple. "So, do you think Mattson had a change of heart? That's what Hiroshi said. I would have thought he'd defend the status quo more as he aged."

"In looking back, as old people do, maybe he felt Asian geopolitics might have been better if he had pushed harder for change. He was a gradualist. In one of his articles in *Foreign Policy*, he wrote that US military bases took too much of America's entire budget. Old-fashioned diplomacy and treaties would be more effective—and cheaper—he argued."

"Japan pays for a lot of it."

"But I wonder how that figures in." Eto Sensei poked his pen around the schematic he was sketching. "Perhaps he didn't want to be known as the man who founded the American empire—800 bases in 70 countries."

"Japan is so small in comparison, isn't it?"

"Yes and no." Eto Sensei examined the possible interconnections on his paper. "I'm not sure his change of heart alone is that threatening. There must be something else. Something he found."

"Hiroshi said he was helping with contracts for cleaning up Fukushima."

"The contracts were all awarded to Japanese companies, though most have little expertise or experience in handling nuclear waste." Eto Sensei started writing again on his large butcher-block paper.

Akiko looked through one of the folders she brought with information Hiroshi had asked her to find. "The Fukushima contracts were worth twenty trillion yen."

"That's what? About 180 billion US? And the cleanup will take decades. That'll keep rising. I won't be here to see the end of it."

"Hiroshi asked me to find what services the contracts were for." Akiko looked at Eto Sensei, deferring to the older man, politely hesitating in case he wanted to take the initiative.

"Radioactive sludge, discarded protective clothing, radioactive rubble, contaminated soil, not to mention nuclear fuel rods. Those are the expensive things. And lots and lots of irradiated water. Without any place to put it, they've had to let it stream out into the ocean now and then."

"Really? That's disgusting."

"That's been in the newspapers."

"Hiroshi told me you read everything. I see that's true."

"If only it were. Time is so limited. My friends in economics tell me the trillions-of-yen budget is going for the most important project in post-war Japan—the restoration of Japan's honor. Others say the money is being doled out to political cronies. The bidding process is closed, with less oversight than usual."

"Honor? They don't think of it as a danger to humans, to the environment? It makes me sick thinking of all the radiation released. I read the reactors could melt down even more."

"The full extent of the disaster is hard to know." Eto Sensei wrote down notes on his large piece of paper, made a square in the corner and wrote down more. "Hopefully, exposing the worst aspects will steer the government ministries towards accountability, if just to save face."

"We can hope."

Eto Sensei smiled at her. "Hiroshi is lucky to have someone like you. You make things easy."

Akiko poked around on the computer. "I hope Hiroshi gets here soon. He wanted to hear everything you know about this."

"It's probably what we don't know that matters most. The number of government documents classified as secret reached an all-time high this year."

They got back to work, Eto Sensei sketching connections, Akiko making sure all the information Eto Sensei handed back to her was kept in order, notated and filed in the right place. Akiko opened the computer files from the archive and Eto Sensei skimmed through it on his computer, stopping to take notes and outline what he found on the huge sheet of butcher paper. Using color-coded arrows and lines, he connected the materials related to the cleanup, SOFA, and other government ministries. The intricate tangle of companies, sub-companies, government ministries, regulations and reports became layered so densely on the paper, Akiko wondered if any sense could be made of it at all.

Both of them were so intent on what they were doing, they didn't notice the early winter sunset coming down, and they didn't hear the doorbell ring.

Eto Sensei's wife came from the kitchen, paused to watch them working, and then went to see who was there. After a brief conversation, she walked back in with a tall foreigner in a long black leather coat.

"Here is the publisher's representative," Yoko announced.

Akiko and Eto Sensei looked up into the blonde hair and keen dimples of Trey Gladius, his blue eyes staring down at them.

Chapter 35

Akiko stepped in front of the table with all the materials. Her eyes searched Eto Sensei's living room for a way out. Was this the guy Hiroshi suspected? He looked like a magazine model, not like a criminal. Eto Sensei's face was covered in a dark cloud of suspicion and Yoko stood rigid on the other side of the table. If only she had returned Hiroshi's calls.

Trey calmly removed his long leather coat and folded it over one arm, smiling at them one by one, slowly, in turn. "*Shitsurei shimashita.* Please excuse my rudeness. I'm from the publisher. My name is Trey Gladius. I'm here to collect Mattson's manuscript and materials." Trey spoke in the politest Japanese, bowing first to Eto Sensei, then to Akiko and Yoko, before extending his name card to Eto Sensei.

Eto Sensei took the name card but didn't look at it or bow in return.

Keeping herself between Trey and the table, Akiko reached for her cellphone. "You're not with any publisher."

Trey held his hand up for her to stop. "Maybe there was some miscommunication with Jamie, but publishing is a very competitive business. If we don't get the first option, there's no point in having a contract at all." Trey unfolded the letter of agreement Jamie signed and set it on the table.

Eto Sensei glanced at it, his face darkening. The phone by her ear, Akiko waited. Eto Sensei's wife turned towards the kitchen.

"Please stay right here," Trey said to her, his voice calmly commanding. "I am from the publisher and I do have a contract. If the publishers agree, they will open the work, later, to academics. But for now, these materials are ours." Trey looked around for a place to put his coat. He folded it carefully over a chair within easy reach.

Akiko pressed the button to call, but would Hiroshi pick up? Hiroshi's phone rang once, twice. With a quick sweep of his arm, Trey snatched the cellphone from her hands. He turned it off and slammed it on the table with a loud clack. His other hand stayed cupped, in the air, his shoulders tensed. He picked the phone up again and slammed it on the edge of the table, cracking the screen.

Eto Sensei stood up. Yoko covered her mouth with one hand.

Trey took a breath and tapped the smashed cellphone with a long finger. "No calls until I ascertain the materials. If you read that letter of agreement, you'll find that all this should be in the publisher's hands, not yours."

Akiko dropped her hands to her sides and backed against the table. She needed to save the materials. She could see the *genkan* entryway, but Trey's long legs and broad shoulders would catch her before she got out the door, with or without her shoes. If she leapt forward to fight with him, maybe Yoko could get to the landline, or out the door, but turning things physical would mean someone got hurt.

Before she could decide what to do, the air-rending blast of a fighter jet overhead rattled the house like a small earthquake. Everyone cringed, waiting for it to pass. When the thundering rumble eased into the distance, Eto Sensei said. "You're not a publisher. Who do you think you're fooling?"

Trey dropped his bag on the table. "You're right. I confess. I'm just the publisher's representative, and I suppose you could say, in this matter, a protector of information." Trey leaned over the table and looked at Eto Sensei's outline with approval. He ripped the large butcher paper off the table, scanning it with an impressed nod before folding it into a small, tight square and slipping it into his pocket. "Very nice work."

He picked up Mattson's notebook of requested materials and flipped through the pages before putting it into his backpack with a flourish. Trey watched everyone carefully, his attention moving back and forth from the materials to where they stood. Trey pulled Eto Sensei's laptop across the table and started scrolling up and down. He stooped down to read the long flow of documents more carefully.

When he did, Akiko moved in front of the other computer. With her hands behind her back, she pointed, as best she could, at the USB drive. Yoko glanced down at it, waiting, cautious.

When Trey leaned forward squinting at the screen, Yoko slid the USB drive out of the computer and popped it into the cherry bark tea caddy, fingering the USB drive down into the green leaves.

Trey finished skimming through the computer documents and slammed the top down, returning his attention to the three as he put Eto Sensei's laptop into his bag. Trey took a step towards the laptop Akiko brought, but Akiko didn't move, trying to shield it from him, and to delay him as best she could.

Trey shoved her aside and she caught herself from falling, and then stepped over next to Eto Sensei. Trey leaned down to the second screen but went through it more quickly than he had on Eto Sensei's computer, satisfied, it seemed, with what was there. He slapped the top down and slipped the second laptop in beside Eto Sensei's. He shook everything in the backpack into place with both hands.

"That's an official police computer," Akiko said.

"Well, I don't officially know that. It looks like documents for Mattson's memoir to me." Trey's blue eyes shone brightly as he examined each of them again. "Well, I think that's everything," he said in a cheery voice. "Or almost. How much of this did you read?"

They stared at him in silence. Akiko glanced at the door, hoping Hiroshi would get there with Sakaguchi and the others. Would her phone still work? She tried to remember Hiroshi's number.

Trey saw her eyes flitter to the door. "Expecting someone?"

Akiko stared at him without a word.

He set the bag down beside the chair and carefully pulled on his long leather coat. The bottom of the coat stretched to his ankles and he flexed his shoulders to get the coat set in place. "Let me ask again. Did you read a lot or a little?"

"Enough to know who you work for," Eto Sensei said, his hands trembling and voice deepening.

"In the end, it doesn't matter too much what you know. Without Mattson's testimony, his proof and authority, this won't have legs. It won't matter what a couple detectives and a retired professor have to say. Much less a secretary."

"You think you can break the law with impunity." Eto Sensei took his cane and stood up. "But you can't. No one can."

"Laws in Asia? They're made to be broken. That's why I like it here." Trey picked up the backpack. "Are there other copies of this?" Trey looked at Akiko with a sneaky face. "In the homicide office? You can tell me."

Akiko's features were as fixed as marble. The sun had started to set, the room filling with evening air and shadows.

"You can steal these computers and materials, but the information won't disappear," Eto Sensei said.

"As long as it stays disappeared long enough, my job's done."

"You can't hide this forever. Someone else will find all this. And soon."

"Japan is a covert culture. Hiding things is an art form. Another reason I like it here. As a professor of politics, you should know that as well as anyone. And you," Trey turned to Akiko, "Working in homicide, you should know that covert dealing is how the game is played."

Akiko glared at him silently.

Eto Sensei took a step towards Trey. "The rule of law rests on openness and transparency. You can't get around that for long."

"If the secrets were all exposed, where would your democracy, your justice, your liberty be then? Well-kept secrets are the oil that keeps the machine running."

"If you're working for one of the American companies bidding for contracts, you're going about it in a dangerous fashion."

"American companies? Because I'm American? You Japanese with your loyalty, your patriotism always amaze me. The only thing you Japanese really care about is which direction the money's flowing. Protecting the environment and helping fishermen catch safe fish? That's all on the surface. What this one boils down to is contracts and budgets. Japan is efficient that way."

"You might speak Japanese, but you understand nothing of Japan's values. You're all surface, no core."

Trey smiled at Eto Sensei and plucked at the flap of his long black coat.

Akiko hoped Eto Sensei could keep delaying Trey until Hiroshi arrived. She was getting sick of Trey's dimpled smile and blue eyes, but there was nothing to do but try to keep him there, braced for whatever he did next.

Eto Sensei leaned forward on his cane. "Every country produces people like you, impetuous, adolescent, pretending the rules don't apply, but actually subservient to authority. Whose orders are you following, little boy?"

Trey strained forward for a moment. He eased back, a smile spreading across his face as he slung the heavy backpack over his shoulder and looked in their faces one by one. "Well, this isn't the time for this discussion. Another time maybe. I appreciate your not needing more persuasion." He turned towards the door.

Akiko said, "You're not going to get far with those."

"I don't need to get too far," Trey said. He walked to the entryway, put his shoes on and walked out, the door slamming shut behind him.

Akiko grabbed her phone and rushed to the door. "I've got to follow him."

Eto Sensei shouted, "You'll do no such thing. Get back here! The police will catch him—"

"He'll move quickly. It's getting dark. I wish I knew where Hiroshi was." She tried to turn her phone on as she grabbed her coat, slipped on her shoes, looked out a crack in the door, and went after him.

Eto Sensei stumbled as he struggled towards the door after her. "Get back in here!"

Yoko steadied him.

"I'm fine, but don't let her go!" he pleaded.

Bowing in apology, Yoko ran out the front door after Akiko.

Chapter 36

Jamie got out of the taxi in front of the Diet offices and walked straight in, pulling her suitcase up the stairs step by step. From her shoulders dangled the small travel bag and backpack she'd so carefully packed. Setsuko said the only time she felt unsafe was when no one else was around. The emptiness of the area, save for a few lingering protestors by the side of the building, seemed to confirm what she meant. Maybe it was better to get back in the taxi. She turned, but it was gone.

Inside the atrium of the Diet office building, Jamie stopped in front of the metal detector, still wondering if she should go in or not. Perhaps it was wiser just to catch the train and go. As she walked up to the metal detector, the guard made an X with his fingers and pointed at her suitcase, shook his head no, and pointed at the coat and baggage check counter beside the door.

Jamie tapped her heel on the marble floor of the deserted atrium. Leaving the bag in a coat check wasn't something she'd considered. The USB was safely inside her bra, but her father's scroll and all that money was in her suitcase.

She would only be upstairs for a short while, just long enough to bluff her way through this last task before getting on a train out of Tokyo.

The old guard at the baggage check counter welcomed Jamie with a sluggish, night-shift nod. The storage shelves behind the counter were entirely empty, but Jamie handed her suitcase to the attendant and slid the claim chip into her pocket. She kept her small travel bag and backpack with her, walked over to the scanner and sent them through on the belt. She breezed through the art nouveau hall and up the shiny brass elevator to Shinobu Katsumura's office.

The secretary showed Jamie into the inner office. Shinobu was sitting by the coffee table talking to an older, rather tall man who stood up, leaning over to grind out his cigarette before facing her. His black suit was like funeral wear and his face a shallow moon with deep-set eyes.

"Jamie, I'm so glad you could come. This is my uncle who runs the publishing house. His name is also Katsumura," Shinobu said.

The older Katsumura removed a name card from his jacket pocket and held it out for her with waxy hands.

"I'm sorry I don't have a name card," Jamie said.

Shinobu translated for her uncle and he nodded his understanding.

"Let's get right to it, since I know you're in a hurry. What time is your train?" Shinobu asked, pointing for everyone to sit down.

"The last train to Kyoto."

"Why such a hurry?"

"I just needed to get away, I guess."

"Kyoto is a wonderful place. You can recover there." Shinobu smiled, easing back into her leather chair like it was a second skin. "You brought your father's notebooks and files?"

"Right here," Jamie said and slung the backpack onto the coffee table. It looked oddly out of place in the office, the only thing practical, youthful or alive. The rest of the office was wood, glass, leather and law books.

"Everything's in here?" Shinobu leaned forward.

"Just like we agreed. I give you the notebooks, Trey edits them, you publish them, everyone reads it, and we all live happily ever after." Jamie said.

Shinobu turned towards her uncle to translate for him. He sat in the chair at the head of the coffee table, keeping his eyes on Jamie as he listened.

"Can we take a look?" Shinobu said, reaching for the backpack.

"The notebooks are all carefully wrapped and taped. Better open them later, at the publishers. You don't want to get them out of order."

Shinobu turned and translated. His eyes didn't move from Jamie and when he nodded, the loose flesh on his mottled face made it seem he existed several layers deeper inside. Shinobu's uncle spoke in a quiet, gravel-crunch voice, impossible for Jamie to pick up anything of what he said. Shinobu turned to Jamie. "My uncle says he trusts you because you're a woman."

"Is that supposed to be flattering?"

"Let's sign the contract." Shinobu glanced at her uncle. He nodded once.

"I thought I signed one the first day I came here."

"This one is more thorough."

A young man came over from the side of the room, startling Jamie. She hadn't noticed him standing back by the bookshelves. He carried over a leather folder and set a document in Japanese in front of Shinobu.

Jamie looked at it and leaned back, feigning surprise. "I thought there would be an English contract?"

"Since you were in such a hurry, we'll have to go with the Japanese for now and send you an English version later. I know in America you would go over the contract, but in Japan we still run on trust," Shinobu smiled, her eyebrows arching.

"I'm not sure," Jamie said. "I'd feel better if it were in both languages."

"We'll have the English contract ready for you by the time you get back from Kyoto. Would that be soon enough?" Shinobu's eyebrows arched to a 'V.'

"I just wanted to be sure about my father's legacy," Jamie said, looking down.

"We're going to do just that," Shinobu said. Her uncle cleared his throat.

Jamie took the pen the assistant handed her and signed the last line. She slid it back across the black lacquer table to Shinobu's uncle who took out his *hanko* seal. The assistant held open a snap-case of red ink with a discrete bow. After stamping his *hanko* above Jamie's signature, the assistant made sure the red ink dried without smudging.

"What you're doing is a great thing for Japanese-American relations and for Asian peace and stability. Your father always knew the right thing to do."

"He definitely did."

"The advance will be sent by automatic bank transfer. Do you have an account?"

"I opened one just for this." Jamie dug in her bag for the brand new account book she set up the day before.

The assistant came over and wrote down the numbers in a small leather notebook he kept in his jacket pocket. He walked back to a laptop on a desk in the shadows and worked at the keyboard for a few minutes. He checked everything again and stood up to give Shinobu a restrained nod.

"That's all settled then," Shinobu said.

"You sent it all?" Jamie asked.

"Most of it. The rest later. After we check what's here. Trust but verify, as one of your presidents used to say."

Jamie stood up.

"And this is just a small token of appreciation," Shinobu said, nodding at a cash-swollen envelope the assistant set on the table. "Kyoto can be expensive, and Tokyo always is."

"Thank you. That's very Japanese. Always so thoughtful. It's appreciated." Jamie picked it up and put it in the pocket of her father's jacket. Back in New York, she would have felt guilty about taking the money. But after hearing how the Katsumuras did business, and having been tricked by Trey, her anger at her former gullibility made any guilt fade away.

"What about a drink to celebrate?" Shinobu said, without making a move to the liquor cabinet.

"I don't want to miss my train. I get lost easily."

"It's easy to get lost in Tokyo." Shinobu rose from her chair in one smooth motion.

"We can celebrate when the book comes out." Which would be never, Jamie knew, especially after they opened the backpack. "But now I have a train to catch." And a couple planes.

In the elevator, Jamie regretted that she wouldn't get to see Shinobu open the bag, but she could picture the surprise on her face. Downstairs, Jamie hurried to the baggage check by the front door. Her suitcase was still there. She thanked the guard and rolled her bag out the door and clunked it down the steps.

Only a few protestors remained to guard the signs stacked against a wall, waiting to restart in the morning. As she tugged her bag over the flat stone toward the street, one demonstrator walked towards her. In her hurry, she hardly noted the oddity of his traditional *hakama* pants and a finely woven *haori* jacket—so unlike the floppy outdoor clothing of most anti-nuke people—and hurried to the street for a taxi. As she waited, she got a call from Shinobu.

"Is this a joke or a mistake?"

"I gave you the book he planned." Jamie waved to a taxi, but it turned down another street.

"Explain this to me."

Jamie looked up at the building with all the Diet members' offices but couldn't remember which direction Shinobu's window faced. "After he died, he said obedience to authority, defending the status quo and insularity were not the parts of Japan he loved. They were the parts he wanted to change."

In a low, angry voice, Shinobu said, "You can't begin to understand what a big mistake you just made. If that's all your father has, the contract is void."

"That's what I figured." Jamie hung up, satisfied to get that off the list before she left Tokyo.

A taxi switched lanes and pulled over. Jamie got in and pulled off towards Tokyo Station. The thought of Shinobu's sharp-angled eyebrows and the pasty face of her uncle when they opened the erotic woodblock *shunga* prints amused her. She had deliberately put in copies of the most explicit of her father's prints. The explanatory notes and descriptive sketches surrounded the graphic sexual combinations, making the details and artistry sharper and richer, and more shocking for being put in words.

* * *

In Shinobu's office, Shinobu's uncle nodded to the assistant to take what would have been an insightful treatise on erotic art out of his sight. He lit a cigarette and pulled deeply on it, his gaunt face placid and unfeeling at Jamie's deception. He looked for an ashtray. Shinobu snapped her fingers at the assistant, who handed Shinobu her cellphone and her uncle an ashtray.

Shinobu called the number for Trey Gladius' phone. "You said there'd be no complications."

"There aren't any," Trey answered, a bit out of breath.

219

"You need to get this taken care of." After a long pause, Shinobu spoke again. "Did you hear me?"

Trey finally said, "I'm a bit busy at the moment. I'll be back in Tokyo later. I have a plane to catch."

"A plane? With everything here?"

"I told you, it's under control. I'm going to Guam. With Jamie tomorrow afternoon."

"She told me she's taking a train to Kyoto. Tonight."

After a long pause, Trey blew out a big breath. "She did? Well, that does change things."

Chapter 37

Akiko followed Trey through the quiet residential lanes towards the station, running at times to keep up, waiting at times to hide, making sure she did not lose sight of Trey. Her cellphone had finally come back on, though the screen was shattered.

After repeated attempts, Akiko finally connected to Hiroshi, whispering, "He's heading to Yokosuka station on foot."

"Almost there. Hang back," Hiroshi whisper-shouted.

"No, Shioiri Station. I'll have to hurry."

"Don't do that!" Hiroshi shouted, too late.

Ueno pulled the car close to Yokosuka Station, but Hiroshi told him to pull around to Shioiri Station, a few minutes' drive. If Trey hopped a train back to Tokyo, he could disappear at any station along the way.

Ueno pulled past Yokosuka station towards Honcho, the main nightlife area. There was no place to leave the car except halfway on the sidewalk, halfway in a lane of traffic. Ueno tried to rouse Sakaguchi, snoring in the back seat after two nights not sleeping, but gave up, left the keys under the visor and hopped out.

Akiko called Hiroshi. "He turned towards that strip of bars. The Honch, I think they call it."

"No closer, OK?" Hiroshi told her as he hurried through the jumble of sports bars, massage studios, DJ clubs, hamburger and pizza joints teeming with off-duty servicemen from Yokosuka Naval Base. Happy hour was still on and the smell of "Navy Curry" filled the air.

Akiko called Hiroshi again. "He should be close to you. He's got the computers."

221

"Stop there. I don't want you any closer," Hiroshi got out of the car just before she hung up on him.

Hiroshi let Ueno take the main street, and he took the first small lane of one-rail bars with handwritten signs in English. It was the old Honch, the real Honch. Karaoke and sports games spilled out in a steady hum. Bar girls with ponytails brought drinks to close-shaved men and everyone waited to cheer the next great play on big-screen TVs. Hiroshi peered down each branching alley.

He emerged from the maze of alleyways and found himself on the highway that separated the bars from the base. Ueno was standing at the next exit down. Trey had snuck through somewhere. They had lost him.

Hiroshi waved at Ueno to go back inside. Hiroshi turned into the next alley, twisting sideways to keep from hitting old wires, signs, and poles holding up low roofs of corrugated scrap. The alley sputtered out to a row of rundown shacks with torn awnings and termite-eaten walls.

A stinging thump on the back of his head sent Hiroshi reeling into the sliding door of an empty, old bar whose wood frame splintered under his weight, its wall raining down bits of plaster, wood and plastic.

Hiroshi rolled onto his back and spin-kicked the air. Adrenaline and high school *kendo* training got him back on his feet, but before he could recenter himself, he heard a whir beside his ear and felt the roof collapse, covering him in wood and tin and blinding him with dust. The next whir sunk into the soft wood post beside his head. He scurried backwards and clawed at a pole he backed into, trying to pull himself up. He could see nothing, choking on the dust, listening intently.

Before he could see again, a hard kick caught him in his stomach. He doubled over, nauseous, sucking for air, red splotches clogging his vision. Another hard kick caught him on the hip and sent him sideways. Hiroshi flailed at the wood and wiped his face, scrambling to his feet. Blinking hard, he saw Trey ready and balanced, sword in hand, within striking distance.

Hiroshi kicked a stack of beer crates at him and lunged for the door. Dusty bottles shattered as Hiroshi looked around for something, anything, to defend himself with. Takamatsu made him swear he'd always carry a telescoping baton outside the office, but he never did. He'd have been happy for the pepper spray Shibata gave Jamie.

From a pile of scrap beside a vending machine, he yanked out a length of old lead pipe and spun around holding it with two hands in proper *kendo* stance, *chūdan-no-kamae*, attack and defense, ready for Trey's next strike.

Trey gripped his *tanto* sword in two hands. In one motion, he rose up and struck with all his force.

Hiroshi parried, staggering back.

Trey struck again.

Hiroshi angled the pipe to deflect the blade, but it landed closer.

He stepped back and moved his feet under himself, resetting his shoulders with the pipe over his head. He lowered the pipe at Trey's throat, gauging the distance. His pipe was longer than the *tanto* but Trey had longer arms. The kick to his gut made it hard to breathe, his guts retching with the pain.

Trey moved his *tanto* sword into the same position, mocking him. "Is this how you *kendo* guys do it?"

"Where are the computers?" Hiroshi said, wiping his eyes on his sleeve.

Trey chuckled. "Safe. Or almost."

"You can't get away."

"I think I can."

Trey leapt forward with a straight downward blow. Hiroshi swung the pipe in a hard half-circle to keep Trey's blade from burying into him. The force propelled him forward past Trey as the sharp blade passed to the side. Hiroshi spun around with a quick swing with the pipe, which Trey sidestepped.

Trey laughed, ready to cut Hiroshi in two, circling him, his laugh turning to a steady, focused sneer. He dominated the crossing of two alleys, giving himself space to work in, maneuvering Hiroshi into the narrower alley.

Hiroshi blinked to clear his eyes, tears streaming out to wash away the dust. He watched Trey's shoulders and the top of his head, the right direction and body position coming back to him as if his old *kendo* instructor was resetting him at practice. Hiroshi slowed his breathing and gauged where he was. He could see what looked like the stolen laptops and materials on top of a junked-out freezer along the alleyway.

A patter of footfalls, soft and faraway, sounded—suddenly—closer. From the side alley, Hiroshi saw a bulky blur dive straight into Trey, flattening him. The sword clattered down the alley out of reach. It was Sakaguchi. He was mashing Trey's head and neck with two hands, his body clamping Trey to the concrete.

Hiroshi dropped the pipe and wobbled over, stamping down hard on Trey's free wrist.

Hearing the commotion, a few sailors from the next alley ran over to watch the fight. They shouted in English and a few doors opened, spilling more servicemen into the alley. One sailor looked down at the sword lying on the ground, confused by what was clearly not the usual Honch punch-up.

Sakaguchi twisted Trey's arm behind him and reached for his handcuffs, but the slight shift in weight gave just enough opening for Trey to twist the other way, swing a punch onto Sakaguchi's ear, and slip out from under him. Back on his feet, Trey kneed Sakaguchi in the temple and stiff-armed Hiroshi, who reeled backwards. Trey grabbed the bags from on top of the freezer and took off.

The American soldiers were not sure who was who. One stepped forward to slow Trey down but could not even get a hand on him. The others looked back and forth between Sakaguchi's massive body and Hiroshi covered in plaster dust.

Sakaguchi clutched his head as he pulled himself up and lumbered after Trey. Hiroshi followed, willing his legs to move, leaving behind the sound of the sailors shouting confused questions and yelling for him to stop.

Alley after alley, corner after corner, he thought he heard Trey just ahead or to the side. Each time he lost the sound of his feet, until he lost him altogether. Hiroshi nearly tumbled over when he emerged onto the wide street along the highway separating the bars from the base. He leaned over to catch his breath as Ueno ran up, shaking his head.

"Where's Akiko?" Hiroshi asked, bending over for breath. Righting himself, he saw Trey, bag in hand, on the other side of the highway, sauntering through the turnstile into Yokosuka Naval Base.

"There he is!" Hiroshi shouted. "I've got him," he yelled at Ueno. "Go find Akiko."

Ueno ducked back into the alleys of the Honch. Sakaguchi, standing at the exit of the next alley down, saw Hiroshi lurching across the highway towards the naval base. By the time they got to the bulwarks, tire spikes and metal gate, Trey was already inside.

Hiroshi knocked on the window of the squat guardhouse. Behind the bulletproof glass and thick concrete walls, a marine guard in dress uniform stared out at them in surprise.

"Can I help you, sir?" the guard asked into the microphone.

"Where did that guy go?" Hiroshi asked, in English. "Tall guy running with computer bags."

"Sir, could I ask who you are?"

"I'm Detective Hiroshi Shimizu." He held up his badge to the window. With the dust, blood and sweat, torn shirt and scuffed pants, haggard and angry face, the badge was the only evidence of being a detective. "The man who just came through here is a suspect. Theft, assault and murder."

The guard pressed the talk button. "I'll call the liaison officer."

"Open the gate, will you?" Hiroshi shouted.

"I'm not authorized. Please wait patiently, sir. We'll be right with you," the guard said.

Hiroshi jammed the call button with his thumb, holding it down.

The guard pressed his talk button without looking at Hiroshi. "Let go of the button, sir. The liaison officer is on his way."

Inside the protective glass, an older man in a badge-speckled uniform listened to the guard's explanation, looking out at the plaster-covered mess claiming to be a detective.

Osaki and Sugamo pulled up and parked the car outside the protective bulwarks of the entry zone a hundred meters away and hurried over to join Hiroshi and Sakaguchi.

"He's getting away," Hiroshi said, straining to look past the gate into the naval base. He held his badge up again. Sakaguchi flashed his.

The uniformed liaison officer buzzed himself out from a side door and stood at ease, looking down from the curb at Hiroshi and Sakaguchi. He was tall but appeared less so with the background of the huge security gate and wall framing him from behind.

"*Konbanwa.* What can I do for you today?" he asked.

"We're detectives, homicide division, in pursuit of a suspect who just went in through this gate. He's wanted for theft, assault and murder," Hiroshi explained.

"We do not allow police onto the base without proper procedures. This is a secure area. You can file a request through the usual channels. We always cooperate with local authorities. You're from Yokosuka?"

"No, Tokyo. Homicide."

The American officer, his uniform spotlessly clean, shook his head at the ragged Japanese detectives. "The request for information must go through the local Yokosuka police station where our application procedures are set up. The chief's named Hirano."

Sakaguchi pulled himself up to his full size, his round, featureless face dripping sweat, and walked up to the officer, staring at the few medals on his chest, his eyes thin lines of intensity. Sugamo and Osaki stood right beside him.

The officer was tall and square-shouldered, and appeared used to being in difficult situations, but just the same he took a prudent step back. He cleared his throat and said, "Sir, I must remind you that this is the border of Yokosuka Naval Base. Different laws apply inside the base. Out there, it's yours. Inside, it's America."

Hiroshi held Sakaguchi back and looked the American officer in the eyes. "What's your name?" Hiroshi pulled out a ploy Takamatsu used at dead ends.

He held out his name pin from his shirt. "Bigston, Colonel Bigston."

Hiroshi said, "Colonel Bigston, you're going to find out you made a serious mistake today."

Colonel Bigston glanced behind him at the soldiers inside. "If I don't follow protocol, it's my ass in a sling."

"Fucking protocol," Hiroshi shouted in English and turned away, pushing Sakaguchi back towards the street.

"I couldn't agree more," Bigston shouted after their dusty backs. "After you route your request through Chief Hirano at the Yokosuka police station, I'll ensure the request is expedited."

Sakaguchi's phone rang. He looked at Hiroshi and hung up. "That was Ueno. It's Akiko. And Eto Sensei's wife."

Chapter 38

Hiroshi flashed his badge at the reception desk, strode through a hallway, a nurse chasing him and burst through the swinging doors of the emergency room. He looked under the bottom of the curtains of the triage exam area until he saw the feet of doctors and nurses in the last space. He batted the curtain back to the surprised faces of a doctor, two nurses and a highly intoxicated Japanese man who wobbled uncontrollably on the exam chair.

"Where is she?" Hiroshi demanded. The nurse pulled the curtain back. Why did he let Akiko go alone? How could he have been so stupid? Hiroshi looked around the emergency room, desperate.

Sakaguchi caught up with him and dropped a heavy hand on his shoulder to pull him away. Sakaguchi bellied him into one of the exam areas and onto a table. "Sit here. I'm used to taking falls, but I don't think you're used to being swung at with a sword. Don't move until these doctors give you the OK."

Hiroshi pushed himself up but Ueno stepped forward and blocked him. Hiroshi sat back down and stared dully at the curtain, taking stock of his pains. His clothes were grimy and scuffed, his knees, elbows and palms scraped rough. Blood dappled his torn, sweat-soaked shirt and bruises were already coloring here and there. Except where he'd wiped it from his eyes, powder from the collapsed shacks dusted his face and hair, and splinters of old wood clung to his clothes.

The nurse and emergency room doctor came in and the two of them forced Hiroshi to sit still as they checked him. His scratches and cuts were not deep, but still in need of bandaging. Akiko pulled back the curtain, and Hiroshi got up despite the nurse's complaints. "Are you OK?" Hiroshi asked. He ignored the nurse and went to Akiko, lightly touching her arm wrapped in gauze and looking her over to be sure there were no other injuries.

"I caught up with him," Akiko said. "And Eto Sensei's wife caught up with me."

"I told you to stay back," Hiroshi said. "You didn't answer—"

"He grabbed us too quickly. He slammed me against the wall and held the sword to my neck. He taped both of us to a pole in an abandoned bar."

"Taped?" Hiroshi leaned forward. "What kind of tape?"

"I don't know, thick grey, no, green, strong. I wasn't paying attention to that."

Eto Sensei's wife, Yoko, bowed as she came into the exam area. Her arm was in a sling, the lower arm velcro-wrapped in place over a hard splint.

"Are you OK?" Hiroshi asked her, shaking his head at getting them into this. "Your arm?"

Yoko wriggled her fingers at the end of the splint. "It was rather exciting, though I'm glad this young man found us when he did." She bowed politely to Ueno, who bowed back. "A few bruises here and there, but the doctor said I need this for a while. Nothing broken."

"Did you call Eto Sensei to tell him you're OK? Is *he* OK?"

"He's fine. Just startled. He never thought his politics would become so, well, real." Yoko laughed. "He said you're his most exciting student."

"Not the right kind of exciting. If I'd had any idea—"

"Everyone's fine. You were doing your job."

"Not—"

"I've got to get back and cook dinner," Yoko said.

"You can't go home yet," Hiroshi said. "You should stay and—"

"You're going right back to work, aren't you?" Yoko asked. "Well so am I."

"I'm—"

"And I could do with a bath. With my arm like this, it will give Sensei a chance to learn how to cook." She smiled.

Ueno said, "I'll drive you home."

"I should go with you," Hiroshi said.

"You're busy here." Yoko looked at him. "But, I do have something for you at the house."

Hiroshi looked confused.

"I saved the USB flash drive. In the tea caddy." She laughed and Akiko giggled.

Hiroshi looked more confused. "Tea caddy?"

"I'll drive her home and bring it back," Ueno said.

Hiroshi bowed to her. "I'm so—"

Yoko patted his arm, gently. "I know, but this is what happens."

"I'll have the local police come by."

Yoko smiled at him one last time and left, Ueno following her out.

Hiroshi turned to Akiko. "I never should have—"

Akiko patted his leg. "Now, at least, we know for sure."

Hiroshi thanked the doctor and nurse and walked out into the hall, trying not to limp from the pain. Akiko, right beside him, looked fine, if ruffled. As they walked, they checked each other's bandages, pointing out each other's injuries, both denying anything was serious.

They walked out the front door of the clinic, across the parking lot and a sealed-off area to the nondescript building housing the Yokosuka Police Station. Hiroshi showed his badge to the duty clerk at the front desk.

They found Sakaguchi hunched over a desk filling in a form in the office of Chief Hirano, the head of the Yokosuka police station. Sakaguchi grunted an introduction and Chief Hirano bowed, but didn't get up. The brown liver spots on his bald head looked like an antique map of unknown islands. His eyelids hung in layers of puffy bluish flesh.

"If you had called me, we could have caught him at the gate. I have men posted near there all the time," Chief Hirano growled.

Hiroshi shook his head at his own thoughtlessness.

"It's good Sakaguchi called ahead. I got the forms ready for him." Chief Hirano showed no sympathy as Sakaguchi sighed at the stack of forms in front of him.

"Let me do that," Akiko said. Sakaguchi made a pretense of waving her away, but gave in, got up—slowly—from the chair and let Akiko sit down to work. She realigned the triplicate forms and started filling in the application for access to a suspect on the American base.

Two young, long-haired guys in *sukajan* silk jackets embroidered with silver and gold phoenixes breezed into Hirano's office and shook their heads. One said, simply, "No sword."

"Where could it go? Could have cut us both in half." Sakaguchi looked puzzled by what the undercover cops in their *sukajan* jackets told him. "Did he pick it up as he ran?"

Hirano said, "Sword cuts are bad. I had one once in Kudanshita, right-wing guy we had cornered. A dozen guys surrounding him but his sword managed to nick me. Shallow, but took a long time to heal. Back when Takamatsu and I were coming up."

"How long will it take?" Hiroshi asked. "We should be back there by now."

The two detectives in their *sukajan* jackets chuckled and shuffled their feet, looking down. Hirano pointed his finger at Hiroshi and one of the detectives went out.

"Pen might be mightier than the sword, but it's a lot, lot slower," Hirano said, pulling open his top drawer for a pill and washing it down with tea from a small cup. "Reason for my high blood pressure. We ask permission. They delay. We wait."

"We won't get on the base today?" Hiroshi asked. "But, that's—"

"You put in your special request," Hirano spoke as if reciting from a written list. "Then you wait for the answer, reassure the American military police that you have evidence, and then wait for one of the military lawyers to answer, and then find one of our lawyers who speaks English, and at long last arrange a sit-down. Then, and only then, can you see the suspect."

"So, impossible." Hiroshi sighed. The undercover detective who had left came back in with a clean white shirt in plastic dry-cleaning wrap for Hiroshi. He took it, but didn't put it on.

"Sometimes they inform us if they prosecute in a military court. Sometimes not." Hirano leaned forward. The liver spots on his bald head stretched and wrinkled as he spoke. "Better bet is to trail him when he comes out. You have a photo, right? When he goes out, we drag him in here and grill him until the military lawyers come."

"This guy is not that stupid," Hiroshi said.

"They're all that stupid," Hirano said.

Hiroshi patted himself down to find his cellphone, worried he lost it in the fight. He winced at the pain of just moving his arms. He held out the photo of Trey and sent it to one of the young undercover detectives.

"Do you watch the entrance to the base all the time?" Hiroshi asked.

"We would if we could. We were told to stand down after the earthquake," Hirano explained.

"By who?"

"American ambassador and a couple of Diet members." Hirano shook his head. "I had to put on my good suit and go up to Tokyo to receive their 'special request.' Someone from the base found a camera we put up across the street to watch the entrance."

"Should have hidden it better," Sakaguchi said.

"We did after that. And, we got a better camera, so we can see faces. The tech guys are amazing."

"Why were you watching after the Tohoku earthquake?" Hiroshi asked.

"We noticed a big increase in the number of American trucks. We thought it was just an increase in Americans sending supplies to Fukushima."

Hiroshi leaned forward. "But the trucks coming back from up north were full?"

Hirano nodded. "Very full. Strange, right? We couldn't figure out what they were bringing back. But after the earthquake, everything was chaotic, everyone pulling double shifts. We were too busy, and too tired to follow up on it."

One of the young undercover detectives said, "Everyone was worried about radiation, so we checked into it."

"From the trucks coming back?" Hiroshi asked.

The other young detective said, "New Geiger counters were all sold out. But we found a big old metal thing in storage. I strapped it on my motorcycle and pulled up next to the trucks."

"What was the reading?" Hiroshi asked.

"Off the charts."

"Where did the trucks go?"

"I dropped a GPS on a couple of them. Our tech guy tracked those back up to Fukushima." The two young detectives knew what they were doing, Hiroshi thought. Their jackets would look absurd in Tokyo, but along the coast, they would help them blend in.

"None went south?" Hiroshi resettled himself, twisting to at least move the pain around.

"Yes, but not the same trucks," Hirano said. "The military trucks went there to here, and Japanese trucks went from here south."

Sakaguchi held up his hand to cut in. "Let me contact that blogger, that young guy who was with Higa in the bookstore."

Sakaguchi scrolled through his cellphone to find the number and made the call to Iino, the pale-faced, intense blogger he met at the twins' bookstore. Sakaguchi reached in his pocket and pulled out the book Higa authored, the one the bookstore twins gave him and showed it to Hirano.

"Wish I had time to read." Hirano sipped his tea. "A journalist I drink with, or used to until this blood pressure thing, is doing a book on the bases. Talk with him." He nodded to one of the young detectives to be sure that happened.

Hiroshi said, "Do you remember the name of the Diet member who pressured you to leave the bases alone?"

Hirano rubbed his bald, dappled head, trying to remember. "Old money, legacy district, pretty woman..."

"Shinobu Katsumura?" Hiroshi asked.

"That's it."

"Was it Katsumura Transportation trucks going in and out of the base?"

"We might have some of the old footage saved."

Akiko said, "The forms are done." She handed them to Hirano.

"Can we hire you down here? We'll raise your pay." Hirano took the forms from her and tapped them on his forehead in a gesture of thanks and respect.

Akiko smiled as she stood up. "Thanks, but I'm good where I am."

"If we can't get on the base, we better find Jamie. With Trey in the open, she's now in real danger." Hiroshi moved towards the door. He was talking out loud about everything now, like Takamatsu.

Sakaguchi pushed himself out of the chair and looked at Hiroshi. He paused, looked out at the hall and then back at Hiroshi. "The guys lost her."

"What? How could Jamie—"

"She gave them the slip."

Hiroshi looked at him quietly.

Sakaguchi checked his cellphone. "Takamatsu's waiting in Yokohama. Wants us to pick him up."

Chief Hirano stood up, stretched his back. "I thought he was on disciplinary leave?"

"More like leave from discipline," Hiroshi said.

"He's always been that way," Hirano said.

Sakaguchi spread his arms to herd everyone out the door. "Ueno's out front, so let's let these guys get some sleep. We'll need some ourselves with the conference coming up."

Hirano gave a curt nod. "We'll keep watching the front of the base. If he moves, we'll know. That kind of guy thinks he's untouchable. But he's not."

Chapter 39

Jamie got out in front of Tokyo Station. Hurrying under the quaint cornices and western windows of the old entrance, she followed the signs for the *shinkansen* bullet train. Right in front of the ticket machine, she stopped abruptly, whipping around to scour the area behind her. Her father and Setsuko knew when they were being followed. But when she went to the archives, or anywhere else, she had never noticed anyone after her.

She stood in the large, open entryway of the station waiting to see if anyone would appear.

When they didn't, she looked up at the colorful spiderweb of Tokyo's rail lines but bought the cheapest ticket to get through the station to the *shinkansen* bullet train counter on the other side. Inside, the *omiyage* souvenir stalls, *bento* lunchbox counters and kiosks were already closed. When she got to the *shinkansen* ticket counter, she bought a ticket to Fukuoka and headed towards the platform.

At the next ticket gate, her cellphone rang. It was Hiroshi. She watched the message record. When it finished, she clicked to listen. He insisted she not go anywhere alone. He demanded she wait for him, call him back, and stay in the house.

She rubbed her finger over the callback button, but Hiroshi had helped her enough already. From here, it was her turn to take charge.

Instead of calling him back, she called his office, ready to hang up if he or Akiko answered. When his message recorder clicked on, she spoke slowly, "Hiroshi, Trey is leaving tomorrow. I was supposed to meet him at the military liaison office in Narita Airport. For an afternoon flight to Guam. I'm not going. I'll call you when I'm safe in New York. And explain everything."

She turned her phone off and scanned the few passengers outside the *shinkansen* gate. She saw nothing and no one out of the ordinary, but she didn't even know what to look for. Crowded or empty, Tokyo seemed to hide people easily.

The departure board's list of departures rotated up one line, the bottom line listing a morning train seven hours later. She remembered telling Shinobu she was leaving on the last train to Kyoto. Perhaps she was being paranoid, but she took the escalator down to the ticket counter and asked to switch her ticket. The ticket seller changed the ticket without a word. The first train left at six a.m., and she would be on it.

She went to the information booth and asked about nearby coffee shops that stayed open twenty-four hours. One was just outside the station, so she walked there, checking behind her on the wide, empty sidewalk. Once inside the bland, antiseptic space full of travelers, night owls and people killing time, she felt safer. She texted Setsuko to let her know where she was and settled into the plastic-covered banquette, ordering a sandwich and coffee, and closing her eyes for an upright snooze like she'd seen Tokyoites do.

At five a.m., she paid her bill, walked across the cold, empty expanse of bus boarding lanes and the taxi line. A few early morning commuters headed to Tokyo trains, fewer still went into the *shinkansen* boarding area. From the platform, Jamie watched the cleaning crew reverse the seats, wipe down the arm rests and inspect the cars to be sure they were spotless. It was hard to imagine how Japanese spent so much energy on cleaning, and yet, let something like radiation go unchecked.

With only minutes to departure time, the barriers slid aside and the train doors opened. Jamie got on and found her seat, pushing her suitcase in front of her. She would be in Fukuoka in five-plus hours, get in a taxi to the airport and take whatever flight got her out of Japan the soonest, just as her father advised.

She settled in to her seat in the brightly-lit, silent train car. She was the only passenger, though others had been waiting on the platform. She put her bag against the wall and the travel bag in the seat beside her. She kneeled in the soft chair with her arms on top of the headrest, waiting and watching both doors.

When the conductor came to check her ticket, he had to turn around for two lanky men who got on right before the doors closed. They were carrying *bento* boxes—an early breakfast. The conductor walked back to where they sat at the back of the car, and with his handheld ticket machine issued them new tickets and took the added charge. When he finished, he doffed his hat, checked the ticket of one other passenger, dressed in traditional Japanese clothes, who had got on after them, and then walked up the aisle towards Jamie.

After her ticket was stamped, Jamie sank down into her seat and let her head loll back as the bullet train picked up speed. Her eyes drooped with the soothing rocking of the train but kept fluttering open. In twenty minutes, Tokyo's urban clutter turned to fields and she snuggled in, her leg on top of her suitcase, willing her eyes to close.

She thought of all that had happened since she heard of her father's death. It was one contorted, confusing dream, welling up into her mind, keeping her awake. She gave up trying to sleep and stared out the window at the rice fields and small towns flitting by in the pastel light of the sunrise.

What had her father written her? Following his instructions was one thing, but what else did he have to tell her on the scroll? She shook herself awake and dug in her bag. Her father's scroll fit on the foldout table in front of her. She rolled and unrolled it as she read.

Right away, she was impressed that her father had done so much. She had been the one who read her book in bed while her classmates snuck out of the dorm to meet boys, smoke pot, or play truth or dare. Maybe that's what he wanted for her—a life far from turmoil, but also far from challenges.

His power to accomplish things, and the directed, principled anger that motivated him, startled and confused her. It was so unlike her and her New York friends. They'd never been angry at anything. Didn't really know how.

As she read, she realized his life *had* been full of drama. Unlike hers, it was real drama—political conflicts and policy decisions, forging alliances and drafting treaties. He wasn't bragging about it, just letting her know. She tried to piece his story together, but there was too much history she didn't know. She knew few of the dates and almost none of the people or places he wrote about.

He was unforgiving of himself about drinking, bemoaning the opportunities and energy wasted. At first in New York she went out every night with friends to the city's best bars but ended up with more forgettable hangovers than memorable experiences.

He never did anything halfway. She herself had done everything that way—except this—taking his manuscript and running with it.

She wiped her tears off the scroll and rolled forward.

She was startled by the sharpness of what he remembered about her as a girl, his words stirring the memories of the pandas at Ueno zoo, museums with ghost *ukiyoe* exhibits, and old workshops where her father talked with the craftsmen before buying her a kite, wood toy, or hand fan. She had forgotten about the handmade boxes he bought her, dozens of them in all sizes, made of paulownia, paper, cherry bark. She stacked and re-stacked them endlessly, rearranging her bracelets, barrettes, and *omamori* charms. She wanted to find those boxes. She'd been a spoiled Tokyo girl, spoiled by him, and she had spoiled herself in New York, at least until her credit cards topped out.

When the announcement came for Osaka Station, Jamie got out of her seat and stretched. It'd be better to get a flight from Osaka instead. She didn't want to ride two or three more hours. She wanted to get on a plane and be gone. Jamie put the scroll back in her bag. She had to pee and wanted to throw her trash away. She got up from her seat and was halfway down the aisle to the toilets before her New York instincts kicked in and she went back for her suitcase.

She pulled on her father's jacket, rolled up the sleeves and tucked the travel bag over her shoulder so she could maneuver her suitcase. She left the seating area, looking back once to be sure she hadn't forgotten anything. She'd soon grab a taxi to Kansai Airport and be gone.

As the automatic doors slid shut behind her, Jamie tugged her bag past the luggage rack, exit doors and washroom to the toilet. She didn't see the Korean man in black pick up his hardshell backpack and follow her. As the automatic door opened for him, he looked back at his partner and nodded yes.

Sitting on the toilet, holding the handrail for balance, Jamie thought it odd that someone fiddled with the lock on the toilet from outside. She made sure the door was locked and pushed her bag away.

The rocking of the train had jiggled it up against her legs, making the small confines of the plastic-lined compartment feel even tighter.

As she flushed and stood up, the door pulled aside and she felt a hand around her throat. She gasped for breath and heard her own head smack the hard plastic wall before an ear-ringing slap on the side of her head made her blank out.

She let her jeans fall but thrust both her arms upward, trying to block another blow. She shook her head and through eyes wild with panic and blurred by tears she saw a short man with a mustache like dried grass raising his hand to hit her again.

She ducked and he shoved her harder against the wall as the door slid shut with scarcely room for the two of them and her bags inside. She tried to scream but choked and coughed as he slapped her again and again. She ripped at his face with her fingernails, but he bent her wrist hard to twist her around.

Then, she felt the grey duct tape across her mouth.

Ignoring her kicking and bucking, he looped tape around her arms and legs and the handrail. She dropped to the toilet floor, breathing deep and fast through her nose.

Her eyes dripping with fury, Jamie watched helplessly as he sliced open her bag with a knife and tossed the scroll on the floor. He pushed his hand down into the bag and pulled out her underclothes and the thick stacks of money, opened the box with the tea bowl, dropping them one by one, taking his time.

The past few days, she'd gone over the assault in her father's house a thousand times in her mind, replaying the scene until she figured out she should have pushed out when they taped her to create slack she could loosen later. This time, she had extended her limbs against the tape.

As the short Korean dug through her bag, she flexed her arms and legs in and out until she could feel the tape wrinkle and loosen enough for her to wiggle her fingers into her front pocket for the pepper spray Shibata gave her. She twisted the small can in the right direction until she could get her thumb on top of the button, waiting for the moment when his eyes moved her way again so she could let him have it.

Chapter 40

Hiroshi barely nodded at Takamatsu when they pulled up to where he was waiting in front of a convenience store near Kannai Station. He was too sore and too tired to do anything other than stare as Takamatsu put out his cigarette in a rusted ashtray, tossed out his can of coffee, and pulled off his camelhair overcoat, folding it neatly. Takamatsu leaned in to set his coat on the backseat next to Sakaguchi and got in.

"What took you so long?" Takamatsu asked.

"He almost got killed today," Sakaguchi said, nodding at Hiroshi up front.

"Sword." Ueno looked back at Takamatsu in the rearview mirror before pulling out of the streets around the station onto the Shuto expressway, a long twisting ribbon of highway devoid of traffic in the desolate hours of the morning.

"Street smarts is one thing you can't teach," Takamatsu said, peering over the seat at Hiroshi. "Was it the American? I know where he's going to be this morning," Takamatsu said, barely able to conceal his glee.

"I don't think so," Hiroshi said. "We left him inside Yokosuka Naval Base."

Takamatsu loosened his tie. "Did you know the Katsumura family is one of the oldest political dynasties in Japan?"

"What are you talking about?" Hiroshi was getting irritated.

"I'm talking about where we're going. Diet office building. Promptly at seven."

"Seven in the morning?" Hiroshi groaned, inventorying his body's aches, wondering if he could stay awake.

Takamatsu leaned to the side and caught Hiroshi's eye. "You tried bottom up, it didn't work, so let's try top down."

"The top's not so easy," Hiroshi said.

"Just the opposite," Takamatsu smiled. "They have more to lose. Reputation is everything for them. That woman I've been working for, Saori Ikeda—"

"The divorce case?" Hiroshi barely muffled his sarcasm.

"She owns and runs the *Kaiko Shukan*, Silkworm Weekly."

"I thought that was a horse racing paper," Ueno asked.

"That's *Kaiko Shumatsu*. Same company. Weekday is investigation. Weekend is racing and porn stars."

"And don't tell me, the owner is pretty and grateful and..." Hiroshi looked out the window.

Takamatsu smiled, pausing to think. "I'd say more handsome than pretty. She's going to Shinobu Katsumura's office this morning for a meeting. He'll be there."

"Gladius?" Hiroshi rubbed his face.

Ueno looked back at Takamatsu in the rearview mirror and said, "You're suggesting we go into a government building and interrogate a Diet member without prior approval?"

"Why not? We catch the killer at the end of the meeting. Everyone's happy." Takamatsu hummed a satisfied note or two.

Irritated with Takamatsu's smug, unruly approach, Hiroshi started to twist in the seat to say something, but the pain made him give up and settle back forward in the seat.

"Your body starting to set up?" Takamatsu asked. "You should keep moving. Don't stay in the same position. One time, I—"

Sakaguchi interrupted. "Chief Hirano is watching the base. The American can't get in or out without being seen, he assured us. So, it's better we catch some sleep, wait for him to poke his head out."

"There's a lot of ways he could get from the base into the city," Takamatsu said.

Everyone waited for him to explain, but he said nothing more.

"Mattson's daughter mentioned Katsumura, too." Hiroshi spoke to the ceiling to avoid twisting again.

"Of course, she did," Takamatsu said. "They have their fingers in everything. Her grandfather got elected to the Diet after the war.

Family owns a fair bit of Okinawa and another chunk of Yokosuka, publishing, transportation—"

"I know all that already," Hiroshi said. "How does the magazine woman know her?"

Takamatsu cracked the window and lit a cigarette. Hiroshi rolled his window down to stream the smoke out of the car and Ueno cracked his, turning the car instantly, bracingly cold.

Takamatsu blew smoke out the window. "She's had a long-running feud with the Katsumuras. Lawsuits back and forth."

"You want us to set up a scoop for a tabloid?" Hiroshi shook his head in the front seat, and even Ueno cleared his throat.

"She gets the scoop. We get the killer." Takamatsu shrugged, and then added, in badly accented English, "Win-win."

Hiroshi started to correct his English pronunciation, but let it go.

Takamatsu said, "This Saori Ikeda isn't afraid of anyone. She's provoked libel lawsuits from the Katsumuras and every corrupt family business in Japan. Her reporters get a bonus if their story results in legal action. She's lost every case so far but writes great retractions."

Sakaguchi growled. "And she's certain this American will be there?"

"The Katsumura family's publishing house is trying to buy Bernard Mattson's work to *not* publish it," Takamatsu explained. "Saori Ikeda found that out from a disgruntled former employee of Katsumura Publishing."

"I know that already," Hiroshi said. He could feel his bruises swelling and muscles tightening.

"Saori Ikeda wants the Silkworm Weekly to print Mattson's stuff as a serial exposé."

"We're not publishers. We're detectives," Hiroshi said.

Takamatsu leaned forward and laughed. "Oh, I thought you were just an accountant? Now, you're a detective? That street fight seems to have brought you around."

Hiroshi squirmed, too tired to quibble. "Trey can't get out of the base and all the way up to the Diet offices without being seen. Jamie left me a message she was supposed to meet Trey at the airport this afternoon for a flight to Guam."

"He's a busy guy," Takamatsu said.

Hiroshi's cellphone rang. He fumbled, stiffly, for the phone. He listened for a few seconds as Ueno accelerated though the light, early morning traffic. "Drop me off in Ginza," Hiroshi said. "I'll catch up with you before the meeting."

"That the Mattson girl?" Takamatsu chuckled.

Hiroshi frowned. "Things are more complicated than one girl."

"If that guy really is military, it gets complicated," Sakaguchi interrupted. "We'll go to the office, then to the airport. After that, we look for the girl. Maybe before then Hirano will call and give us a real tip." Sakaguchi rolled his coat up, put it under his head and went to sleep.

Takamatsu flicked his cigarette butt out the window. Once the smoke cleared, no one rolled their windows up, letting the air continue whipping through the car fast and cold.

* * *

Ueno let Hiroshi out in front of a department store in Ginza. Without even a wave, Jim Washington headed along the elevated train tracks at a quick pace. The small restaurants, bars and eateries under the tracks were all closed. Hiroshi's body was aching too much to catch up with Washington, who waited under the arched brickwork of a passageway. "Amazing the brick has held up all these years. Look at the ironwork bolted in. Great craftsmanship."

Hiroshi said, "Can we talk here? I'm worn out."

"Not enough sleep?"

"Sword fight."

"Really? I don't see you as a street fighter."

"I'm definitely not."

"Swords. Well, Japan always impresses me. But that kind of thing is all the more reason you need to come over to Interpol. You have a talent for getting things done in the office—out of harm's way."

"That sounds really good right now." Hiroshi looked down along the closed store fronts to see if anyone was following or not.

"This story will give you some street cred. Slip it in during your interview. My guy in Singapore found a whole lot of nothing on Trey Gladius."

"Nothing at all?"

"More nothing than any one person has a right to, so we changed tack. It's hard to expunge everything. We figured his records were missing for a reason."

"Which was...?"

"To cover up a smuggling operation through the military bases."

"Drugs?"

"You're thinking too small. Found a notice in Stars and Stripes that Gladius was supervisor of waste disposal."

"Waste? Disposal?" Hiroshi tried to stifle his confusion as he twisted this new piece around to see where it fit.

"The military keeps extensive, detailed records in multiple places. We also found his name as a military contractor."

"Contractor? For what?"

"Record keeping."

"Records? He's an accountant?"

"Like you. Or rather the opposite of you. Remember all that stuff that went missing in Iraq? Hundreds of thousands of weapons, shrink-wrapped stacks of cash, large weapons. Seems Gladius knows how to clean up the records—sales, supply stock, shipments, whatever needs to disappear. Including his past, apparently."

"I know the game. Deliver it, sell it, erase the record, move the cash, cover the trail."

"All with plausible deniability—accounting error, auditing oversight. The army doesn't want to be embarrassed by acknowledging that taxpayers' money, and the expensive military stuff it buys, can just disappear. Not a headline they want."

"But the stuff has to be somewhere."

"It disappears inside military bases."

"Disappears?"

"The records disappear. That's enough."

"Anything else you found?"

"We checked juvenile police records in Japan and Korea. Hits on both. He was an army brat. Yokosuka in Japan and Osan in Korea. Long police record for juvie stuff near Subic Bay. Quite a list there, assault, weapons sales, drugs. Maybe where he learned to street fight."

"He learned more after that."

"Martial arts?"

Hiroshi touched his aching body. "He must have learned Japanese and Korean when his father was stationed all around."

"Mother. I found a record for a lieutenant colonel, a single mother, Theresa Gladius. No record of anyone else with that last name. You say he killed someone?"

"Three people. And tried to kill me."

"That's why I want you over at Interpol. Use your brain, not your body."

Hiroshi followed Washington's gaze towards Shinbashi and back towards Ginza.

"One more thing. If he's military intelligence with a high clearance, there's not much you can do about him."

Hiroshi's cellphone buzzed. He patted his pocket but let it ring through.

"Asian Interpol chief's arriving from Singapore tomorrow. We've got your interview all set."

"I'll be ready."

"You'll be a shoo-in," Washington said and walked off along the tracks, the only person moving towards Shinbashi in the cold winter streets before dawn.

Chapter 41

When Hiroshi got back to the car parked near the Diet building, he saw Ueno walking back from a convenience store with a plastic shopping bag. Even at a distance in the foggy morning, he could see the bag was full of *onigiri* rice balls and hot cans of tea. Hiroshi felt suddenly, immensely hungry. Ueno plopped the bag on the hood of the car and went back to the convenience store. He came out carrying three large instant noodle cups, steam rising from them into the humid air.

Hiroshi helped arrange them on the hood of the car and dug through the rice balls, pulled out his favorite flavor, salmon, and opened the layered plastic wrap. He stirred the boiled water in one of the noodle cups and bent the top back down to let it simmer, wrapping his hands around the cup to warm up.

Sakaguchi tumbled out of the back seat of the car, rubbed his face and stretched muscle group by muscle group in the middle of the empty street. Squatting and rising, he performed a few *shiko* leg stomps, slapping his thick thighs, until sweat beaded on his brow. Finished with his routine, he plucked a pair of chopsticks out of the bag, nodded thanks to Ueno and dug into the noodles, slurping loudly in the early morning silence.

Takamatsu returned from a nearby glass-partitioned smoking area, but didn't even look at the food, instead frowning at how rumpled and wrinkled everyone was. Takamatsu's European suit and tailored shirt were clean and pressed, his camelhair coat pristine.

Sakaguchi took the last *onigiri* rice ball, dunked it in and slurped down the rice-broth in big gulps. Ueno gathered the trash and threw it out in the convenience store trash bins.

Sakaguchi opened the trunk and took out a small side-handle baton, a *jutte* sword catcher, and kevlar gloves, then set them back.

"What if he has a sword?" Takamatsu asked.

Sakaguchi said nothing but handed Ueno and Hiroshi telescoping batons and handcuffs.

"Wish I had these with me the other day," Hiroshi mused.

Takamatsu patted his coat to check on his baton.

All four of them looked at the two New Nambu .38 special pistols holstered in a locked rack.

"You're going to call the chief?" Ueno asked.

Takamatsu shook his head. "He'll have the whole department over here."

Hiroshi said, "I've never passed my shooting certification."

Sakaguchi looked longingly at the pistols. "If Gladius *is* in there, we can't shoot up the office. If he isn't in there, we'll have a major violation to explain. Sword or not, batons and handcuffs only." He shut the trunk with the pistols inside and the four detectives walked to the front door of the Diet Office Building.

Hiroshi, Sakaguchi, Takamatsu and Ueno flipped their badges and walked straight through the metal detector. It sounded off—loud—and Takamatsu told the guards, "It's just our badges. Don't worry."

The guards followed them to the elevator, flustered, demanding they sign in, but Sakaguchi pressed the button and held up his badge. One of the guards called his superior on his headset, but when the elevator arrived, the four detectives got on. Upstairs, the carpet-muffled hall was quiet and empty in the early morning.

At Shinobu Katsumura's office, Sakaguchi flashed his badge at the secretary, who stood up from her desk in the high-ceilinged waiting room, waving her hand for them to stop. Sakaguchi breezed past the startled secretary and pulled open the large oak door into the office. The other detectives came in after him, ready.

Shinobu Katsumura disguised her surprise at the four detectives with a look of poised contempt.

The other woman in the room—publisher, magazine owner and recent divorcée, Saori Ikeda—tried to look surprised. Her chic suit and knit sweater fit tight over her compact, well-toned body. Hiroshi thought Takamatsu had, for once, understated a woman's attractiveness. He snapped back to surveying the room, but there was no sign of Trey Gladius.

In the politest Japanese, Sakaguchi said, "Katsumura *san*, we are from the Tokyo Metropolitan Homicide Division and we have a few questions."

Shinobu straightened herself and said, "Homicide? That's a new one."

Saori Ikeda glanced at Takamatsu with apology in her eyes that Gladius was not there.

"Ikeda-*san*," Shinobu said. "Could we continue our conversation another time? The secretary will show you out."

"I think I'll stay. As you just told me, you don't have anything to hide." Saori Ikeda straightened up and looked interested.

Shinobu's tight lips forced a thin smile. She took Sakaguchi's name card, read it and invited them to sit down with a polite wave of her hand. "What is this about, detectives?"

The four detectives remained standing and instinctively spread out a step or two. Hiroshi stepped forward, letting Sakaguchi and Takamatsu stand to the side, a little behind, with Ueno by the door.

In the most formal Japanese, Hiroshi asked, "Could you tell us the nature of your relationship with Trey Gladius?"

"Trey Gladius works with several ministries and Diet members finding materials and translating them for Diet members. He's fluent in Japanese. It's rare to find an American like him."

"He may be involved in serious crimes. Trey Gladius introduced you to Jamie Mattson for what purpose?" Hiroshi asked, though he knew the answer, or thought he did.

"My uncle's publishing firm is going to publish Bernard Mattson's works. Jamie signed over her father's work for publication. Maybe she just wanted the money, but my impression was she wanted to do something good for her father, and for Japan. Gladius is, was, helping with that."

Hiroshi cleared his throat and straightened his jacket, wondering if his clothes looked as bad as he felt. "We have to examine every possibility related to Mattson."

Shinobu's eyebrows peaked to a "V" and she shook her head. "Such a loss to both countries, his death. Have you found who did it?"

"We're looking at why." Hiroshi paused, staring at Shinobu. "Mattson uncovered evidence of collusion and corruption at the American bases. He was going to reveal what really happened after the Fukushima meltdown."

Shinobu looked unperturbed. "It seems you must be reading Ikeda-*san*'s scandal magazine! I haven't read what Mattson wrote, so I'm not able to say, but I can't understand why you're coming to my office so early in the morning to ask about this."

"We believe that Mattson, and two other people, were killed," Hiroshi paused to let the words sink in. "To suppress his book. Buying the rights to his work means you could be in danger."

"Now you're saying you're here to protect me?" Shinobu's voice went up a pitch. "All I know is that my uncle's publishing house planned to edit and publish the work. You said someone else was also killed in connection to this?"

"Surely, you know the name, Higa?"

"He was a worthy adversary, misguided as he was on the issues. He published articles with your magazine, too, didn't he?" Shinobu looked at Saori Ikeda.

Saori Ikeda smiled. "He always wrote under a pseudonym. He was a bit paranoid."

Hiroshi said, "Higa was going to be Mattson's editor. It would seem the publisher might be next on the list."

"That seems fanciful," Shinobu said. Her voice rose higher. "How does this connect to Trey Gladius?"

Hiroshi held her gaze without replying.

Shinobu frowned and shook her head. "As for Trey Gladius, if he broke laws, arrest him. For us, he was a translator and go-between. I don't know much about him other than that."

"Oh, there's more you might know," Hiroshi said. "You are involved with the renegotiation of the American bases and treaties next week."

"It's one of my duties in the Diet," Shinobu said.

"With the protests gaining steam, the Americans must be willing to offer something new, something more, to keep the bases in Japan."

Shinobu stood with her hand on the top of the leather chairs in the center of the room, her face unrevealing. "The negotiations are always smooth."

"But with Mattson's death so close to the conference, it might be different this time. For you, I mean. And for your family's businesses."

"As the Silkworm Weekly always reminds everyone, my family runs a diverse range of businesses. But I'm in the Diet, not in business."

Hiroshi continued, "Your family's waste management company bid on a contract to transport and store waste from Fukushima. That's billions of yen."

Shinobu laughed. "Well, I see the police conspiracy theories are as absurd as those silly protesters. At least the scandal magazines make a profit from speculation." Shinobu took a breath and recomposed herself. "Look, every politician helps with contracts that benefit Japan. All of this is public record."

"Gladius helped negotiate many of the contracts," Hiroshi knew he was moving away from what he knew for sure but pushing her was important. "If he's involved, and he's connected to you, it's not going to look good for your political career, or for your family's reputation."

Shinobu's penciled eyebrows, delicate features and refined gestures closed down. "The status quo is more powerful in Japan than in any country in the world. Japanese tend to change their ideas slowly."

"But they change," Hiroshi added.

Saori Ikeda, who had been listening quietly and attentively to all this, spoke up. "When Mattson's work comes out in print, people will be able to decide for themselves."

Shinobu patted the top of the leather chair she was standing behind. "Well, you'll have to find what he wrote, because I don't have it. His daughter, Jamie, didn't give us anything more than her father's sketches."

Hiroshi looked confused. He felt sure the Katsumura's had the work, rightly or wrongly. But maybe they didn't. Maybe they'd been tricked. But by Gladius, or by Jamie?

Sakaguchi's phone rang. He picked it up and his stony sumo face broke into a barely concealed grin. He hung up and nodded for them to go.

"Trey Gladius told me he was catching a late afternoon flight to Guam," Shinobu said.

There it was. Finally. Takamatsu was right again, Hiroshi had to admit. With the right pressure, she coughed up a scapegoat to put distance between her and trouble. She was old-school politics, survival of the safest.

Shinobu smiled confidently. "We nominated Mattson for the honorary Japanese Order of the Rising Sun. Sad that it's posthumous, but he deserves it. I heard he'll receive a Japan Foundation award too. The media will be all over this story."

"Japanese do love happy endings," Saori Ikeda agreed with a shrug. "Maybe because there's so few of them."

"Can you tell me where Jamie went after she talked to you last night?" Hiroshi asked.

"How do you know she talked with me?" Shinobu frowned.

Hiroshi waited for Shinobu's answer since she was dispensing information so freely to keep herself insulated from trouble.

Shinobu leaned forward on the leather chair propping her up. "Jamie told me she was going to Kyoto. She must be there already. She left last night."

Sakaguchi turned to the door, his thick arm waving them out.

"It must be hard in politics to know who to trust," Hiroshi said, as Sakaguchi tugged him and the others towards the door. "But it's even harder as a detective."

The detectives filed out one by one, Ueno, the only one who bowed, going last.

Chapter 42

Leaning up from the floor of the *shinkansen* toilet, Jamie cocked her arm and shot a stream of pepper spray straight at the short Korean. The bright orange goo slathered across his face like a poisonous orange snake. Startled, he wiped it downward—fatefully spreading it—and looked down at the orange resin cupped in his hand. In the second before it kicked in, he dropped Jamie's stuff and looked at her. Jamie flexed against the duct tape and splattered another thick orange ribbon right across his eyes.

He dropped the backpack, the initial surprise over. He clawed at his face. His eyes and nose erupted in tears and mucus. He doubled over hacking and spewing and flailing his arms for a sink, for a towel, for toilet paper, but his hands found only useless air in the small compartment. As on all *Shinkansen* bullet trains, the sink, with its flow of water, was located in a separate area outside.

Jamie watched him struggling before managing to pull the corner of her father's jacket over her face in protection. She coughed and spit as she pushed her hand to her mouth to pull the tape off far enough to breathe through her mouth. The pepper spray spread through the air of the small cabin.

The short Korean finally found a T-shirt from Jamie's bag to wipe his face, but that only worked the swelling, choking, burning deeper. He tossed it down, completely blinded, twisting and banging against the walls of the toilet, cursing in Korean, fumbling for the door handle. He kicked her hand by accident, and the spray can rolled out of reach.

Jamie heard the other Korean outside in the passageway, so she tried desperately to prepare for him. When he squeezed himself in and yanked the door shut, Jamie sighted as carefully as she could through the glaze of tears, coiled herself and aimed a kick at his balls. Her tight-taped legs sprung and connected but only reached his thigh.

Before she could try again, a straight-on punch ricocheted her head against the wall. She felt the pain deep inside her skull, felt him straddling her body. Her head felt distant, spinning and throbbing. She heard the crack of something opening and felt air roar in from some outside vent, making it easier to breathe. When she got her eyes to refocus, she saw the shorter guy's face knotted into one tight, red, wet glob.

The taller Korean pulled the door open, looked both ways into the hall and—careful not to touch him—led the shorter man to the small curtained-off sink in the corridor. He pushed the faucet to start the water flowing. Back inside the toilet, he tied a handkerchief over his face, careful not to touch any of the vicious orange goo and tossed clothes over Jamie's head.

Jamie's ears stopped ringing and her head started to clear. She heard the empty can of pepper spray rolling back and forth with the rhythm of the train, and twisted her wrists in the manacle of tape, loosening them, but not enough to free her arm. She heard the taller Korean moving the scrolls from her bag, the wood rods clacking. She listened, helplessly, as he pulled out the stacks of tight-wrapped cash and tucked them into his hard-shell backpack, going through her stuff right beside her.

Outside, a train conductor passed by. Hearing spluttering and sniveling, he peered behind the curtain of the sink area to find a short guy rinsing his face and washing his hands over and over. The conductor sniffed the strange smell in the air, and let the curtain fall back. He checked his watch. Ten minutes to Osaka. The conductor reset his cap, ignoring the guy who was no doubt still drunk from the night before.

Inside the toilet, Jamie kept her eyes on the tall Korean going through her things. She felt like she was underwater and out of breath, her body soaked with sweat. She blinked back the stream of tears and stared at him furiously. When he knelt down and pinched her jaw, she spit in his face.

He reeled back and she coiled and tried to knee his stomach, but he dodged and she felt the punches on her head again and again until her body flopped out motionless. The sound of the train, of the man, of the air rushing in, fell to a distant hush. Her body started rocking gently with the sway of the train.

* * *

The tall Korean thief tied her tightly against the handrails and dropped a shirt over her head. He went through her pockets and patted her down, finding nothing.

The announcement for Osaka came over the speakers: "Ladies and Gentlemen, we will arrive at Osaka Shinkansen terminal in a few minutes. Those passengers transferring to local Osaka train lines should please detrain here. After a brief stop, the train will continue, making stops at Kobe, Okayama, Hiroshima, and Kokura before the final stop, Hakata. Please do not forget your belongings."

He looked at his watch, two minutes to Osaka, and went through her pockets again. He then unbuttoned her pants and dug around inside her underwear, looking for what he had been tasked to find. He pushed up her sweatshirt, unbuttoned her shirt, pulled up her T-shirt, and there, tucked inside the full, round swell of her bra was what he wanted—the USB drive.

He snatched it, admiring her for a moment, but the pepper spray was catching up with him. He tucked the USB into his front pocket and reached up to a small cabinet by the ceiling, pried it open with the pliers, removed the "Out of Order" sign. In the passageway, he slid the sign onto the handle and twisted the outside lock to "Occupied" with the pliers. He tossed the pliers and handkerchief in the trash by the door and pulled the backpack over his shoulder.

The few passengers getting off in Osaka were already lining up at the doors as the train slowed from three hundred kilometers an hour to zero. The short Korean had his cap pulled low over his face and his jacket collar up. He zipped up his leather jacket to hide his shirtfront drenched with tea, tears and snot. As the train came to a halt, the short Korean, unable to see, rested his hand on the shoulder of the tall Korean and followed with mincing steps.

They rode the escalator down and crossed the open lobby of the station. But before they could get onto the escalator back up to the Tokyo-bound platform, a sturdy bonsai of a man dressed in Japanese *hakama* stuck the sharp point of a small sword into the back of the taller one, far enough to let him know there was a lot more blade, not so deep as to make him cry out. The loose, low-hanging sleeves of the traditional jacket kept the sword well hidden from view, but a shake of the arm would ready it for a full swing.

"Over to the toilet," commanded Suzuki, the Shinjuku sword-dealer. "Slowly and carefully."

Driven by the sharp pain of the metal in his flesh, the taller thief moved forward with the shorter following in dainty, uncertain steps, doing what he was told, what the blade ensured.

When the taller Korean entered the bathroom, he lunged forward to get the tip of the sword out of his back, but Suzuki reeled back and drove the butt of his sword into the back of his skull, midway between ear and spine.

The quick, sure blow sent him sprawling. His head careened off the toilet bowl as he thumped face down on the floor of the stall. Two quick follow-up strikes rendered him immobile.

Suzuki watched the tall man slide into unconsciousness and then turned to the shorter Korean, blindly swaying in front of the stall. Suzuki stepped back and stabbed the meat of his shoulder to guide him into the stall. He stumbled on his partner's feet and put his hands out to steady himself. A single pop with the sword handle on the back of his head dropped him like a *tameshigiri* practice mat on top of his partner.

Slipping his sword back inside his Japanese overcoat, Suzuki reset himself and smoothed down his neat-cut ponytail before looking through their pockets. In the last pocket of the taller guy he found the USB drive. He put it inside the sleek hardshell backpack, an odd contrast with his crisp-pressed pleats, black jacket and *zori* sandals.

At the sink, he rinsed off the remains of the pepper spray from the pack, wiped it down with paper towels, and walked out of the toilet into the human tumult of morning rush hour, the other commuters around him beelining to their destinations inside the indifferent orbits of their own day's business.

Chapter 43

Hiroshi slapped the retractable baton in his palm all the way to Narita Airport. Ueno slowed the car and eased around the hotel buses, shuttles, private cars and taxis unloading suitcases and passengers. Hiroshi thought back to his *kendo* at college, and then stopped thinking about it. He had to act, not think.

Sakaguchi finished his cellphone call and turned to the others. "Chief Hirano said Trey slipped out on a military shuttle. They caught sight of him on a camera at the tollbooth for the Tokyo Bay Aqua Line. He must be here already. Airport security's supposed to meet us."

Out of the trunk, they pulled handcuffs, batons, kevlar gloves and *jutte* sword catchers. Takamatsu and Ueno went with airport security guards to the check-in counters while Hiroshi and Sakaguchi headed downstairs to the military liaison office.

In the second basement, a small square sign, "DOD L.O.," pointed down a deserted hallway with plate glass windows covered in paper. At a T-intersection, a new sign pointed to the only office along a vacated hallway that smelled of fresh paint.

Hiroshi pushed open the doors with Sakaguchi right behind.

Trey was leaning on a counter with a cup of coffee in hand. Behind the counter, three American officers in uniforms and buzz cuts stood up straight from their desks when the detectives slammed in. The officer nearest the counter asked, "Can we help you? This is a restricted area."

Hiroshi ignored him, staring at Trey. "Three murders, two assaults, stolen goods and illegal exports."

Sakaguchi stepped towards three large vinyl duffel bags on a cheap black couch beside a water cooler. Across the bags was Trey's long black leather coat.

Hiroshi walked up to Trey. Under the harsh gleam of lights, Trey's dimples looked shallow and worn, his light blue eyes filmy and distant.

Hiroshi said, "You're coming with us to the station."

The officers cleared their throats and looked from Hiroshi to Trey. One of them picked up the phone to call for orders while Trey closed his eyes and slowly opened them into a glare. "You Japanese just don't get it, do you?"

Hiroshi pulled out his handcuffs. "Turn around!"

Trey didn't move. Sakaguchi stepped forward as Hiroshi reached for Trey's arm.

"Sir, this is a restricted area belonging to the US Military—" one of the officers behind the counter said, as Hiroshi grabbed for Trey's arm. Before Hiroshi could even touch him, Trey spun his body and caught Hiroshi hard in the nose with his elbow. Hiroshi reeled, the pain reigniting the other lingering pains.

Hiroshi wiped his eyes and saw Trey leap towards his coat. Hiroshi grabbed Trey by the shoulders and pulled him backwards over the coffee table, scattering copies of *Stars and Stripes, Guns and Ammo,* and *USA Today.* Hiroshi fell over the duffle bags on the couch. Beneath him, Hiroshi could tell the odd, long, shifting shapes inside the bags were swords.

Sakaguchi shoved his arm into Trey's chest, unbalancing him, and repeated *tsukidashi* arm thrusts until Trey was backed against the wall. In the blur of the attack, neither Trey nor Sakaguchi saw the sword come out. Hiroshi held the gleaming silver blade straight at Trey's throat and everyone froze.

"Like being on the other end of a sword?" Hiroshi said.

Trey sneered. "Don't pull a sword unless you're ready to use it. First principle."

"What's the second?"

"Hiroshi," Sakaguchi said, his hand out towards Hiroshi's arm.

"Sir," one of the officers said as they stood on either side of Sakaguchi. Hiroshi held the sword steady on Trey's neck. Hiroshi felt ready—very ready—to accept the consequences of his actions. His rage flowing into the blade, Hiroshi held Trey transfixed.

Trey's eyes moved from the tip of the blade to Hiroshi's stomach, hands and head, searching for the slightest inattention that might let him dodge away. The sword stayed a wrist-flick away from Trey's jugular vein and carotid artery.

"You killed them, didn't you?" Hiroshi said.

"Them?"

"Mattson—"

"I didn't, no."

"So, you ordered him killed."

Trey looked at Hiroshi. "Treason is a crime. Releasing classified documents."

"Mattson was researching the bases, opening their secrets."

Trey swallowed. "If he released what he planned to release, he would have scuttled SOFA and jeopardized the bases. Mattson knew better."

Hiroshi held the sword without a quiver. "And the thief in the alley? The writer Higa?"

Trey kept his head steady, trying to control his breathing. "Higa's work? Paranoid anarchist rants. And the thief? You'd have put him in prison."

Hiroshi pressed the blade onto the flesh of Trey's neck.

Trey looked in Hiroshi's eyes. "You won't use the sword. I know your kind."

"Sakaguchi, open his bags and get Mattson's stuff out," Hiroshi commanded.

From inside the first duffel bag, Sakaguchi pulled out five swords wrapped in silk. He set them on the coffee table.

His eyes still locked on Hiroshi's, Trey held his body stock-still except for the strange smile spreading across his face. Sakaguchi dug inside the other bags. The first held clothing, the second, scuba diving equipment.

Sakaguchi turned the clothing inside out and then did the same with the masks, fins, snorkel, and wet suit. Out of the corner of his eye, Hiroshi could see Sakaguchi's empty hands.

"Where are they?" Hiroshi demanded, the tip of the blade against the skin of Trey's throat. "The computers, the documents, everything you stole?"

Trey looked at Hiroshi, without moving.

"You thought you could keep it all secret," Hiroshi said, resetting his feet. "But you can't hide radiation."

"No one cares about that. They only care about being told the right bedtime story. Everyone's slept well so far."

"They won't any longer."

Trey turned his head and looked at Sakaguchi, and in the flicker of an instant Hiroshi's eyes followed. Trey high-kicked Hiroshi in the ribs and dodged sideways.

As Hiroshi swung, Trey shoved the water cooler forward and the sword plunged into the large plastic jug, sending water cascading over the bags and across the floor.

Hiroshi swung again as Trey lunged for one of the swords on the table. Before he could get one, Hiroshi swung straight down, barely missing Trey's arm. Trey pulled back against the wall and Hiroshi reset the tip of the blade against his neck. His body stock-still, Trey's face tensed.

"You killed them, didn't you?" Hiroshi said, louder. "Mattson, the thief and Higa."

Trey looked Hiroshi in the eye.

Sakaguchi said, "Hiroshi, put down the sword."

Hiroshi held Trey where he was, unflinching in his control, soothed by the surety of the sword, the sharp finality of its edge, its ease of use.

"Hiroshi," Sakaguchi said in a low, even voice. "The documents aren't here. Put the sword down."

The outside door swung open. In the doorway was a tall American officer with the angry look of someone used to commanding situations. His epaulettes and gold buttons glinted as he raked the cap off his head. Another American officer stood behind him. Everyone looked his way except Hiroshi, who kept his eyes on Trey.

"What's going on here?" the officer shouted, his tours of duty written in the lines on his face, his rank in the colored pins on his chest.

No one moved.

"Gladius! What is this?" the officer shouted at Trey. "Every time I work with you something goes wrong."

Sakaguchi said, "Hiroshi, put it down."

Hiroshi kept the sword against Trey's flesh.

Jamison barked at Hiroshi. "I'm Major Jamison, ranking officer here, military intelligence, and I'm telling you to put that sword down. Now. This is a secure area."

Sakaguchi said again, "Put it down."

Takamatsu, Ueno and two Japanese officers in dark blue suits burst into the room.

Hiroshi didn't waver. He could sense Takamatsu taking a step towards him, one hand up, but Takamatsu, for once, stayed silent.

Hiroshi stood there in a space that was in Japan, but not of Japan, wavering between languages, societies, times, codes of justice— oppositions poised on the sharp edge of the blade in his hand. His mind raced between what he felt and what he knew, what he knew and what he could prove. All he really knew was that the sword caught the light from the harsh overhead bulbs and measured the distance between him and another man, between another man's life and his blood-soaked death.

And then, Hiroshi lowered the sword, slowly, in one hand, every- one in the room watching it descend until the point rested on the linoleum below.

As soon as the sword touched the floor, the American soldiers lunged at Hiroshi. Sakaguchi and Takamatsu leapt at the soldiers, everyone slipping on the water spilled from the cooler across the floor. Ueno picked up one of the soldiers by the arm and shoved him aside. The soldier slipped, scrambled and leapt onto Ueno's back. Takamatsu fumbled for his baton but a too-quick punch knocked it from his hands and he started swinging with his fists for all he was worth. The Kevlar gloves and defensive tools stayed uselessly in the pockets of the detectives. Everyone pulled, grabbed, shoved and punched each other in one great mass in the middle of the room, shouting—"Stop," "*Yamero*," "Bastard," "*Ii kagen ni shiro*," "Enough," "*Yurusene*"—in a dense tangle of limbs and languages that careened in one direction and then the other.

Finally, Sakaguchi rose up from the middle of the pack, spinning his arms and elbows in a circle to separate them all. The Japanese detectives and American soldiers stood back separated, breathing heavy, hands at the ready, facing each other.

Major Jamison shouted. "All right, all right."

"This man is not going to leave the country," Hiroshi said, panting for breath.

"Our policy is to cooperate with the police in all matters, but to question him you need to file an application," the major said.

"He'll be charged with murder and attempted murder."

"This office is part of the extraterritoriality agreement," Jamison said. "It's American territory. Even if Trey were formally charged as a suspect, we would still need to question him first. That's how it's been for sixty years."

Sakaguchi stood back, pulled out his cellphone and dialed the chief.

"He's a military employee? What's his status?" Hiroshi demanded.

Jamison turned to Trey, exasperated, "What is it this time around, Gladius?"

"I work for IARPA under the ODNI," Trey said.

"A string of letters?" Hiroshi asked.

"IARPA is Intelligence Advanced Research Projects Activity. And ODNI is the Office of the Director of National Intelligence. Senior Specialist in the East Asian division," Trey explained.

"As an operative, you killed those men on orders, or you did it on your own?" Hiroshi demanded.

Jamison sighed and shook his head. "The agreements clearly state, any American service member accused of a crime must be handed over to United States jurisdiction, and shall remain in that jurisdiction, until charged. Gladius goes with me. He's translating in Korea at nineteen hundred hours."

Jamison looked directly at Hiroshi, who hadn't budged, and continued, "Article nine, section two says: Members of the United States Armed Forces shall be exempt from Japanese passport and visa laws and regulations."

The two Japanese officers in dull blue suits who'd come in earlier with Takamatsu and Ueno, nodded at the swords and went to inspect them. Trey jumped towards his luggage. "Whoa, hold up there. Those are my bags."

"Customs office," the two men said simply as they started inventorying what Trey had planned to carry out of the country. One of the officers pulled out a confiscation order from his breast pocket and tossed it at Trey. Hiroshi was glad to see the customs officers, knowing they had received an anonymous tip about national treasures being smuggled out of the country.

Trey tried to block the officers, but Jamison yelled at him. "Gladius, back off! Your swords are the least of it. Our Air Mobility Command Flight leaves in three quarters of an hour and it takes that much time to get to the gate."

The two customs inspectors wrapped up the swords. Hiroshi nodded at Trey's leather jacket. The officers pulled out the short sword tucked in its lining and placed it next to the others.

Jamison turned towards the door. "We have a flight. North Korea's starting something. We need to be in Seoul ASAP."

Sakaguchi put away his cellphone and shook his head no at Hiroshi. "The chief says if he's military, we can't hold him unless you have evidence in hand."

Trey stuffed his clothes, and what he could of the scuba gear, into the bag, and slung it over his shoulder. With the heavy bag weighing him down, Trey never saw the roundhouse punch coming. Hiroshi socked Trey so hard his head rebounded off the wall and his knees buckled. He slouched down on one knee, clutching his head, stunned.

Hiroshi pulled back for a second punch, but Takamatsu and Sakaguchi were there in an instant, holding Hiroshi back by both arms.

"You done now?" Jamison asked. "Gladius, you are more trouble than you're worth."

Trey stood up and spit a bloody wad of thick saliva into what was left of the potted plant and followed Jamison and the other officer out the door.

Hiroshi watched them go.

Takamatsu lit a cigarette and inhaled deeply, patting Hiroshi on the back. "You know, maybe you *can* teach street smarts."

Chapter 44

Hiroshi met Suzuki in front of the *shinkansen* ticket counter inside Tokyo Station. They both tucked the heavy black bags they carried behind them and bowed to each other in the middle of the congested passageway, commuters politely sidestepping the most fundamental Japanese ritual. Amid the gleaming tiles and chrome pillars of the station, the pressed suits and bright overcoats, Suzuki's *hakama* and sandals looked straight out of old Edo.

"I couldn't be in two places," Suzuki said. "So, it was better to leave her on the train. I called the transit police as soon as I could."

Hiroshi set his bag down with an understanding nod. "The police called from Fukuoka."

Suzuki handed the hardshell backpack to Hiroshi. "That little computer thing is in there, too. No swords, though."

"My miscalculation." Hiroshi swung the black duffel bag of swords confiscated from Trey onto the floor in front of them.

Suzuki lifted the bag, gauging its weight. "Six swords."

"Five. We took the *tanto* as evidence."

Suzuki pulled the duffel bag over his shoulder. "I'll buff these up. Then we can decide where to send them."

"You were right about not being Japanese until you use a sword," Hiroshi said.

"Did you use one?"

Hiroshi looked away. He pictured himself using the sword on Trey's neck, the body crumpling on the ground, split open with the vital life pumping out until the corpse was dry and cold and unmoving.

Suzuki smoothed his ponytail. "Miyamoto Musashi said the ultimate aim of martial arts should be *not* using them. Mastery over the self is harder than mastery over the sword."

Hiroshi thought that over, knowing it was true.

"How did you know the girl would go to the Diet office?" Suzuki asked.

"Lucky guess. All my other guesses were wrong."

"One is all you need sometimes."

Hiroshi waited for a smile or some change on Suzuki's face, but none came. Suzuki said, "Stop by the shop after I refurbish these. We can try them out."

"I will," Hiroshi assured him, and promised himself he would this time.

Suzuki settled the duffel bag over his shoulder, turned neatly and walked off into the stream of commuters. They swept around him, parting and rejoining until Hiroshi could no longer see his black *hakama* and grey ponytail in the endless human flow of the station.

At the *shinkansen* gate, Hiroshi showed his badge to the conductor. On the platform, he watched the long white train glide into the station as if floating on air. It was one of the new models, with a scoop-nosed design that was even sleeker and leaner. He walked along the platform looking at the numbers of the cars. The cleaners rushed onto the train wiping and straightening the interior in a flurry of sprays, rags and mini vacuum cleaners, readying it for its return journey.

And then, at the far end of the platform, her hair tangled, eyes swollen, arm in a splint, she was there. She moved so stiffly, like a ghost in an old woodblock print, that he wasn't sure for a moment if she really was there. But she was. Limping and unsteady, but there. Hiroshi had to make an effort *not* to look away. She set down the bag the police had lent her and stretched her neck.

Hiroshi walked towards Jamie. She had not seen him yet. When she saw him at last, she moved towards him and embraced him. With hesitant motions, he wrapped his arms around her. Her body felt frail and light, and she shook slightly. He held her for a moment, wondering why no police officer had escorted her. Jamie gathered herself and pulled her head back to look in his eyes, stalled for words. Her face, covered in bruises, looked like a purple-green-yellow version of herself. In one eye, the white had hemorrhaged to a dark red.

"Why didn't you answer my calls?" Hiroshi held her shoulders and looked in her eyes, unbalanced by the blood in one, and tried to understand what was going on inside her. Was she as beat up inside as she was outside? Hiroshi hugged her again.

Jamie looked away. "I wanted to get to New York, but I didn't even get to Osaka."

"Why didn't you let me know? What were you going to do?"

Jamie looked up at him, her eyes searching for a way to explain.

"You just left?" Hiroshi sounded angrier than he meant to.

Jamie shook her head no. "I didn't *just* leave."

"Was it Trey?"

"It was the USB. With the manuscript. His speech. I lost it all."

Hiroshi slung around the backpack Suzuki had just handed him and held it out towards her.

Jamie looked up at him, and whimpered with relief, pain and gratitude, leaning forward hands outstretched for the backpack. Hiroshi set it down on the platform in front of her. She zipped open the top and ruffled through it. She pulled out the scroll from her father, clutched it to her chest and rocked back and forth.

Hiroshi looked at the scroll. "What is that?"

"It's my father."

Around them the platform was quickly filling up with passengers for the next train lining up inside the boarding marks painted on the platform.

Hiroshi took her arm, delicately, his own body hurting as much as hers. He slipped the backpack over his shoulder and started slowly walking her towards the brick exit of the old station. Halfway there, she stopped.

"It's in the pack," Hiroshi said, gently pressing her to keep moving towards the exit. "I sent someone to change the locks and install a security system at your father's house. Before I take you there, we need to make one stop."

They got in a taxi and rode in silence, each looking out the windows on their side. Hiroshi had the odd feeling they were stuck in one place and the city was rushing by. He was too exhausted to tell what was moving and what not. Tokyo looked different, felt different, but whipped by outside as if it would never change.

When the cab pulled up in the circular drive, Jamie looked confused. "I don't need to go to the hospital. I need to go home."

"Just come inside," Hiroshi said, helping her out.

Hiroshi led Jamie along the antiseptic hallways until they got to the room. He stopped at the door and steered Jamie inside.

In the bed, Shibata opened his eyes and, seeing Jamie, smiled. "You okay!" His round head, swathed in bandages, bobbed with relief. One of his arms was in a cast and the other had an IV held by white strips of tape. Tugging against the tape, he held both arms out as wide as he could.

Jamie hobbled over to give him a careful hug. "I went by the club. I thought—"

"Little misunderstand," Shibata said, fiddling with the bed adjustment button. "Your father got in big fight one night after war. I try help. My arm got broke. Your father sneak me in army hospital. Save me. Second time broke arm. You not hurt?"

Tears started as she spoke. "They hurt you looking for me, right? I should have—"

"Always bad people. That is life."

Jamie held Shibata's hand and turned to Hiroshi. "I don't know why I tried to do it alone. I wanted to *do* something, for once, by myself."

Jamie turned back to Shibata and leaned over him, her tears falling.

"You getting my bandage wet," Shibata laughed.

"Where's Ken?" Jamie asked, wiping her nose with her hand.

Shibata looked away.

"*Where is he*?" Jamie said, stricken.

"He lose two fingers. Sword." Shibata wiggled his fingers in the air.

"In the fight? Because of me?" Jamie asked.

"His family rich, take him to hospital, Sendai, hometown." Shibata patted Jamie's arm with his one good hand, consoling her over his loss.

Jamie looked at him, still crying, and then slipped to the floor. Hiroshi dropped the backpack and caught her before her head hit anything. Barely able to bend over himself, he struggled to pull her up, but maneuvered her into the bedside chair. Her body went slack, tears coursing down her face. He started to call a nurse when one entered from the hall. Jamie could no longer answer. "Keep talking to her," the nurse said and went to get a doctor.

"Just relax. You better get checked out. And you need to sleep. You're safe now. Your father's stuff is here," Hiroshi murmured to her, softly, soothingly.

The nurse returned with a doctor and another nurse and a wheelchair. They slid Jamie into the wheelchair and wheeled her to a room at the end of the corridor. Hiroshi followed, standing aside as they checked her vitals and scrutinized the bruises on her head. The nurse gave Hiroshi forms to fill out, but he did not know many of her personal details. The doctor said Jamie needed an MRI and Hiroshi nodded okay.

The two nurses put an IV in her and pulled the curtain to get her out of her clothes and into a gown. When they wheeled her out, Hiroshi took her hand.

She rubbed Hiroshi's hand with her thumb, slurring her words. "You know Setsuko kept Mattson as her name? Never changed it back...even though my mother did...she wouldn't stay...but I am. Call Setsuko?" Her monologue sputtered out and her eyes shut, her head sinking into the pillow. She looked even more beautiful than the last time he watched her sleep. He tucked her hand under the sheets, kissed the less bruised side of her forehead and watched her wheeled off for the MRI.

In the hallway, he called Osaki and Sugamo to send additional police to guard the hospital rooms. Then he returned to Shibata's room where he set the backpack against Shibata's bedside table.

"Take a look." Shibata's voice was a dry croak.

Hiroshi pulled out the scroll.

Shibata said, "You should read that."

"It's private."

"Don't leave it here. Keep it at the station."

Hiroshi pulled out a bundle of cash and a wood box. When he opened it, the broken pieces of the tea bowl rattled around like splotches of color from three separate bowls, matte yellow, pale orange, reddish pink.

"You can get that fixed. Keep the money safe. Take the USB to the Endos to publish. You're the only one who can walk." Shibata patted Hiroshi's arm and reached for his morphine drip.

"I never imagined the past could be so dangerous," Hiroshi said, putting everything back in the backpack.

"Nothing more dangerous," said Shibata, pressing the morphine drip again.

Chapter 45

When Akiko got to the office the next morning, Hiroshi was asleep on the futon chair with Jamie's scroll unspooled across his chest, one side rolled open all the way to the wall. Sighing in exasperation, Akiko started rolling up the scroll and Hiroshi spluttered awake.

"You were reading all night?" she asked.

"I dozed off at some point." He sat up wincing and groaning, his body stiffer and sorer than he ever remembered it being. He wondered if he'd ever be in so much physical pain working at Interpol.

"Did you find Jamie?"

"Hospital. With Shibata. MRI was fine. There's a lot of money in the bag. USB is in there too. We have work to do," Hiroshi said.

"I'm not sure those are all connected." Akiko opened the wood box and cringed at the broken pieces of the bowl inside.

"Can that be fixed?" *Can I?* Hiroshi wondered.

"*Kintsugi,*" she said. "Traditional repair method. I'll take care of it. What was on the scroll?" Akiko closed the box gently and set it on her desk.

"Politics, profit, corruption, contamination, a short history of Japan. Mattson knew everything."

"So, what do we do about...*everything*?" Akiko stared at Hiroshi.

Hiroshi tugged at his sweaty, half-buttoned shirt. His bandages needing changing. He could feel them sticking. He started to stretch, but it hurt too much. "We start by getting copies of the manuscript to the Endo brothers," Hiroshi said. "Make backup copies for us. It's too late for the conference, but at least they'll have it. The speech should be on the USB."

Akiko wrote down what he said.

"Katsumura Transport. We need to raid their offices for their records."

"Chief's not going to like that," Akiko held her pen poised over her notebook.

"The bureaucrats above him are going to like it even less. That's why we have to make the proposal airtight."

"I love going on those raids. Pushing aside company security, carrying out the files, the employees' indignation." Akiko chuckled.

"We can't get onto the American bases, but we can take the evidence right up to the gate. Past there, it's politics, not police work." He paused. "And then we get Trey Gladius on every watch list in the world."

Akiko sat down at her desk and got to work.

Hiroshi took a towel, toothbrush and clean clothes down the hall to the shower room. He thought of how Mattson must have been horrified as the research for his autobiography led him to stumble on corruption on a vast scale. Or maybe he knew all along? Denying the noble defeat of his life's work. Hard to be clear-eyed at the end. Hard to change course. That took courage.

In the shower, Hiroshi washed off the crusted blood and dried sweat, being careful to avoid scrubbing where it hurt, which was pretty much everywhere. As he redressed his scrapes and cuts with bandages and put on the first clean clothes for days, he thought about how to ensure Gladius was brought in. Street smarts were one thing, but office smarts were another.

Akiko was waiting for him in the office, ready. "I sent the files to the Endo brothers."

"Call them later to be sure they got them. Did you print out the speech he was going to deliver?"

"The speech was nowhere I could find."

"Check again. Next is Katsumura. We need to trace the last verifiable point of the trucks. For that, I need outside help."

"You're sounding like Takamatsu."

"You're not the first person to tell me that," Hiroshi said, holding up his hand as he called Iino—the long-haired blogger from Okinawa who'd been Higa's protégé.

Sounding pleased to talk, Iino said, "Thank you for putting me in touch with Chief Hirano in Yokosuka. His detectives helped us out, as did that journalist."

"Do you have routes for the trucks?" Hiroshi asked.

"Trucks carried supplies to Fukushima, picked up debris, trash and soil from there, and then carried everything to a truck stop where the loads were attached to other rigs. After the switch, the newly loaded trucks headed south. Some went into bases nearby. Others went into bases farther south. Some all the way to Okinawa." Iino's voice was a youthful mix of outrage and overconfidence.

"And you have dates?"

"Quite a few."

Hiroshi wondered if he should offer them protection. "You should be careful until we get all this in place."

"I realize that. But Mattson went it alone. We're a community. All the investigators on our site get online backups of everything at pre-arranged times. If something happens to one of us, all the others have a copy. If we had known about Mattson, we'd have kept him and the information safe."

"The public speech was what really threatened them."

"He was a dynamic speaker." Iino hummed disappointment. "There's going to be a funeral for Higa in two days."

"Email me the info." Hiroshi hung up and started on the application for confiscating the Katsumura Transport Company's records. Akiko put it onto the official forms. They worked for hours until they had a complete file on what they knew. The Katsumura Transport files would provide the rest.

"The thought of all that radioactive contamination is horrifying." Akiko straightened the forms.

"There are a lot of American bases all over Japan," Hiroshi said.

"Poisoning the groundwater, draining into the ocean."

"It's slow murder."

They looked at the thick stack of application papers.

Akiko said, "You should mention an increased budget."

"What?"

"The chief will go for this if he can get extra operations budget. And Takamatsu always had me put duplicates at the end to make the file look longer and heavier."

"So, the chief won't read it?"

Akiko giggled and printed out an extra copy of everything and added it at the bottom. "I'll get started on Trey Gladius while you talk with the chief."

Hiroshi groaned as he set out to the chief's office, aching with each step but knowing he needed to keep moving. As he walked the long tunnel, he was happier than ever to be in the annex building, in a quiet office, with a sane, competent assistant, and a functioning espresso maker. He would never leave the office again.

The chief groaned when he saw the stack of papers for the raid on the Katsumura Transport Company's records. "I don't have time to read a report this long." The chief shoved the stack back towards Hiroshi. Saito looked on from his chair at the side of the chief's desk.

"We need to think a little *outside the box*." Hiroshi used the English for the last phrase.

"What does that mean?" The chief looked insulted. "English phrases can mean anything."

"Katsumura Transport and Storage has been contaminating the country. They're dragging radiation everywhere. It's all in my report." Hiroshi tapped the thick folder. "We need to confiscate their records—technical financial stuff, accounting procedures, delivery dockets. I'll go through it all, don't worry."

"We have to wait until this conference is over. Every one of us has to be there to protect all those foreign delegates. Already, there are protests outside the forum hall."

"I've been bringing you cases of financial fraud connected to homicide and they've all been airtight, right? *Airtight*." Hiroshi repeated *airtight* in English.

The chief mumbled a begrudging agreement. Saito, ensconced as usual in the chair by the chief's desk, mumbled an echo.

Hiroshi straightened up as straight as the ache would allow and continued, "We ask for expanded funding. The budget directors will get on board if the American embassy and the Ministries are satisfied."

The chief nodded approvingly. "A raid like this has to be carefully planned in advance—"

"Saito, you'd be the perfect point man for the raid," Hiroshi said. Saito sat up. "You've done this kind of raid of companies before." Hiroshi knew this was the kind of safe action he liked.

"Let's do it combined with the tax office," Saito suggested and the chief nodded. "A joint raid is safer." Saito called on his phone as Hiroshi summarized the application.

Saito hung up and said, "They've been after the Katsumura's for years. They'll bring a dozen officers. We bring the same. Best to do it early in the morning. Catch them off guard."

"Can we spare everyone from the conference?" the chief asked.

"Conference doesn't start until the next afternoon," Saito said. "We do this tomorrow morning."

Hiroshi feigned being impressed.

The chief pulled out the top form, put his *hanko* seal in the first box at the bottom of the page and handed it to Saito, who put his *hanko* into the next box. "Akiko will do the rest." He pushed the file across the desk to Hiroshi.

Hiroshi bowed on the way out and took the forms to Sakaguchi, who was talking on the landline on his desk. Sakaguchi dropped his *hanko* on the form without stopping his conversation.

When Hiroshi walked back through the underground corridor his legs felt like hardening concrete. The rest just hurt. Maybe he should have taken the pain pills the clinic gave him, but the pain was keeping him awake—and focused.

Hiroshi set the forms down in front of Akiko, who got started while he looked through the forms for placing Trey Gladius' name on every suspect list in every country he could. He'd contact every police bureau in every country he'd collaborated with on cross-border crime cases. He'd send it to Interpol, too.

Akiko filled the forms out in English, correctly and completely, and better than he would have done himself. When she was done, Hiroshi put the paperwork into a folder and trudged back through the tunnel to the chief's office again, and then to Sakaguchi, who looked surprised. "You're over here more today than the past year."

"I want to get Gladius in Japan."

"Better outside than not at all." Sakaguchi put his *hanko* on the form. "You need anything else from me? This conference hasn't even started and is already sucking time."

"There'll be a funeral for Higa day after tomorrow."

"I'll go with you," Sakaguchi said. "I finished reading his book."

Back in his office, Hiroshi sent an email to Jim Washington at Interpol. Instead of an email, Washington phoned: "We usually go with a Yellow Notice first, but I can bump it up to Red. Frankly, it's doubtful Gladius'll be extradited back here, but it'll keep him hopping."

"If he keeps traveling on military visas, he'll be free to come and go, right?"

"He could slip in and out anywhere, potentially, but Red Notices go out to almost two hundred countries. Just a matter of time before someone grabs him."

"Sooner the better," Hiroshi said.

"You'll learn to play the long game at Interpol. If you can't get them in person, you get them on paper."

"It has to be in person in this case."

"That'll be even more paperwork. Your interview's scheduled for the day after tomorrow at four."

"I'll be there." Hiroshi hung up and looked around his office. The smell of cleaning supplies seemed fainter. In its place, the room had soaked up the espresso, the perfume Akiko wore, the sharp smell of printer toner, and the aroma of *bento* meals. Hiroshi slumped back in his chair, too tired to open the files on banking scams, embezzlements and illegal offshore accounts that had piled up over the week. He felt content just to be in his office.

Chapter 46

"Why didn't you call me?" Hiroshi yelled at Akiko from the door of his office the next morning. "You know how much we have to do."

Akiko smiled and held her watch up towards him. It was ten in the morning. "You should have seen the look on their faces when we marched in. I think they really didn't get any tip-off. For once. Took them completely by surprise."

Hiroshi hung his coat up on the rack. It was an old coat he'd found at the back of his closet at home, one he'd forgotten about, a much warmer one. He had time to actually look through his closet after he woke up that morning, the first time in a long time he hadn't rushed out the door or slept in his office.

"You needed to sleep," Akiko said. "The raid went smoothly." She stood up from her desk to go make the first espresso of the day, first for Hiroshi. She'd been up since six.

For the first time in a week, Hiroshi smiled, not sure if he should be angrier or not, but grateful to have slept in, like the process of healing the injuries had begun. He wanted the Katsumuras exposed almost as badly as he wanted Gladius in prison. It didn't really matter how it happened. They had too much to do to squabble about the lack of a wake-up call. He let it go.

Hiroshi and Akiko worked all morning on the files from Katsumura Transport. The documents they'd confiscated showed truck routes, security and safety precautions, receipts, dockets and invoices. It wasn't everything, but it was enough, and it led right to the gate of the American bases.

A little before two p.m., Akiko reminded him of the time, and Hiroshi left the trail of documents on his computer and desk and hurried off to the main building. "I'll meet you there," Akiko called out after him.

Hiroshi stood waiting in the main building's meeting room—the one for outside officials—and precisely at two p.m., the door opened and in walked Colonel Bigston, the officer at the gate who denied them entry to the Yokosuka Naval Base. He looked taller and more broad shouldered in the confines of the office than he had at the gate. But it was hard to remember. Hiroshi'd been pumped full of adrenaline and covered in dust the time before.

Bigston had many fewer medals than the Major at the airport, but his seasoned manner was far superior. Bigston stood politely, though not stiffly, behind a chair at the conference table, waiting to be invited to sit, showing respect he was on Japanese territory. The aide behind him stood awkwardly, taking his cues from Bigston, clutching a briefcase, new at this.

Hiroshi walked over to shake hands with Bigston. "We meet again."

"We do, indeed," Bigston said. "In better circumstances." A flicker of a smile crossed Bigston's mouth, as he bowed his head just enough to follow Japanese custom, but not too much to cease being American. They both waited patiently as Sakaguchi, Saito and the chief walked in, bowing before seating themselves quietly at the round conference table. Bigston waited until the end to sit down, followed by his aide, who took out a notepad and pen.

After everyone was seated and introduced, Colonel Bigston spoke first. "I would like to apologize on behalf of Yokosuka Navy Base for the misunderstanding with your detectives. After reviewing the material your detective, Hiroshi Shimizu, sent us yesterday, we have a proposal."

The Japanese remained unresponsive, even after Hiroshi translated. Akiko came into the room, and bowing deeply, walked around the table and slid into a chair, opening a notebook to write down whatever was needed.

Bigston made eye contact with everyone in the room. "We're going to establish a computerized system to expedite requests and exchange information. No more triplicate forms, no more waiting time. After the initial interview, we can mutually decide how to proceed. We will not block the arrest of a suspect if evidence is compelling and can be heard immediately."

"Thank you. That will be an immense improvement," Hiroshi said.

Bigston nodded agreement. "We want soldiers to be afraid of Japanese jail time. We will have more officers in the liaison office starting next month and we've hired a translator." Bigston leaned back, pleased with himself.

The chief asked why the change was coming now after so many American suspects were not handed over to Japanese authorities in the past. Hiroshi translated this as a question, not as the accusation it clearly was in the chief's phrasing.

Bigston nodded. "Not a change in the rules, a change in enforcement. New people are in charge. My Japanese is good enough to order a beer, but nothing more, so that was part of it. I appreciate you translating today."

"I can speak for my chief here," Hiroshi said in English, nodding at the chief. "And the chief in Yokosuka when I say your proposal is highly welcome." Hiroshi added, "I should apologize to you for my rudeness at the gate the other day."

Bigston smiled. "Your command of the American idiom showed me I could trust you. That's why I'm here."

Hiroshi returned his smile. "I learned a lot in America."

"What you sent me about this case has moved us to make this change in policy. If I can speak frankly, the US military has grown so huge, a few rogue players are inevitable. That's no excuse. It's explanation. We're working on this guy, Gladius, too."

Hiroshi paused, letting all that sink in for everyone. Then, he said, "We'll share the rest of the evidence on him with you when it's certain, but until then, we do have a little more today if you could stay for the next meeting. It's related to Trey Gladius."

Bigston looked at his watch.

"It won't take long," Hiroshi said, looking at Akiko, who nodded.

Settling back into the chair, Bigston said, "If you feel it's important, we can stay. What's this about?"

Akiko went out to the hall and then ushered two people in to the room. The older of the two, Shimabukuro-*san* was in his seventies, with grey hair and mottled cheeks. He wore a black *kariyushi* shirt with long sleeves. Just beneath the surface bubbled sunny island energy and the depths of Okinawan culture. The younger woman, Kaneshiro-*san*, looked as lively as her orange flower-print shirt. Hiroshi watched her eyes take in the room at a glance.

He introduced the two Diet members from Okinawa to Bigston and everyone exchanged *meishi* and shook hands and bowed before sitting down.

Hiroshi spoke in English. "After the Fukushima disaster, American waste management companies came to assist with the transportation and storage of hazardous materials. These documents are from Katsumura Transport, who acquired nearly all the contracts, letting some Americans assist as subcontractors." Akiko handed around photocopies of the contracts. "At the time, the central government and the nuclear industry wanted the problem of radioactive waste disposal to go away. Katsumura Transport offered to do just that."

The Okinawan Diet members quietly scrutinized the documents Akiko handed them one by one.

"Bernard Mattson, who was killed in his home, stumbled on a lot of this information while doing research in the national archives. The Katsumura Company, along with several other Japanese firms, no doubt made a plea to keep the clean-up in Japanese hands, but they still had a major problem."

"Which was?" Bigston asked.

"They had no place to put the radioactive debris."

"Couldn't they just leave it there? Build concrete containment?" Bigston asked as if he had an idea of the answer.

"Too expensive and too short-term. They still needed to remove waste from a vast area around the nuclear plant if full-scale reconstruction of the Fukushima area was to ever begin. So, where to put it?"

Shimabukuro and Kaneshiro nodded as if they already knew where it went.

Hiroshi took a breath and continued, explaining in detail all that he had learned, how the trucks were loaded, where and at what times, what routes they took and the last places the trucks with radiated debris had been seen.

"Where did the trucks go finally?" Kaneshiro asked in flawless English.

"That's why we invited you here today."

Bigston turned to his aide to make sure he was getting all this written down.

"You mean the American bases in Okinawa?" Kaneshiro asked.

Hiroshi continued. "The bases are huge. Just as all military personnel are free from passport restrictions, Japan has no right to inspect anything inside the bases."

Bigston nodded.

"Mattson found pieces of what was going on, even though everything was secret. Before he could publish what he found, he was killed." Hiroshi nodded for Akiko to hand around the information from the blogger Iino and from Chief Hirano in Yokosuka. "These are independent verifications of radioactive loads going in and out of Yokosuka."

Bigston frowned. "So, that's where Trey Gladius came in? I wouldn't be surprised. He's been in and out of every base in Asia, leaving a trail of problems. But how is the storage of radiation connected to Mattson's death?"

"He understood the entire scam."

Bigston leaned back and shook his head, his jaw tight.

Shimabukuro tapped the documents. "So, you're saying the American military turned a blind eye to storing radioactive debris as incentive for allowing the American bases to remain in Japan, smoothing the renewal of SOFA."

Hiroshi nodded. "The radioactive waste flowing into the Pacific Ocean was an open disaster they couldn't hide. But on land, putting it inside the American military bases kept it out of sight, out of mind."

Bigston shuffled through the documents in front of him, checked the notes of his aide.

Shimabukuro continued. "And Mattson figured this out before anyone else. The companies would have divided the process up into separate pieces, all disconnected from the others so no one ever saw the whole operation."

"Two others were killed too. Higa and another man," Hiroshi said.

Bigston looked furious. "And Gladius set all this up? I'm taking a transport to Okinawa right now." Bigston nodded to his aide to call to make arrangements.

"Aren't you the liaison officer?" Hiroshi asked.

"I'm doing liaison now because I've got a bad ticker." He tapped his heart. "Before taking what I thought would be a less stressful job, I was in charge of base operations in Okinawa. I'll find what's been stored, where, when and by whom." Bigston stood up and saluted. "Detective Hiroshi, Shimabukuro-*san*, Kaneshiro-*san*, I thank you for your time. I will see this is cleared up."

The Diet members stood and bowed to the two American officers as they left.

There was not much more to say, but Shimabukuro's eyes sparkled and his gentle face wrinkled in pleasure. "This might change the negotiations. It's just in time. But we'll need to hurry. How much of this is for public consumption?"

Hiroshi shrugged. "It's all on Iino's blog."

Chapter 47

At the International Forum, Hiroshi took an earphone and read the printout of responsibilities. He found his name and where he'd been assigned. From his position just inside the wings of the stage, he could see about half of the audience, and all of the backstage area. Sakaguchi stood stoically on the other side. Hiroshi settled in for a long day of standing in place.

Diplomats of every description and rank, from every country in Asia, Europe and North America filled the hall, leaning over the plush seats, exchanging name cards, catching up with colleagues, their murmur and buzz echoing off the walls. The press had set up cameras on both sides of the stage waiting for the opening speech, the one Bernard Mattson should have been giving.

At least they were not outside, where police had erected barricades to separate protesters from opposite sides of the political spectrum. Earlier, when walking into the sprawling complex, he wondered why protesters, no matter how complex the issue, always divided neatly into two opposing groups, when there really should be dozens.

Hiroshi saw Pamela from the U.S. Embassy walk out into the wings from backstage. She was helping organize the event. But when Hiroshi saw Setsuko step out and look out at the crowd, he was very surprised. Setsuko ducked back into the wings while Pamela patted a young woman on the back to send her out as emcee in the middle of the wide stage. A hush fell over the hall as the audience returned to their seats and the media clicked on bright video lights.

Then, in the opposite wings, Hiroshi saw Setsuko talking quietly to Jamie, one arm around her. How had she recovered so quickly? The last time he saw her she was sprawled out on a gurney, going for an MRI.

The emcee's voice projected loudly: "We welcome you today to this conference on Asia. Bernard Mattson was going to give the keynote address here today, but I'm sure you have all heard the tragic news of his death." The emcee stopped as murmuring filled the hall. "Sadly, we lost a true diplomat, one who understood all sides, knew the past from personal experience and envisioned a better future." The crowd's whispering brought the emcee to a halt. "Mattson's work is not lost, though. A short biography is included in today's program, along with a timeline history of this conference. Let me just recite a few of the high points."

Hiroshi listened for what seemed like a long time to the list of Mattson's achievements and the conference's history. A brighter, livelier tone echoed through the hall. The introduction came to an end amid a flurry of expectant whispers. The emcee waited patiently for quiet, and finally said, "Bernard Mattson lives on in his writings and in his ongoing influence on our decisions. And in one other way, too. We are honored today to have his daughter speak in his place. Please welcome Jamie Mattson."

Was she really going to speak? She said again and again she couldn't stand being in front of people, but there she was, nodding as Setsuko whispered to her. Jamie walked unsteadily into the lights. The stage and media lights caught the indigo blue of her one-piece dress and shone off the white shawl over which her hair tumbled in a thick drape of shiny black. Watching her move to the center of the stage, Hiroshi felt again what he felt when he first set eyes on her—that she was ravishingly beautiful.

By the time she got to the lectern, every person in the hall was on their feet applauding. Even with the lights and the distance, the blue of the bruises on her face were only half concealed by makeup. She didn't smile or acknowledge the applause but studied the room. Her hands quavered, clamped around a printout of the speech. She blinked at the bright lights, as if they hurt. And then she spread out the pages on the lectern in front of her and tapped the microphone awkwardly.

Jamie looked in Hiroshi's direction at the edge of the stage but didn't seem to see him. She looked the other way, and Hiroshi saw Setsuko nod reassuringly. Jamie faced the audience and took a big breath, steadying herself with her hands. The hall fell into respectful silence as she leaned forward to the microphone.

"I am sorry that my father could not be here—" she paused to slow her breathing. And then continued. "I can not hope to do him justice, but this is what my father wanted to say. This is his speech. I changed only the pronouns. He wanted so much to be here today to tell you what he found, to express his disappointment not in humanity, but in the mistakes and misconceptions humanity falls prey to. He wanted to change the root and practice of politics. I hope you will listen until the end."

Jamie brushed back her long hair, touched the bruises on her face, and blinked again in the bright lights. Channeling her father's will and spirit, she looked around the hall, and commenced to read.

"My father believed the American system of worldwide military bases had become derailed. He wanted America and its allies to start decommissioning the bases, all six hundred of them in thirty-some countries, beginning with Japan. Under American pressure, every country in the world has been pushed to spend more and more on defense. Those expenditures drain the budgets of every country, destabilize economies and siphon money from unmet needs. The bases appear to be securing safety in the short run, but actually ensure conflict in the long run. Asian countries built defense systems and defense mentalities that provoke anxiety and encourage antagonism. It's a state of mind that selfish political actors on all sides manipulate to their advantage. The lack of transparency covers up the corruption on which the system thrives. As one horrifying example, my father stumbled across evidence of the storage of radioactive debris from Fukushima on American military bases." The crowd murmured but Jamie didn't stop. "For him, that was the final straw. It confirmed his opposition to the renewal of SOFA. That was the reason he was killed. And I hope it will become the reason to change."

The audience listened, rapt by her—his—honesty.

"He wanted to speak up not just to criticize, but to insist that the world can be cleaned up, can be made safe and secure, and can thrive in complex co-existence. He believed that Asian countries share a deep heritage and have more in common than politicians admit. He believed Asia could get along without America but could still get along *with* America as friend and ally. He believed that America should be a force for uniting countries, not for profiting military corporations."

Jamie paused, wiped her nose, and looked out at the audience in the huge hall. The audience members all rose to their feet, the initial patter of applause swelling to a roar of approval.

Hearing a faint voice in the earphone, Hiroshi tried to tune in the signal. Saito was calling the detectives to the back entrance hallway. He heard his and Sakaguchi's names called through the earphone, Saito ordering them to stay where they were in the wings of the stage.

Hiroshi glanced out at the crowd, still on their feet, applauding. Jamie surveyed the crowd, confident now, pleased at the people responding to what her father wanted to say. Suddenly, she stopped and her smile faded. Jamie's eyes fixed on one place in the hall, midway to the back doors. She squinted and blinked and stared. Hiroshi followed her sight line to the figure of a tall man rising from his seat and turning towards the exit.

It was Trey Gladius. His tall body, blonde hair and overly assertive posture were unmistakable. He was heading up the aisle to the exit.

Hiroshi skirted around the curtains and hurried down the stairs at the far side of the stage. Hiroshi sidestepped the people still applauding Jamie on stage, the aches and pains returning along with his fury, his mind racing through explanations for what he saw. Gladius must have returned on a different passport. Or through a military entry point. Or perhaps had never left at all. But how could that be?

Hiroshi burst through the exit door into the huge open hallway. Light poured down from four floors of framed glass rising to the ceiling. Hiroshi could hear the chants of protestors outside. He looked in both directions, saw Gladius moving up the central three-story escalator. Hiroshi sprinted up the escalator past a row of people admiring the Forum's architecture and looked back to see Sakaguchi climbing up after him.

At the top of the escalator, the doors leading out into the street were just sliding shut. Hiroshi paused for the doors to slide back open and found himself outside between two factions of protestors held back by barricades and policemen. As Hiroshi pushed through, the line broke and the orderly crowd surged forward with a shout of victory. The police and barricades were overrun.

The opposite group of right-wing protestors, corralled into a small lane opposite, broke loose and charged forward. The formerly rhythmic chants disintegrated into random yells and screams and then the painful sound of bodies pummeling each other. The opposite sides crashed together—as if magnetically pulled—right in front of the glass doors of the Forum. The police at the door pushed back, but there were too many people moving in too many different directions.

Hiroshi turned sideways to struggle after Gladius who hurdled a barricade—toppling a policeman—and dove into the crowd. Hiroshi ran after him, examining each possible exit as he went, and caught a glimpse of Sakaguchi splitting the crowd with his huge arms.

They both pushed through another jam-packed block of surging protestors until they could see far down the wide sidewalks of Ginza. Hiroshi ran a few steps in one direction, then in the other, before coming to rest by Sakaguchi, who had stopped at the last corner, sullenly scanning the meandering weekend shoppers.

Gladius was nowhere to be seen.

Nearer the forum, protestors obediently boarded police vans to be carted off for booking, herded along by riot police with *keijo* batons. As each van pulled off, more police trucks took their place, stopping all traffic and squeezing people away from the Forum. Atop one of the trucks, a police spokesman with a bullhorn ordered everyone to disperse. A few tussles continued, but police quickly surrounded each one to quash it.

Along the usually neat, tame streets of Ginza were scattered broken blockades and crumpled protest signs, plastic bags and random trash, a few lost shoes, making it seem like a different city altogether.

"Was that him?" Sakaguchi asked.

Hiroshi caught his breath, looking back one more time.

"You're not sure?"

"It looked like him."

"The local cops are going to be too busy to chase him. You want me to call it in?"

Hiroshi shook his head at the hopelessness of it. "Maybe put something out to the airports. We might get lucky."

"That's what it's going to take. Luck. And patience."

Hiroshi kicked at the debris at his feet. "Is that all we're doing from now on—chasing maybes?"

"Maybes can lead to certainties," Sakaguchi said. "Even when they don't, it doesn't mean we shouldn't chase them."

Chapter 48

Jamie straightened up when Hiroshi slid onto the chair across from her in the dim light of the jazz *kissaten* coffee shop in Shinjuku. The bruises on her face had lightened into a coloring that no longer detracted but seemed to accent her vitality. Her silk shirt, a deep indigo blue, was pulled tight over her breasts. Their eyes met before they said a word, and they both looked away.

"One of the few jazz coffee shops left in Tokyo," Hiroshi said, asking the waiter for a cappuccino. "It's been here since the 60s."

"I love the album covers on the walls. They still play records here?" Jamie looked around the brick-walled underground shop.

"Vinyl never went out in Japan." Late-fifties jazz played over the speakers, Miles Davis—sad, slow, spare, elegant.

"I thought you were trying to avoid me," she said.

"It's been days of spreadsheets, bank accounts, calls to London, New York, Singapore, Nairobi. I was so far behind."

"That's my fault." Jamie looked down at her coffee cup.

"The speech was fantastic."

"I want to explain what happened," Jamie said, frowning at her coffee cup.

"I should have ordered several cappuccinos then."

Jamie smiled and looked into Hiroshi's eyes. "I never thought Japanese had a sense of humor."

"Learned it in America. Self-defense." Hiroshi leaned back as the waiter set his drink on the table.

"That's where I *lost* my sense of humor," Jamie said. "I remembered laughing all the time when I was a kid."

"That's because you were a kid."

"Thank you for sending the money and the scroll to me. And the will and other documents. Ueno brought them to the house. Why didn't you deliver them yourself?"

"I was busy," Hiroshi said. "I had to—"

" 'Busy' is what people say when they don't want to do something," Jamie said as Hiroshi sipped his coffee. "I don't know where to even start," she continued. "What made it so scary was I knew the guys on the train were the same guys who tied me up at my father's."

"The police report didn't say where you were going after Fukuoka."

"New York."

"You took a train to Kansai to get to New York?"

Jamie took a breath. "It sounds stupid. But I was scared. I found the scroll, a lot of money and his manuscript. On the scroll, my father told me that if he was dead, I should get out of Japan. I was going to take the manuscript to New York and get it published."

"The ticket was for Fukuoka."

"I planned to fly to Seoul or Hong Kong or wherever I could. Then I decided to get off in Osaka and leave from there. I thought that would be safer. But they knew where I was all the time."

"If you had told me—"

Jamie held her hands up. "I know, I know, I should have. I apologized in all the messages I left on your phone. You didn't listen to them?"

"I listened to every one." Many times. It had interrupted his work. He had pressed reply and canceled every time. He had been happy to sink back into work, without distraction, but thoughts of her kept rising in his mind, popping up on his mental desktop.

"I was trying to be a good daughter. For once."

Hiroshi watched Jamie look around the *kissaten*. The room was smoky and the bar well-stocked. The two wait staff idly polished glassware.

"But why didn't you tell me what you were going to do?" Hiroshi finally asked, angrier than he meant to be. "I would have—"

"I didn't want to get you involved."

"I was already involved." Hiroshi set his cup down and pushed it, half-finished, to the side. His anger was maybe something she deserved, but not something he wanted to let out. He needed to keep it in place, at least for a while longer. He pulled his coffee cup back towards him and took a sip. "You went to see your father's lawyer. Did the will get settled?"

Jamie sighed. "You don't want to hear what I'm telling you."

Hiroshi looked at a Charles Mingus album cover on the wall. It was an abstract painting of two people made of colorful cubes and spheres, or maybe not two people at all, just strung-together shapes.

"The will, then, OK. Setsuko took me. The will stated the house was mine, which Shibata already told me. There were multiple savings accounts. I tried to give something to Setsuko, but she refused everything except our relationship. I decided to stay in Tokyo. That's about it, practicality-wise."

"What about New York?"

"I quit my job. An easy email to write. I'll get my stuff moved to storage. All I had were overpriced clothes anyway." Jamie looked at him, her eyes asking forgiveness or at least understanding. Not seeing that, she continued. "The Endo brothers are helping me sell a few of my father's prints and tea bowls. Ones I don't want to keep. I'll make more from that than from my old job in New York, which I hated anyway. I'm going to help Setsuko with her school. She's been more like a real mother than my own."

"Did she help you with the speech?"

"No, that was my father's."

"Where did you find it? On the USBs, there was no file for his speech I could find."

Jamie squinted at him and drank her coffee. "It was his speech."

"But where—"

"Thank you for the home security system."

"You wrote it yourself, didn't you?" Hiroshi started to smile, impressed. She had written it, he realized.

Jamie shrugged off the question. "With all the locks, cameras, alarms, and devices, I could catch up on my sleep. But it takes me ten minutes to get into the house."

"*Your* house. Your bruises are better."

Jamie touched her face. "It doesn't hurt to smile now."

Hiroshi looked at the thick layers of Jamie's hair, freshly cut in a new style, and at her cheeks, glowing and radiant again. He took a sip of his cappuccino. He sighed, trying to think what to say, how to organize the file of what he wanted to tell her.

Jamie bounced a little in her chair. "So...the English version of the book is coming out first, and then the Endo brothers are publishing it in Japanese through a new media company set up with Saori Ikeda's funding. She's a force of nature. It seems like the powerful Japanese women, few as they are, are really powerful."

"They have to be." Hiroshi looked at Jamie. "Your father never knew who Trey was, though, did he?"

"He was there, wasn't he? At the speech?"

"I'm not sure."

"He'll follow me forever."

"He's not following you, he's following orders."

"That's worse. Some shadowy organization."

"But you understand who he is now, don't you?"

"He killed my father. Or had it done."

"We'll get him even if it takes time," Hiroshi said.

"Will you?"

"Yes."

They both looked at the album covers and the framed photos of jazz greats along the walls. Hiroshi stayed quiet.

"So...the Endo brothers are building a site to go with the release of the book. It'll create 'synergy,' they keep saying. I was asked to give a couple more speeches. Your professor is helping with background. He's something."

"I'm glad he's helping," Hiroshi said. "He called and told me."

"You answer his calls, but not mine? Just how many apologies do I have to give you?" Jamie brushed her hair back. She looked at Hiroshi, and then at the brick wall.

Hiroshi tuned in to a solo from Miles, each of his notes falling and spreading like raindrops in still water.

Jamie looked back at Hiroshi and reached under the table. "I wanted you to have this." She handed him a thick book wrapped in Japanese *washi* paper.

Hiroshi pulled back the thick, pulpy paper. It was titled, simply, "*Shunga.*" The cover featured a woman in kimono, her smile half-covered with her sleeve while a young man with a topknot pushed his hand deep inside her kimono.

"I wrote something in the front."

Hiroshi opened the front cover. In Japanese characters, it said, "*Shogyo Mujo Shoho Muga.* Love, Jamie." It was the same saying Mattson had on his wall, above where Jamie put his ashes: All things must pass and nothing stays the same.

"Is that your brush work? It's impressive."

"My father taught me calligraphy at the kitchen table, on newspaper, but I haven't held a brush since I was a girl."

"I have something too." Hiroshi reached in his bag and took out the wood box.

Jamie smiled as she lifted the bowl out of the box and unwrapped the silk lining. The yellow, pink and dark orange glazes were lined with bright gold where the pieces were sealed together along the cracks.

"I thought this was lost."

"They redo the cracks with gold paste. The craftsman told me repair is just part of the life of the bowl. It marks the event of breaking and becoming whole again."

Jamie marveled at the tea bowl and looked up at Hiroshi. "Is this real gold?"

"Repaired bowls sometimes have greater value."

Jamie smiled and turned the bowl in her hands. "This is the bowl I ate breakfast from when I was a little girl. I guess I can't anymore."

"Quite an expensive bowl for a little girl."

"Even for a big girl."

Hiroshi listened to the jazz playing in the background, Miles Davis, one of the late fifties quintets, he wasn't sure which one. He would get a stereo and buy CDs of the records he used to have. He left all his records behind when he went to America, not that he could afford many. Or maybe he'd go for vinyl instead, recover what he lost. He wrapped the book back in the soft paper and slipped it into his bag.

Jamie took his hand. "I was thinking we could stop by and see Shibata. And maybe get some *yakitori*. I loved that place we went. My treat."

"I've got a funeral to go to." Hiroshi squeezed her hand and looked along the row of record covers, reading the colorful, styled titles over the crisp, shadow-heavy photos of John Coltrane, Art Blakey, Sonny Rollins, Lee Morgan, music trapped in time, in faces.

Jamie let his hand go and leaned back. "All my life one side of me fights with the other. Too open for Japan, too delicate for America. You'd think just once the two sides could—"

"We're the same that way," Hiroshi said.

"You mean, too much to—"

Hiroshi touched her hand. "I've got to go."

"Let me get the coffee." Jamie snatched the check off the table before he could get it.

"You're becoming more Japanese."

"I'm becoming more myself."

Hiroshi waited while she paid and they climbed the steep stairs to the busy sidewalk outside.

Jamie turned to face Hiroshi. "I'm going on a pilgrimage. Two, in fact, to Shikoku and Chichibu. For my father."

"That sounds wonderful."

"When I get back, maybe we could—"

"Get together. Yes."

They stood there, both looking past each other at the Shinjuku crowds passing by.

"Do you have to move the bones at the funeral you're going to?"

"That part's finished already. Today's just the memorial service."

Chapter 49

Hiroshi and Sakaguchi joined the long line of people waiting to pay their respects at Yushima Seido Temple. Higa's mourners were an odd mix of stiff funeral suits and designer black-on-black, but they stretched along the outer temple wall of stacked flat stone and down the sidewalk to the corner.

"Look at all these people," Sakaguchi chuckled.

"I thought he was a loner," Hiroshi whispered.

Inside the courtyard, the mourners clustered around a large circular urn with a thick forest of incense smoldering to ash in the fine sand. A gentle wind dispersed the smoke in light grey wisps that rose up past the temple's black pillars. Along the green copper roof, statues of squat dragon-fish and burly lion-cats glared and snarled at the milling crowd of humans below.

On the altar of a glass-fronted building to the right, nestled between pyramids of *mikan* oranges, *mochi* rice cakes, and large *sake* bottles, sat an old photo of a handsome, energetic young man who looked nothing like the sallow, angry man Sakaguchi had met in the Endo Brothers Bookstore. But it was him.

Hiroshi and Sakaguchi waited patiently in line for the two cushions on which everyone kneeled to pray for the departed spirit of the writer, activist and—according to some website posts—martyr, Higa. When they got to the front of the line, Hiroshi and Sakaguchi knelt side-by-side on the cushions, put their hands together and offered a prayer. They both groaned in pain getting up.

In the open area by the urn, Hiroshi saw the Endo twins, Seiichi and Shinichi, and Sakaguchi pulled out Higa's book, *Complacent Japan*, as they walked over to them. "It makes a lot of sense what he says in here," Sakaguchi said to the twins, who bowed in unison. Each wore a black tie, button shirt and suit coat, making them look more alike than before.

"Are these his readers?" Hiroshi asked, gesturing at the mourners.

"He sat on a lot of committees, advised NPOs, NGOs," Seiichi said. "They like to network. Even at funerals."

"Especially at funerals," Shinichi said.

Sakaguchi nodded at a long horizontal banner hanging between the pillars of the main temple building. In elegantly written characters, it read: *Reveal and liberate. Conceal and enslave.* "That phrase was in his book!"

"We thought that would be a nice twist on the usual Buddhist pieties," Shinichi said. "The priests found it amusing."

"It applies to detectives too," Sakaguchi said.

The twins talked over each other. "With all this attention, we're doing full print runs of his older works."

"He wouldn't have known what to do with the money."

"We don't know either."

"Saori Ikeda bought us out and made us chief editors."

"She told us to publish whatever we like, as long as we make it sting."

"Good editorial policy," Hiroshi said, trying to slow them down. "But, you gave up your bookstore?"

Shinichi shook his head no. "We expanded. The insurance was enough to remodel. We moved the rare books to safe storage and switched all book sales online. A friend of Iino's built us a website. Gives us more time for publishing."

"We have a website for that now too." The twins chuckled.

From around the smoking incense burner in the middle of the temple, Iino walked over with a lively group of nerdy-looking twenty-somethings. Two of them started talking to the Endo brothers about a publishing possibility and Iino handed a copy of *The Silkworm Weekly* magazine to Hiroshi and Sakaguchi.

"Here's the first exposé. Our blogs are getting more hits than ever. The photos of the base entrances went viral. The Okinawans had cameras in place, too, so we combined them all. The government shut down our cameras, but the footage had already circulated, so it'll be out there forever."

"People won't want to buy the book if the info's all online, will they?" Sakaguchi asked.

"Just the opposite. They don't want to buy the book *unless* it's online." Iino shook his head with amusement. "Next up is an exposé on consumer finance companies. Guess what family owns one of the biggest loan companies in Japan? And guess which Diet member refused to support a cap on the 25% interest rate for personal loans?"

Hiroshi laughed. "I thought she looked like a loan shark."

"Rumor has it, Shinobu Katsumura's resigning." Iino tip-tapped his laptop bag and rejoined his colleagues.

The detectives looked around the bustling temple courtyard. Higa's spirit hovered over the proceedings, and Mattson's too.

"Where's lunch?" Hiroshi asked Sakaguchi.

"A ramen place in Jinbocho. Takamatsu will meet us there. Akiko, too. Feel like a walk?"

"Might do our aching bodies some good."

Another wave of mourners made it impossible to exit at the main gate, so they headed through the still-billowing incense smoke towards the side gate. Hiroshi stopped in front of a moss-covered statue of the wrathful deity, Fudo Myo-o. The solid stone hands held a sword upright for cutting through ignorance and a curling rope for binding up evil. Elaborate flames, the stone worn by weather, crackled behind his fierce countenance. Suzuki had told him that a sword always had a history, but held no secrets. Hiroshi bowed to the deity before hurrying through the gate to catch up with Sakaguchi.

The two detectives continued down a street of musical instrument stores, which turned into an area of splashy-colored snowboarding shops pumping loud music into the street. At the bottom of the hill, a quiet row of bookshops with people standing and reading led left toward the Endo brothers' store. The detectives turned the other way towards the Yasukuni Jinja Shrine, Kitanomaru Park and the Budokan martial arts stadium. An earthen rise lined by craggy-barked cherry trees, their willowy branches heavy with new green, swayed over the moat below.

Sakaguchi said, "In his book, Higa wrote that people are still dying from World War II."

"Maybe Higa and Mattson were the last," Hiroshi said, hoping that was true, knowing it wasn't. They turned onto a small street.

Takamatsu was standing on the corner of an intersection smoking a cigarette at a designated smoking area. Takamatsu waved them over to join the line for a ramen noodle shop where Akiko was holding their place.

"Look at this line." Sakaguchi shook his head with impatience.

"Means it's good," Akiko said.

As the line plodded closer, Takamatsu blathered on about how much money he was making from photographing people having affairs. He said love hotel receipts were the easiest thing to get and phone records not much harder.

Inside, they bought tickets at the vending machine and sat down with Sakaguchi on the outside. Takamatsu hung his coat on a wall hook and slipped a paper bib on to protect his shirt and tie from splashes of oil or broth.

Hiroshi faced the kitchen, and watched the main chef shake the noodles free of water with fierce strokes of his arm before easing the noodles into the broth in two neat folds. The prep chef layered beansprouts and bamboo shoots on thin slices of roast pork and fanned three sheets of black seaweed along the rim of each bowl. The waitress, a pretty young woman with an earful of piercings and a head scarf carried the bowls over one by one.

They cracked their chopsticks apart and rubbed the splinters off, took up their Chinese-style spoons and entered a meditative, culinary silence. The next fifteen minutes passed without conversation—just four people, four bowls, a pitcher of iced water, lip-smacking slurps and the drone of the television on a high corner shelf. The other customers kept their own silences.

When he got to the bottom of his bowl, Takamatsu removed his paper bib. "I'm off suspension in April. It'll be a pay cut."

"Don't come back. Open your own investigative service," Hiroshi suggested, sarcasm thick in his voice.

"Don't encourage him," Sakaguchi said.

Hiroshi pulled out the copy of *The Silkworm Weekly*.

Akiko put down her chopsticks and took it from him. She held up the grainy photos of trucks coming out of Yokosuka, traveling down the highway, delivering their poisonous loads to the Okinawan bases. "Wow! Right into the base!"

"Unlike us. We were stopped at the gate."

"Unfortunately, transporting radioactive debris is not a crime," Takamatsu said.

"In Japan, it doesn't have to be a crime. It only has to be disgusting," Akiko said, flipping the pages.

The waitress came over and Sakaguchi nodded for a refill of broth and poured his rice in, mushing and mixing the grain with his spoon.

Hiroshi drank a glass of ice water. "I still can't believe Gladius got away."

Takamatsu laughed. "Don't get obsessive. Worst thing you can do in this line of work."

"If I wasn't obsessive, I would never have taken this job in the first place. All accountants are obsessive."

"Did those guys who attacked Jamie roll over on Trey?" Takamatsu asked Sakaguchi.

Sakaguchi poured and drained another glass of ice water and held up the pitcher for a refill. The waitress came over with a new, full pitcher. "The ones on the train haven't said a thing. And I made sure they had every incentive to talk."

"The gang's forcing them to take the rap?" Hiroshi asked.

Sakaguchi and Takamatsu looked at him as if he was naive.

Sakaguchi wiped the sweat off his face. "The two Koreans confessed to killing the thief, Sato, in Golden Gai. Who knows if they really did it or not, but the prosecutor wouldn't let them take the rap for Mattson or Higa. Not yet, anyway. The prosecutor convinced the chief to wait for the real murderer."

"The *tanto* sword we took from Gladius was clean as a whistle," Hiroshi said.

Takamatsu shook his head. "He certainly waltzed out of the airport."

"He won't waltz back in," Sakaguchi said. "Or not again. Or not so easily again."

Takamatsu frowned, wondering what more he didn't know.

"The Red Notice from Interpol will catch him somewhere," Hiroshi said.

"That's why they have fifteen days in every sumo tournament. You don't have to win every day, just more days than everyone else."

Hiroshi filled his glass from the pitcher and slurped it down, then got up pulled on his coat. "I have to run."

Takamatsu had a smirk on his face. "Going to see Mattson's daughter?"

Hiroshi shook his head. "You always think you know where I'm going."

Takamatsu looked at him. "You don't ever seem to know."

"Ah, but this time, I do."

Chapter 50

Hiroshi crossed over the thick, Edo-era bridge gate into the huge gardens of Kitanomaru Park, once part of the Imperial Palace. A few people strolled in the first non-wintery day of the year, slowing their pace amid the greenery, talking to each other in the afternoon sun. Past the Budokan, he found a bench near the central fountain and speed-dialed Jim Washington, who had left several messages during lunch.

"Hiroshi? Where have you been? I wanted to let you know we got a hit on Gladius. He was detained in Spain."

"They won't send him here, will they?"

"Doubtful, but even if he gets out of this, he'll be on the *persona non grata* list for all EU countries. He won't be able to set foot anywhere else without the possibility of being detained."

"I guess that's a first step."

"Need a first before you can have a second. You know, one of our undercover guys was killed in Macau last year. The killer was high up in some agency or other."

"You got him and he did time?"

"No, but we made his life a living hell," Washington said, chuckling. "He was yanked off planes, held in custody, detained in airports, put on watch lists. We froze his bank accounts."

"Any way to get a hold of Gladius' accounts?"

"I can look into that. Or you can, once you're here at Interpol."

"I'd still rather see him in jail."

"We can work on getting his security clearance revoked. We do whatever we can, however we can."

"Justice delayed is—"

"Justice still. That's what I like about you, Hiroshi, not easily satisfied. You'll be a great asset to our team here. You ready for the interview?"

"Actually, I'm sorry, but I won't be coming to the interview."

"But we're all set. The Asian bureau chief is here. What happened?"

Hiroshi frowned. "Just, well, things have changed."

"We're locked in pretty tight time-wise, but we can reschedule."

"It's not that. It's that I've decided to stay where I am for now."

"Listen, I'll make some excuse for you. We can do the interview next time he's in town. I'm not going to let your cold feet now ruin your chances later."

"With so much to take care of—"

"You're just tired from that case. It sounded rough. Take some time. We'll talk again."

"Thanks, Jim, but—"

"We need you and you'll have far greater impact here, more reach, more resources. Take a little more time. We can wait." Washington clicked off before Hiroshi could answer.

Hiroshi put his cellphone away. Washington was a good man, and he would talk to him again soon. He felt bad to say no. It wasn't something he'd done very often.

Hiroshi got up from the bench and followed the dirt path leading to the hill above the moat. The wide sidewalk circled through the park before veering through lush tracts of thick bamboo grass. He walked off the path to a higher ridge where he could see the moat walls, an intricate pattern of tightly set stones that extended around the entire palace grounds.

These days, the moat was a place for couples to rent boats and row across the tranquil surface of murky, green water. He watched them for a while, amused that so few even knew how to handle a boat, their oars flailing and splashing as they mostly just floated along too happy to even think to take a photo.

Hiroshi carefully searched each bench before finding her. She sat looking across the moat calmly eating her lunch. Hiroshi sat down on the next bench. He wondered how long it would take her to notice him. She was lost in an afternoon daydream, enjoying the freedom of lunch break. Hiroshi stared at her to draw her attention. Surely, she would look up eventually.

He watched her chew an *onigiri* rice ball wrapped in black *nori* seaweed. She self-consciously brushed back her hair from her face. When she took a sip of tea, she finally looked over to see who was sitting so near.

"Hiroshi!" Ayana laughed. "You startled me! Oh, I thought it was some *chikan* pervert."

"Ayana! What a coincidence meeting you here. So close to the archives."

"Why didn't you call?"

"Thought I'd surprise you."

"How did you know I would be here? Are you investigating me?"

"Just following up." Hiroshi moved over to her bench. "You said you had lunch here most days."

"Did you need something from the archive?"

"In a way."

"Mattson's documents?"

"Not exactly."

"What then? Lunch?" She held up a rice ball.

"I just had ramen."

"So, you need something, but you don't."

"That's it exactly."

"What's the book?" Ayana nodded at the large book Hiroshi set in his lap, the one Jamie gave him.

He held the book up in both hands. "Oh, well, maybe I'll show you later."

"Secret?"

"In a way." Hiroshi looked at the cherry trees at the edge of the wall. Their trunks were gnarled and mossy, twisting and bending, the older limbs bulging with younger limbs branching up towards the sky. "When are they supposed to bloom this year?"

"Are you going to sit here and wait for them?" she asked.

"I might. What about you?"

"I could sit here until then."

Hiroshi looked up at the trees to see if there were any buds. "No buds yet."

"Last *onigiri* rice ball." She waved it back and forth.

"I might have half." He unwrapped the plastic, bit off half and tried to hand it back, but she waved it back to him. "Why are there so many cherry trees here? Emperor planted them?"

Ayana spoke in a mock NHK documentary narrator's voice. "Planted four hundred years ago, when this was Edo Castle, the hundreds of trees along Chidorigafuchi—"

"You've been watching too much television."

"I have, actually." She blushed at having too much time to watch TV in the evenings. "These are some of the oldest and most beautiful in Japan. They planted them right on top of the defensive perimeter for the Imperial Palace."

"As good a place as any," Hiroshi said. "Beauty and violence are so intertwined, aren't they? Swords, moats, martial arts, they're so lethal, they become beautiful."

"Do you do *kendo* anymore?"

Hiroshi laughed. "I hadn't even held a practice sword for years, but I guess I haven't completely forgotten. What about you?"

"When I lived in America, I was one of the best at the *dojo* hall. But all the time I was doing *kendo*, I found out, my husband was cheating on me."

"When you went to *kendo*?"

"Gave *kendo* a kind of bitter taste."

"I'm sorry about that."

"I quit for a while, but back here, I realized it was the only thing that kept me balanced."

"Where do you practice now?"

"A *dojo* hall near my place."

"I don't even know where you live."

"Not far from here, Kagurazaka."

"Little Kyoto in Tokyo. Must be expensive."

"I had a good settlement from my ex-husband. He was a big executive and...well...at least he didn't cheat on the divorce terms. You said you did *kendo* recently?"

"Sort of. It's complicated."

"How complicated can it be?"

"Painfully complicated," Hiroshi laughed. "It all comes back, though. I guess your body remembers."

"Yes, bodies remember," Ayana said and looked away.

The wind from the palace grounds and through the park blew in alternating layers of warm and cool, the last of winter and first of spring. They could hear the clunk and creak of rowboats in the moat, but not the rowing couples' whispered conversations.

"I always like those little red things that fall after the blossoms are gone," Hiroshi said.

Ayana laughed. "What are you talking about?"

"You know, the little red things that cover the outside of the blossoms."

"You used to say nonsense like that all the time." Ayana laughed. "The blossoms are the beautiful part."

"The blossoms are okay..."

Ayana looked at the trees. "I like the moment right before they burst out full. You see them straining."

"You'd have to climb up in the tree to see that, wouldn't you?"

"Why don't you climb up and take a look for me?" Ayana pointed to the row of large cherry trees whose branches reached over the water. "Take a close-up photo."

"The water might be a bit cold if I fell."

"Like that time in Kamakura."

"Jumping in the ocean at sunrise."

"After sleeping on the beach. It was cold on cold."

"But we didn't feel it at all, did we?"

"We were too young then."

"Do you feel the cold more as you get older?"

"Right now, I feel like a walk." Ayana hopped up, balled up the trash and looked at Hiroshi.

"Don't you have to go back to work?"

"The books and documents aren't going anywhere. I can be a little late. What about you?"

"The spread sheets and investment accounts aren't going anywhere. I can be very late. Once around the Imperial Palace?"

"It's a long ways, but why not?"

Hiroshi pointed both ways with his fingers down the curving row of cherry trees, gesturing to ask her which way she wanted to go.

Ayana swirled her finger once in both directions to tell him it was all a big circle and they would come back around to where they were supposed to be, no matter which direction they went first.

If you enjoyed this book,
please consider taking a minute to write a review.

About the author

Michael Pronko is a professor of American Literature and Culture at Meiji Gakuin University in Tokyo. He has written about Japanese culture, art, jazz, and politics for Newsweek Japan, The Japan Times, Artscape Japan and other publications for 20 years. He has appeared on NHK Public TV, Tokyo MXTV and Nippon Television. His website, Jazz in Japan, is at: www.jazzinjapan.com. His award-winning collections of essays about life in Tokyo are all available at online retailers and from his website: *Beauty and Chaos: Slices and Morsels of Tokyo Life* (2014), *Tokyo's Mystery Deepens: Essays on Tokyo* (2014), and *Motions and Moments: More Essays on Tokyo* (2015), in addition to three essay collections in Japanese. When not teaching or writing, he wanders Tokyo contemplating its intensity and reaching out for the stories to come.

* * *

For more on the Hiroshi series: www.michaelpronko.com
Follow Michael on Twitter: @pronkomichael
Michael's Facebook page: www.facebook.com/pronkoauthor

Also in the Detective Hiroshi series:
The Last Train (2017)
Thai Girl in Tokyo (coming in 2019)

A book is a group project, and I have a large group that helped me with this one.

Thank you to my university for a sabbatical and support. Thank you to my students for teaching me more about literature than I could have learned on my own.

Thank you to my editors, CR, HZ, and NLF. Their input and help brought out so much.

Thanks to AA who read numerous versions.

Thank you to Paul Martin for his knowledge and insight about swords.

Obrigado muito to Marco Mancini for talk, design and energy.

* * *

And a special thank you to my wife. For being there. Words can't...but can a little.